Desta

AND THE

GREAT MYSTERY

The Great Mystery

Getty Ambau

Book five of the epic adventure series of
an Ethiopian shepherd boy in search of his
ancestral family's twin Coin of Magic and Fortune

Published by Falcon Press International
P. O. Box 8671
San Jose, CA 95155
Cover Art and design by Philip Howe of Philip Howe Studios
Library of Congress Cat. No. 2010927259

Desta and The Great Mystery, novel/Getty Ambau—1st Ed

Volume 5
356 P. Manufactured in the United States of America

ISBN: 978-1-884459-13-9

The setting—fiction. 2. school—fiction. 3. Desta and David Hartman's camping trip—fiction. 4. Desta's National Junior College cross-country championship and win—fiction. 4. The Johnsons' Christmas vacation in Deer Meadows, Vermont—fiction. 5. Desta's New York City subway tunnel escapade—fiction. 6. Desta's summer job—fiction. 7. The Parents- of-the-Breast ceremony—fiction.

This is a work of fiction. Names, characters, places and incidents are either the products of the author's imagination or used fictitiously. The author's use of the names of actual persons, places and characters are incidental to the plot and are not intended to change the entire fictional nature of the work. The cover illustrations are based on the characters and events described in the book.

Manufactured in the United States of America

PREFACE

Although this book is a sequel to the previous four volumes, every effort has been made to make each volume independent of every other. Still, to get the most out of the Desta stories, the first four volumes should be read ahead of the fifth.

This ambitious book series follows the adventures of a young man named Desta, the places he discovers and the people he meets along his way through life.

The first four volumes were set in Ethiopia and as such serve to document the Ethiopian people, history, land and culture. This volume, set in the early 1970s, is about Desta's first year in American society and college. The challenges he faces and his efforts to overcome them would be an inspiration to anyone, particularly students. Although the story is fiction, the setting and historical facts are true to life.

I hope you have a fun ride with Desta's adventures. – GTA

ONE

Fresh out of high school, guided by mystical talismans and an ancient prophecy, Desta, at five foot nine inches, slender young man with fine features and curly hair, had finally made his way from Addis Ababa to New York City. The journey had taken nineteen hours; he'd never imagined it would be so long. Nor had he thought he would feel this afraid and alone or that the dull, intractable pain in his head would follow him here and resurface with a vengeance. He felt unprepared for this new world. He had only murky impressions of America, gleaned from magazines and the foreigners he'd met as a tour guide in Ethiopia. No one back home could have told him what to expect when he stepped off the plane onto American soil, and into a society so far removed from his own. Everything had happened so quickly, it seemed he'd barely had time to blink or think.

When his plans to start medical school on a full scholarship in Bulgaria fell apart, he'd felt compelled to seize the unexpected opportunity to come to this dreamland to start college at the end of August and continue his search for King Solomon's Second Coin of Magic and Fortune.

He still lamented what should have been. He wanted to scream *Why me?!* A twist of fate had taken him from his Bulgarian mentor and benefactor, Dr. Petrov, who had inspired his pursuit of medicine to help his country.

The prophecy had compelled Desta to follow the sun westward to find the missing magic coin, twin to one Desta had inherited from his family. Its image was tattooed above his heart by his grandfather's spirit for his protection and counsel.

By the prophecy, he had to find the missing relic and unite it with his own to benefit all humanity, and so he'd followed the historical clues and omens to America, as his conjuring rod had forecast.

David Hartman, a Peace Corps teacher who'd befriended Desta in high school, had helped salvage Desta's shattered dreams. David had arranged Desta's trip to America, found him a host family, and helped him enroll and finance his first year at Abraham Lincoln Junior College in Rye, New York.

Desta had crossed Africa, the second largest continent, and the Atlantic, the second greatest ocean, which Desta thought was a good omen. In flight between catnaps, Desta's mind had been a cauldron of thoughts and emotions. He'd gazed out the plane's window at the clouds, sun, land, and sea by day, and the plane's wingtip light and the brooding darkness at night.

These formed the backdrop to a stew of fears, disquiets, and fleeting excitement about what he would see in America, especially New York City.

His friend David had driven Desta home from the airport in New York and fed him his first pizza and Coca-Cola. They'd talked until Desta couldn't keep his eyes open, and he'd gone to bed, hoping he wouldn't wake until noon the next day.

But he had woken at 4 a.m., the time his body clock was set to, no matter where or how tired he was. A knife seemed to needle his head from the inside. Pain radiated to his fingers and toes. These familiar sensations had resumed after Desta's abusive brother Damtew visited him a year ago, and now it seemed his affliction had followed him to the new land. Before Desta woke, he'd dreamed Damtew was chasing him, threatening to kill him.

With the help of the magic coin's image on his chest, Desta quieted the pain to a dull ache. As he lay with a soft cotton sheet on his face, Desta thought about his new life, and all the concerns he'd had the day before on his flight across Africa.

It all seemed precarious. He had no financial security beyond his freshman year and didn't know how he would find another family to support him after that. He didn't want to rely on his friend David again. And he still had to face the vast, daunting task of finding the coin.

He fretted that his high school education, without books, library, or laboratory, hadn't adequately prepared him for college.

He had expected to return home from Bulgaria at the end of his education there, but now that he was in America, he couldn't return home before finding the second shekel. And he wouldn't ask his friend to pay for his return plane ticket if his adventure in America proved unsuccessful.

He'd been used to visiting his family over holidays, or for a break from his problems in his school town. But there was no bridge over the Atlantic Ocean, or a highway to walk or ride on from Rye, New York across Africa to his home in Ethiopia. Many thousands of miles lay between him and his family, and he realized there was no chance of seeing them anytime soon.

Desta felt like an orphan in America, and his heart sank in despair.

Desta would face all the hurdles that awaited him in this new land without the support of someone who understood his heritage and his challenges, to share his joys and sorrows with, and to rely on if he got sick. All Desta's worries settled in his chest like a winter cold. He tightened his arms and pressed on his heart. His eyes brimmed with tears.

Desta felt stripped of his resolve. The confidence to overcome all adversity that had been his bedrock was now shifting sand. Terrified by the very image, Desta squeezed his eyes shut to make himself sleep.

He woke an hour later when he felt the bedsheets slipping off his face. He opened his eyes but saw nothing in the charcoal-deep shadows of the night.

"Uhh!" Desta uttered, realizing he was not alone. A form white as cotton, tall as one on a stilt, stood at the foot of his bed.

"You have yet to see your first sunrise in this country, and already you worry about a future you can't know," the figure said.

Desta lifted himself on his elbows to better see the stranger. Human in form, insubstantial as a cloud, with definite features of nose, mouth, and eyes, an oval face below a round head. He had an enveloping aura that instantly put Desta at ease. "Who are you?"

"I will wait for a better time to introduce myself," the stranger continued. "I came only to relate an important message.

"Treat your time in America as a gift of opportunity, not one of insurmountable difficulties. You are still capable of applying your fine qualities of determination, perseverance, and ingenuity to accomplish your purposes in this country.

"The pain that afflicts you is neither a disease nor bodily injury, and nothing can be done for it just yet; you must learn to cope with it." The white figure abruptly vanished.

Desta fell back as if in a trance. Could that have been Tsadok, his spiritual guide and King Solomon's high priest, in disguise?

He went to the bathroom, mind still reeling with the strange man and his cryptic message. From a small porcelain tray at the sink, he picked up a green bar of soap with a soothing herbal scent.

He opened the faucet and let the water run warm. He lathered his hands and gazed into the mirror. Dark circles surrounded fearful eyes, and his pale skin and ashen lips disturbed him. He poured water into cupped hands and dowsed his face with it, massaging his cheeks and brow.

He dab-dried his hands and face with a towel and returned to his room. He got back under the covers, begging sleep to come, but he still thought of his worries and the encounter with the strange spirit.

WHEN HE WOKE two hours later, morning light had seeped from the edges of the curtains and brightened the room, a comforting change from hours of darkness.

Desta's eyes roamed the walls. A bookshelf stood to his left, and a round table and chair sat in the corner. Carpeting, curtains, window seat cushions, and a lampshade, all in tan, contrasted with pristine white walls. A light on a silver stem and stand shaped like a tulip, stood alongside a built-in desk and chair.

Would his new family give him a room like this? What would they be like?

And his schoolmates? Desta made an educated guess. From the *Newsweek* and *Time* magazines he'd read in high school, he knew that five kinds of people lived in America: Whites, American Indians, Blacks, Hispanics, and Orientals.

If the family he was going to live with was Black, would they reside in a town like David's, or Harlem, where Desta had heard most Black people in New York lived. Then a strange thought came to him.

Abraham Lincoln was the president who had freed Black Americans from slavery. Desta's new college had been established to honor the man, and Desta imagined most students there would be Black.

Lincoln College was in a town called Rye, which reminded him of his favorite bread his mother used to make. His lips tightened in a thin smile at the memory, surprised by the connection.

The white bookcase caught his interest. He wanted to browse its volumes but felt he should first get David's permission, a rule he'd learned at home. So, he studied the shelves from afar.

Some of the books stood in rows, others lay on their sides. The model of a white-haired man in gold-rimmed glasses, a black coat, and a white shirt perched at the top right corner of the bookcase, like a high chief presiding over his domain. A miniature guitar on the second shelf from the top looked out of place, *like me when I step outside today,* he thought.

He dropped his eyes to the second shelf from the bottom where an old round-bellied straw basket with a conical top sat between half a dozen standing books. It reminded him of the simple baskets woven by beginners in Ethiopia.

He rose, walked to the window, and parted the curtains. His spirits brightened at the ethereal glow of the early day that fell across the manicured grass and hedges. He looked across the street to the large, beautiful homes with pitched roofs and projecting windows, some with columned entrances. Lush trees rose high above the houses; Desta was struck by how green the neighborhood was.

His mind reeled again. "It's been an incredible journey," he said to himself, thinking of his trip from Ethiopia, and the journey of his whole life.

In his mind, he traveled back to the beginning. A little shepherd boy in a remote village of round, dried mud and wood buildings with grass roofs and dirt floors, who'd trained to be a farmer, and dreamed of climbing the mountains encircling his valley to touch the sky. Ultimately, he'd discovered a bigger realm, and a chance for a modern education.

That was the start of Desta's epic adventure in a more expansive world. Now he was somewhere entirely different, his purpose far from what his family intended.

In his mind's eye, Desta returned to that first trip he had made to the mountaintop with his oldest sister, and all the discoveries and adventures that followed.

Desta sighed. He had seen and done so much in ten years; it had been an extraordinary journey for an ordinary boy, he mused. He returned his focus to the present and caught sight of a couple in T-shirts and shorts strolling up the sidewalk alongside a dog with a golden coat.

Suddenly, everything around him felt like a dream, and he felt dizzy. He sat down on the window seat. Resting an elbow on his knee, he pinched the insides of his eyes with thumb and forefinger to hold back a surge of emotion.

"I may be unremarkable in many ways," Desta said, "but I've also been given extraordinary abilities to connect with ghosts and spirits and uncover secrets hidden from most people. Through these gifts, I found the remains of my missing grandpa, and our Solomonic Coin of Magic and Fortune." He felt his cheeks pull into a smile.

He'd endured his family's wrath and physical abuse and, later, by people in the towns where he'd studied. He survived privation, abandonment, and homelessness. Desta's lips hardened, and his pulse quickened. He dispatched his dark memories with the toss of a hand over his shoulder.

How was it possible that only months ago he'd had an entirely different plan, and yet ended up in America, where he knew little of the people, land, and culture, to look for a coin that had gone missing thousands of years ago? He felt like a bird blown off course by a strong wind. Desta shook his head in wonder.

Desta sought inspiration and courage from his past to face his future boldly and do his best to accomplish his goals. He needed to take the white figure's counsel to heart. It was up to Desta what he did with it. He sighed again, closed his eyes, and tried to envision his prospects.

He heard a knock on the door. David poked his head in.

"Come on in!" Desta said. He rose and headed toward the door. They shook hands.

"Did you sleep well?"

Desta said that he'd slept as much as his body wanted.

"Breakfast will be ready in twenty minutes."

"I'll take a quick shower and be down shortly."

TWO

Desta hurried to the bathroom, peeled off his pajamas, and stepped into the shower, a spacious cubicle of glass and teal tiles with a soap niche on the facing wall. He pulled and twisted the shower handle, and cold water pummeled him. He sidestepped the flow until the water turned tepid, and then stood directly below the showerhead to cleanse himself and relieve the tension he held inside.

After he lathered up his body and thoroughly rinsed himself, he stepped out and dried his body with a thick white towel he grabbed from its rack.

Limbs relaxed, senses awakened, Desta became more aware of his surroundings. Exotic birds and fuchsia-and-purple flowers filled twisting branches on the wallpaper. He scanned a lustrous silver tissue holder and towel rack, the patterned linoleum floor. The fresh spring scent of soap tickled his nostrils, and the plush bathmat soothed his feet.

Returning to his bedroom, Desta dressed in his new cream-colored shirt, khaki pants, and brown leather shoes. Checking himself in the door mirror, he brushed the wrinkles from his shirt and pants and patted down his hair.

As he descended the stairs and crossed the large living room, the piercing aroma of garlic and onions hit him first, followed by the smell of sautéed meat, teasing his appetite. The skimpy pizza he'd eaten the night before had long vanished from his stomach.

Through parted window drapes, natural light splashed the beige leather sofa, walnut coffee table, plump chairs, and gold-flecked brown carpet. At the far end of the room, above a chestnut dining set, pendants of glass in a silver chandelier sparkled in the sun's long rays. The luminous calm and aroma of breakfast cloaked Desta in ease and comfort.

"We'll sit outside on the patio," David said, emerging from the kitchen archway with two plates of food. In his blue apron, he looked more like a cook than a college instructor. His arms, chest, and shoulders bulged from the faded yellow shirt he wore. It seemed his friend had filled out since a year ago.

Desta followed his host out to the backyard. A circular glass table with an umbrella stood on a cement slab whose meandering borders edged a lovely green lawn. Half a dozen yellow folding chairs and two loungers spread across the grass and concrete.

On opposite ends of the table David had placed two sets of forks and knives on white paper napkins, alongside teacups. He put the white plates next to the place settings and went inside.

Desta regarded the yard, some forty feet deep, bound by a curved concrete walkway. A border of multicolored flowering bushes fronted a weathered wood fence. Beyond the wall, a tall, leafy forest momentarily transported Desta to his parents' wooded grounds in the countryside.

He tilted his head, straining for the sounds of birdsong, the hum of bees, or the throaty call of colobus monkeys. But he saw no bees among the flowers and heard no birds or monkeys in the tableau before him.

"Sit," David said, waking Desta from his blissful reverie. His friend held a tray with a hot kettle and a stack of toasted bread on a plate. He set the tray down on the table between them.

Desta sat before his breakfast. He glanced at the kettle and inhaled its rich, spicy aroma. Steam rose from the spigot and lid before rising lazily and vanishing.

David sat, looked at his food, and then at Desta. "This is your first American breakfast," he said with a grin.

Desta studied his plate for a bit, then looked up and said, smiling, "I need a formal introduction."

David Hartman picked up a fork, pointed to each kind of food, and named them. "This egg dish is made with finely chopped broccoli, mushrooms, cauliflower, garlic, and onions. The golden sticks are French fries. These strips of meat are bacon. The bready squares with little holes in them are waffles."

The bacon looked and smelled different from the *tibis*—sautéed beef or chicken—he was used to eating at home.

Desta asked about it, and David Hartman explained.

"We don't eat pig meat," Desta declared, his appetite suddenly vanishing.

"Oh, that's right," David said. "Sorry, I forgot. I'll take it off your plate."

Desta struggled to eat the remaining food, feeling as if the bacon had soiled his whole plate. His brow grew clammy from anxiety and the muggy air. He passed his hand over the coin image on his chest, calming him, and he comfortably resumed his meal.

David said, "I talked to my parents last night, and they were delighted to hear that you've arrived safely."

"Oh, thank you," Desta said, heartened by their concern.

David explained that his parents, Jean, and Hal Hartman, had gone to Hawaii for a two-week vacation. On their way back, they'd stopped to attend a physics conference in San Francisco. Hal was a professor at Columbia University.

"They should be home in two days."

"I look forward to meeting them," Desta said. "You mentioned in your letter that I'm to live with a family you know in the vicinity."

"Oh, yes," David said. "The Johnsons."

"Are they far from here?" Desta asked.

"Just the next town, very close. We'll head there afterward."

Desta's heart lurched. He would have preferred to be fully rested before meeting his future benefactors. But realizing this date was prearranged, he said nothing. He tapped his fingers on the table and studied his host.

David Hartman seemed to sense Desta's ambivalence. "The Johnsons are nice people," he said. "According to my father, well-traveled. Mr. Johnson's father was a diplomat, and they lived in many different countries, including Egypt. Mr. Johnson knows a lot about Ethiopia. The very reason they were interested in hosting you."

In silence, Desta absorbed David's portrayal of his host family.

"Is that so?" he finally said. His fingers stopped their play on the table.

"Yes," David replied. "Mrs. Johnson is originally from England. My dad says she is also a world traveler, having spent much of her childhood in India, where her father worked for a British company."

"Interesting," is all Desta could say. He didn't know what to do with this report, or whether to ask David to expand on the story of his future hosts.

David went on. "They have three children, but only two will be at the house when school starts, as one daughter will go off to college in New Jersey. Of all the families my father and I considered, we thought the Johnsons were the best fit."

"Is that so?" Desta said. Now he couldn't wait to meet them. He already felt at ease knowing that they'd traveled the world.

"Yes!" David said, raising his voice a little more than necessary. "I know you came to the States reluctantly, which was understandable. For the present, I think you will be okay here. The future we can't know, of course."

"You're right. I'm more interested in having a good beginning at this point than worrying about the rest," Desta said, "but many thanks for all your help getting me this far. My gratitude is boundless."

"It's nothing," David Hartman said. "You're here because of your own struggles. You've paid dearly to get this lucky break." He studied Desta. "Do you think I didn't know all of what you went through?"

Desta dropped his fork on his plate and gazed at David. "You did?" he asked. "But I never told you about it."

David looked up from his plate. "Why do you think I sent you those 100 birrs when you were stuck in that little town after the fourth grade?" he said. "I knew that without help, you couldn't go to bigger towns like Finote Selam for your higher grades. As it turned out, my initial effort to help you move forward became a means to your independence, and for you to manage your future."

"I know," Desta said, remembering those times in all their detail. "How do you know everything else that happened to me? And why have you been so kind to a stranger like me?"

"I came by the details of your life story in some . . . strange ways," David said with a faint smile. "Also, it seems I am one of the small cogs that keep your wheel of prophecy moving toward the Second Coin of Magic and Fortune."

Desta shook his head in wonder. He felt as if he had met his friend for the first time, like the spirits who once appeared to him out of thin air. "I hope you can elaborate on this sometime," he said. "All this is a mystery to me."

"I don't know the details," David Hartman said. "It's just a feeling I had, and the little message I received through the air that got me involved in your mission."

Desta's head spun.

David glanced at his watch. "In an hour, we will go to the Johnsons'," he said. "I'll need to take a shower first."

After they finished eating, they cleared the table and went inside. David Hartman went to his room, and Desta upstairs to his.

THREE

Desta sat on his window seat, waiting for his friend to go meet Desta's host family. The mid-morning sun caressed his back, easing his nerves as the movie reel of his childhood played in his head.

He thought about the Johnsons, and David's mysterious remarks. *Is this family I will live with part of the prophecy?*

Strangely, he was now possessed by the same fear and ambivalence he'd felt before meeting an earlier benefactor, Colonel Mulugeta and his family, in Finote Selam.

If one of the Johnson family members didn't accept him, what challenges would he face in their home? What would they expect him to do in exchange for room and board? Being indebted to others was the last thing he wanted. That was why he'd tutored merchants' children during high school and paid two years of school expenses with the proceeds.

In Ethiopia, he'd read about the problems between Whites and Blacks in America. Desta did not know how he'd handle the problem if encountered it.

Where could he go to get a haircut? Desta broke out in a sweat. He sighed. He was now an adult, and he wished he no longer feared the unknown and could better grasp his situation and future.

He crossed his hand over his heart and pressed his constant companion, to help protect him and ease his troubled mind. Instantly, the hobbling worry he'd felt departed like a wind-blown mist. He felt calm again.

"Ready?" David said, standing at Desta's door.

"In five minutes," Desta said. He dashed to the bathroom, brushed his teeth, combed his hair, and went downstairs. He found David waiting for him, wearing gray slacks and a dusty blue short-sleeve shirt. It looked like a dart had split his brown hair into two unequal piles, passing along the left ridge of his skull. David Hartman reminded Desta of a movie actor, with his prominent nose, high cheeks, and sharp hazel eyes. He held something navy blue in one hand.

"Thank you," Desta said. He inserted each hand in turn into the sleeves while David held the jacket. He wiggled his shoulders to ensure it settled well on his body.

"It looks good on you," David said, stepping back to fully assess Desta's new look. "The salesman helped me select it, and we couldn't have made a better choice."

Desta moved his shoulders a little and patted down the front of the jacket. He liked the color and the way it fit.

David smiled. "Come take a look at yourself," he said, leading him down a short hallway to a guest bathroom.

Desta had never seen himself before in such a large mirror. With both hands clutching the lapels of the jacket, he studied his reflection. The clothing was loose on the shoulders and all around his body. He extended one arm and then the other, examining the sleeves, slightly longer than if they'd been custom-made. Desta thought he could live with this; he might still grow a few inches.

Desta finally turned to one side and the other, craning his neck to view himself from behind. He studied the image, from his wooly hair to the back of his knees, like he was gazing at a curious object or an alluring woman. His hunched back, boney shoulders, and lean buttocks all signaled a body long neglected.

He pulled up from his waist and pushed his chest out, striking a more erect and symmetrical pose. Desta liked what he saw and determined that from here on he must always be this image of himself. He turned to face the mirror again, opened the faucet, wet his hands, and patted down his hair. Satisfied with himself, he stepped out and closed the door behind him.

"What do you think?" David asked, fixing Desta with a curious gaze.
"I like it."

"Good," David said. "I was worried it might be too big on you."

"Just a little, but I'm glad to have it," Desta said. "Thank you."

They walked out the front door, David locking it behind them, and headed toward the car in the driveway, blue with BUICK on its hood.

David opened the side door for Desta, then got in and cranked the engine to life. He turned to Desta.

"We will first go to the Johnsons' house, your future home, and then we'll drive by Abraham Lincoln College," he said.

"That is fine," Desta replied mechanically. He was feeling anxious again. Crossing his hand over his chest and pressing his fingers on the spot above his heart, he sighed, and relaxed.

David backed the car into the street, reversed gears, and gunned it east. Several minutes later, he looked at Desta and said, "I don't know the Johnsons well, but my father says they're good people."

It seemed David had registered Desta's apprehension. He had said nearly the same thing earlier, and Desta didn't know what to make of his continuing assurances.

"That's good to know," he eventually replied. "Where do they live?" he asked.

"Rye City, very close to here," David replied, keeping his eyes on the road.

David glanced at Desta again and said, "That means we can visit you often." He smiled.

"That is nice," Desta said. "You are the only one I know in America, and it would certainly be good to see you when you can manage it."

"You should know a bit of our geography," David continued. "There are two Ryes: Rye Town, where we live, and Rye City, where you'll live and go to school."

Desta perked up, hardly believing his ears. "That is interesting," he said, while thinking how a pair of Ryes underscored the duality that had always been present in his life. "Where exactly is Rye City?"

"Next door," David said. "They are like the front and back of a hand, two different places with a common name."

Desta shook his head and curled his lip. "You could say the head and tail of a coin, too," he said. How remarkable that he'd come so far to live in a town with its own twin, like the two coins.

Thank you for that information," Desta said, turning to his friend. He kept his thoughts of twins and pairs to himself, even as he felt more at ease, like a greater power was watching over him, ushering him to his next abode.

They drove through winding streets and wooded neighborhoods to a six-lane road. David sped up to keep pace with the other cars that seemed to fly by like the wind. Beyond a ditch to their left, cars raced along at top speed in the opposite direction.

Desta looked at the traffic ahead, turned to David and said, "It's amazing how fast people drive in America."

David grinned. "These roads are called expressways. Cars can travel 65 miles per hour, legally. But people don't often obey the law."

"This whole area is like a forest," Desta said.

"Yes, because here people are not allowed to cut down trees, farm the land, or use it for any other purpose."

For a moment, Desta was taken back to the forest that once sur-rounded his parents' home, which they later cleared for farmland. He shook his head in sadness for the many animals gone with the old forest. His reverie briefly quelled the concerns about his future and the host family they were heading to meet.

David soon left the freeway for a curving local road bordered by trees. A few turns later, they entered a vast, well-traveled road. At the corner, a sign read "Boston Post Road."

"The Johnsons live a few miles down," David announced.

Desta sighed, while butterflies stirred in his stomach.

"I bet they are anxious to meet you," David said.

"Me too," Desta replied, forcing a smile.

A wrought iron gate bracketed by stout stone pillars guarded the en-trance to the Johnson residence. The house looked enormous and sat about fifty yards from the gate. The compound appeared to be several acres, bordered by shade trees, flowering bushes, and vines twined in the iron fence. Desta imagined himself enjoying the clipped, green lawn, like the field below his childhood home in the springtime.

"This place doesn't look like Harlem," Desta half-whispered.

"Harlem?" David's eyes narrowed and brow knit.

"Yeah," Desta said. "Isn't that where most Black people live?"

"Not most, but . . . " David paused when he noticed the closed gate.

David stopped the car and got out. Walking to the gate, he pressed a button on the left pillar, prompting a dog's deep, resonant bark. David paced back and forth, occasionally peeking through the grill of the gate.

Inscriptions on the left pillar caught Desta's eye. Three names appeared on the rustic post, separated by paired double lines like tree rings. They read, in ascending order: Johnson Manor, in fancy cursive letters; Johnsons' Estate, in caps; and Johnsons' Place, in regular lettering, higher up but well below the sizeable square capstone.

Above these words was the number 147, printed prominent enough to be read from fifty feet away; perhaps the address, Desta thought.

Atop this post, the statue of a lion gazed out to the driveway, while a lioness sat sphinxlike at the summit of the opposite column, it too, warily looking in the same direction. Moored to the two posts, a pair of black wrought-iron gates of intricate design barred entry. In the middle of each iron panel, two birds balancing on twigs faced each other. Leafy vines crawled up the sides of the pillars and the curving stone walls around the property.

Desta studied all these wondrous things, mind spinning, nerves tense. He focused on the numbers in the address once again, and then it hit him. The number 147 was made up of three sevens that added up to twenty-one: the number of legends in his magic coin. The number seven had always been a key part of Desta's life, too. He took his discovery as a good omen, and it softened the edges of his fears.

He stepped from the car and walked to the gate. Inside the vast compound loomed an enormous stone mansion, crowned by several narrow ridges and pointed structures that reminded Desta of the jagged mountains of home.

Except for the sounds of the street, the place seemed like a cathedral in its serenity. Yet something in the air tantalized Desta and put him more at ease. Did the Sweet and Sour woman and King Solomon's Coin of Magic and Fortune live here? he pondered. The ancient prophecy hadn't described a home or setting like this. He must wait and see.

If that weren't true, why would such a family living in this grand place want someone like him living among them? They wouldn't need Desta's help with the house or its grounds; they could afford to hire anyone. The realization dampened his hopes.

If they'd planned to offer him room and board in exchange for work, would they reconsider once they saw his scrawny condition? Why would they take a stranger—sight unseen? The Johnsons must have decided based on David's account. Had his friend exaggerated Desta's abilities?

The gates swung open as if by magic. David and Desta jumped into the car and drove in. The driveway terminated in a circle, with a twenty-foot island of flowering creepers and a life-size statue of a partly clad woman at its center.

The barking resumed, this time louder and more strident. The wild protests echoed as if from an empty cave. Desta's gut knotted.

"If that dog is as mean as it sounds, we may be in big trouble," Desta said.

"Aha." David breathed. "American dogs sound more threatening than they are."

David rolled the car around the circle and stopped near its outer edge. He got out, strode to the entrance, and pressed the doorbell, which only incited the dog even more. He waited, and then pressed again.

"Give me a minute!" From behind the closed door, a voice rose above the dog's din. "I need to put the dog away."

Suddenly, all was quiet. A topless young man in shorts opened the door and stood at the threshold.

"Good morning, I'm Jake Johnson," he said, extending a hand to David, who reciprocated.

"Have you been here long?" Jake asked apologetically. "We're all in the back by the pool."

"I've someone with me. . . . be right back," David said, hurrying to the car. Returning with his companion, David introduced Desta and Jake.

"Nice to meet you," Jake said to Desta, his face lighting up. Fine tufts of mossy golden hair edged out of his tight waistband and spread around his navel to his chest, resuming on his chin and above his temples. Desta was startled by the young man's half-naked welcome.

He was a well-formed fellow, with a sharp nose and intelligent brown eyes. The morning sun beamed golden on his unblemished skin. Jake appeared never to have seen hunger or hardship.

"The same here. Thank you," Desta said, smiling back, his chest easing.

Jake ushered them inside, and Desta stood motionless at the foyer. He glanced over the drapery of forest green and gold and found the same lustrous sheen in the couches and chairs, the landscape and portrait paintings, and the expansive carpet. Projecting from the ceiling, stems of light glimmered gold and pearl, with crystal pendants suspended from each.

Everything was pristine and seemed carefully arranged to be admired but not touched. The gap in the curtains framed a symphony of colors in the garden beyond.

"This is our living room," Jake said casually. "But we hardly spend any time here. Let's go to the back where everyone is lounging."

Opening a door, they came to another large room, which Jake called the family room.

Here, too, gold predominated. It adorned the walls, the coffee table's paw feet, the hooped light shade, and the statue of a dog on a corner circular table. It painted the frame of a portrait of mother and child on the mantel and threaded the ornate rug beneath it.

A touch of gilt glinted in the brown divans, two chairs, and the elegant floor-to-ceiling curtains; it embellished door panels and window frames.

Beyond this opulent space, Desta saw more green. At the far-right side of the room, Desta caught a glimpse of the kitchen, its spacious counters, a large table-like fixture at the center, and a dining table and chairs farther off to the left.

Jake drew his guests' attention back to the family room. "This is where we spend most of our time—if we aren't by the pool, that is."

David, too, seemed awestruck by everything in this sumptuous house. "I can see why," he said. "The view is breathtaking."

"And also because the kitchen's nearby." Jake smiled. "Now, let's go out to see the folks," he said. "They're anxious to meet Desta."

"Really?" Desta said under his breath. His palms dewed. *Like I'm the new family pet*, he thought. How he conducted himself now would seal his fate with them. But how should he behave? He wasn't sure what American families expected. For the present, he would rise or fall being his authentic self, the Ethiopian shepherd boy with a modern education.

Once outside, Jake stopped and looked around. "Where did Mom and Dad go?" he called to a trio of girls draped in long chairs by the pool.

One of them sat up and said, "They went in to change."

On the wide patio stood a canopy of yellow and white umbrellas over a large round table and six chairs. Jake gestured toward the table.

"Have a seat . . . my parents should be out in a minute." He excused himself and left.

David and Desta sat side by side, facing the turquoise pool. The vast green field beyond, with its colorful blooms, trees, and verdure eased Desta's nerves even more.

Like the house itself, there was something surreal about these grounds. The perfectly manicured grass, the trimmed trees, and plants along the fence, and on the patio near them, rose bushes, and other unfamiliar ones in large brown pots that David called planters. Everything showed a controlling hand and seemed designed to please the eye. Desta wondered what machines did the job so beautifully, and who did the work.

Jake returned with the leashed dog, a beautiful creature with fluffy brown hair. To Desta's surprise, the animal was now calm and quiet.

"This is Kooper with a K," Jake said, bringing the animal over to the visitors.

"He's got a completely different personality now," David said. "I thought he might eat us alive when we arrived." The corners of David's mouth pulled up into a smile.

"I'm surprised he's so calm," Jake said. "He normally stays excited until he gets to know new people."

Just then, Kooper dropped and rolled belly up at Desta's feet. He didn't know what to make of this show of affection from a dog he had barely met.

"I've never seen him do this before with any visitor," Jake said.

"It's a good sign," David said. "Animals sense a lot more about people than we do."

Desta bent down and rubbed Kooper's belly. The animal appeared in a trance. The three men watched intently, thoughts playing on their faces.

"I agree," Jake said finally. "This is reassuring."

David nodded.

Then Jake tugged on the leash, and Kooper rolled over and stood.

"Kooper and I will go for a walk," Jake said. "You two keep company. My parents should be out shortly."

Desta and David nodded at Jake, who left with Kooper in tow.

"For a start, you will have one good friend," David said to Desta, and smiled. "And I know his feelings will be unconditional."

"You could say that," Desta said. "When I was little, I had a dog who sacrificed his life for me." His eyes suddenly moistened. He sighed, turned away, and wiped them with his hand.

"Sorry," David said. "Dogs touch us in ways that no human can."

"Kooper sounds almost like Kooli, my dog's name. An interesting connection that you might call a coincidence—but it isn't," Desta said.

"Oh, hello!" Mr. Johnson said, coming behind the pair at the table. He was a tall, striking man dressed in a white short-sleeved shirt and khaki trousers. Desta and David stood up, their shoulders snapping out. They introduced themselves to the man and shook his hand. Behind him stood a woman no more than five foot six, with short, full hair and bangs on her forehead. She wore a cream-colored skirt and a sleeveless yellow pastel top.

"This is my wife, Beverly," Mr. Johnson said.

Mrs. Johnson lightly shook hands with the guests and said, "How do you do?" Her reserved smile and her greeting reminded Desta of the English and French women he'd taken on guided tours for the hotel in his high school town.

"Sit down, sit down," Mr. Johnson said, and pulled out a chair for his wife and himself. They both sat, the umbrella shielding their faces from the late morning sun.

"Did you have trouble finding us?" Mr. Johnson began and chit-chatted with David a bit.

Desta observed Mr. Johnson's manners and disposition as he talked. He seemed to be a worldly man of good breeding who'd seen a lot, understood peoples' differences, and accepted them for who they were.

He appeared stern, disciplined, even-tempered, and scrupulous. Desta sensed that man's wealth was a means to a fulfilling life, not the end, and that he was not defined by the luxury that surrounded him. Desta could see this in the easy and relaxed gesture of his hands too.

Jake and Kooper returned. The animal jumped excitedly at Mr. Johnson, interrupting his conversation with David.

"Jake, take him inside," Mr. Johnson commanded.

"He'll calm down, Pa," Jake said. He tugged at Kooper's leash and went over to a low circular bin near the house entrance. Jake picked out a red disc and walked past the seated group to the lawn. He tucked the red object under his arm and unleashed the dog, dropping the coiled rope near a clay flowerpot. He then slid the red circle from under his arm, the dog eying the thing excitedly.

They walked to the edge of the lawn, and Jake sent the object flying with his left hand. During high school in Bahir Dar, Desta had seen Peace Corps volunteers at the grassy airfield play with this plastic thing, which they called a Frisbee.

The dog took off after his prize. When it landed, he sank his teeth into the Frisbee's lip, ran back, and dropped it before Jake, who threw it again. Once more, the dog took off after his toy. The game went several rounds, while Desta watched dreamily, imagining himself playing with Kooper, if the family took him in.

All the girls were in the pool now, tossing a soft ball twice the size of a soccer ball among themselves and filling the air with their splashing, giggles, and laughter.

"We need Aida and Jake included in this conversation," Mr. Johnson said, glancing at his wife. He excused himself, got up, walked toward the pool, talked with one of the girls, and returned. Shortly after, all three girls left the pool, their hair matted, bikinis and bodies dripping and glistening in the sun.

Mr. Johnson then approached Jake. "Stop playing with the dog and come visit with the guests," he said.

Jake flung the Frisbee as far as he could, and Kooper flew after it. The dog returned with his catch to find his partner leaving the field.

"Aida is an interesting and historical name," David said.

Mrs. Johnson smiled at the visitor. "Out of place and context, you could add."

"A beautiful name for a lovely girl," Mr. Johnson said, grinning wide.

Mrs. Johnson stole a glance at her husband, her eyes mischievous. She turned to David. "I'll let you in on a secret," she half-whispered, suppressing a giggle. "My husband had a big crush on Sophia Loren, who played Aida in the Italian movie of the opera named for her character. I was pregnant with our third child in 1954 when we first saw the film. At her birth, my husband insisted we name her Aida."

"Actually," Mr. Johnson piped up, with a tinge of seriousness on his dignified face, "Egypt inspired me. I fell in love with the culture and

history when I lived there as a youngster." His eyes grew misty. "And
Sophia Loren was brilliant in that film."

Aida and Jake now stood before their parents and the visitors. "Go
get changed and sit with us," Mr. Johnson said.

Aida's two girlfriends dab-dried themselves with their towels. They
slid their feet into flip-flops, threw damp towels over their shoulders,
and waved vigorously to the Johnsons. "Thank you for the swim," they
said together, off-key.

"Our pleasure," Mr. Johnson said. "See you next time."

Jake returned in faded jeans and a button-down, light blue shirt. He
pulled out the empty chair alongside Desta and David and sat down.

Aida came next and sat between her father and Jake. Her hair, still
damp and stringy, framed a blotchy complexion. She had a prominent
nose and sensitive blue eyes and wore a sleeveless dress of pink-and-red
roses on sky-blue fabric.

Kooper came last, panting and clutching his toy. He dropped it near
Jake and sat expectantly on his haunches, still like a statue. When his
friend ignored him, he laid his snout flat on the concrete next to his
best friend.

Desta was touched by Kooper's bond with Jake. He thought dogs
spoke to people in so many ways. He felt a sudden desire to grab the
Frisbee and send it soaring into the vast green field to watch Kooper
run after it.

He wished he could spend time with Kooper and prayed that the Johnsons would agree to host him. The image of his dog Kooli flashed before
him again and he felt a deep sadness, drawing notice from Mrs. Johnson.

In the meantime, the Johnsons continued chatting with David, the
husband doing most of the talking. He asked David about his time in
Ethiopia in the Peace Corps, his impressions of the country, its people,
and culture.

David described Ethiopia as an ancient country that went back to
Biblical times. He explained that in the highlands where he taught and
where Desta came from, the people were gentle, soft-spoken, dignified,
and of high moral character. His young students were always polite, respectful, and eager to learn.

David glanced at Desta. "Desta and I have known each other for six years. I visited his village and stayed with his family for a few days. The place was very remote and inaccessible; we had to walk a full day to get there. Desta's father, Mr. Abraham, impressed me as a brilliant man. His mother was kind and a good host. I met a few of his brothers and their wives who lived nearby, all nice people.

"After I left Ethiopia, Desta and I stayed in touch by letter and phone. You can ask him more about himself, of course," David said, glancing at his friend again.

"Very interesting," Mr. Johnson said. "Yes, we are keen to learn more about Desta."

All eyes were on Desta now. He clenched his palms and took a moment to thank God he'd had the opportunity to speak English before large groups. He assured himself that he'd do just fine sharing his personal story with this eager audience.

He crossed his hand over his chest and pressed his thumb to his heart to calm himself. He cleared his throat and began. "I grew up in a valley where the mountains eclipsed the sun and walled my world, along with my seven siblings, who were all bigger and older than me."

Then he told them how he had achieved his boyhood dream to climb those mountains, and how this led him to leave home to earn modern education. He continued.

"My parents couldn't pay for my schooling, so I supported myself with errands and domestic work after classes, nights, and weekends, in exchange for room and board with no less than seven families in four different towns, from elementary school through eighth grade, in four separate schools.

"When I got older, I made my way by tutoring wealthy children for pay. I let nothing stop me from getting ahead. I even built a kind of airplane to keep moving toward my goals. My opportunities came with many challenges: hunger, poverty, homelessness, abuse, and abandonment."

When Desta finished his story, everyone was speechless.

"Your journey is remarkable," Mr. Johnson finally said. "Most American kids don't leave home in childhood, let alone live with strangers, and don't accomplish a lot, much less get into medical school and travel the world. Your story is an inspiration to the youth of our country." He glanced at Jake, and then Aida.

Mrs. Johnson found her voice. "I should think so! In your shoes, most American kids would have quit early on." She tapped her fingers on the table thoughtfully.

Mr. Johnson turned to Jake and Aida. "You two certainly could benefit from Desta's example."

"Exactly what I've thought for a long time," David said. "Once I got involved in Desta's life, I insisted he come to America," David said, "not just for a good education, but to be an example to others."

"Were you ever tempted to quit after all those bad experiences? Aida asked.

"No," Desta replied, "because I treated those bad things as obstacles to overcome in order to achieve my goals. I tried not to let them get in the way of my purposes."

"Should Desta come live with you," David said, "I think his life story could inspire you to reach your own goals." He looked one by one at his hosts.

Mr. Johnson beheld his family. "No one in this household, or anyone else we know, has a story like Desta's. We have much to learn from such experiences.

"These are changing times, and our children must adapt to them, and learn how to live with all kinds of people to thrive. And when we pass, we want them to leave the world better than they found it.

"Because my father was a diplomat, I lived in other countries and had a well-rounded upbringing. My schoolmates came from many backgrounds, and I learned to appreciate people's differences. For example, at the American International School in Egypt, I had classmates from thirty countries.

"Now, when we travel, we feel at home wherever we are. Whereas our children," he said, fixing his gray eyes on Jake and Aida, "have had no such experience. That's why when Dr. Hal suggested we host an international student, Bev and I readily entertained the idea."

Mr. Johnson turned his attention to Desta. "And so," he said definitively, "after consulting with my family, we have decided to host you for the coming year."

Desta dipped his head in gratitude and said, "Thank you so very much."

"We hope that from you, Aida and Jake will gain a greater appreciation of how disadvantaged people live in the world, and how fortunate they are to be Americans. And it's equally important that they learn to accept all people as their equals, regardless of their origins."

Aida rolled her eyes, while Jake shifted in his seat, clamped his lips, and stared at his father. Both children didn't seem to take their father's remarks well.

"You're right," David said, leaning forward to get up. "It's important for young people to adapt and grow." He tapped Desta's shoulder.

"You're not going yet," Mrs. Johnson said abruptly. She signaled to Aida who got up and went to the house. "Your young friend would wonder what type of people we are to let you go without offering you something to eat."

David hesitated.

"Something light," Mrs. Johnson insisted.

Desta's friend sat back. "If it pleases you, Mrs. Johnson," David said.

Aida and a woman in her thirties with dark brown hair arrived with fruit salad on small plates and forks and a pitcher of iced tea and stacked drinking glasses. The woman passed the plates and Aida poured the iced tea and placed them in front of the visitors and the parents. The woman returned with the trays; Aida sat down.

After their meals David informed the Johnsons that he and Desta would be traveling for a few days, and after that, David's father would bring Desta here to live with them. They all shook hands, and the visitors thanked their hosts graciously and left.

FOUR

David Hartman and Desta exited the opened gate, down the long driveway and into traffic on the Old Boston Road. They headed toward Desta's school.

"The Johnsons' home is not far from Abraham Lincoln Junior College. Some students call it Abe Lincoln for short," David said. "After you get a look at your new school, if you feel up to it, we can visit Rye City's big amusement park, called Playland." David's face lit up as if the name itself brought back happy memories.

"Look forward to it," Desta said. His fears about his host family had abated; he was eager to explore the campus where he'd be spending the coming year.

David headed north to Playland Parkway, and then southeast to Forest Ave. The driver flipped his left signal, and after about three-quarters of a mile, Forest Ave became Independence Road. Desta remembered the name from his college application. 1865 Independence Road was his school's address. Desta suddenly filled with anxiety and excitement. He sighed under his breath.

He turned to David, who'd been quiet awhile, and seemed preoccupied. Desta pointed to a road sign at the first traffic stop. "I recall that name. We should be there soon," he said.

"In a few minutes," David noted.

They turned left on a nameless street that ended in a vast asphalt field, where a few dozen cars shimmered in the midafternoon sun. They parked and followed a walkway lined with flowerbeds of purple, pink, white, and red, toward an imposing gate joined on either side by straight stone walls that ran both ways and vanished into woods.

Desta thought this must be someone's home, but the enormous red and blue arching sign ABRAHAM LINCOLN JUNIOR COLLEGE belied that notion.

Unexpectedly, a man in uniform stepped from the shadow of a pillar, and asked, "Can I help you?"

David addressed him. "This young man arrived from Ethiopia yesterday to study here. We came for a look at the campus."

The man looked appraisingly at Desta and then asked, "Is his English good enough? Some foreign students who come here fail their first semester because of the language."

David's face hardened. "The admissions office thought so—can we go in, please?"

The guard asked for David's ID. This little business done, the man let them pass the gate.

"Oh, my goodness!" Desta cried, as he looked up at a towering building, unlike any he had seen before.

David answered the question on Desta's mind. "It's a castle," he said. "A long time ago, a rich family lived here. After the owners died, their children left it empty until about twenty years ago, when a wealthy man bought and converted the whole estate to a junior college, named it for our sixteenth president, and had its street and address changed to Independence Road, number 1865, the year our civil war ended. Today, the castle houses administrative offices and conference rooms."

Desta had gotten a bigger answer than he'd bargained for. "Fascinating," he said. His eyes went from the central tower to wings on either side, and then to the immaculate grounds of thick grass, lush trees, and blossoming plants bordering the buildings and stone wall. Just like the Johnsons' property, everything was trimmed, shaped, and patterned to please the eye. The whole campus seemed serene, almost magical, a sanctuary for contemplation.

Many questions bubbled up, requiring too many answers of David, and Desta chose to silently enjoy what he saw.

They turned left, following a wide paved path that went west along the back wall of the building. When they turned the corner, they found modern structures of stone and brick, and glass and wood. David said some were classrooms, and others housed the library, bookstore, dining hall, and gymnasium. Beyond these buildings were a sports stadium and facilities for track and field.

In the center of a large circular courtyard stood a bronze statue, which David said was that of Lincoln. With his downturned face and right hand extended, Lincoln appeared to be speaking, or entreating passersby. The angular jaw and deep-set eyes said much about the man, and Desta was taken with him. Desta imagined students sitting on the surrounding benches, listening to an address by this stately figure.

"Come, let me show you something interesting from America's past," David said. Desta was not quite finished communing with Lincoln and the solemnity of the place, but cheerfully followed his friend. David proceeded along a footpath that went south, parallel to the left wing of the castle. The path snaked around lush trees, manicured rose bushes, and many flowering plants Desta had never seen before, which he paused to admire.

After about a hundred yards, they reached a garden of life-sized sculptures of men and women, arrayed in the earth's cardinal directions, set apart from an oversized statue of Lincoln at the locus. Each sculpture faced another, positioned in a different cardinal direction, and each pair seemed to chat as casually as neighbors at a garden party.

Plaques at the outside of each directional line identified the statues, which David said portrayed figures of importance in the American Civil War and the history of the United States.

"I think you're going to enjoy this place, Desta," David said. "Its only drawback is that it's not coed."

"Coed?" Desta asked.

"A school for boys and girls," David Hartman said with a grin.

"Is this so the boys can focus on their studies?" Desta asked, lighting up.

"You could say that . . . and it's partly just old Puritan mentality."

Desta thought of asking what exactly was a "Puritan mentality," but David was already on to his next thought. "Abraham Lincoln was founded as an elite two-year, or community college for rich students who didn't have the grades or achievements to get into Ivy League schools like Columbia, Yale, and Harvard.

"If they do well here for two years, they have a chance to transfer to one of the top schools and get a good job when they graduate. You, too, have that chance. Lincoln is one of the top transfer schools in the country."

Desta was not thinking about academics or even next year, but instead whether he would fit in with the Johnson family, or in a school of wealthy students. He'd have to find out for himself, and so he kept his troubled thoughts to himself. He said to David, "That is good to know."

David turned to his companion and said, "You know, instead of going now to the amusement park, I think we'd better go home, you rest, and then we can talk about a plan I have for the next few days."

This was good news for Desta, already tired from the day's activities. He needed to think about everything he had experienced today, and integrate that with his own life experiences. He had to formulate his own path forward to face his challenges without undue worry.

They left the Lincoln campus. The pair said nothing while driving back to David's family home. Desta was lost in thought, and David seemed to sense that.

Desta was jolted from his musings when David finally said, "I was thinking you and I would go camping."

Desta didn't know what camping was, or where people went to do it. And Desta didn't want to ask, either, and risk the kind of humiliation by others that he'd felt long ago for not knowing what a tomato was. He had hoped his first sightseeing trip would be to New York City. He thought for a moment how to reply.

David continued. "Camping is a nice way to ease you into American life, get some country air and beautiful surroundings before you start the grind of academics. And you and I can have more time to talk about your search for the coin.

"You know, I have been wanting to go camping for years, but my studies and travels have prevented me, and so I'd planned to do it before I start work. Now that you might join me makes my plans doubly attractive."

Desta could tell from David's enthusiasm that camping would be fun, and felt it was important to grant his friend's wishes.

"Whatever you say is fine with me, so long as I get to see New York City before I start school." He glanced at David and grinned, his thoughts now freed from more serious matters.

"I plan to take you to the city," David said, "after you get adjusted to your new environment. New York can be overwhelming, even for me, a regular visitor, let alone for a newcomer."

"You have been reading my mind about such things," Desta said. "Thanks for your consideration."

"I see your stay with the Johnsons working out well for you."

"I like them," Desta said. "And their dog."

"I think that dog is a dealmaker," David said, smiling. "Jake seemed very happy to see you scratching Kooper's belly. It was like the dog had already approved you."

"We'll see," Desta said.

FIVE

Upon their return in the early afternoon, David Hartman parked the car in the driveway. He pulled down a rectangular visor above his head and pressed the button of a pocket-sized plastic box strapped to the visor. Then a broad door before them lifted like the jaw of a giant beast, to reveal a room housing two gleaming cars—a hunter-green station wagon and a four-door black Mercedes Benz sedan.

David closed the garage by pressing a button next to another door that opened into the kitchen. The smell of onion and garlic from their breakfast still hung in the air.

"Go rest if you like, Desta," David said, "while I make our lunch."

"How about I help you?" Desta suggested.

David welcomed the offer and instructed Desta to slice some tomatoes and chop a red onion while David toasted the bread and set out cold cuts of meat and a green salad.

"Thanks for helping," David said. He served the piled sandwiches and salad, opened two brown cans labeled Root Beer on the side, and set them next to their plates.

Desta took a sip of his drink, and quickly put it down. He found the strong, unfamiliar flavor, like bark-steeped water, disagreeable.

As they ate, David glanced at Desta occasionally as if expecting him to comment about their earlier visits.

"So, you like your new family?" David asked finally, breaking into Desta's silence.

"I do, and their dog," Desta said. "You're right, Kooper is my bridge to the family. The dog's approval was important to me."

"Yeah," David said, "Kooper set the tone because Jake immediately reacted with pleasure when he noticed the dog wagging his tail as he came to you. The atmosphere around us instantly brightened."

"If Kooper were human, he would have smiled wide and shaken my hand."

"It was a great relief to me," David said after he swallowed his last bite. "It means we can go camping on a happier note and enjoy ourselves."

After Desta washed the plates and forks and put them on the rack to dry, David said, "Go rest. We have a long day tomorrow."

"Thank you for the lunch," he said. "I certainly can use more sleep. . . . I'm looking forward to our trip."

Desta's fatigue felt like morning fog that wouldn't lift. And he had that leaden, ominous discomfort in his head. He turned and went upstairs.

Inside the room, he took his shoes off and lay on the bed, hoping sleep would whisk him away. But he found himself staring at the ceiling, mind on a train of thought.

With everything he had seen and heard today, it seemed he was on the cusp of a new world, where he had no clear idea what skills or talent he would need to adapt and thrive in it.

Strangely, as Desta struggled with these thoughts, he could feel his past woes—his privations, fears, loneliness, yearnings to connect deeply with someone or something—sloughing off like an old skin, as if by some hidden force.

He knew that the ancient prophecy charted his course to America, where millions before him had come to find freedom and a better life. But Desta was here foremost to search for King Solomon's Second Coin of Magic and Fortune.

A poem from the Statue of Liberty's booklet he'd once read came to him: *Give me your tired, your poor, your huddled masses yearning to breathe free, the wretched refuse of your teeming shore. Send these, the homeless, tempest-tossed to me. I lift my lamp beside the golden door!*

He wanted to believe that somehow these words would be true for him, too, and Lady Liberty would shine her lamp over his path to his education, and to discover the coin. Her message was his glimmer of hope, leading to his redemption.

The thought comforted him that he would soon be free from want and have space to think as he wished, without others forcing their beliefs or politics on him. Several months back in high school, a group of students had beaten him up for not joining their demonstration against the

Ethiopian government. Now, for the first time, he would be free to express feelings he'd denied himself for so long. He would enjoy *the luxury of feeling good.* Desta fell into a deep sleep.

SEVERAL HOURS LATER, he woke and went downstairs to find David standing before several objects he had spread out on the living room floor. He had a notebook in one hand and a pencil in the other and seemed to be taking inventory.

Desta couldn't make sense of the scene, a hodge-podge of things whose function he couldn't tell. Save for the two tissue paper rolls, most of them looked like throwaways, their shabbiness in stark contrast with the plush cream-colored carpet and beige leather sofa nearby.

"Oh, you're up," David blurted out, looking puzzled. "What you see is what we need for our camping trip." He continued checking items in his notebook.

Desta appraised the things before him. There were two old mummy-like sacks, which David said were their sleeping bags, an equally worn rolled pad pair, a rusted stove, a beat-up, small aluminum cooking pot, two plastic bottles and a plaid thermos flask fitted with a brown drinking cup, and a pile of faded forest green fabric inside a small, dusty open sack, which David said were part of their tent gear.

In addition, there was an assortment of other things: a brown matchbox, small paper plates, a half-pint kerosene can, and a linen pouch containing their tent gear.

A pair of backpacks with dented metal frames leaned against the wall near the front door. They, too, appeared to have just been brought out of retirement. Two neatly folded plaid shirts, four new T-shirts, and two rolled gray socks sat on the couch.

Having completed his camping checklist, David placed the notebook and pencil on the arm of the sofa. "Let's go—" he began to say, only to stop suddenly and stare at Desta.

"I see that you don't seem too thrilled about camping," David said. "Let me explain. A few days before you arrived, I had this message, as if it came from above. It said to me, 'Before anything else, you should show Desta America's natural, unspoiled beauty.'

"I know you want to see New York City. You will have many chances to go there, but not to go on this camping trip.

"In high school, I belonged to an outdoor club. We went camping often, and the things you see here are from those days. I borrowed an extra back-pack for you from an old camping buddy. Now, let's get to other things."

"Don't worry," Desta said, "I'm fine with this trip, now that you've explained your reasons. I appreciate that." Desta followed his host to the kitchen.

David stopped before the round white table in the breakfast nook. "Here are our daily rations," he said.

Nuts, seeds, and dried fruits, a bag of dried beef strips, white utensils, and a box that said marshmallow on its cover, occupied different bowls and plastic containers on the table. Two packages shaped like a cooking pan announced "JIFFY POP . . . As Much Fun to Make as It Is to Eat!" Desta looked at them with curiosity.

"There are corn kernels in there," David said. Desta's family called these maize, though the kind back home didn't pop.

David mixed the seeds, nuts, and dried fruit in a large ceramic bowl. Afterward, he transferred the mixture into plastic bags.

"These and the beef jerky will be our trail snacks," David said, hold-ing up a bag of each. He placed them back on the table, pointed to two glass jars, and said, "When we are starving, we'll make peanut butter and jelly sandwiches." He grinned.

Desta didn't have much to say about all this; the whole idea of a 'snack' was new to him.

"Here," David said, handing two bags to Desta. "I'll take the rest."

They brought their food to the living room and set it next to their camping things. Next, David clutched the edge of the piled green fabric with both hands and stretched it out on the carpet.

"This is our tent," David said. "To keep out insects, dampness, and fallen leaves. He doubled it over four times until it was small enough to roll and fit at the bottom of a backpack.

David then brushed and stretched the mummy-shaped sacks one at a time, folded them lengthwise, and tightly rolled and strapped them. He put the plastic bottles and thermos into a pouch and placed them next to the rolled bags.

The corners of David's mouth twitched, his big brow tightened and relaxed, and his eyes looked wistful as he arranged the different items.

He glanced at Desta. "Linda, my girlfriend, had planned to come with us," he said, "but something unexpected related to her Ph.D. thesis in anthropology took her out of the country. She plans to defend her work at the end of the fall semester." He shook his head.

"That's too bad," Desta said. "I would have liked to spend time with her too." He looked up at his host. "One thing about your camping puzzles me. When travelers in Ethiopia need food and shelter, they present themselves at strangers' homes as 'guests of God'; don't Americans do this, too? Or are we unable to do this because we are going so far from where people live?" he asked.

"No. Americans don't generally ask strangers for shelter and food when we travel," David said. "And yes, campers usually stay in places far from cities and towns."

"Where are we going?" Desta asked. "I don't know much about the geography of this country, but I'm curious."

"To the Green Mountain National Forest in Vermont. This place is in the wilderness. So, we need to bring our own supplies."

Desta scratched the back of his head. "Are there wild animals in the forest that attack humans?" he asked. He remembered at home people didn't dare spend the night in a forest without a gun.

"There could be bears, but they are generally not aggressive."

Desta hesitated and then said, "It sounds like it will be an interesting adventure. I'm looking forward to it."

"And who knows," David added, lightheartedly. "A physical and mental challenge like camping could be useful to your search for the Second Coin of Magic and Fortune."

"That would be a bonus," Desta said. "But I'll be happy just to see a part of your country. I need to go to my room now." Desta turned to go.

"All right. I'll call you when I have dinner ready."

Desta opened the window in his room to let in the cool air. Although it was nearly five o'clock, the sun was far above the western horizon, and Desta wondered if dusk in America came later than 6 p.m., when it did in Ethiopia.

He found himself gazing at the lovely, whitewashed homes and trimmed front yards across the street. He thought, *could camping in the woods really be that much fun?*

He would carry a load on his back and walk through the forest all day. All he had wanted to see after arriving in America was the forest of tall buildings in New York, not wilderness. Sleeping in the woods like a bandit was beyond him.

Desta tried to reason what he could gain from this strange escapade. He would see the American countryside. He could learn about American plants and trees, and see strange birds and animals, that hopefully didn't attack or eat campers.

He thought that his American life seemed like a new language or musical instrument to master before he could feel confident and comfortable. Including all the camping equipment, and a weekend spent wandering in the woods like an animal. He was on a precipice of change unlike any before.

David called Desta from the bottom of the stairs, taking him from his thoughts.

Coming to the living room, Desta noticed two pairs of rugged shoes with tangled laces next to the camping gear, now packed and ready to go.

"Please try these two pairs of boots," David said. "I bought, 10 and 9D. I'll return the one that doesn't fit you." Desta chose size 9D.

David then picked up the smaller backpack. "Turn around," David said, "Let's see how it looks on you." He appeared anxious and businesslike. He lifted the pack and let Desta slip his arms through the straps, one at a time. David adjusted the pack so it sat squarely on Desta's lean frame. Desta sagged a bit, like a donkey with its first load.

"You wanted to see how I handle the weight?" Desta asked with a strained smile.

"Yeah, and how the whole thing sits on your back."

For Desta, harder than the weight was the pack's bulk, and that he had never carried anything like this on his back.

They brought their backpacks out to the green wagon in the driveway. David unlocked the tailgate and opened it. He folded down the back-facing yellow bench seat and dropped his pack on top. He removed Desta's and shoved it in the trunk as well. While David fussed to fit the packs neatly, Desta got the hiking boots. David set them in one corner of the trunk, closed up the car, and they went in.

After dinner, they made their final plans. David said it would take four hours to reach the Green Mountains. They would get up at 5 a.m. and leave half an hour later to arrive by 10. The trail was a loop; they would hike part of it that day, camp overnight, and finish the next day. Their plan made, they went to bed.

SIX

The next day Desta stirred to life at four. Once he was fully awake, he switched on the light, jumped out of bed, and went to take a shower. The warm water invigorated his senses and brightened them even more. Afterward, he dried off and dressed, and followed the smell and sounds of cooking downstairs to the kitchen.

"I was going to wake you, but then I heard the shower running," David said with a smile. "Thank you for rising promptly. Breakfast's in ten minutes."

He dropped two slices of bread in the slots of a stainless-steel box. He then cracked five eggs and dropped them into a pan where onions and garlic slowly sautéed. He turned up the heat and stirred vigorously with a wooden spoon.

Once done, David split the eggs between two plates with a slice of toast on each one. Then he slipped two more slices into the metal box and set down the dishes next to napkins and utensils on opposite sides of the white table.

"Let's eat quickly," David said, and sat down. His urgency was apparent in his rushed handling of things and tense hazel eyes. They scarfed down their food, washed their dishes and utensils, and stacked them on a rack. Then David brought a metal box containing their food and drinks and returned.

They readied themselves to leave and headed to the garage, where David took keys from a wallboard and locked up. David marched down the driveway and got in the driver's side of the station wagon, eager to leave. Desta sat down next to him, feeling anxious about their weekend in the woods.

David started the engine and let it warm for several minutes. He glanced at his watch. "Let's hope we get there by ten."

He wheeled the car from the driveway into the street and headed east. Barely above the horizon, the sun splashed the tops of trees with dreamy golden light. Traffic trickled into the roads like a summer creek. After a few turns on local streets, they entered the expressway—Highway 237, first going east and then north on interstate highway I-95.

David seemed less harried. His cheeks flushed, eyes glistened, and he spoke in cheerful notes.

"Could you open that box near your feet?" David asked, extending his arm and pointing. "And pass me the first tape."

Desta bent down, lifted the box's cover, revealing two rows of four hard plastic cases, which resembled small books.

He pulled out the first with a colorfully dressed group of people on its cover and inspected it. "What's this?" he asked.

"It's an eight-track tape that contains music recordings," David said.

"Pass it to me," David said finally, his left hand on the wheel. He gripped the tape by its edge and inserted it into the open port under the dashboard.

"In America, we don't just listen to music on the radio.," David said. "You can listen to what you want on demand." He smiled.

First a click, rough and loud. Then a hiss, followed by a slow, upbeat musical instrument followed by a man's strident voice, accompanied by more instruments.

David harmonized with the vocal on the tape. He seemed to float in happiness.

He turned the volume down a little, glanced at Desta, and asked, "Ever listened to the Beatles?"

"No, not really. Chuck Berry and Elvis Presley were popular at home."

"My mother installed the tape player so she could listen to Frank Sinatra and Mozart. I brought my favorite Beatles tapes for us to enjoy.

"It's great you can have this music wherever you go," Desta said.

Desta had missed the song's next three verses while he and David were talking. Now he paid close attention to the song once again.

David tuned out everything else. Eyes straight ahead, hands on the wheel, he made subtle adjustments as the tires of the big machine pushed them forward, past trees and road signs.

Click.

The song had not finished when David pressed a button below the dash and advanced the tape.

As the music played, David moved his head and tapped the wheel with his fingers. He seemed in another world.

Click.

When the third track, "Lucy in the Sky with Diamonds," began, David was not just listening to the music but imbibing it. The station wagon now felt like a bubble sailing through the air.

A small two-door car sped past them on the right and the driver flashed his middle finger toward them.

"People don't like it when you drive slow in the fast lane," David said. "The music made me forget to move over to the right lanes, to let him pass."

Desta wondered about the man's middle finger, when David said, "When someone flips their middle finger like that, don't be tempted to do the same to them. It's a big insult, and you never know how they might react."

The tape played on. The Beatles were growing on Desta. The melody, brassy instruments, and reedy voices played on his senses, and the bright, happy choruses, seductive rhythms, and brisk tempos drew Desta like a bee to honey.

"Words that would be boring to read over and over on a page sound so compelling when sung and played in a beautiful melody," Desta said.

"This group does a fantastic job of it," David said.

"They sound great to foreign ears like mine," Desta said.

The grey landscape continued to bend past them as if driven by a storm. Trees and highway signs sped by, thrilling Desta by validating in action Newton's laws of force, mass, and acceleration.

The scenery, the big green-and-white signs, the swirling ramps leading to bridges spanning the highway, the orderly cars and trucks, great and small, sharing the road, all of it impressed Desta that America was a great country.

David remained mute, buoyant, and seemingly lost in the music. At one point, he looked at his watch, and then moved to the fast lane to pass a string of slower cars. Moments later, he looked in the rearview mirror and exclaimed, "Oh shit!"

Desta didn't like the way his friend looked. "What happened?"

"A cop!"

Desta glanced at the side-view mirror. A red light gyrated atop a black and white car that looked official.

David turned the music way down and eased the car across two lanes to the shoulder and stopped. The official vehicle moved in tandem with the station wagon and stopped behind them. David waited stiffly, hands on the wheel. Desta watched as the cop in black uniform, gun hanging from his belt holster, approached cautiously, and said, "Do you realize how fast you were going, sir?"

"No, not really," David replied awkwardly.

"I clocked you at 87 miles per hour. Can I see your driver's license?"

David fumbled for the wallet in his back pocket, took out his license, and passed it to the cop.

"Be right back," the cop said and left. After a few minutes, he returned with a slim yellow pad that he handed David to sign.

Stiff-lipped, the lawbreaker scribbled on the bottom page and handed back the pad to the policeman, who tore out the page and gave it to David.

Desta's friend folded the slip twice and put it in his wallet. He turned toward Desta. "This can happen to you when you drive over the speed limit," David said. "Always try to obey the law."

They drove more on the I-95 and then got off the expressway and onto a local road. David pulled to the shoulder and parked. He took a map out of the glove compartment and studied it. He then folded it to show the area where they were headed. He set it on his lap and kept driving.

After several roads and a string of towns, they reached a parking lot where a sign announced GREEN MOUNTAIN NATIONAL FOREST, Stratton Pond Trailhead, in painted dark brown wood. A dozen cars occupied the gravel lot, but no one was in sight. David parked between two trucks. They got out of the car and stretched their limbs. The air was warm and fragrant.

David looked around. "It seems everyone is out on the trails," he declared. "We need to get going pretty soon too." He walked around to the trunk and opened it. He took out the two backpacks and leaned them against the side of the car.

"It's about four and a half miles to the pond where we'll make camp," he said.

"How long will it take us?" Desta asked.

"Three and a half to four hours." David peeked at his watch. "It's nearly eleven o'clock now. Let's have lunch," he said.

David brought two cold sandwiches and a couple of Fanta drinks from the metal box in the back seat of the car. He gave one to Desta and kept the other for himself. They perched on the car's rear bumper.

"The first pair of our four meat sandwiches," David said, smiling. "We'll have the other two for dinner."

They washed their meals down with their drinks, and disposed of their bottles and wrappings in the trash can at the edge of the parking lot. Returning to the car, David checked that everything they needed for camping was in their backpacks and then locked the trunk.

David helped Desta mount his pack on his back and tightened the straps in front. Desta wiggled his upper body, so the weight sat evenly on his back. It was heavier and more cumbersome than anything he had ever seen his brothers carry. David threw on his own pack like a sack of feathers and tightened the chest straps.

Desta shook his head and wondered if he'd make it even halfway there without collapsing. He sidled one way and the other, testing the pack's stability on his sinewy back. For now, his energy intact, he could control its bulk. He passed his hand over the tattooed coin image above his heart. *Please seed energy and courage in me to make it to our destination.*

He couldn't shake the thought that this trip was pointless. In the countryside where Desta grew up, people carried loads on their shoulders, head, or back for a purpose. But here, he bore this load only to walk along a trail for hours and spend the night. They would do the same tomorrow: walk all day, camp someplace, and eventually go home. Was this supposed to be fun?

They strode side by side on the road for a mile, and then got to a trail marked by a sign bolted to a stout weathered post that read, "Stratton Pond 3.2 miles."

Desta's back and knees had begun to hurt, but he didn't mention this to David. This was his first challenge in America, and he would endure it to achieve his goals.

Right before they entered the trail, Desta told David he wanted to shift some items in the pack to better balance it on his back. David took down Desta's load, opened the back pouch, and adjusted the contents at the bottom of the pack.

Desta took the moment to rest and rub the coin, praying it would give him strength and make his load as light as a pack of leaves.

"It should be okay now," David said, and helped Desta strap on the pack.

Desta felt better; although the load was still heavy, his back and knees were okay now. They entered the wooded trail, Desta following David. After a while, his shirt felt clammy on his back, and the skin dewed around his hairline.

Desta looked around for a tree or plant to remind him of Ethiopia, but nothing resembled those back home. He tilted his head to listen for bird calls, and scanned the trees for monkeys or other animals, but he saw none. This vast forest was so serene that Desta wondered if there was any life here. It seemed the only things these woods had in common with those back home were its earthy fragrance, luxuriant undergrowth, and the mottled sunlight on the forest floor. All of it delighted and soothed him and made him forget his heavy load.

Suddenly, Desta heard thrashing leaves and looked toward the sound. A golden brown, white-tailed beast stood, turned its neck, and gazed at them. The two hikers halted and stared at it. "How about that!" David whispered. "You've just seen your first deer, Desta," David said, lips parting into a smile.

"It resembles the *goma*—antelope—in Ethiopia, but without white on its tail," Desta said, excited to see this lovely creature.

"I don't think the two are related," David said. Soon the deer began to walk at first, her head moving nervously back and forth. Then it took off at top speed, her white tail flashing like a burst of light. The hikers continued moving, and Desta returned to his thoughts.

After journeying restlessly for seven thousand miles, his first trip was to a forest, his back burdened like a mule. Desta had yet to discover how this trip would advance his education or search for the second coin.

David turned to his friend and asked, "Does the backpack feel better now?"

Desta said it was fine, and David continued. "I was thinking last night how lucky you are that your new plans worked out so smoothly—the flight to America, college, the Johnsons."

Desta said nothing. David's comment only reminded Desta that he was still a child of charity, and it hurt his pride. He wished by now that he were independent.

David sensed Desta's antipathy, and quickly added, "I'm just glad everything worked in our favor so you can be with us.

"When you mentioned the connection between the two Ryes and your two coins, I wondered if your being here is a part of a bigger mystery."

"Yes," Desta said. "It's also a mystery why we came here when my dream was to see New York City."

"Well," David began. "Speaking of mysteries, there are things I'm baffled about myself. Perhaps we'll talk about them tonight under the stars."

"Your father finding the Johnsons for me is no coincidence," Desta said. "Or why they named their daughter Aida."

"What do you mean?"

"It's the name of an Ethiopian slave girl."

"But as Mr. Johnson said, she was a princess, too."

Desta did not want to argue with his friend. "I look forward to learning why you think my presence in America is mysterious."

Their footpath met the Stratton-Pond Trail, where a sign pointed north to the pond. They now passed lush undergrowth, and flowering and fruit-bearing plants.

Desta's load began to bother him again. His energy was good, but his legs wouldn't hold up much longer. Yet his surroundings were enough to distract him.

They came upon a shrub with big, tongue-like leaves that lay flat or arched on the ground; it bore the bluest round fruit Desta had ever seen. They stopped to study the plant. David bent and picked about a dozen plump berries and put them in his pocket. "They may be edible. We'll rinse them at camp."

Only a few yards ahead, Desta tripped and fell forward, nearly smashing his nose, and drawing blood from his arms and forehead.

"Oh my God!" David cried, turning around. "What happened?"

"That rock," Desta said, pointing to a sharp stone half buried in the ground.

"Sorry to see this."

David got the first aid kit from his pack and bandaged the cuts. He suggested that they rest for a while before resuming their hike.

After their break, they passed a dozen people returning to their cars. Right away, Desta felt the presence of someone following them. Yet, looking around, he saw no one. Just then, Desta felt his energy return. Even his backpack felt lighter.

Desta and David finally reached the pond, an enchanting, peaceful place surrounded by pine trees and bushes. Desta was sweaty but no longer tired.

David led their search for a camping spot. The heat and humidity grew more apparent here in the open. They found a great site at a clearing near the pond, below a ridge of rocks. It had a beautiful water view, easy shore access, and fortress-like surroundings.

David took off his backpack and leaned it against the rock wall behind them. Desta removed his pack with relief and stood it a few paces from David's.

The afternoon sun had turned the lake's surface glassy, and the water near the shore was so clear they could see fish at the bottom. David hopped onto a boulder and sat. He removed his shoes and socks, rolled up his pants legs, and stepped into the water. He closed his eyes and purred with pleasure.

He turned to Desta and said, "The water's delightful. Let's have a swim."

"Go ahead," Desta said. "I'll look after our belongings."

David didn't need prodding. He undressed, leaned forward, and tore into the water like an arrow. Some distance from shore, David surfaced and swam farther out, then returned to the shore. Out of his clothes, David looked leaner and taller.

His skin glistened in the afternoon sun, water beading his hair and muscled shoulders and arms. Droplets clung to the hair furring his chest and legs. Desta thought his friend would make the perfect subject to sculpt the ideal human form.

"Now it's your turn," David said, looking down at Desta.

Desta squirmed. "But I don't know how to swim."

He explained how his older brother nearly drowned him while pretending to teach him how to swim. Since then, he'd had an aversion to deep water.

"That's too bad," David said. "If this were a swimming pool, I would give you lessons. Perhaps you can do that at college."

They set up the tent, and then laid out their mats and sleeping bags inside it. Then they sat down and ate their trail snacks with bottles of Fanta.

Desta looked up to the western sky and asked, "Why does the sun set so much later here than in Ethiopia?"

"America is much farther north of the equator. During our summer, the sun is in the northern hemisphere and the days are longer."

David decided to visit some of the other campers. Desta sat facing west, wondering how far he would have to follow the sun before he found the owner of the second coin. He sighed deeply. Now that he was sitting, he felt the brunt of their hike. His feet, legs, and shoulders ached. He decided to lie on his sleeping bag and rest a bit. He woke an hour later to the tap of David's fingers.

"I met people from my town," David said. "They suggested places to hike tomorrow. And they offered that we could leave most of our stuff with them."

"Great!" Desta said. "Then we can sleep here in this nice spot tomorrow night."

"Yeah, that's what I thought too," David said. "Let's make a fire. You go collect wood while I make our dinner."

Desta was used to collecting firewood from the forest when he lived in the countryside, and he quickly got to work collecting dry branches and twigs. He soon returned with an armful. He first made a bed of twigs and dry leaves and then arranged the larger pieces of wood into a cone over it. He struck a match and carefully lit the kindling. Orange and brown flames erupted, casting a golden glow before them.

"Here," David said, and handed Desta a variation of their lunch sandwich. "They kept well in our cooler with ice cubes."

The last rays of sun flickered over the water like candlelight in a draft. Night soon fell, draping the world far and near in shadow. Desta's little mound of flames reflected in the pond like dancing spirits.

"Let's toast marshmallows," David said, and picked up a twig. He sharpened one end of the stick with his pocketknife, then opened the plastic bag of foamy white cubes and stuck the twig's sharp end into one of them. He twirled the stick over the flames so the marshmallow would brown evenly. When it began to char, he took it from the fire. He cut a slice of bread in half with his red utility knife, sandwiched the roasted marshmallow in the bread, and handed it to Desta.

"Here's your dessert." David now roasted another marshmallow for himself.

"Thank you!" Desta said, and bit into it. "Delicious!" he exclaimed.

"We used to do this at campfires in high school," David said, as he chewed his marshmallow sandwich. His expression grew wistful. He opened another Fanta, poured half into a Styrofoam cup for Desta, and drank the rest out of the bottle.

Finishing his drink, Desta rose, collected more wood, and dropped it on the fire. He picked up a stick and began poking the embers with it. He thought about his aborted dream to study medicine in Bulgaria.

"What a difference a month makes," he said, glancing at David. "Only a few weeks ago, I was fretting about my dashed plans for medical school. Now look where I ended up." He smiled.

"I'll say something about that after I take a leak." David grabbed the flashlight and briefly disappeared into the dark. When he returned, he announced, "I'm still hungry. Let's have popcorn."

He grasped the round covered Jiffy tray by its metal handle and removed the cardboard lid to reveal a pleated aluminum cover. He held the tray over the fire and continuously shook it. Gradually, the contents began to pop, and the aluminum sheet rose until it resembled a big balloon.

David pierced the balloon with his knife, exposing puffy white kernels. He curled back the foil. "Dig in," he said, setting the tray between them.

Desta took a handful of the cracked corn and tossed it in his mouth. He loved the crunchy, sweet taste.

Desta watched as David ground the food in his solid jaw, eyes thoughtful and distant. "To continue what I said earlier," David began, "you and your mission are shrouded in mystery."

Desta jerked his chin and narrowed his eyes. "Shrouded in mystery?"

"Yeah! It turns out, I was in Ethiopia for your education and search
for the coin. The Peace Corps job was only a vehicle for that purpose.
During my first Christmas break in grad school, a strange woman appeared in my dream and urged me to join the Peace Corps. Days later, a
man on a white horse came in a dream and suggested the same. That's
why I came to Ethiopia." David paused a moment.

"Then halfway through the first semester teaching at Debre Marcos
High School, that same woman appeared at my doorstep and advised I
send you a hundred birrs so you could continue your education and
search for the coin in Finote Selam.

"At the end of high school, you wanted to go to Bulgaria to study
medicine. Still, after you resisted my suggestion, the map and compass
sent you to America. So, what can I say? My life is somehow entwined
with your mission. Coming here instead of New York City also seems
for that reason. And how else can I explain why my girlfriend canceled
this trip at the last minute? You were meant to be here with me, to see
the true America."

Stunned, Desta put his hand over his mouth and gazed into the boisterous fire. "I take it the woman you're referring to is Eleni?" he asked
and glanced at his friend.

"Yes!"

"And the man on the white horse?"

"I've no idea who he is and never saw him again."

Desta sighed, leaned against the rock, and stared at their dimly lit haven. An oblong moon rose above the trees. He thought for some time.
His mind devolved to another world, but he could still hear David
munching his popcorn, and the water lapping against the rocks. He lifted
his head, glanced at his neighbor, and said, "I thought these things were
behind me." His face hardened. "When will I ever live my life and pursue my dreams?!"

"Take it as a dispensation from heaven, not a punishment," David
said, as if channeling the advice of Desta's spiritual guide, Tsadok,
who'd helped chart Desta's course to America.

"It's easier said than to live it," Desta responded.

"Here is what we'll do," David said. "Go to bed now, rise early, and hike to the fire tower, uphill west of us. We'll come back and hike around the pond, and then I'll teach you how to swim."

"I'll go with you, but no swimming lesson, please," Desta said. Suddenly Desta was underwater again, drowning at his brother's hands.

"We'll talk about it tomorrow. Let's go to bed," David said. "I'm sore all over." He got up, and said, smiling, "If we don't want a bear to visit us, I need to collect the trash." He gathered it in a plastic bag. "We'll take it home with us this way."

Desta arranged their bedding in the tent. Then undressed and crawled into sleeping bags. They said good night to each other and went to sleep.

SEVEN

When Desta woke at 4 a.m., David was fast asleep. He thought of getting up, but didn't want to wake David, and turned over. He woke again at 7 a.m. when David nudged him to get ready for their hike.

The morning was cold, and Desta blew warm breath over curled fingers. David had the hood of his college sweatshirt over his head. Still, he seemed unfazed by the biting air, and busied himself lighting the kerosene stove, boiling water in a pot, and pouring in oatmeal to cook.

A lazy mist spread over the pond, partly screening the silent pines on the opposite shore. To the east, a grey cloud shrouding much of the land drifted away, letting the young sun light the mist in ghostly glow.

While David prepared breakfast, Desta rolled up their sleeping bags and pads. He brought them out and set them to one side. Following David's instruction, he took down the tent, folded it multiple times, and rolled it too.

They relished their warm cereal and hot tea with sugar as they watched the changing scene before them.

Afterward, David and Desta loaded their backpacks with snacks and drinks. David brought their gear to his acquaintances for safekeeping. When he came back, they hoisted their backpacks and headed for the fire tower atop Stratton Mountain. The air was cool, the forest enveloping, but the climb tested Desta's stamina; his back was sore from yesterday's hike.

Tall pine trees covered the peak, obscuring views of the surrounding country. They arrived at an ingeniously designed tower that shot fifty feet into the sky. The brand-new open structure of four main steel frames was anchored to concrete blocks, crisscrossed with metal braces. Stairs led to a domed glass enclosure, offering viewers a panorama in every direction.

Desta and David climbed the stairs, passing other visitors, and reached the glass lookout. They joined a dozen people moving around the large space admiring the sweeping landscape.

Beyond the veil of green around the peak, the land tinted brown and lay in bumps, folds, and valleys. A couple of lakes, one a crescent, the other elliptical, broke an otherwise uniform vista.

Desta was astounded that there was not one farm or cattle field in this sprawling terrain, seemingly untouched for eons. His mind leaped to his valley in Ethiopia, once a dense forest full of unique birds, monkeys, antelopes, and other animals, a magical world that faded into memory when farmers cleared the land and tilled it.

"Why is all this land not used for anything?" Desta asked David.

"Forests like this all over the country are protected by the government so that people like us can come and enjoy their natural beauty."

Desta shook his head wistfully. He wished his own country had done the same.

They descended the stairs and headed back toward the pond. Going down was more challenging than the climb for Desta. It felt like gravity was pulling him and his backpack downhill. He retightened the strap on his chest with David's help to keep the pack from shifting.

On their way, they stopped and sat at the picnic table outside a shelter to rest and have snacks. David made peanut butter and jelly sandwiches, which they relished with bottled water.

They progressed downhill to the pond, rested under a tree overlooking the water, and snacked on mixed nuts. They continued on the trail that looped the shore, walking in tandem, Desta behind David.

The area was full of dense bushes, some with blossoms, offering, it appeared, food and shelter for insects, birds, and ground animals. On a dried twig, they saw a faded blue bird that reminded Desta of one he'd seen along the shores of Lake Tana, in Bahir Dar.

They stopped to admire the creature. "That's a blue jay," David explained. The bird flew off, and they resumed their walk. David turned to Desta and said, "I think we must defer your trip to New York City until next weekend."

"Why?" Desta asked, disappointed. He had hoped to go right after they returned to Rye Town.

"We'll get home tomorrow afternoon," David said. "Sunday, you move in with the Johnsons, and Monday, college registration begins."

Desta clamped his lips and stared at the ground. Now he'd have to wait a *whole week* to see the city of his dreams. "Okay," he said finally.

At a clearing, they saw two crows feeding on a dead animal. Soon after, a mother quail with her chicks scurried across their path into the bushes, and a hummingbird danced in a frenzy over an orange blossom.

"I think the Johnsons are pragmatic and far thinking," David said, surprising Desta with another compliment about his host family.

"What do you mean?"

"With everything happening in this nation: the Civil Rights movement, the antiwar protests, and our problems with race relations, they felt they must adapt to changing times."

"That is interesting," Desta said. The question of why such a wealthy family was willing to take in someone like him who would contribute little to their household was becoming more apparent to him. But the last thing he wanted was to be considered a token by the family or his classmates.

"Also, Jake is not a motivated student. He couldn't get into Yale or Harvard as he had wanted because of his grades in high school. His parents hope your presence will inspire him to do well and improve his chances of transferring to a top Ivy League school."

"They aren't expecting me to tutor him, are they?" Desta asked, amused at the prospect. "Although I do enjoy that. I tutored many students back home."

"No, I think they just want him to be around another student who takes his studies seriously."

Desta was relieved. He felt uncomfortable speaking English with native English speakers, and he still wasn't sure how well his high school had prepared him for an advanced American education.

Before they finished the trail loop, they saw a handful of monarch butterflies fluttering over the bushes, and a bumblebee feeding on a yellow flower. They returned to the campsite and unloaded their backpacks. They were hot and sweaty, and David suggested that they cool off in the pond. He collected their gear from the nearby campers and took out a pair of new blue swim shorts from his backpack.

"Here," David said, handing them to Desta." I bought these for you."

Desta thanked his friend and took them. David stripped off his clothes and put on his faded gray set. "Change into your swimsuit, Desta," David said.

Desta shook his head and said, "But I don't know how to swim." Feelings from childhood came rushing back again.

"Come," David said, and walked to the pond's edge. "Nothing bad will happen to you. We'll practice in the shallows where you can stand with your head above water."

Reaching the water's edge, David said, "Look, it's easy and fun," and dove into the pond. Several yards ahead, he surfaced and swam on his back, his arms cartwheeling through the water. Then he stood in the pond and walked toward the shallows. "We'll practice here," David said, extending one hand toward Desta.

Desta reluctantly undressed, put on his suit, and came to the shore's edge near his friend.

One person from a group of campers overheard David and Desta's conversation had asked, "Why is he afraid of the water?" Desta turned to look at them.

"The water will feel good on a hot day like this, son," the oldest of the group said.

With all those eyes on him, Desta felt trapped. He needed to go in. He took a deep breath, crossed his hand over his heart, waded toward David, then stopped.

"C'mon," David said, holding his arms straight out. "Lean forward and lie on my arms, face down." Desta complied. "Keep your legs straight and move them up and down, one at a time." Desta followed his direction. Then he had Desta stand and showed him how to move his arms. David rotated his own arms alternately, dipping each into the water, turning his face out when his hands entered the pond. Then he had Desta lie on David's arms again and practice the strokes he had shown Desta.

To Desta's surprise, this exercise came to him easily. He swam parallel to the shore in one direction, turned, and swam in the other. David clapped with enthusiasm. Desta overheard the others applaud too. Now confident in his ability, Desta turned and headed to the deeper part of the pond. David followed him. After swimming thirty feet, he returned to shore with David, but found the hikers had gone.

David tapped Desta's shoulders. "Great job!"

"Thanks," Desta said. "I just never thought I could."

"You're a natural athlete," David said.

Desta had discovered something he never knew he had in him. He was thrilled and brimmed with emotion. In his growing years, he had never taken up sports because he had to work for his benefactors, or else was so hungry that he didn't have the energy to spare.

The two friends removed their shorts and spread them on the rocks to dry. They shivered some as they toweled down and dressed.

The late afternoon breeze from the pond turned the air cooler. David made peanut butter and jelly sandwiches, which they devoured. Afterward, they munched on snacks and watched the setting sun. The water rippled the reflections of cattails and water lilies along the shore.

"Let's talk about your new situation," David said. "I think first you should focus on adjusting to life with the Johnsons and college. You can also get into athletics like swimming, basketball, track and field, or soccer, which you know from home. American schools offer so many different sports. Right now, you can search for the coin, using the library, and by talking with people you meet. But this will be too much to tackle once school is in session."

"Honestly, I don't even know where to start."

"That's what I mean," David said. "America is vast. Many immigrants from Europe and Russia are scattered, and many more live in big cities."

They both agreed that Desta must wait for whenever the time was right.

The sun turned a brilliant red. Its ghostly reflection throbbed on the pond's surface. Desta wondered why it lacked tinges of blue, orange, purple, and gold, like the sunsets at home.

"You go get dry wood and make a fire, and I'll start dinner," David said.

Desta gathered dry wood and kindling and piled them neatly on last night's fire pit.

He struck a match and lit the kindling. Soon, the wood grew into a bonfire that lit up the pond, flaming orange and white.

David boiled water and poured a box of macaroni into it. Once the pasta had cooked, he strained the water and added yellow powder, which he said was cheese. He blended the macaroni and cheese until it was creamy gold. He filled one plate for himself and handed Desta his own dinner.

"Bon appetit!" he said.

"Thank you!" Desta said, although he had never heard the words before.

A silvery moon edged out of the clouds above the pond, barely full and not yet fully luminescent. Its presence enchanted Desta.

The last rays of sunlight from the nearby treetops flickered and dimmed as the sun slipped behind a shrouded sky. Moments later, it vanished as if blown out by the evening breeze. The temperature dropped rapidly.

David retrieved the tent and the aluminum rods, and then he set up their shelter and their sleeping things inside it. He slathered his skin with lotion to ward off the insects buzzing about them. He handed Desta the bottle and reminded him to do the same.

Afterward, David asked Desta to toast marshmallows while he made hot chocolate. Desta retrieved the sharpened stick from last night and four marshmallows, pierced each one, browned it over the flames, and set it on a paper plate.

David, in the meantime, boiled a pot of water on the stove, and once it was piping hot, he tore open a packet of chocolate powder and poured it in. He added three spoonfuls of sugar and served the bubbling drink in Styrofoam cups.

Desta toasted two pieces of bread on the tip of the same stick. Once done, he folded the bread around two toasted marshmallows and gave it to David, saying: "Bon appetit." He kept the second batch for himself.

David passed a cup of chocolate to Desta. "Enjoy," he said.

David sank his teeth into the sandwich of bread and marshmallow, took a sip of hot chocolate, and let his jaws go to work. "The best for body and soul," David said, sipping more of his drink. His face beamed with happiness.

Desta felt good as well. "I couldn't have asked for a better drink on a cool evening like this."

After they'd finished, David said, "I need to leave for a bit and will be back." He smiled.

Desta smiled back. "My father used to say two of life's pleasures are filling and emptying an organ." David grabbed the flashlight and a roll of tissue paper and left.

Desta stared at the pond's reflection of the fire. Occasionally he looked up at the sky and the nearly round moon, now bright. But his mind was elsewhere. Despite all the horrors of his early life and his school years, he'd depended on the goodwill of so many strangers all along. He still marveled at how he came to be here in America, in this remote forest, by a campfire, in the company of a man offering him the love and kindness that he couldn't get from his relatives.

"It shows that the world is benevolent and that the union of the two coins is important," he said to himself. "How else could I have traveled so far from home?" But his heart darkened to think of how unclear his life's goal remained.

Desta's musings gave way to the sound of hoofbeats on the trail. He turned to look, but saw nothing, and felt uneasy.

"Now, your turn," David said, handing Desta the flashlight and tissue roll.

On the way back from his outing, Desta stopped and turned when he heard the same sound of animal's hooves. He cringed. A man on a white horse rode toward him. Desta was about to flee when the man said, "Stop!"

Desta was not new to apparitions. But now, his feet were immobile, as if struck by a spell.

"Hello, young one," the white figure said, "I'm glad you obeyed my command." His voice was soft and pleasant but vanished after a transient echo.

"One of my many names is The Great Mystery," the ghost said. "My horse, Flying Wind. You and I have met before. I come tonight to welcome you to this great land that once was ours. Your arrival to our continent is in our legends. Although David doesn't know it, he brought you here for us to meet. He came to your country because of me, and I helped advance your mission."

Desta gently rubbed the flashlight as his mind whirled. "How is that possible?" he said lastly. "You're so far from where I came from."

"I'm part of The All-Knowing entity called God. I know most of what occurs around the world. I'm also referred to as Wakan Tanka, so don't be confused if you see this name."

"Does this mean, then, you know where the owner of the second coin is?"

"I can't answer that," the spirit said. "That is the mystery you have been assigned to solve."

Desta wanted to say, *What good are you for me then?* but decided against it.

"But I will say that I arranged for your friend Eleni to come to your continent and reside in Washaa Umera," the ghost added. "She is originally from here."

"This is getting more cryptic by the minute," Desta said. "If you arranged for Eleni and David to come to my country, you must know about the second coin and its owner."

"I have given you my answer. That is part of your life's mission. You have been given the tools to find its owner. The prophecy intends that the person assigned the task solves the riddle.

"One last thing," The Great Mystery said. "Kooper is the reincarnation of Kooli, who is also connected to the coin. Add the letters in the two dogs' names to determine what I mean."

Desta froze, speechless, eyes fixed on the lake he didn't see.

"Again, I welcome you!" the spirit said, and Desta turned back to the apparition. "Be good! Do well! Good luck!" Moments later, The Great Mystery was gone.

Desta's feet came unglued, but they felt like lead. Back at camp, he found David snoring. He quietly tiptoed around him and got into his sleeping bag.

To unravel the dogs' connection to the coin, Desta added in his head the number of letters in each and came up with 11; he imagined the two shekels would look like this when they came together and lie next to each other. The sum of the two numbers corresponded to the two coins, and the head and tail of each one. Time slowed, his senses congealed as his head swirled, trying to make sense of this astounding connection. He couldn't call this a mere coincidence, of course. He thought long and deep about this discovery and the mysterious man before he eventually fell asleep.

David prepared hot cereal and tea in the morning while Desta took down the tent. He rolled their sleeping bags and pads, and then secured them with a rope to each backpack. After breakfast, they loaded up their cookware, slipped their packs on their backs, grabbed the trash bags, and traveled to the parking lot.

As they walked, Desta told David about meeting The Great Spirit the night before.

"Impossible!" David said.

"I think I have been fated to live in the spirit world and the human realm," Desta said. "How else to explain that these otherworldly creatures are constantly revealed to me?"

"I think it's the spiritual legacy of the coins," David said. "It's a rare honor, and a big responsibility for you, I know. But you will be very proud of yourself when all is said and done."

"I've said before, I am generally optimistic, but I often wonder if it will ever be said and done."

"There must be a purpose to all the roads you've traveled and challenges you've overcome."

They reached the parking lot at high noon. They dropped their trash in the silver bin and loaded their packs in the back of the wagon. They wiped sweat from their faces, got in the car, and drove away with the windows rolled down. The cool wind on Desta's face felt terrific.

Desta's thoughts turned to his moving day tomorrow, and the trip to New York City on Thursday, and his heart leaped with excitement.

Back home, David and Desta parked the car in the driveway and walked in the front door to find Dr. Halford Hartman in the living room opening his mail.

"Oh, hello!" Dr. Hartman said, smiling broadly. He left the envelopes and rose.

"Hi, Dad," David said, voice ringing with happiness. "You're back!" The men hugged, and David introduced Desta to his father.

"Welcome!" Dr. Hartman said warmly and shook Desta's hand. "So glad you're finally here!" The doctor's hair was grey and thin on top, his pate like an arid plain.

Mrs. Hartman emerged from the kitchen and came straight to the campers. She hugged and kissed David and shook Desta's hand.

"We have heard so much about you," she said, holding Desta's gaze. Her full head of brown hair, shaped in a bowl cut, showed no trace of white.

"When did you arrive?" David asked his father.

Dr. Hartman glanced at his watch. "An hour and a half ago."

"We would have beaten you home if we hadn't stopped along the way," David said. "How was your vacation?"

"Let's sit down," Mrs. Hartman offered. "We're more eager to hear about yours."

"Yes," Dr. Hartman said. "And why you took this young man camping so soon after he arrived." His sharp, bespeckled eyes rolled like marbles between his son and his wife.

He picked up the empty envelopes from the sofa and set them on the coffee table next to the unopened mail and a slender silver knife with a bright gold tip.

Desta sat beside the doctor, and David with his mother on the opposite sofa.

"You both look great!" David said.

"Thank you," Mrs. Hartman said. "We had a wonderful time. Now, coming to your trip, wouldn't the city have been the best introduction to our country for Desta, rather than camping?" Her brow hardened.

David glanced at his mother. "What better place to go to experience the beauty of America than our national forests?" he said.

"What's important is they had a good time and learned something about the country," Dr. Hartman said. He eyed his son over his glasses.

"Did you enjoy yourself, Desta?" Mrs. Hartman asked, locking eyes with him.

"It was great experience, and I learned a lot," Desta said.

David detailed where they went, what they saw and did, and how much he enjoyed Desta's company and teaching him how to swim.

While David spoke, Desta studied his parents; they looked to be in their late fifties. Unlike his son, Dr. Hartman did not have a prominent, commanding nose. Still, his high forehead, pointy chin, measured tone, and calm demeanor made him appear learned and wise. His close-cropped moustache and beard distinguished him.

Jean Hartman was striking in other ways. Her long, narrow face was copper-toned, and etched with fine lines. She had a dainty aquiline nose and high cheeks. But it was her slender neck and big, brilliant eyes Desta found attractive. Like her husband, she bore little resemblance to their son.

"Please take Desta to the Johnsons' tomorrow at two, Dad," David said. "I've an appointment then."

"Glad to," Dr. Hartman said. "Then I can catch up with Skip and Bev, too."

Butterflies usurped Desta's stomach once again.

"We're glad you're here, Desta," Mrs. Hartman assured him. "Consider our house your second home."

"Thank you very much," Desta said, his stomach easing.

David mentioned that he'd stocked the fridge before the camping trip. "Well, then, I should see about dinner," Mrs. Hartman said, and left for the kitchen.

"You catch up on your mail, Dad, while we unload the wagon," David said.

"Certainly," the doctor said, and picked up an envelope and his knife beside it.

The two campers brought their gear to the basement and stowed it on a shelf in a gray metal closet. They gathered their personal belongings and went upstairs.

While Desta perched on his bed and thought about all the mysteries of his new life, David appeared at the door holding a familiar musical instrument.

"It occurred to me that you have no access to Ethiopian music here," David said, "particularly living with the Johnsons. I bought this bow and *Masinko* while I was in the Peace Corps, and I'd like to loan it to you. Playing it is one way of staying connected to your own music. If you don't play, try to practice a tune or two."

"How thoughtful of you," Desta said happily. "Never got to play it, but it's a favorite instrument of mine. As you probably remember, the *azmaris*—minstrels—widely play this single-string instrument in bars, weddings, and other events in Ethiopia, and it certainly would be fun to practice some of our country's classical songs on it. Thank you!"

"You're welcome," David said, and handed his friend the instrument. "Dinner's in thirty minutes, Mother said. Come down then," David said and left.

After a satisfying meal of steak, pasta, and vegetables, Desta lay on his bed, unsure why he'd been so anxious when David mentioned going to the Johnsons tomorrow. But on reflection, he'd always felt that way when he'd gone to live with strangers. He was still haunted by all those bad experiences.

Then he remembered that The Great Mystery had said that his dog, Kooli, was reborn in the Johnsons' Kooper, and he couldn't wait to see the dog again. With this thought last in his mind, Desta fell asleep.

EIGHT

Jake and Aida waited by the entrance. Dr. Hartman parked his Mercedes at the head of the driveway. "Here we are at your new home, Desta," he said, and got out.

"Thanks for bringing me," Desta said. He pushed open the heavy door and followed his host. Inside, Kooper barked gently, the way Kooli used to welcome him home.

"Father thought you might need help," Jake said, approaching Dr. Hartman's car.

"That's very thoughtful," David's father said.

He opened his trunk. "Perhaps you could carry one of these suitcases."

Jake took the carry bag and a large suitcase while Desta lugged another big travel bag.

Kooper's bark had shrunk to a whimper when all of them walked in. He sniffed Dr. Hartman but jumped up and down and wagged his tail when he saw Desta.

The Johnsons emerged from the family room. "Good afternoon, Hal!" Mr. Johnson said. Dr. Hartman returned the greeting in kind, and they all shook hands.

"How was your vacation?" Mrs. Johnson asked.

"Missus and I had a fabulous time."

Mr. Johnson eyed the suitcases and asked his children, "Why don't you two take these upstairs and show Desta his room?"

"Please come have a sit," Mr. Johnson said to Dr. Hartman. The three adults moved to the sumptuous leather sofa and sat down, the couple facing the visitor.

Aida, Jake, and Desta brought the luggage up the wide spiral staircase and down a long hallway to a corner bedroom on the right. Jake pushed the door open with his foot, and they set down the bags.

The room seemed easily large enough for three people. A beautiful walnut bed stood head to the wall, right of the entrance. It was neatly made with a light blue spread and topped with two small, patterned beige pillows. A gray lamp with a silver base sat on a nightstand right of the bed, while the opposite stand held a big clock radio.

"This room was our older sister Shae's, who's in college now," Jake said.

Aida piped up. "It's much bigger than our rooms and has the best backyard view."

"Not bigger, but the view is the best," Jake said.

Desta noted a large window on the wall to the left of the door; a generous gray desk and chair sat directly across from the bed to the right of another large window. A cantilevered lamp angled over the desk like the beak of an exotic bird.

Jake opened two doors against the right wall. "This is your clothes closet."

Desta peeked, and his eyes grew.

"I wish mine was that big," Aida grumbled.

"This one's no bigger than yours," Jake corrected. "You just have way too many clothes."

"That's not true," Aida protested. "But that's okay."

"Good," Jake added. He turned to Desta. "Make yourself at home. I will give you a house tour in the next few days so you know your way around."

"Particularly the parts Mother's picky about," Aida chipped in, and Jake agreed.

Desta's brow knotted, and he slowly breathed out. *What's Mrs. Johnson picky about?*

They went downstairs to the living room.

"Did you three have a good visit?" Mr. Johnson asked.

"Not much of a visit," Jake said. "We just showed Desta his room."

The parents and Dr. Hartman had tea and cookies. Mrs. Johnson handed the tray of sweets to Jake to share with his sister and Desta.

Dr. Hartman said he needed to prepare for a talk the next day and rose. Desta despaired, without knowing why. As he thought about it, he realized he felt like it was not only the doctor, but David who was leaving him behind, with a family he knew little about. But Desta had to admit that living with strangers had always been his fate. He followed Dr. Hartman outside to the car.

Dr. Hartman tapped his shoulder. "Cheer up. You couldn't ask for a better family to live with."

"I'll be fine, Dr. Hartman. I appreciate it."

"I'll tell David to call you often, and we'll come see you when we can."

"Thank you," Desta said. He watched the doctor's car roll past the gate, down the long driveway. Once he'd lost sight of the man, he returned to the house. He found Jake standing by the entrance, as if he'd been watching Desta the whole time.

"Have you ever played Frisbee?" Jake asked teasingly.

Desta said he hadn't. Just now, he was more eager to see Kooper.

"Let's go to the backyard, and I'll teach you. First, I'll get Kooper," Jake said, as if reading Desta's mind. He opened the door and called the dog.

With Kooper alongside him, Jake led Desta down the cement path bordering the plantings along the wall on one side, and the grass and flowering shrubs on the other.

Jake got the red Frisbee from the bin on the patio. They walked across the flagstone pavers, past the pool, and stood near the edge of the lawn.

"You hold the Frisbee like this," Jake said, bending his wrist and curling his fingers around the lip of the disk. "Bring it toward your chest and then toss it as if you were casting a fishing net." He sent the Frisbee sailing a short distance. Kooper ran after it and returned with it in his mouth.

Desta used all the techniques Jake had explained, and the Frisbee spun flawlessly through the air and landed a few yards away.

"Great job!" Jake exclaimed. Kooper brought back the disc once more. Jake had Desta throw it, and again, the Frisbee flew smoothly, but higher and farther.

"Sure you haven't done this before?" Jake asked, incredulous. "That was one of the best throws I've ever seen. Now, let's you and I play." Jake handed him the disc, and once he'd trotted about thirty feet away, had Desta throw it to him.

Desta gently tossed the red saucer toward his partner's chest. Jake caught it and flung it back to him, and he jumped in time to grab it. Jake moved farther away. Desta locked his eyes on Jake and snapped the Frisbee harder to reach its target. Jake caught it quickly and sent it back to Desta. He ran still farther from Desta, and again, he hit the mark exactly.

They began a running game, throwing and receiving, shifting locations and directions. Now the receiver didn't always catch the Frisbee, so Kooper got into the act. The game became such a spectacle that Jake's parents and Aida stood mesmerized at the edge of the field.

For Desta, the Frisbee seemed like an extension of his dreams of flying, a mark of his freedom, just as his old flying craft had been.

"That was quite a show!" Mr. Johnson said, smiling.

"We had fun," Jake said. "Desta is a natural at the game."

"I concur," Mrs. Johnson said. "From here on, you two play as much as you want, and we'll enjoy being your audience." She grinned.

Aida tightened her lips, and Desta saw a hint of envy in her eyes.

"We'd better shower; I'm all sticky," Jake said.

Desta bent over and tenderly stroked Kooper. He wished he could speak with him privately, to verify The Great Mystery's claims about Kooli and Kooper. But how to speak with a dog?

Desta had his doubts. Kooper didn't resemble Kooli, and he was much bigger. And the idea of a past life returning in a new form, thousands of miles away, made Desta doubt the spirit. He shrugged off his thoughts and went inside.

In the shower, as the warm water spattered his head, Desta regretted that circumstances in his early years hadn't allowed him to enjoy sports.

While a country shepherd, he'd had no friends to play with, and at school, he'd spent his free time working for his room and board. Even when he'd had the rare opportunity to play sports, he'd had no energy to spare for anything beyond his necessities. He shook his head for all the fun he'd missed in childhood.

He stood at his bedroom window and looked out. He noticed a white pebble path that went around the perimeter of the backyard, between the lawn and the hedges and flowering bushes that hugged the fences. Desta thought the space within it was the size of a soccer field. A bench sat in the center of each section of fence, facing the lawn.

He caressed his chin absentmindedly. His eyes no longer saw, and again he felt like this new world was a dream he would wake from, and it would vanish. He closed his eyes, held his face in his hands, and sighed deeply, to somehow assure himself that he wasn't dreaming.

He lay on his back on the firm bed. Snatches of images came to him: bare dirt floors where he slept on a leather mat with a skimpy *gabi*—a shawl-like fabric used for shoulder wrapping for cover, in all the towns where he'd lived from first to eighth grade; his bug-infested bed the last two years of high school.

His eyes wandered over the beautiful things that surrounded him. Desta would not regret or berate his past. He was grateful for all the hardships and challenges he had faced. They'd made him strong and resilient, and paved the road to where he was now.

The significance of his current situation had not yet sunk in. He didn't know where it would lead him; he could only take one step at a time. He believed that nothing that happened to him was random. Would coming to the Johnsons' home be the next rung on the ladder of his journey to that second coin? How else could he explain all the links to the coin he'd already found—the two Ryes, the house address, Aida's name, and Kooper's connection to Kooli. Exciting as these discoveries were, they also frustrated and even scared Desta.

Desta's heart leaped with hope. Whether or not the Johnsons would play a role in finding the second coin, he had to proceed cautiously. He must keep secret his magical possessions: the compass, magic wand, stone tablet, and his coin and coin box. They would only invite probing questions, and his explanations could spread through the community.

Jake knocked on the door, and Desta started, vaulted from bed, and went to the door.

"Dinner's in an hour," Jake said. "We're looking forward to our first meal together."

Desta glanced at the clock on the nightstand. "Thanks," he said. "I'll be down at seven-thirty."

He closed the door, dragged his suitcase from the closet, and opened it. He took out his cream-colored cotton shirt and blue pants and placed them at the edge of the bed. Then he quickly showered and returned to his room and got dressed. Afterward, returning to the bathroom, he brushed his teeth and combed his hair, and near seven-thirty, he went downstairs to the family room, from there to the kitchen. The curtains were pulled back, and sunlight filled the room. The family gathered from outside and in different corners of the house.

Jake introduced Elsa, a plump woman who was dishing out food on white porcelain plates and laying them on the island counter. Jake and Elsa brought them to the dining table and set them down before each chair. Next, Jake fetched an opened bottle of red wine and a carafe of ice water and placed them at the center of the table.

At seven thirty, Mr. and Mrs. Johnson entered the kitchen through the family room. Desta had learned from Jake that his parents spent Sunday evenings before dinner in the library, Mr. Johnson reading newspapers and business articles, his mother with her Bible.

The large dining table stood fifteen feet from the kitchen, parallel to the large windows facing the pool and the green yard. Seats were assigned with small rectangular name cards. Desta and Jake were on the side of the table with their backs to the windows. Mr. Johnson sat at the table's head while his wife was on the opposite side, where with just a slight turn of her head could fully see the kitchen. Aida sat across from Desta and Jake, with a full view of the outdoors.

This strict protocol intrigued Desta. The white cloth napkins were folded, and silverware and glasses placed precisely. The water tumblers were to the right of the plates above the napkins, and the wine glasses on the left near the tips of the forks and knives.

The children sat primly, the parents less so. Mrs. Johnson hardly uttered a word. It seemed she was not given to frivolous banter. Her words, like her mien, were precise and to the point.

Jake filled his parents' glasses with wine and poured water into tumblers for the rest. Mrs. Johnson brought her hands together, their tips touching her nose. "Let's pray," she commanded.

"Father, we have gathered to share a meal in Your honor. Thank You for bringing us together as family and thank You for this food. Thank You for meeting our need of food and drink. Forgive us for taking that simple joy for granted, and bless this food to sustain us as we fulfill Your will for our lives. We pray that this meal will renew us and inspire us to work for the glory of Your Kingdom. In Jesus's name, Amen."

Desta didn't know the rules for eating and decided to mirror Jake. Nobody spoke while they ate. It was as if they were in mourning, or else mouths at mealtime were dedicated to eating. Mr. Johnson now and then lifted his eyes to survey the family. Occasionally he sipped his wine; Mrs. Johnson drank hers sparingly. Her expression thoughtful, her eyes shifted between her plate and the kitchen, as if monitoring Elsa's efforts.

The helper arrayed five white bowls on the island counter. Aida, busy eating, occasionally looked across at Desta and Jake, but her face registered little. It seemed the unspoken code of silence was how the family honored God and their meal.

Once everyone was done, Elsa collected the plates and glasses. Afterward, she served the parents coffee and the children tea. Evidently this was a household ritual, too. Desta was happy for the tea; coffee was his least favorite. Suddenly everyone was in a talking mood again.

"Do you have brothers and sisters?" Mrs. Johnson asked Desta.

He replied he had four brothers and two sisters, and he was the last of seven children. Mrs. Johnson asked his family's religion and denomination. Desta said that they were Christians, and they followed the Ethiopian Orthodox faith. Jake asked if Desta played any sports, and Desta groped for an answer.

"I've imagined playing soccer, track and field, and basketball," he said finally. "I hope to make that a reality here in your beautiful land."

Mr. Johnson chuckled. His wife smiled.

"What's mealtime like for you at home?" Aida wanted to know.

Another tough question. Desta tightened his lips, mind searching. "In our culture, children generally eat separately, after the adults have eaten." In the country, he told them, he often ate alone, or with his sister, while in the towns, he ate with his hosts' children or their servants.

Mrs. Johnson seemed surprised and glanced at Aida and Jake. "What do you think of that?" she asked.

"That's strange," Aida said. "But like you told us, we're not supposed to judge other cultures."

"I think that custom would make me run away from home, first chance I got," Jake said.

"How did you feel about it, Desta?" Mr. Johnson asked.

"I didn't think about it. I just accepted that it was our way of life. Now, I know better."

"Thank you," Mr. Johnson said. "We hope to learn more about your culture so all of us can be better-informed citizens of our country, and the world."

Mrs. Johnson nodded, seconding her husband's comment. The children said nothing but looked thoughtful. Jake stroked his chin absently, his left arm resting across his chest. Aida curled her lip and kept her eyes on her brother, as if assessing his reaction to Desta's unusual life.

Mr. Johnson rose and retreated to the library to read. Mrs. Johnson went to the kitchen and spoke with Elsa, and then vanished through the same door her husband had.

"Very interesting background you have," Jake said. "You can tell me more about it some time."

"Be happy to," Desta said.

"School registration for our fall courses starts tomorrow, a week before classes on the 24th. We should go in at nine a.m. You'll have more forms to fill out, so bring all your documents."

Jake and Desta rose and went upstairs. In the hall, Jake said, "Once I've straightened up my room, I'll invite you in. Till then we'll say good night and good morning in the hallway."

Desta said good night. As he lay in bed, he felt excited at the thought of spending time alone with Kooper, and to see New York City with David the following Thursday.

NINE

The registrar of Abraham Lincoln Junior College was on the castle's second floor. Jake and Desta climbed a broad staircase to the office. Desta, anxious to see the castle's interior, was disappointed to find that it had been extensively modernized and looked like an ordinary office building with several offices and meeting rooms. The polished hard-wood floors and wall paneling looked new, and the ceilings had been smoothed and painted white with cool recess lighting.

Students scurried across the floors and hallways. Jake and Desta joined a line of a dozen pupils inside the registrar's office to pick up their enrollment forms. When their turns came, the matron at the counter gave Jake his forms, but directed Desta next door to Mr. Trent Shaw, the international student counselor.

Jake sat down at a round table nearby to fill out his forms. Desta perched on the chair next to his host brother and followed all the activity around them, trying not to feel like an alien just arrived from another planet.

Jake scanned his forms, then brought them to the woman at the counter, who gave him a course catalog. Jake and Desta left to see Trent Shaw.

A pleasant and welcoming man, Mr. Shaw shook hands with Jake and Desta. After a brief introduction, the counselor asked for copies of Desta's Certificate of Eligibility, official high school transcript and diploma, passport, and declaration of his finances. Desta hadn't brought any of these papers with him, so they made an appointment to return at 2 o'clock, shook hands with Mr. Shaw, and left.

After lunch at home, Jake and Desta returned to Mr. Shaw's office to find one student waiting at a table, and another talking to the counselor. When Desta's turn finally came, he handed Mr. Shaw a folder with the documents he'd requested.

Mr. Shaw flipped through the folder, looked up at Jake, and said, "You're Mr. and Mrs. Skip Johnson's young man?"

"Yes," Jake replied, his brow bunched into a question. "Why do you ask?"

"I'm aware of your young man," Mr. Shaw said, smiling a little. Your father and another man came in June, asking us to make an exception to admit him to this fall class, although our admissions were closed. His voice and bearing grew softer and respectful. "I didn't make the connection earlier." Mr. Shaw opened a drawer, took out a set of forms, and handed it to Desta.

With Jake's help, Desta completed the application at the table. The reference to "major" stopped him. He liked all the sciences, but he eventually settled on biology. After checking over the documents, he signed and returned them to Mr. Shaw. The man carefully reviewed the pages, looked up at Desta, and said, "Good job!" He shook Desta's hand. "Welcome!"

Next, Mr. Shaw gave Desta his course catalog and added, "There is a sheet in there for your courses. Make sure to complete and return it before the deadline." Jake and Desta thanked Mr. Shaw and left.

Outside, they sat on a bench facing Lincoln's sculpture and browsed their catalogs. Desta glanced uneasily at the bronze figure, half-expecting him to speak.

With Jake's input, Desta chose the courses to take first term: trigonometry, chemistry, physics, biology, and English. Jake had yet to decide on his classes.

"Are you afraid of Mr. Lincoln?" Jake inquired.

"No," Desta said, "But it's strange to be near this towering man. And I think I saw his mouth move."

Desta's host jerked his chin and looked at him skeptically.

"What can I say," Desta said. "It might just be my imagination." He smiled.

"Let's go to the bookstore."

Inside the bookstore, each inspected the textbooks they might buy for their courses. Desta was astounded at how many titles there were in the store, and in his curriculum, and that he was supposed to buy these books and keep them for himself. Up until now, Desta had only borrowed books from school, and watched his teachers read from them in class. He didn't have spare money just now, so he satisfied himself by browsing one book after another, until Jake suggested they go.

Back home, Desta went to his room. He stood by the window overlooking the lawn and pool thinking about his day. Everything went smoothly at school, and Desta would have plenty of books for his classes. He stared for a long time. "If this is not a dream, how long will it last?" One thing was sure: he couldn't take any of it for granted. But for now, he couldn't deny his happiness either.

He went to the closet and took out the suitcase that contained his most valued possessions: the magic wand, the compass and map, the painting of the two coins, the stone tablet, the magical coin, the scroll containing the shekel's twenty-one legends, and the coin box.

He needed to talk to Tsadok about his new life in America, as he had promised. He picked up the magic wand and studied it; the circular disc in its center contained the Star of David, inside of which appeared a large 9 made of blue stone. Above and below the circle, along the rod, were smaller versions of the number nine.

Desta put down the device and thought for a moment. Did he want to engage in what might seem like witchcraft to his hosts?

His door had no lock, and Desta might have to scramble to conceal his magical things if someone came to the door. The whole idea made him uneasy. He decided to resume at midnight when they all had gone to sleep. Desta put the magic wand and its companion pieces back in the suitcase and returned it to the closet.

The whole matter made him nervous. He lay on his bed, pulling and stroking a pinch of hair at his temple, wondering what would happen if he were discovered practicing magic. Of all the people in the household, Mrs. Johnson would be most upset. She was so much into God and her Bible, she'd find Desta's involvement with a magic coin and wand blasphemous, and she'd prohibit such practices under her roof, if not ask him to leave. Desta understood pious people; his mother, Ayénat, was one. The scenario he'd just imagined made his gut twist. Shortly after, he fell asleep.

He woke when Jake knocked on the door for dinner. His parents were out, and Desta dined with just Aida and Jake. They ate less formally, even chatting between bites. Afterward, each went to their own room.

Desta took out his magic wand and set it on his nightstand, still wrapped in cloth. He went to bed immediately and told himself he must wake up at midnight.

He woke at the expected hour, sat up, and switched on his lamp. He retrieved the magic wand from the nightstand, unwrapped it, and set it next to him. Then he sat legs folded and overlapped before him, back pressed to the headboard. He placed the pillow on his lap, and the magic wand on top.

He crossed his arms over his chest, closed his eyes, and sighed. He concentrated on Tsadok, imagining him as Desta remembered. After several moments of effort, he opened his eyes, stared at the big 9 at the center of the wand, and said three times, "Accept and transmit this message to his honorable Tsadok." It took a while, but finally the wand glowed green.

With his eyes still on the big number and his thoughts on Tsadok, Desta said,

Dear Honorable Tsadok, High Priest of the Ark:

> *I apologize I did not send a message sooner. I wanted to wait until I got a clearer understanding of my new life. And I could not find the right time until now.*

> *Before anything else, thank you beyond words for all your guidance during my years in Ethiopia. I don't know what my life would have been like if not for you.*

> *My flight from Addis Ababa to New York was problem-free but exhausting. My friend David picked me up at the airport and took me to his parent's home.*

> *Soon after I arrived, the vague future I faced—my education, and the coin—preoccupied me, and being far from home weighed on my mind. I had wanted to see New York City, but my host thought it better for me to see America in the wild: woodlands and wild creatures. We walked mountain trails, instead of concrete and asphalt. And breathed its pure, healthy air. So, on my third day, David and I took a weekend hike in the forest, carrying all of our supplies.*

> *I had a good time with David. I learned to swim, and met a spirit being who calls himself The Great Mystery. I don't know if Eleni has*

mentioned him. I think he is America's leading resident spirit. He was
very kind to me.

The trip was the break I needed from my worries. I returned with a
clear mind and good attitude.

I live with a family of five whose home I couldn't have imagined in
my wildest dreams. I'm not overwhelmed by the luxury surrounding
me, but I wonder how things will turn out in the days and weeks ahead.
We are in a mutual experiment.

I registered for five classes yesterday, and Jake and I will buy our
books tomorrow.

I hope to share more in the future.
Please send me your news in any way you know how.
Thank you so much again.

Yours, Desta *Abraham.*

He secured the magic wand and stowed it in the closet. He undressed
and got under the covers. The wand and Tsadok were his last thoughts
before he drifted off.

In his dream, Desta was with Tsadok. The spirit sat on a golden bench,
next to a sky-blue book trimmed in burgundy and embossed with gold.

You're not ready for my messages because you don't have the neces-
sary medium yet. He gestured to the tome and said, *"Like this journal."*

Desta wrestled with the ancient spirit's meaning as he continued.

It will be presented to you when you purchase your school supplies
tomorrow.

AFTER BREAKFAST Tuesday morning, Jake and Desta sat at the
kitchen table with a calendar opened to the week of August 17th. Jake
explained what he called an "activity-packed week."

That day, Jake gives Desta a tour of the house. The following day,
they submit their registration slips and purchase their school supplies at
the bookstore.

At two o'clock on Wednesday, Seth Kaplan interviews Desta for the
school paper.

Thursday, David Hartman takes Desta to New York City.

Jake rose and said, "Let me now familiarize you with our home—indoors and out—and share our house rules."

The put their slippers on and went outside through the main entrance, which Jake noted was generally for guests. The family entered from a room adjacent to the three-car garage on the left.

The family rarely used the basketball hoop at the right corner of the large, paved driveway. Across from it, near the other end of the garage, stood a small building, Jake's mother's second office. Jake said she was a real estate agent dealing exclusively with million-dollar homes and had many famous clients. His father was president of a big bank in New York City. Mrs. Johnson was not in, but Desta met Mary Winslow, her secretary, thirtyish with shoulder-length blonde hair.

Returning to the main house, they entered through the side door into a room of roughly twelve by fifteen feet that reminded Desta of shoe shops in Addis. It had sky-blue walls and a grey floor. Shoes and slippers in different colors and sizes lined the shelves, the space under the benches, and inside a glass-fronted closet.

"This is our mudroom," Jake announced. "From now on, you'll come into the house through here. You'll get your own key." Desta tried to grasp what this immaculate space had to do with a room of mud.

"We leave our shoes here when we come inside," Jake said, as if trying to clear Desta's confusion. He picked up a pair of flip-flops. "In the rest of the house, we wear these, or just our socks."

Jake removed his slippers and tossed them into a box with others that he said needed to be washed before they could be reused. Desta did the same. Wearing new ones, Jake and Desta walked through a hallway into the family room, and finally, the kitchen.

"Our parents have several house rules," Jake said, leaning against the island. "The most important is tidiness. My mother is obsessed with it. Leave nothing on the counters, floor, or in the sink. The house gets cleaned twice a week—Monday and Friday. The housekeepers do their best in this big house, but we children are responsible for cleaning up after ourselves."

Jake showed Desta how to load the dishwasher. He opened the refrigerator, described how the groceries were organized, and pointed out the cleaning towels and chemicals in a small closet next to the pantry.

Afterward, they went to the formal dining room through a door from the kitchen. A table with a smooth walnut finish and eight chairs of the same hue occupied the center of the room. A crystal chandelier with a couple of dozen candle-like bulbs hung from the ceiling above the dining table. A large rug in hues of gold and faded blue and green sat on the hardwood floor.

"This room is used maybe four times a year, but we still keep it like this all the time," Jake said. They walked around the room. Jake looked up at a large oil painting of Abraham Lincoln on the wall that led to the kitchen. "This room is dedicated to that man."

"Why, is he your relative?"

"No, but an ancestral grandfather, five generations past, was a Union general in the Civil War, and he admired Lincoln. When my grandfather decided to open the junior college, he named it after this man."

"Interesting," Desta said, surprised by this revelation. He stood before the paneled window, admired the view of the backyard and the cloaking serenity, and thought of the good fortune that had led him to the family who founded his new school. Here, like everywhere else in the house, order and austerity reigned. Desta felt he must tread cautiously in these rooms.

"Just make sure to obey the rules: clean up after yourself and put away the things you use."

Desta said he would do his utmost and went upstairs. Coming to his room, Desta sat at his desk and thought about Jake's advice. It astounded him how hard the family worked to maintain their comfortable life, almost excessively, it seemed to him.

IN THE AFTERNOON, Jake came by Desta's room to find out if he had a dress suit and tie. Desta opened the closet and showed him what he had brought from home: a hunter green shirt and pants, a light blue and cream-colored cotton shirt, two pairs of khaki pants, and a safari jacket, but no ties.

"You will need clothes more formal than these," Jake said. "Mother said if you don't have dress clothes, we need to go to town and buy you some."

Afterward, they drove to town. They parked behind a row of buildings and walked down a side street and onto the main road that split the
town in half. They went inside the PHILIPS BROS MEN'S CLOTHING
store. Beautiful shirts, jackets, pants, suits, ties, and shoes hung on rows
of racks, and were piled on large tables.

"See what you like," Jake said. "I'm going to do the same."

Desta walked around admiring the apparel, enjoying their colors, textures, cuts, and styles, not yet choosing any for himself.

"Did you find any you like?" Jake asked, coming from behind.

"There are so many good-looking clothes, it's hard to choose,"
Desta said.

Jake suggested that Desta concentrate on the styles and colors he
liked. Desta tried on several suits, shirts, and shoes, as Jake remarked,
"It's becoming" or "it looks good on you." They settled on two tweed
jackets—one light blue with flap pockets, another a shade of brown with
patch pockets. The shirts were straightforward: button-downs in light
blue and cream. Pants: dark gray and golden brown. They decided on
dark brown shoes. Jake said he had plenty of excellent ties that Desta
could choose from, even keep.

On the drive home, Desta's new clothes surfaced feelings from deep
in his mind that he couldn't articulate and needled his conscience. In the
store, while looking at himself in new clothes in the mirror, he'd felt
like an imposter. He liked them, even thought they looked good on him.
Yet his reflection wasn't him, but rather a caricature of his former self.
Jake was right that Desta might be *becoming*, through his new clothes,
someone he never was—for better or worse. On the first day of class
Desta would prefer to introduce himself wearing his national dress.

As much as Desta wasn't close to his family, his bond with his heritage was profound. But to transition smoothly to his new life, earn his
education, and find the second coin, Desta had to assimilate. He had to
dress, act, and talk like Americans, even while he held fast to his roots
in his heart.

Jake parked the *Impala* outside. They went through the mudroom, exchanged their shoes for slippers, and went upstairs.

"Thank you so much," Desta said to Jake as they parted ways in the
upstairs hall. He clutched the plastic bag with his new clothes.

In his room, he took out his purchases one by one and shook out the wrinkles. Then he hung each one in the closet. He placed his new shoes next to the black pair he'd brought from home. He stood before the full-length mirror on the closet door and held his new clothes to his frame, one a time, to see how they looked.

They were nice. Despite how conflicted he'd been in the store, now he saw himself in them. He realized that he must accede to a situation which he had no power to change. "I'll accept this new man in a new country," he said and smiled.

TEN

On Wednesday morning, Jake and Desta went to their school campus and submitted their slips to the registrar for the courses they were taking. Afterward, they went to the bookstore. They browsed the texts for their classes. Desta's books for trigonometry and three science courses—physics, chemistry, and biology—all had titles prefaced by "Introduction to," and they seemed straightforward enough. But the requirements for English 101 gave him pause. He had to analyze and write expository essays with brevity and clarity using *standard American English grammar and usage*. And the course demanded much more.

His work as a tour guide had improved his spoken English, but he hadn't written any assignments in English in high school; the books he'd read were basic. He had never heard of the writers in the syllabus: Hemingway, Faulkner, Joyce, Conrad. He would have to work harder in English class than his other courses.

They headed to the cashier with their books, school supplies, and schoolbags.

A young man approached Desta. "You'll need this, too," he said, holding a faded sky-blue oversize book with dark burgundy trims. His name tag said Timmy Dawson.

"No, he doesn't need that," Jake said, waving the man away.

"Don't ask me to explain why, but he does," the clerk insisted.

The exchange confounded Desta. Jake took the book from Timmy and leafed through it.

"This is a journal," Jake said. "What makes you think my friend needs this book?"

"I had the impulse to give it to him on my own intuition," Timmy said.

"Can I see?" Desta said. It was the same book he'd seen in his dream. He fingered its cover and leafed through to the end, page 567. He noted that these digits added to 18, and then again, reduced to 9—the numeral on the Magic wand.

Jake glanced at Desta. "Do you want it?"

"Yes, I would like to have it."

"Be sure to record your experiences in America—the good ones." Jake smiled.

"We'll take it," Jake said, "How much?"

"It's free, sir," Timmy said.

"Free?"

"Yes," Timmy flashed a perfect circle between thumb and index finger.

"That's very kind," Jake said.

"Thank you very much," Desta said. He pressed the tome against his chest.

Jake paid for their purchases, and they went out and drove home. Enroute, Desta tried to make sense of the journal, but no plausible answer came to him.

Back home, Jake and Desta climbed the stairs. "As I said earlier, a student named Seth Kaplan will come at 2 pm to interview you for the school paper," Jake said. He suggested Desta and Seth have the interview under a canopy by the pool.

Desta dropped his book bag on the floor of his room. He thought about his interview. He figured most of what he'd want to say would come out in the conversation.

He wondered whether to bring up the magic coin. It would be an easy way to spread the word; someone who read the interview might know about the coin. He decided he would talk about the shekel as much as Seth wanted.

He lay on his bed, closed his eyes, and imagined what else he'd discuss. Shortly before two pm, Jake woke Desta.

Desta thought his masinko would add a cultural dimension to the interview, and he retrieved it from the closet. He made his way to the pool patio with his instrument and sat under the canopy. He pressed on his heart, to help him play his best for Seth, and practiced as he waited for the young man.

At two sharp, Jake brought Seth to Desta. He rose and shook the visitor's hand.

"Be gentle with him," Jake said with a smile and left.

The newly acquainted men sat across from each other and chatted.

A slight fellow with a narrow face, pale skin, and light blue eyes, Seth asked if this was Desta's first trip out of Africa and how long his flight took. Desta replied it was his first time, and the flight took five hours less than a full day.

In response to Seth's further questions, Desta touched on his family, childhood, and sports. When Seth asked why he had come to America, Desta said for his education, and then mentioned his search for the twin of an ancient coin.

Seth's expression grew serious. "I'm quite familiar with the Old Testament," he said. "And I believe that King Solomon's ring may exist, but not a pair of coins."

"They were always hidden," Desta said, "So they wouldn't be in the Bible."

Seth was not convinced. He closed his book. "I think I have enough information for my article," he said. "But I'd like to take your picture before I go."

Desta picked up his masinko and bow and pulled his chair out of the canopy's shadow. He sat back down, wedged the resonator between his thighs, and rested his left hand on the lute, fingers open.

"This is called a *masinko*," Desta said, patting it with his hand. "I would like to sing a traditional song for you. It's called *Tizita*—remembrance." Desta passed his hand over his chest once again.

He turned the peg to tighten the string. Then he grabbed the bow, rested it on the lute, and drew it back and forth slowly as he tapped the cord above with alternating fingers:

Eheh eheh eheh eheheheh eheh eheh eheheheh the masinko sang. The music wasn't exactly lyrical, but he was surprised that he could draw such good sounds. *Something else I've discovered about myself in America*, Desta thought.

He continued to bow the string, improving as he went, his hand moving gracefully. He paused the bow slightly and began harmonizing: *eheh eheh eheh eheh eheh ehhhh*, imitating the masinko, pausing, and then *nena nena nena nena hhhhhh . . .*

Another slight delay, and:

Tinan'tenant'so, zaren tentereso
Kenegem teweso, amna'nem adeso
Yemetal Tizitash guazun agbesbeso
Fikerens shegnehut wetiche ke'dege
Mabarer yalchalhut tizitan naw enji

"What do the words mean?" Seth asked.
Trouncing yesterday, bolstered by today,
Borrowing from tomorrow, renewing yesteryears
Comes your Tizita (remembrance) hauling its goods.
I escorted love out of my premises.
The difficulty I face is chasing away the Tizita.
The instrumentation felt moving, melodic, and transporting to Desta's ear.

"What a wonderful song!" Seth said, seeming genuinely enchanted.

He took three pictures of Desta from different angles. "Thank you very much," he said, and shook Desta's hand. "*Tizita* will be great for my article."

"You're very welcome," Desta said. "It was great to share this little piece with you, and through your article, with the rest of the community."

Seth left. Desta slid the bow into the neck of the masinko and leaned it against the chair before him.

Jake came out to the patio. "I was watching from the family room. How do you think it went?" he asked. "The music sounded great."

"It went well," Desta replied, with his hand still on his chest. He then grabbed his masinko and got up.

They went inside. Desta's head teemed with hope and worry as he climbed the stairs. Whatever this interview meant, he hoped it would open doors of friendship and new acquaintances who would help him adapt to his new life and advance his search for the missing shekel.

ELEVEN

Desta was already at the driveway waiting for David. He was finally going to New York, the city he had heard and read so much about in Ethiopia. And he could look for the person who owned the Second Coin of Magic and Fortune while they were there.

He wore his light cotton shirt, khaki pants, and polished brown shoes. He didn't know how people dressed in a glamorous city like New York, but he thought his outfit would withstand scrutiny; hopefully that included the coin's owner.

David pulled up his car, reached over and unlocked the passenger door for Desta. As they drove off, David explained that they would take the train to the city, to avoid the troubles of traffic and parking. They got to the Rye railroad station lot and heard the approaching train. They parked and ran up several flights of stairs to the platform for the city-bound train.

They had barely caught their breath when the train screeched to a halt. The doors opened; the waiting crowd rushed in like a gale of wind, and scrambled to their seats.

David tugged Desta's sleeve, leading him to two empty orange seats by a window. The doors slid shut and the train hissed as the brakes released, metal grinding metal, wheels hurtling forward.

Desta's heart filled with excitement. He would soon be in America's most beautiful city, that he had long wanted to visit.

But his enthusiasm dimmed as he considered that finding the second coin's owner might be one more unrealized dream. Even so, he wouldn't stop believing in miracles.

He pushed against his seat and closed his eyes. *First, I must believe that this Sweet and Sour woman has come to America,* he told himself. When he had prepared to study medicine in Bulgaria, the magic wand

and compass guided him toward America as the place where the coin owner likely lived. Desta had already learned that thousands of Jews had immigrated in the early 1900s to America, and New York in particular, and so Desta assumed that the coin owner must live in this city. This might be false hope, but that was all he had right now.

Desta's eyes wandered around the car. He saw heads buried in newspapers draped over arms. Women with scarves around their necks sat meditatively, purses tucked under their arms. Others chatted with their neighbors. White, red, and blue ads lined the gray walls at the ceiling.

Outside, green foliage still followed them, but the gray rooftops of buildings predominated as the train moved on. Soon the palette shifted to a dreary rust-brown and charcoal gray. Tall brick buildings looked hundreds of years old. They seemed long neglected and worn by weather and pollution.

The picture near the ground was the same. Piles of old bricks, boards, twisted metal, and shards of glass in an empty lot seemed like the aftermath of some natural calamity. Streets and empty lots were littered with abandoned cars missing headlights, chassis smashed, like the skeletons of prehistoric creatures. Letters and symbols were scrawled on buildings like the messages of ancient tribes. Children in shabby clothes played on trash-strewn sidewalks.

Desta's excitement ebbed with these developing scenes, and he wondered how this could be America, much less New York. David chatted with a man next to him, as Desta's troubling questions multiplied. He squirmed in his seat and shot glances at David.

"Enjoying the ride?" his companion asked, seemingly sensing Desta's unease.

"Let me ask." Desta weighed his words. "Are we going to New York, or someplace else?"

David seemed surprised. "Of course we are going to New York City," he replied, and glanced at his watch. "We should be there in about twelve minutes. Why do you ask?"

Desta explained to him what he had seen from the train.

"Well," David began, eyes thoughtful, "Sorry that what you see around us colored your impression of our city. New York has had big financial problems for some time. What you see reflects that. But the center of the city is still an exciting place. You'll see."

A tunnel, deep and dark as a cave, swallowed them. Its noise and novelty arrested Desta's thoughts, and now he was anxious to find out where they might end up.

After some time, the train conductor announced: "Welcome to Grand Central!"

The doors slid back, and the passengers poured out. Desta could only see a platform, pillars, and walls lit by fluorescent fixtures on the ceiling. There was no sign of land, buildings, or sky.

First the raucous sound, then the hurrying feet, animated hands, and the hum of voices made it all seem he had entered another world.

"Follow me," David said. "We'll go up three flights of stairs before we reach the street."

Here. too, strange characters and symbols covered the walls and pillars. Though these works seemed illegible, their meaning obscure, and their artistry mediocre, Desta found the intentions of their creators intriguing. He wondered if these recesses held a colony of alien artists.

They passed a great many people descending as they climbed the stairs. On the second level, people streamed from all directions, like converging rivers, as if they were all denizens of these subterranean chambers.

After passing through arches and passages, they reached an airy, barrel-shaped concourse. It was well lit; the sun added to its brightness through the hall's high arching windows. For a moment, Desta lingered on the sidelines and watched the mass of humanity move like cattle in a vast field. If the person who held the second coin were among this throng, how could he possibly go about finding her? He hung his head in despair.

Somewhere beyond his pressing thoughts and the stream of people before him, Desta heard David say, "Let's go see some of the exciting places of the city." His friend pressed his shoulder.

They followed the crowd through the double doors and into the bright sunlight and warm air. The sidewalks and streets teemed with people and traffic, and the air carried the scent of cooking, cigarettes, and exhaust fumes.

"We'll go to Times Square first," David said. "It's one of New York's most famous landmarks."

They headed to the corner of Vanderbilt Ave, and turned left onto East 45th Street, heading west. Desta kept glancing at the sea of cars and people, feeling he might drown any moment. Cars of all shapes and sizes, some as long as a bus, jammed the roads. They came in white, blue, brown, and green. Many yellow cars had *taxi* written on their sides and a sign on their roofs. To behold the kinds of vehicles he knew only from magazines filled him with excitement.

The people, too, came in all shapes and looks: tall, rugged, small, and round. And their faces varied; White, black, brown, and yellow. Desta probed the crowd for a sign of the second coin's owner. His hand slid over his chest, and he prayed that the magic power imprinted there would connect him with the coin's twin and its keeper.

Desta looked at David, wide-eyed. "Do all these people live in New York?" he asked.

"Many are visitors like us," David replied.

Desta's heart sagged. He sensed that his chances were remote to find the coin's owner on the streets of New York, where people were too pre-occupied and, in a hurry, to chat with strangers. But then again, miracles did happen, he thought. He hoped for one today.

When they got to Seventh Ave, David stopped abruptly. Desta felt like a car that had suddenly jerked to a halt.

"We have a good family friend who works on this street," David said, face thoughtful. "He is well-connected with the Jewish community, and he could be helpful in your search for the coin. I was thinking to see him after Times Square, but let's do it now. Then we can go where we want."

Desta found the prospect of this helpful friend encouraging. They walked south on Seventh Avenue to 42nd Street.

"Did you just think of it?"

"I planned to bring you here," David said. "His name is Robert Krause; he's a lawyer. His family owns the largest plumbing supply store in the Bronx, started by his grandfather when they came from Russia in the early 1900s."

Robert Krause's business meant nothing to Desta, but his background piqued his interest.

They entered a handsome building just before the corner and took the elevator to the 7th floor.

"I have an appointment with Bob. Is he in?" David said to the square-jawed young man who greeted them across the counter.

"Please sit," the young man said. "I'll put a call to him."

David and Desta sat side by side on the burgundy leather sofa. A few minutes later, David's friend came through a door to the right of the counter. The visitors rose, and David and Mr. Krause shook hands warmly. Then the man shot his gray, deep-set eyes at Desta. "This is the young man you told me about?"

"Yes," David said, smiling at his companion. "His name is Desta."

Mr. Krause gave his hand to Desta, which he shook gently. "Call me Bob," the man said, tapping the visitor on his shoulder. "Let's go to my office," Bob said land ed them to a spacious office overlooking Seventh Avenue. Bob pulled out two chairs before his sumptuous desk and invited David and Desta to sit.

The two friends chatted about family and work. Bob seemed pleased that David was now an assistant professor at New York University. "That means we'll get to see you once a year instead of every five," Bob said, cracking a gap-toothed smile.

"Sorry," David said, "with the rigors of graduate school and my travels, I've had very little time to visit friends. But my parents kept me posted about you and your family."

David then explained what Desta was looking for and how Bob might help him.

"As you know," Bob responded, "this city is largely 2nd, 3rd, and 4th generation immigrants, many of them from Europe and Russia."

"Yes, I know," David said. "Would you know anyone who might have brought with them a treasure like that one I described?"

"Most people wouldn't talk to others about such a precious object," Bob said. "A coin from King Solomon's time would be worth a lot of money."

"You're right," David said.

Desta hadn't considered that an ancient treasure like his coin might be very valuable. This made him think of it in a way he never had before. He had to guard his coin with his life, indeed!

"Do you have any clues about the coin's owner?" Bob asked.

Desta briefly fixed his eyes on Bob. "According to an old family member, the person's name means Sweet and Sour, and they were born on January seventh." He hoped he wouldn't need to say any more about the relative in question, who was his grandfather's spirit.

Bob tightened his lips and knotted his brow. "The parents of the coin's owner must have suffered some personal calamity to give their child a name with such a meaning," he said, the corners of his mouth pulling up. "The Jews in Europe and Russia experienced many trage-dies. Most parents wouldn't give their children a name that reminded them of their troubles. I think that tracing the owner with that evidence alone will be difficult."

Desta rubbed his chin. He realized that the clue he had counted on might not lead anywhere. He thought to mention that the owner might be a hermaphrodite, but quickly dismissed the idea. Who would admit their sexual identity to strangers?

"Do you know which Jewish sect this person comes from?" Bob asked.

Desta was at a loss; he didn't know what this term *sect* meant. He glanced at David.

David turned to his friend "Like Catholics or Orthodox Christians," he said.

Desta perked up. "Someone else in my family line says the coin was owned by a Karaite."

"That helps," Bob said, brightening. "The Karaites are only a thou-sand people in this country, and many live here in New York."

"Is that so?" Desta asked, a flicker of hope rising in him.

"Yes," Bob said. "If a Karaite in the United States now owns the coin, you should be able to find them." Bob added, "I'm part Karaite. Many of my family once lived in The Bronx."

Desta studied the host as if expecting him to say, "I'm the person you've been looking for."

"That could make the search a lot more manageable," David said. "Perhaps you can share this information with your family and friends and see what develops."

"My gratitude would have no bounds," Desta said.

"We have places to go today," David said. "Thank you so much for your time." They all rose, shook hands, and Desta and David left.

Desta's head swam. Was the coin owner really a Karaite? He didn't remember who had told him. Was it one of the blue spirits in the Washaa Umera caves, or Tsadok? *I'll have to confirm this with the old priest of the Ark.*

They got on the elevator with half a dozen others. At the first floor, they shuffled across the lobby. David turned to Desta and said, "I need a bathroom. Wait for me outside if you like." Desta exited the building and walked south to the corner of Seventh and West 42nd Street. What he saw there stopped him cold.

An oversized rectangular plaque framed by dancing yellow lights proclaimed, "Live Strippers." He let his eyes travel west along 42nd Street. Several entrances announced, "25 CENT MOVIES" in big letters on one side of the door, "ADULT MOVIES" on the other, and suggestive sketches of women above. A lean, balding man with a folded newspaper studied the display. By and by, a young man with dark glasses stopped at the building, studied the pictures for a few moments, and went inside.

Then a slew of men and women passed by, blocking Desta's sight, and he couldn't tell if the man also went in or joined the crowd. Most people moved along without even a casual glance, seemingly oblivious to the lurid offerings, as if they were a common occurrence.

Desta was not unfamiliar with women who sold their bodies for a living. He had lived with prostitutes in elementary and junior high school. But these women never showed their bodies publicly or talked about what they did behind closed doors.

Diagonally across the street near the southeastern corner stood a movie theater. Above the entrance, its big marquee displayed:

MATURE ADULTS ONLY
SUITE FOR THE SWEET
TEXAS FEMMES IN COLOR

Desta didn't know what to make of this public show of sex. Where he grew up, people believed that sexual activity defiled them, and promiscuous people were considered sinful.

Then, at age fourteen, he began having wet dreams. When Desta told his father, he explained what it meant, and also told Desta not to yield to his body's urges but wait until he got married.

As if to reinforce the taboo against sex, a boy in seventh grade received ten lashes while lying on a board in front of the whole school for kissing a girl on her cheek.

Now here he was in America, where sex was on display, bought and sold, right here on the corner where Bob Krause was helping him pursue the magic coin. On that journey, Desta knew that such challenges were part of his mission, and that he must accept this one like all the rest.

David joined Desta. They traveled west on 42nd Street and headed up Broadway. As they walked along, Desta sought out people in bell-bottom pants with stringy or spherical hair that he remembered from his magazines, but to his surprise, there were few in the crowd.

The ads here were bold and loud: CANADIAN CLUB, COCA-COLA, and CASTRO CONVERTIBLES looked down from a tall building at the north end of Times Square, above where Broadway and Seventh Ave crossed. Around the plaza, people wandered in and out of coffee shops, lunch spots, and clothing stores. Others looked up at the sky-high buildings and studied the giant billboards on their facades. Desta and David browsed the shops, then turned left on West 43rd Street.

"Are you hungry?" David asked, stopping at an entrance.

"I'm getting there," Desta said with a smile.

"Let's have a New York pizza."

Desta followed his friend in, and a waitress took them to sit at a corner table at the window.

"Perfect," David said. "We'll be more relaxed chatting here, away from the noise."

When the waitress returned, David ordered a medium chicken pizza with cheese, mushrooms, and black olives.

"Are you having fun?" he asked while they waited.

"I'm learning a lot," Desta said. "There is so much to see just in this one place."

"Yes," David said, measuring his thoughts, "If you stop to notice, New York is enlightening and shocking, particularly with all its problems now—the porn movies, prostitution, drugs, gangs, vandalism. And culturally, it's so rich. People from all over the world are here, even the Karaite Jews. I'd never heard about them before."

"Yes," Desta concurred. "That was an interesting discovery for me too. If all the stories and facts add up, then tracing the coin owner could be easier here." Desta continued. "I need to confirm with my spirit guide that the coin owner has a Karaite background," Desta said. "And I also realized something remarkable when we left Bob Krause's office."

The waitress brought them a steaming platter of pizza, paper plates, and a small black spatula. Another woman set down two Cokes and a bottle opener at the corner of the table.

David Hartman beamed. He set the heels of his palms at the table edge and gazed at the pie, as if he were about to dive in. Desta sat back and watched his friend.

"We should let it cool off a little," David said. His eyes flickered. He grasped the spatula and shoveled the nearest slice onto a paper plate for Desta, and one for himself. Then he picked up a glass jar from the table, flipped the cap, and sprinkled what looked like grated cheese on his pizza slice. Then he handed the jar to Desta, who followed David's lead.

The pizza was warm, succulent, and crusty. They enjoyed every bite along with their drink.

Desta wanted to finish his earlier thought, but a boisterous group sat down at a big table next to them. The neighbors laughed and spoke loudly, making it nearly impossible for Desta and David to carry on a conversation. They quickly finished and left.

"Next, we'll go to the Empire State Building," David said. "It's a fifteen-minute walk."

They took Forty-third Street back to the corner, and turned south on Seventh Avenue, which reminded Desta of his unfinished thoughts.

"Do you know the most important part of our visit so far?" Desta asked, glancing up at David.

"Tell me," he said.

"The recurrence of the number seven. Bob Krause's office is on the 7th floor and his building is at the intersection of Seventh Ave and 42nd Street."

Desta might as well have said, "the sun rises in the east and sets in the west." David's face was an unreadable mask. Desta explained that the number seven held great importance for his family. Forty-two, or six times seven, was his birth year in the Ethiopian calendar. And 49, his birth year in the Western calendar, was 7 and 42 combined, and also the sum of seven sevens. Adding the seven in Bob Krause's floor gave eight sevens.

Eight was twice four, corresponding to the four faces of the two magic coins.

David appeared to be lost. "It's a bit complicated, I know," Desta said. "I can show you on paper when we get home if you like."

"That's fine," David said, "But do you believe all this stuff?"

"I guess I didn't tell you before," Desta said. "My life has been inter-twined with certain numbers. Seven seems the most important of all."

"What has all this to do with anything?"

"The first place we went in this city was marked by numbers that re-fer to my birthdate and the two coins. I take this as a sign that the second coin is in this city."

"I hope so. . . that'll be some coincidence!"

"Coincidence is an unknown concept in my world," Desta replied. "It seems all that has happened to me is by design. But why those pictures of nude women confronted me when I left Bob's building is a mystery. What it signifies, I will never know."

"We don't believe in numerology or fate in America," David said. "But I hope these things have meaning for you."

David's skepticism was a splash of cold water. Desta saw that he couldn't make his friend believe in something he didn't relate to, and he changed the subject.

"Tell me about the Empire State Building."

David said, "They completed it in 1903. And it took a year and forty-five days to construct it. It was the tallest building in the world at that time."

They walked leisurely, and Desta occasionally looked up at the build-ings that towered over the streets and watched the pedestrians moving in every direction. It had been a while since the sun crossed its zenith, and now the shadows of the buildings marched like soldiers, taller and broader with time. They reminded him of the mountains around his birth valley, and for a moment he was there, watching them cast their forms on the eastern peaks as the sun set. But here he was, moving through a colorful world of people, cars, and buildings.

At West 34th Street, they turned left and headed toward Fifth Avenue. A block and a half away stood their destination: the Empire State Building. Each halted in his steps and looked up.

The enormous base looked like a launch pad for the mammoth four-faced structure it supported, like the Apollo rocket to the moon, which he'd seen in magazines. It tapered as it rose to a vanishing tip. Desta loved its simplicity. His eyes glided over its sleek, light gray vertical lines until they, too, disappeared into the blue. It looked nothing like the buildings around it.

"Let's go in," David said, bringing Desta back to earth. They went through the revolving doors.

A long line meandered to the ticket counter, where David bought their tickets and followed the crowd to the nearest elevator. Desta and David squeezed into the packed space. One passenger pressed the button near number eight-six on the panel by the doors. They slid shut, and the capsule shook a little and rose. White floor numbers showed behind a glass cover.

Once they reached their destination, the doors opened, and the visitors spilled out. A sign displayed Observation Deck above a silhouette of the tower and left of the sign they could see stairs with a stainless steel railing.

The interior halls of this floor held a gallery of images from the building's construction. David and Desta looked at black and white photos of the building under construction, of city dignitaries, and the laborers on the job site, some defying gravity hundreds of feet in the air.

The deck seemed more exciting. Desta followed his friend out of the doors, where most visitors congregated. For a second, the inward-turned, latticed glass enclosure, great height, and panoramic view gave Desta the sense that he had stepped into a rounded basket that might float away.

Desta brought his face close to the glass barrier and looked out. "This is fantastic," he said. He gathered his thoughts and tried to articulate his feelings. David stepped closer and said, "Let me describe what we see before us." He pointed and said, "South of us is Lower Manhattan. That way, you see the construction of two buildings that will be the tallest in the world."

He pointed again. "Over on the left are Brooklyn and Queens, two of the five boroughs of the city. "Let's go to the next side." They turned left and made their way through the crowd. David gestured again and said, "There is Midtown Manhattan; and farther away a fuller view of Queens."

Desta had to take David's word for it. They continued their circuit of the observation deck. "Here you see more of Midtown Manhattan, Central Park, and Upper Manhattan farther away."

They walked around to the earth's fourth quadrant. "This is the west part of Midtown, and that stretch of water is the Hudson River. The land beyond it is New Jersey, one of our fifty states."

"Thank you for the tour," Desta said. "I'd like to walk around and study each view again."

Thoughts of the coin were still on Desta's mind. He rested his hands on the wide cement ledge and peered at the vista before him. He faced the direction the sun rose, the way he would go home. Desta found his bird's-eye vantage point thoroughly engaging, but its detail dreary and obscured, like the anxiety that now crept into his heart like a bad dream. On the left, a large cluster of high-rises soared like Greek columns. Below were boxlike buildings spreading along a riverbank and across the sprawling land that vanished into the gray haze.

Water towers, chimneys, and indistinct projections dotted the lofty rooftops, above walls of many colors, some dark brown to gray, others tan and light gold and white, beaming in the afternoon sun, the whole view as jumbled as the questions about the coin that roiled his thoughts.

Soft music piped to the deck eased Desta's mind. Cameras clicked, feet shuffled, and voices chattered behind him, but his thoughts mostly shut out the din as he gazed at the view. When he'd seen all he could, he straightened up, and looked around at the wall of people, faces and cameras pressed against the protective glass.

The spire cast a shadow over Desta's side of the deck and set off the brightness beyond, which glowed like a full moon on a cloudless night.

Desta now stood at the north face of the deck. When the crowd shifted, he stepped forward for a closer look and gazed out. The height and density of the buildings got him thinking of how thick and tall his parents' crops grew on their farm. The summits of many of these buildings weren't far below where Desta stood. Towers threw shadows like fallen trees across buildings farther east.

Desta scanned the buildings from one side to the other; they stretched for miles north into the silvery miasma. His mind entered another world as he gazed at them. People must occupy nearly all of them, from floor to roof. Among this forest of towers, *how could he possibly find the one person with the second coin?* He rose and walked westerly, following the curving deck.

He planted his elbows on the ledge at the next unoccupied space and looked out. Many of the high rises here were a block and a half away, veiled in haze. The gauzy, charcoal shadow of a cloud covered the foreground. Most structures were old brick, a few steel-framed; some of glass towered over the others. Here too, practically every inch of the earth seemed filled up, all the way to the gunmetal gray waters and beyond, on the ridge edging the Hudson River.

The afternoon sun shone brightly over the smooth surface of the river, its countless rays bouncing back into the air, bathing the surrounding buildings. Just then, Desta remembered what his grandfather's spirit and Tsadok had both told him: the keeper of the Second Coin of Magic and Fortune lived near a body of water where the sun set. *Is this the place?* Desta wondered. If not here, how much farther would he need to follow the sun? To India, or even a full circle to Saudi Arabia?

He'd come from Ethiopia, given up his chance at medical school, and blindly accepted another course set by a compass, a map, and a magic wand! All for a path and a clue no better than this?

As he gazed at the glorious scene, his eyes teared. *Why was I chosen for this?* he wanted to say, but he swallowed that thought. He knew his fated mission; it was a privilege. He wouldn't complain; it wasn't in his nature. He wiped his tears and sighed deeply. The breath he released from his body was the opiate he needed.

David placed his hand on Desta's shoulder. "How is it going?" he asked.

Desta's body jerked. "Good," he replied animatedly.

"Let's go home," David said. "We can always come here again."

"Okay," Desta said. He turned to fully face his mentor.

"Did you have fun?" David asked.

"Yes," Desta said, and paused to gather his thoughts. "But it was also overwhelming," he added.

"Yes," David said, "New York City can be both."

Desta took another deep breath.

David said. "Glad you enjoyed yourself."

They headed for the elevators, where a horde of people waited. The gleaming doors slid open like an accordion, and Desta and David piled in. They stood side by side, feet together, David towering over Desta, a long-haired Indian woman on his other side.

Desta held his breath. The heat, the odor of bodies tinged with chemicals and perfume, and the tight space were too much for him. Desta exhaled and took another deep breath. Once the doors opened at the ground level, he let it out.

Through the lobby and out the revolving doors to 34th Street they went and headed for Grand Central.

On the crowded sidewalk, a pale old man with a long, tangled mess of hair, shriveled skin, and milky blue eyes stepped in front of them and asked, in a low, pleading voice, "Would you have a quarter?"

David and Desta stopped. "You nearly tripped us," David said. "What made you stop us?"

The beggar turned to Desta. "This young man," he said, his ancient eyes probing deep into Desta's. "I want to welcome him to America." He extended his bony hand for a shake.

Desta took it. "Nice to meet you." The hand felt rough and leathery.

"Equally so," the old man replied. "I won't delay you two," the stranger said. "Go on. I just needed a moment with him. Hope to see you again."

David reached for his wallet in his back pocket, pulled out a dollar, and handed it to the man.

"This was not my main purpose, but thank you," the old man said with a slight bow.

"Good luck to you," David said, and waved.

"I can always use good luck," the man said in a tired voice. "Thank you very much."

Desta and David resumed their walk. Moments later, Desta turned to see if the beggar had stopped anyone else, but he was gone. When Desta told David this, they retraced their steps to find him, but the old man had vanished. Desta and David looked at each other and shook their heads.

They continued for some time, face down but looking up ahead occasionally. Shortly before they reached the corner of 6th Avenue and 34th Street, David glanced at Desta. "That old man either went inside the building or got lost in the crowd," he said.

"He's not unlike the supernatural beings that have always been a part of my life," Desta mused.

"Supernatural?" David asked. Just then, a lively group outside a restaurant drew his attention. Part of 6th Avenue was closed for some kind of event. Many round metal tables stood scattered in the street, but oddly, none had chairs. A big sign atop a tall building north of where they stood declared HERALD SQUARE.

"I'm hungry. Let's get something to eat before we catch the train," David said.

"Sure," Desta said, and followed his mentor to a small sandwich shop. Not knowing what to get, he told his companion that he would eat whatever he ordered for himself. David bought two pastrami sandwiches and bottles of water. They went outside and claimed a table and chairs at the quiet end of the patio, near the street.

"A good spot to enjoy our meal quietly," David said. He smiled.

Desta faced the street, opposite David.

"Good idea," Desta said. "I have a few questions for you."

Desta loved the smell of the rye bread and the pink meat with charred tips. As they ate, Desta took in his surroundings. The balding, cracked street, a mother with long black hair crouched to attend to her baby in stroller, while a little girl in a cream-colored top and pastel yellow pants looked on. Two heavy-set women strolled north, one with polka dot top and black pants, the second with a Prussian blue calf-length dress. They appeared to be chatting from their hand gestures and glances at one another.

Most of the crowd was at the north end of the block. Desta spied a stocky man in a short-sleeved shirt with bold sunflowers in pale green field. He wore a straw hat and flip-flops; his faded blue jean shorts seemed too tight. He stood near a large planter of aster flowers. He held a cigarette in one hand and a cup in the other.

He stood half turned toward Desta in profile and stared into space; he seemed utterly lost in thought. Desta studied the man, and wondered what might be bothering him, whether the smoke and drink would fall from his hands at any moment, or if he would come out of his trance. By all appearances, even a bomb blast couldn't move him.

Might he be searching for something precious, too? Desta wondered. He was tempted to walk over to him and ask if he was looking for a missing coin. The man reminded Desta of himself. When deep in thought, Desta saw and heard nothing around him, just like his father.

"So, how have you found New York so far?" David asked, breaching Desta's distraction.

"No streets paved in gold, or hippies, or people wearing bell-bottoms," Desta replied, and broke into a broad smile. "But I have seen so many amazing and daunting things in this city."

David's face tightened. "Daunting?"

"Yes," Desta said. "How many people live in greater New York?"

"Roughly sixteen million."

"That's a daunting portion of humanity for me," Desta said. "If the coin owner lives among so many people, how do I find her?"

"One thousand Karaites," David corrected. "Remember what Bob Krause said?"

"One thousand Karaites who live among sixteen million people."

"You overthink," David said. "Let's see what Bob comes up with. Besides, you won't have to walk the entire city to find her. There are many ways to reach sixteen million people."

"Like?"

"Post a want ad in Times Square, or place a small notice in a newspaper—"

"These things probably cost a lot of money, and I don't have any."

"That's true," David said. He wiped his hands on his napkin. "But your coin is supposed to bring you good fortune."

"As legend has it . . ."

David rose. "Let's go," he said. "This is rush hour, and the trains will only get more crowded."

Desta took one last look at the man in the sunflower and green shirt. Smoke poured out of his nostrils, veiling his face. Desta couldn't tell if he was still lost in thought, or just enjoying a moment of bliss.

The Rye-bound train had just arrived when David and Desta reached the platform at Grand Central station. When the doors opened, David dashed in, Desta in tow. They sat together by the window. A short while into their ride David glanced at Desta and said, "I'm glad you got a chance to realize one of your dreams."

"Me too," Desta replied. "It's a great trip full of challenges and mysteries."

At the Johnsons' gate they said goodnight with a hug. Desta was glad to finally be home, but not without that dull pain in his head, which he assuaged by pressing the coin image on his chest.

TWELVE

"Are you ready for your classes?" Jake asked, appearing at Desta's door on the eve of their first day of classes. He carried clothes on hangers in one hand and a folded newspaper in the other.

Desta sat at his desk, overlooking the backyard, pondering his new academic life about to begin thousands of miles from home. He turned to face his host brother.

"I have all my notebooks and writing things in my backpack," Desta replied. "I'm not sure how else to prepare."

"Good," Jake said, "I have these for you. Can I come in?"

"Please do," Desta said.

"These clothes are for you," Jake went on, spreading them out on Desta's bed alongside the paper. "They were mine, but I outgrew them. Mother recently picked these out from my closet for you and had them cleaned."

Desta rose to inspect his windfall. "Thank you," he said, glancing up at six-foot-tall Jake. Desta felt awkward; he still had to try them on to see if they fit him. *His words of gratitude* were enough for now, he thought.

"Go through them," Jake said. "I'm sure you'll find a few that fit you. If not now, soon." Jake smiled.

Desta thought Jake meant that a good American diet would bulk him up. "I'll do that," Desta said.

"Oh," Jake said, and picked up the paper. "There's an article here about you."

"About me?" Desta's heart leaped.

"Seth's interview was published today."

Desta had forgotten about it. He got up slowly and unfolded the paper with the deliberation of someone not ready yet to receive their verdict.

Jake abruptly shifted gears. "By the way, do you know how to put on a tie?"

"No. . . . I never had one."

"Choose one from these that goes with the new clothes you bought last week."

Desta picked out a red and blue striped tie and handed it to Jake.

Jake slung the tie around his neck so it fell onto his chest with the wide end hanging low. His fingers moved methodically until he had pulled it through a knot at his throat and tightened the knot with a tug on the tie's ends. He patted down the collar of his shirt and turned toward Desta.

"That's how you make a simple four-in-hand knot." He opened the left closet door and checked himself in the mirror. He stroked his handiwork while fixing his eyes on his reflection.

"Did you follow that?"

"I may have to practice."

Jake loosened the short end of the tie and slid it over his head.

"Leave it this way," Jake said, laying the knotted tie on the bed. "Tomorrow, all you have to do is slip it over your head and adjust the knot.

"Let's consider the clothes you'll wear tomorrow," Jake said. From the closet, he took out the navy-blue jacket, khaki pants, and white shirt they'd bought at the store. "I think this set of clothes with the tie will look good on you."

"Thanks for your help," Desta said. "I look forward to wearing them tomorrow." He hung the clothes in the closet and closed the door.

"You're set," Jake said, smiling. "See you at breakfast at 7:30, dressed and ready for school." Jake turned to leave.

"Good night," Desta said. He turned to his bed, briefly surveyed the clothes Jake had brought from his closet, and then glanced at the newspaper. Its masthead read *Lincoln's Weekly* in slanted bold letters above two double lines. The first column had an article about the school's plan to admit women next year.

Not that it mattered to him; but it was interesting that girls were excluded from the same academic space as the boys. Many thoughts crossed his mind, in the time it took his eyes to land on the column containing his interview.

Lincoln's New International Student, it began in large, bold print. *Airplane inventor, Talented Musician, Antique Coin Hunter*, it continued in smaller letters.

Below, a grainy, two-by-four inch black and white photo showed Desta, his masinko positioned on his thighs, its neck and tuning peg resting on his left arm. His right hand held the bow. He resembled a virtuoso *azmari*—a minstrel.

He clamped his lips and eagerly read the reporter's assessment of him.

"Desta Abraham is Lincoln College's international student from Ethiopia, our first from Africa," the article began. *"A unique and likable guy, Desta comes from a remote highlands valley where, he tells me, partial eclipses of the sun occur every morning and evening when the mountains drape his valley in shadow.*

"Desta has a fairy-tale background that most of us couldn't imagine. He became a shepherd at the tender age of seven, the first duty a boy his age assumes before becoming a farmer. But then things took a sudden turn. A sage in his family told Desta that an ancient prophecy chose him to leave home to be educated and to search for an ancient gold coin, the missing twin of one his family owns. The union of the two is predicted to benefit all humanity.

Desta is a courageous and imaginative fellow. When he was barely eight, he scaled the mountain above his home to touch the sky and clouds; in school, out of necessity, he built a hand-operated airplane and used it to travel far and wide to look for clues about the missing treasure.

While still in high school, Desta was accepted on full scholarship to study medicine in Bulgaria. But shortly before he was to start there, he found clues that the missing coin was in America. Desta sacrificed medical school and came to the United States to search for the coin and study at our college.

Desta is a talented musician who plays an Ethiopian single-string instrument called a masinko. He performed a classical song of his country, called Tizita (remembrance), which I enjoyed.

Desta has overcome many hardships and challenges to be where he is today. He is highly motivated and has definite goals and a purpose for his life, and we are lucky that they have brought him to our school.

We at Lincoln tend to see the world through the prism of our personal lives, culture, and history, and sometimes we take what we have for granted. Having someone like Desta among us, with his unique talents, heritage, and life story, can inspire us to reflect on our lives, broaden our perspectives, and face with confidence our own difficulties.

As I prepared for this interview, I discovered much about Desta's country. Ethiopia is an ancient nation with a unique calendar, alphabet, and number system. They were the first country in Africa to adopt both Christianity and Islam.

Desta inspired me to learn more about our world. If you get to know Desta, I'm sure he will inspire you, too. So, when you see him on campus, come say hello. And who knows, maybe you'll be the one with the clues he needs to find his ancient coin.

DESTA WAS ACCUSTOMED to waking at four a.m. SHARP to study for a test or do homework, but this morning, it wasn't schoolwork on his mind, but what he would wear today to present himself to his new college—his traditional white Ethiopian clothes, or the jacket and tie that his school's dress code required.

Desta tossed and turned, and when the day finally broke, he rose and sat at his desk, his thoughts weighing on him. His concern was mainly not to offend his host family and the school. Elbow on the desk, Desta reached above his right temple and began pulling and stroking his hair, his device of escape.

On his first day of school, he didn't want to feel like an impostor in his American clothes, but he also felt a duty to his national and cultural identity. This Monday—August 24, 1970—also marked the beginning of Desta's journey into an American education. If Desta went by the numbers, this beginning seemed to bode well. The two numbers in the day plus the first day of the week added up to seven, the most crucial number in the coin's legend and Desta's life. The individual numbers 1970 add up to eight, double the four faces of the two shekels. So, introducing himself to this new school in his national dress was essential to Desta. There would be no question to any onlookers who he was.

If I wear my national dress, many people will remember me, and some will come to ask me about it. Then those who read my newspaper interview might be curious to learn more about me and the coin I want to find.

Also, his host family and the school might find his unfamiliar dress intriguing. He placed his right hand over his chest and pressed his thumb above his heart. He prayed the magic coin would help him with his dilemma. Soon, Desta felt a warmth in his heart, the signal he sought that he should wear his national outfit to school that morning. He sighed with relief and laid his national dress and his brand new white sandals on the bed.

Shortly before 7 a.m., Desta showered and returned to his room wrapped in a towel. Jake knocked on the door. Desta opened it, flushed with anxiety. After they greeted each other, Desta invited his host brother in.

Jake's eyes landed on the white costume, and then moved to Desta. "Are you all right?" Jake asked, puzzled.

"Yes," Desta replied. "I just have a bit of a dilemma," he said, and explained it to Jake.

"You shouldn't agonize over this," Jake said. "Our dress codes are not cast in stone. Let me see what you got."

Jake walked around the bed and stood before Desta's national costume. "What's what here?" he asked.

Desta picked up each piece of clothing, held it before them, and explained the name and function of each: the long breeches, the long shirt, the wool vest, and the *netela* or shawl.

"They're nice," Jake said; he seemed weighed by Desta's problem. He turned to Desta and said, "You're not planning to wear them every day, are you?"

"No," Desta said. "Just today, so there's no question who I am. And it's one little thing the students and teachers will learn about Ethiopia."

"You're a good ambassador for your country," Jake said, lighting up a bit. "On further thought, most people will probably find them interesting. Go ahead and put them on and come down for breakfast. We need to leave for school by 8 o'clock."

"Will do," Desta said. He exhaled deeply.

Excited, he put on his traditional clothes. First, he struggled to get the openings of his breeches past his arched feet, just like his father and brothers. Then he put on his knee-length shirt and the wool vest on top, finally draping his shoulders with the *netela*. Checking himself in the closet mirror, he felt happy and proud. He grabbed his backpack and sandals and brought them down. He set them on the bench near the entrance and walked to the dining table.

Aida's eyes turned to stone when she looked up from her bowl of cereal and saw Desta. Beverly Johnson, her hands wrapped around a white coffee cup, stood frozen by the kitchen counter, staring at Desta. Mr. Johnson, already at work, was spared the surprise.

"Come sit," Jake said, and pulled out a chair for Desta. "We'll start with cereal. We can have scrambled eggs and toast if you want more."

Jake walked to the other side of the table and sat across from Desta. Dry, curled yellow chips submerged in milk filled the bowls.

Aida didn't appear to get over her shock at Desta's all-white clothes. She looked him over every so often as she ate.

Beverly was now at the sink washing something; a gold and green scarf wrapped her head, its ends tied in the back like a ponytail, with bird images on the fabric. Aida took her bowl to the sink, rinsed it, and set it in the dishwasher. Soon Desta and Jake followed suit.

Desta went to get his backpack, when Aida and Beverly stopped him. "It's beautiful," Aida cried, studying the netela's intricate embroidery. "It's so white. At home, do you wear this every day?"

"Just on special occasions—like holidays and weddings."

"In India, men wear white cotton tunics they call kurta pajamas," Mrs. Johnson said. "Very light like yours, just as long as the shirt and pants, but no vests." Mrs. Johnson ran her fingers over the netela, "or this shoulder wrapping."

"Ours is a bit complicated," Desta said. "Probably one reason we don't wear this every day."

"We need to go," Jake said, coming down the stairs with his backpack. He wore a wheat jacket, light cotton shirt, brown slacks, and a tie in gold and navy stripes. Jake looked to Desta more like a businessman than a student.

"Have fun!" Aida said.

"Make sure Desta goes to the right classrooms," Mrs. Johnson said. "First day of school can be confusing for American kids, let alone some-one who is entirely new to our schools."

"Will do, Ma," Jake said, waving at his mother.

In the mudroom, they exchanged slippers for their brand-new shoes—Desta for his white sandals, Jake his black. Jake picked up a set of keys from a blue bowl on a pedestal by the entrance, opened the door, and they went out. Walking to the far end of the three-car garage, already open, they came to a small red car that looked like it had been delivered from the factory overnight. ALFA ROMEO announced the vehicle's name above the right taillight.

Desta had never heard of the name. Jake put their backpacks in the trunk, got in, and motioned Desta up front. Jake turned the engine, let it warm, and slowly pulled out of the garage. He then reversed gears and headed to the open gate, passing the four-door Chevy Impala that looked like a boat to Desta compared to the Alpha Romeo.

As Jake powered the red car down the long driveway to the Boston Post Road, Desta glanced around at the velvety leather seats and panels that smelled sweet and earthy, with a hint of dry bark.

Is this how I'll go to school every day? How long will this last? Hopefully, through *the end of the school year and beyond*, he thought.

He was not overwhelmed by all this luxury, but instead, like many previous experiences, Desta would need to get used to this.

Silent and expressionless, Jake drove with his eyes on the road. He occasionally turned toward Desta, as if assessing his state of mind.

"I may not go to all my classes," Jake said. "As Mother suggested, I'll help you find your classrooms, and introduce you to students, teachers, and the librarians."

"That's very kind of you and Mrs. Johnson," Desta said, "but it's un-necessary. I don't think I'll get lost. From my impression, the campus isn't very big."

"I know," Jake said. "But you'll probably get a lot of attention for your clothes, and we thought it would be easier for you if we spent the day together."

"I appreciate that," Desta said. "I thought my English was good enough, but I noticed that people here speak fast, and some accents are difficult to follow. So, I may need an interpreter." He tried to smile, but feelings of inadequacy sabotaged his attempt.

"You'll do all right," Jake said. "Dad said David Hartman told him you're a top student. You're supposed to . . ." The remainder of Jake's thoughts vanished in air.

He briefly glanced at Desta. "Do you like this car?" he asked unexpectedly as if to erase his unfinished sentence.

"I like it," Desta said. "It's beautiful."

"It's my dream car," Jake said. "My grandpa bought it for me when I graduated high school last June."

"That's nice," Desta said. "Your grandpa is very generous."

"To tell the full story, and finish what I started to say before," Jake continued, "my grandfather promised to buy me this car if I got good grades, got admitted to Yale University, the school he graduated from. When he found out I was wait-listed, he thought his connections at the school would help my chances. He bought this car and had it delivered here on graduation day. We found it parked in front of the garage when we came home that evening, with a personal note from Grandpa. Jake's eyes moistened.

"Unfortunately, in the end, I didn't get in. My grandpa was disappointed, and I was sad for days. I didn't drive the car the whole summer, to distance myself from the bad memory," Jake said, shaking his head.

"Sorry to hear that," Desta said. He shook his head, feeling sorry for Jake and his grandpa.

"No problem now," Jake said. "I've got a second chance. If I do well at Abe Lincoln in the next couple of years, I can still transfer to Yale or any other Ivy League school. You're supposed to inspire me to do well." Jake smiled.

Desta wanted to shake his head, afraid of the responsibility placed on him. Instead, he held his face stiff, eyes fixed on the lustrous dashboard. When he thought of how much work he used to do in exchange for room and food, he felt this obligation was so tiny. And he saw a ray of hope in it: if Jake improved his grades this year, Desta could be offered a second year of scholarship, and extend his stay with the Johnsons.

"That will be fine," Desta said, finally. "We can motivate each other. I've done things alone all my life. It will be a nice change for me to have somebody to study and do things with."

Jake flashed a warm smile but said nothing. When they arrived, the parking lot was busy, and he drove to the last space near a tree and parked.

"I'm parking this far from the entrance to protect my new car from someone opening their door and denting it," Jake said. They got out and collected their backpacks from the trunk.

Desta brushed down his long shirt. As they walked, he felt like a bright object that had just dropped from the sky. Students arrived in their cars as others walked to the entrance after parking.

"Good morning," a well-dressed man with sandy hair said, "I'm Keith Parker, an instructor here. I'm also the school's dress code enforcer. I make sure the students come properly attired: jacket, dress shirt, tie, slacks, and good shoes."

Desta could feel his face tightening, eyes fixed on the man.

Mr. Parker sized up Jake. "You meet the code," he said. The man moved on to Desta, and his eyes hardened. "Now, here is what I call a complete violation of our rules," Mr. Parker said. His eyes ran up and down Desta's lean frame.

Desta felt like a boy who had broken some sacred promise. He dropped his head to avoid eye contact with the man.

"Sorry I didn't introduce myself," Jake said. I'm Jake, and this is Desta, our international student from Ethiopia. You may have read Seth Kaplan's article in the Weekly.

Keith Parker's face relaxed. "So, you're that young man?" he asked, his eyes perking up. "You weren't dressed like this for the picture in the paper."

"I know," Desta said, looking up. "I don't wear these clothes every day."

"Good," The dress code enforcer said. "Tomorrow, come dressed like Jake. Are you a distance runner?" Desta's mind went blank. "If you are, you can join my cross-country team."

"I've never been part of a team," Desta said, "but if I had the chance, I'd probably do well." Desta was surprised by his own response. He couldn't fully articulate where his confidence came from. His only experience running was shepherding animals in the countryside, and racing to elementary school when he feared punishment for being late.

"Come see me, both of you," Keith Parker said, "My office is at the Field House. I'm there most afternoons. Now, I need to check these other students."

Mr. Parker eyed Desta, "Tomorrow, you'll come dressed like Jake, right?"

"Yes, sir."

"Wouldn't it be nice if we ran on the school team?" Jake said. "Mr. Parker seems like he could be a good coach, too."

"Nice of him not to send me home and change my clothes," Desta said, smiling.

Desta checked the course catalog and saw that his trig class was in the science building—West of the Castle and past the humanities building.

"Jake," Desta said. "Really, you don't need to come with me. I'll find my way around. I know exactly where my first class is."

Jake and Desta parted, but with a plan to meet in front of the cafeteria for lunch.

When he arrived at his first class, he found twenty students already in the room. Their faces froze and their mouths stopped when they saw Desta walk in, as if he was an alien who had just landed in their midst. As he walked up the first rows of seats, their eyes came to life, following him until he sat behind them. Several students arrived after Desta and sat in the first rows.

The last to arrive was the instructor, a wide-girthed, cherubic-faced man. He had a book, a wooden box and folders in his right hand, and sidled in as if he were lame. Curly red hair with a hint of yellow haloed his head.

He set down his things on the gleaming brown table. Then he turned to the board, picked up a stick of white chalk with his left hand, and wrote Stu Brown in caps to the left on the blackboard, boxing it in a zigzagged rectangle.

He set down the chalk and said, "Good morning!"

"Good morning to you, Mr. Brown," the students said.

"I'm Stu Brown, your trig instructor. I will do my best teaching, and you do your part learning." He smiled and sat down. He took roll call from a sheet in his folder, each student answering "Here" or "Yes." Desta just raised his hand like he used to do at home.

Mr. Brown pronounced Desta's name as Dasta A-braham, like his Peace Corps teacher used to. He didn't wince or correct the man; he couldn't possibly correct every person who misspoke his last name with such an off-key sound. He told himself he must accept this too.

Afterward, Mr. Brown rose. "I know many of you at this college hope to transfer to the Ivy League and other top schools. The only way you will achieve that is with top grades. This school was founded to give students like you a second chance, and graduate with a good education under your belt.

"How many of you applied to an Ivy League school and didn't get in?"

Mr. Brown counted the raised hands. "Sixty percent. It's roughly the same number every year."

With further questioning, Mr. Brown determined that the rest of the students also hoped to transfer to the Ivy League.

"I'll give you the hard facts," Mr. Brown continued. "You'd better have a 3.8 or better grade point average to transfer to Harvard, Yale, or Princeton, and 3.6 for the rest. If you are an excellent athlete, you have a better chance at the top three, even with a lower GPA. We aim to give you an excellent education to help you improve your opportunities, but as I said, you have to play your part by studying hard and doing well."

Desta squirmed in his seat. With so many things to get used to, he was still determining how to achieve those numbers. He tapped his desk and thought hard about his academic future. He tipped his head back, drew air as much as he could and let it out slowly with a hiss.

"I assume you all have taken geometry," Mr. Brown continued. Everyone, including Desta, raised their hands.

"Good," he said, and drew several figures: a rectangle, a square, a circle, a right triangle, a trapezoid, cylinders, and spheres.

Of all these shapes, his course dealt with only one: the triangle, or more precisely, the right triangle.

He opened the box and took out a beautiful, wooden version of the triangle. He raised and held it, with the longest side to the right.

He pointed to the three interior angles, one at a time, and said, "Trigonometry is the relationship of these angles to the figure's three sides.

This relationship is called trigonometric functions or ratios, designated as sine, cosine, and tangent. He wrote out on the board three such ratios for each of the two smaller angles.

Desta and the rest of the class took notes. The man spoke fast, face to the blackboard, and was sometimes hard to understand. Desta's difficulty writing legibly, which started after his brother's visit in high school, returned, but somehow, he managed. He knew it was connected to his head problem and wondered what he could do if it got worse.

Mr. Brown placed the chalk on the board's ledge and blew the dust from his fingers. Then he gathered his things and said, "See you next time."

The students rose and started to file out. Desta remained seated. One student in the row before him came and introduced himself to Desta as Tor Gardner. "Seth Kaplan said you built a flying craft. Is that true?" Tor asked.

"Yes," Desta said, his eyes holding Tor's. A couple more students lingered and listened as Desta and Tor spoke.

"And you're searching for a coin that once belonged to King Solomon?" a second student inquired.

"That's true," Desta said. He clamped his lips and looked at the eyes before him with anxiety.

The second student shook his head. Desta couldn't tell whether that was a sign of disbelief or reverence.

The Biology 15 instructor started his class with a wave of his hand, a hello, and an introduction–he was Bret Nelson, new to Abe Lincoln College, but had been teaching this course at other colleges for twenty years, which explained his salt and pepper beard and hair. He didn't bother with a roll call; he said he would get to know his students over time.

"I'm generally a hard-working instructor," he said, "This year, I will probably work harder than ever in my career. Your course curriculum is far more advanced than at any other school. That means you, too, must work hard to earn your grades for this class. Reading assignments and lab reports must be timely."

Then Mr. Nelson launched into his first lesson: cell structure and function. He drew two circles, one inside the other, representing the cell. He filled each with its components—the DNA and its parts at the center, and all the rest in the space between the inner and outer circles. He spent the remaining time describing the function of each cell component in such detail the man might have lived inside it.

He spoke clearly and deliberately. The man seemed driven to do his best and expected the same from his students. After covering all he had planned to teach that morning, Mr. Nelson gathered his things, and left, and the class dispersed.

Since Desta had an hour before he met with Jake, he decided to sit on a bench near the Abraham Lincoln sculpture. He needed to know if the man's lips moved, or if it was his imagination, as Jake made it appear.

When Desta got there, he found himself alone, and sat across from the bronze figure with his backpack beside him. He gazed at Lincoln's face, his hands gripping the edge of the bench. The lips didn't seem to move, but the moment he looked away, he saw them part from the corner of his eye. When he refocused on them, he saw only a closed mouth. He did this three times and swore he saw Mr. Lincoln's lips move each time. The third time, the man's eyes also moved. Baffled, Desta left for the cafeteria to meet Jake. He was outside waiting for Desta.

Jake came up to Desta and asked, "How did it go?"

"Well," Desta said, "I learned that students here simply say "yes" or "no" during roll call; that they go from room to room for their classes, like nomads; and that I'll be learning about the right triangle the whole semester."

"Things are done differently in America," Jake said, "You'll get used to it."

The long line at the cafeteria moved along. Other waiting students studied Desta's all-white clothes. Just about everybody in the dining hall could see him, but nobody came over to ask where he was from, or about his clothes or the coin or his flying craft.

"I won't ask you what you want to eat, since you haven't seen the menu, and you don't know a lot of our dishes," Jake said. "But once we get to the food, choose whatever looks good to you." Jake handed Desta a brown plastic tray and a white plate when they reached the serving line.

Desta watched his host brother pick a reddish cut of meat, on which the server poured a thick brown sauce, cubed carrots, and green vegetables, and added rice and a square of soft bread, which Jake called a brownie. He wanted to try a chicken leg but didn't want to overeat, and so he stuck with his choices.

Many eyes followed them as Desta and Jake made their way to the only unoccupied table at the far end of the dining room. Jake put his tray on the table, and said, "I'll bring us a drink. What would you like?"

"Fanta or Coca-Cola would be fine."

Jake returned with the drinks, and they began to eat. Recalling the Johnsons' rules not to talk while eating, Desta put off his questions about Jake's morning suggestion of doing sport at school.

Unruly hairs from Jake's mustache quivered. He seemed thoughtful. "So, would you like to join the school cross-country team? Jake asked, looking up from his plate.

"That would be great," Desta said, out of courtesy. He had never run just for its own sake and couldn't see the value.

"We can go one afternoon later this week and talk with Mr. Parker," Jake said.

"Do you mind if I sit with you? All the other tables are taken," Tor Gardner said, a full lunch tray in his hands.

"By all means," Jake said, gesturing to an empty chair.

"I'm interested in chatting with Desta," Tor said.

"How nice," Jake said. "As you know, Desta is new to the country and can probably use as many friends as he can find." Jake grinned at his housemate.

"That's true," Desta said, happy that someone he had barely met wanted to chat with him.

He felt a little less afraid of America and Americans. Maybe there were more like Tor Gardner.

First, Jake and Tor talked about their high school years and what led them to Abe Lincoln Junior College. Tor had gone to the Hackley School in Tarrytown, New York. He played varsity field hockey, lacrosse, and tennis in his junior and senior years and played the clarinet in the school band.

He had a high-grade point average and good SAT scores, but he'd needed higher to get into Harvard. His twin brother, who had similar stats, had applied to Princeton, and gotten in and was now a freshman at the University. So, Tor came here, to study hard, and improve his transfer chances to the school of his dreams.

Jake had gone to Rye Country Day School, where he competed in varsity golf, and tennis, and was on the swim team. His grades and SAT scores were not high enough for Yale. His grandfather, who graduated from the school and had contributed a lot of money to it, was upset when he was not admitted. Jake's parents decided that he would attend Abe Lincoln, significantly improve his grades, and try to transfer to Yale.

Both Jake and Tor admitted that they were not disciplined students. Tor turned to Desta, "And you?"

Desta had already been feeling he needed adequate English to talk at the same level with these classmates. Also, listening to Jake and Tor talk about sports he had never heard of, let alone played, Desta felt like he had landed in a completely different world. He groped for an answer, straightened up, and cleared his throat. "During high school, I worked part-time for the people I lived with, and didn't have time for sports," he said. "But I did well enough in my studies to get into medical school in Bulgaria.

"Medical school?" Tor asked incredulously.

"Yes, in Bulgaria and Ethiopia, students study medicine right after high school. I decided to come here for a complicated reason."

Tor shook his head. "And you invented a flying craft."

"Which I did out of necessity," Desta said. "It became useful later for some expeditions I made."

"And the coin?"

"It's an ancient treasure that I'm supposed to find. That's the very reason I came to the United States instead of Bulgaria."

"Amazing!" Tor Gardner said. "My grandfather collects ancient coins. Since I read your article in the Weekly, I thought of him and wondered if he might have such a coin."

Desta suddenly perked up. "Really?"

"Yeah, but he is a recluse and hard to reach. He's an old man from Russia."

Desta hadn't thought finding the Solomonic coin would be this easy, but he considered this hopeful lead. "Thank you for the information," he said. "Please let me know what you find out from your grandfather."

As Jake and Desta drove home, David's advice to defer the search for the coin until he was adapted to his new life now made more sense to Desta, particularly considering the effort he must devote to his challenging English class. School was his priority, and he had to do well, and motivate Jake to do well, too, if he was going to earn another year's stay with the Johnsons.

Before he went to bed that night, he recited the legend and prayed to God to help him fulfill his dreams.

IN HIGH SCHOOL, Desta's favorite science subject was chemistry; he'd earned nearly perfect scores in all his exams. How he would do in college chemistry was as unclear as the rest of his unfolding life in this country. Like everything else, he'd have to find out by going through it, and make sure he did his best to earn the grades he needed.

Dr. Juan Gabriel, the Chem 10 instructor, arrived with sweat trickling down his face, and kept mopping it with his handkerchief. It was a warm, humid afternoon, and the AC in the room was not working. Everybody in the class was sweating too.

Dr. Gabriel seemed not to heed the dress code; his pastel blue shirt and brown pants showed wrinkles, and his carelessly knotted tie hung cock-eyed. Dark curly hair framed his bespeckled brown face. His intelligence and seriousness gave Desta hope he'd receive a quality education from the man. He knew to get into medical school he needed a solid foundation in the sciences.

After roll call, Dr. Gabriel spent much of his time discussing his course syllabus, reading assignments, grading system, and their lab experiments.

"I know most of you are in this college to improve your chances to go to the Ivy League school of your choice," the man said. "If you want me to give you the grade you need, you'll have to meet all my requirements by studying hard and doing well with all of your homework and tests."

With these warnings, Dr. Gabriel went directly into chemistry. "Generally speaking," the man began. "Chemistry is the study of the chemical compositions of substances, their structure and properties, and the changes they undergo. Like the other physical sciences, there are natural laws that govern and describe these changes.

"Atoms and molecules are the fundamental players in chemistry. They combine to create a substance or form from the disintegration of a raw material. These are done by a chemical process in solution where energy is consumed or released to effect the changes. These changes can be noticed in the ingredients of a baking cake or a cooking sauce or in a chemist's lab by the appearance of dramatic color or evolution of gas."

Dr. Gabriel then pulled down a rolled screen, showing the periodic table of elements, organized as rows or periods and as columns or groups. He briefly described each. He then sketched the atom and talked about the protons and neutrons found in its nucleus, the electrons that spin around it on different levels or shells, and how energy is emitted or absorbed as electrons are excited.

These electrons, which often came in pairs—like the two coins Desta one day hoped to see together—occupied different rings or levels, corresponding to the elements' positions in the periodic table, which Desta had studied in high school. The minimum number of electrons at the bottom circle was two, and the maximum at higher shells was eight.

A substance with unpaired electrons at the outer ring was unstable and needed another unpaired electron to become stable or form a molecule. Dr Gabriel said that massive amounts of these molecules created the matter we see and feel around us. Fire and chemical agents are the facilitators of many of the chemical processes that take place in a lab.

With this introduction, Dr. Gabriel gathered his things from the desk, reminded the students to complete the first syllabus reading before next session, and dismissed the class.

"How do you feel about your courses?" Jake asked as they drove home.

"Overall, I'm okay with them," Desta said, "But some teachers and students spoke too fast."

"You'll get used to the way we talk," Jake said. "It'll be okay." He smiled.

That night, Desta lay in bed and wondered how he could get a 3.8 GPA when he felt so unprepared for his English 101 class. He shuddered and thought he might drop physics to devote more time to English, which was sure to be challenging for him.

THIRTEEN

In this second day of college, Desta wore his new royal blue jacket, blue and gold striped tie, brown pants, and shoes.

"Good to see you dressed like the rest of the students," Mr. Parker said to Desta when he saw him inside the gate with Jake.

"I'm happy to comply with your dress code, Mr. Parker," Desta said. "Thank you for accepting me in my national dress yesterday."

"It was a pleasure," the coach said. "It'll be even more so, if you fellas . . ."

Jake interrupted. "We are still thinking about your invitation for Desta and me to join your cross-country team, Mr. Parker," Jake said. "We'll let you know in a day or two."

"Good!" Mr. Parker said, "My roster is filling up but should have room for you two." The man moved on to check other students.

Jake and Desta went to their classes.

ENGLISH 101. While waiting with the rest of the students for their instructor to arrive Desta thought about the title of his first class. It sounded mysterious and intimidating. Why 101? And why such a high number? Should Desta have taken the first 100 English courses before enrolling in this one? He wouldn't agonize over it. He would just have to wait and see how this course unfolded.

Dr. Quinn Donovan confidently strode through the door and stood before the class. She was a petite woman of about thirty-five. She wore high heels and a knee-length beige cotton skirt. She had twisted her brown hair into a pile on her head in no particular style, seemingly to appear taller.

"Good morning!" she said. A chorus of good mornings came from the students.

Dr. Donovan set down a single folder and a book on the desk before her. She wrote her name in big, slanting letters on the blackboard. She returned to the desk and took attendance.

She passed out the course syllabus and reviewed each topic she planned to cover in the first semester. "This class is designed to teach students how to write intelligent essays clearly and effectively," she said. Her class would start with grammar and syntax, paragraph development and organization, and formulating a thesis statement to achieve that goal.

She said she expected each student to read the six books in the syllabus, and showed the class one of them, *The Portable Conrad* by Joseph Conrad. They were to write critical essays on four books of their choice.

Dr. Donovan made clear that she expected the essays to be original. She cautioned that if any student presented someone else's work as their own, this would violate school ethics rules against plagiarism, and would be punished, by at least a failing grade for the course, up to expulsion from the college.

Desta realized the challenge he faced competing with students who grew up speaking and writing the language. If he failed any course, he feared it would be English.

English had been one of his favorite subjects in Ethiopia, and he'd earned top marks. But expectations were different here. He knew basic grammar and had a good vocabulary but had never written anything original or read literature. He sighed. Just as quickly, his resolve took over. "No matter what, I must work hard and get a good grade," he said under his breath.

They were to read the assigned pages in *The Portable Conrad* for homework. With that, she collected her folder and book and left, her shoes echoing in her wake.

PHYSICS 12, Desta's other class of the day, was held next door to English 101. After he gathered his writing things into his backpack, he left to find the physics instructor, Chuck Fernsby, standing by the entrance, introducing himself, shaking hands with every student, and invariably asking, "Your good name?"

Desta found the unique and intimate roll-calling intriguing and liked Mr. Fernsby, a lean, bearded man of about forty. Then the instructor came to the desk and passed out two sheets containing the course syllabus and reading and homework assignments.

Mr. Fernsby not only seemed to have amity for his students but also for physics. On the board, he had already outlined the topics he would cover and the weeks he planned to do them, giving his students a clear course roadmap. Desta noticed that his Indian instructors at home had covered many of the topics on the list. He would have to wait and see how American teachers dealt with them.

"Physics," Mr. Fernsby said, "is the study of the physical world— both the visible (like objects around us) and the invisible (atoms and molecules)."

"Luckily," he said, "as vast and complex as these worlds are, they can be explained by simple and unified sets of physical laws and mathematical equations. With these tools, we can describe the relationships of many things in the physical world, for example, energy and matter, and time and space which can be measured and studied. Then he listed the different units that help quantify them—from the motion of an object on a plane to electrical charges in matter to the photons that come from the sun."

Mr. Fernsby drew a simple square object on the board that he moved with an arrow to the right. He assumed the space and time for the thing moved in meters and seconds, respectively. From these numbers, he created a relationship between the meter/second or speed of the object and the meter/second plus the direction or velocity of the object. After this simple illustration and mathematical representation, Mr. Fernsby talked more physics, the laws that were determined by a famous English mathematician and physicist name Sir Isaac Newton.

From this simple illustration he went on to describe acceleration, and Newton's Laws of Motion.

"We'll have fun learning about these things and all the topics outlined in the syllabus," he said as he put away the chalk on the ledge.

Then, Mr. Fernsby gathered his things, waved to the class, and left.

DESTA AND JAKE MET outside the bookstore, where his host brother said they would purchase their textbooks. Each picked up a basket at the entrance and headed to the Academics section. They collected their required texts, Jake paid for them, and they left. They went to the library to do their homework.

Near noon, they gathered their books and went to the cafeteria for lunch. Jake met friends from high school, and they sat and talked until one o'clock, when everyone headed for their classes.

Later, as Jake drove them home, Desta closed his eyes, tipped his head back, and thought about English 101.

"So, do you think you'll join the cross-country team?" Jake asked, pulling Desta from his thoughts.

Desta considered the question. "What exactly would we do?"

"We'll have running practice every day after school with the team."

"But I have lab classes on Tuesdays and Thursdays."

"That would be okay," Jake said. "You can make up those two practices on weekends."

"And how far do we run?"

"To be honest, I don't know."

"Let me sleep on it and I will tell you tomorrow."

Arriving home, Desta and Jake went upstairs. Desta put his backpack on the window seat in his room and lay on the bed on his back. He crossed his arms over his chest and stared at the whitewashed ceiling as thoughts filtered through his head. His momentary concern was what he must do to earn top grades to transfer to a good school with a scholarship, God willing.

Desta felt the English course, with all the reading and essays, would be his hardest. He could handle trig and science, but he had to excel in all his courses. He owed it to the people who helped him come to America—David's family, the Johnsons, and the Catholic charity that paid his tuition.

Then the idea of joining the cross-country team had not sat well with him. Earlier while walking between his classes, Desta thought that practicing with the cross-country team after school would be a waste of his valuable time. It went against his training and drive to be productive and fed his fear of punishment that he'd learned from his family and hosts in Ethiopia.

Throughout his education, Desta had always left school promptly after classes to work for his host family and later, in high school, to support himself tutoring merchants' children. Despite this, he'd always wished he could spend more time and play sports with his classmates.

Here in America, Desta didn't expect to be punished for this, but he was still unsure about committing his time for cross-country workouts. The Johnsons had never told him what he must do in exchange for his one-year stay. He wanted to send a message to Tsadok for his assistance with his dilemma, but he decided against it. Desta was now big enough to make his own decision.

That night after dinner, Desta sat at his desk and took out his English syllabus, assignment, exercise sheets, and *The Portable Conrad*. Though the next class wasn't for two days, Desta was eager to get his work done.

From the teacher's worksheet on grammar and syntax, he rewrote sentences to be corrected. Then he checked the syllabus for the first reading, *Heart of Darkness*. Desta liked the mysterious title. His assignment began on page 490, as if the first 489 pages weren't important. He waded through the sea of words from the beginning to his destination; it was divided into sections.

Heart of Darkness.

Like this thick volume's other titles, it was a book within a book, near the end of its contents. Desta stared at the title, turning it over in his thoughts for some meaning. It was something neither here nor there, as elusive and confusing as Sweet and Sour. Desta closed his eyes and pronounced the title, seeking shades of meaning. He thought of the Ethiopian phrase *sem ena work*—wax and gold, the literal and the figurative. He split up the words; Did darkness have a heart? Taken together, the meaning was abstract, intangible.

Desta had never heard of Joseph Conrad or his stories. He put out the light and went under the covers. But he was wide awake and once again, he thought about the idea of practicing with the cross-country team after school. Somehow it all felt like a right-handed person trying to write with the left hand, like he'd felt a year ago when his fine penmanship became mere scrawls. He switched to his left hand, which was clearer but painfully slow. He put out the light and closed his eyes for a journey to 4 a.m. tomorrow.

In the morning, waking up at the usual hour, Desta did his homework for his science and trig classes and even read a few more pages of Conrad. He had about an hour before breakfast and then school, and he turned off his desk light to lie down and nap for a while. It was then when Desta saw white light shimmering over *The Record*. Excited, he turned the light on, picked up the journal and leafed through to find Tsadok's new entry.

Why do you agonize over an opportunity you have been offered, one you never had while living in Ethiopia? Accept it and see what develops from it. Your life is evolving. Don't let your past hold you back. I'll share what a wise man told me as we contemplated leaving the Elephantine Island in Egypt and coming to this beautiful land twenty-five hundred years ago. "Opportunity has a tail in the front but none in the back." Grab its tail while it has presented itself to you. Once it passes, you may have nothing to hold on to.

Desta was happy to read these words of wisdom from his ancient counsel. He quickly took out his magic wand, set it on his desk, sat down before it and said three times, "accept the following message and transmit", while fixing his eyes on the big 9 at the center. As soon as he saw light emerge from it, he said:

Dear Tsadok, the Honorable guardian and transporter of the Ark,

I cannot thank you enough for this message. It helped lift the dark cloud that has hung over me for the last two days. As you know, I'm just starting here. I've not figured out yet what would be suitable for the pursuits that brought me to this country. Your advice will now make it easy to accept the coach's offer. Thank you very much. Desta

FOURTEEN

On the third day of classes, as Jake and Desta drove to school, the host brother turned and said, "What have you decided about our joining the cross-country team?"

"I don't have a definite reason or a clear view of its value, but I'm willing to explore the opportunity. What's your reason, considering that you were in completely different sports in high school?"

Jake turned and eyed Desta. "I know," he said. "You've never played any of my favorite sports, and cross-country is one we can do together. We both have good legs." Jake smiled.

"Well," Desta said. "That's good of you to switch to running on my account. As a kid, I wish I had played soccer, but I never got a chance."

"Soccer never appealed to me. But I ran a lot playing tennis in high school, so I'm okay with cross-country."

"I've mulled over the idea of running since yesterday. Although I'm not experienced at it, I like the freedom of the sport; it's like flying without leaving the ground. So, let's join the team."

"Great!" Jake said, "I think we'll have fun."

MR. PARKER STOOD AT THE GATE in front of the castle with a clipboard and pencil. "Good morning, fellas!" the dress code enforcer said. "So, have you two decided to join my cross-country team? We've only got a few more spots."

Jake and Desta eyed each other. "Matter of fact," piped up Jake, "we were talking about that on our way here. Yes, we'll give it a shot."

Desta wished Jake had answered Coach Parker with an emphatic *yes!*

"In that case," Mr. Parker said, pencil poised over his clipboard, "give me your names."

The coach jotted them down and advised them to come to the gymnasium that afternoon at 3:30. "I'll give you your lockers. If you want to practice with the team afterward, bring shorts and running shoes."

The men smiled at Mr. Parker.

"See you later, Mr. Parker," Jake said. "We'll bring our running clothes."

"Okay then," Mr. Parker said. "A pleasure to have you on my team."

Jake and Desta went off to their morning classes. At lunch in the cafeteria, they discussed their running outfits, and agreed to meet after classes at 2 pm at the campus All-purpose School Department Store.

After his last class concluded, Desta went to the store directly and found Jake on the second level. Both grabbed their shopping baskets and went to look at sportswear.

They considered shirts, shorts, sweatpants, and tennis shoes in various colors and sizes. Jake suggested that Desta get a T-shirt and a couple pairs of shorts for the warm weather, and sweatshirts and pants for cooler days. Desta picked out gray cotton shorts and a matching shirt, and they both filled the baskets with their choices.

All the clothing was emblazoned with a version of the school's name and logo: a stylized image of a dog with stout legs, big head, and a rumpled face. It carried an axe on its right shoulder, its sharp blade aimed at the viewer. "Rail-splitters" was inscribed dark as night below the dog, the letters touching his front paws.

Desta wondered what the words meant, but life had taught him not to ask unnecessary questions of others, and he kept his thoughts to himself.

Jake chose similar clothes, only blue and bigger. He paid for the two of them, and they left the store.

They still had an hour before the team met at 3:30. Jake suggested they browse the bookstore until then. Desta felt he could spend hours on end among those bookshelves.

Desta gravitated toward novels. Jake headed for history and biography. Several new releases were propped up on stands and stacked on shelves, and also lay on tables near the cashiers. Among them were *The Bluest Eye* by Toni Morrison and *Bury My Heart at Wounded Knee* by Dee Brown.

He read a page or two, skimmed headings and chapter openings—whatever caught his fancy. As unfamiliar as their authors, stories, and characters were, their magic drew Desta into these books. He promised himself that when he could afford to buy them, he would read them cover to cover.

Jake came over. "Time for the meeting with Mr. Parker." Each carried his bag of clothes and left.

"So, you were serious?" Mr. Parker said, feigning surprise. He looked at the watch on his burly forearm. "On time too." He smiled.

"Of course!" Jake said.

Desta liked his host brother's confidence.

Mr. Parker wore shorts too tight for his muscular legs, and a T-shirt that could have been roomier for his broad chest and sturdy shoulders. He held a clipboard with a pen clamped at the top. He smiled at Desta. "How do you like it here?"

"Very much," Desta said.

"Let's get you some lockers," Mr. Parker said.

The door to the gymnasium opened to a big basketball court with wood benches rising to the top of opposite walls. Several students practiced shots at the basket. More sat on benches, watching the players. The sun filtered through a high window, making the floor shine.

Jake and Desta followed the coach alongside the court and entered a long, narrow room, where grey metal panels with doors and padlocks studded the walls. Desta held his breath against the stuffy, humid air, filled with commotion and noise. At benches, students changed from school clothes into T-shirts, shorts, and running shoes. Others scurried in and out of the showers, some wrapped in towels, looking pensive and harried, hair ruffled and sticking out as if they had just come in from a damp windstorm.

Mr. Parker stopped at an empty bench halfway down the left wall of lockers, and gestured toward two that were empty. "These are yours," he said. He handed each recruit a paper slip from his clipboard with his name, locker number, and padlock instructions.

"Get changed and come outside," Mr. Parker said and left.

Desta first watched Jake use the strange lock with a dial, and then unlocked his own. He stripped off his clothes and shoes, hung them inside the locker, and changed into his running outfit.

They locked up their things and went outside to find Mr. Parker and a dozen students, some stretching arms and legs on the grass, others pacing or running in place. Two others arrived after Jake and Desta, bringing the roster to sixteen.

"Shake hands and introduce yourselves," Mr. Parker said.

The students made the rounds with one another. Desta felt alone and exposed under the glare of attention of these easy-going, carefree young men.

He hadn't worn shorts since he was a kid, and he was smaller and skinnier than most. He'd barely tipped the scales at 115 pounds when he'd last weighed in at a doctor's office in Addis Ababa.

Despite his teammates' much lighter complexions, Desta regarded them no differently than his schoolmates at home. He wasn't sure how they saw him, but he was completely comfortable in his own skin.

"Follow me," Mr. Parker said, and strode across the open field to the north side of the school grounds past the stadium, the runners trailing their coach like ducklings after a mother hen.

They came to a tree-shaded trail, which Mr. Parker explained went around the perimeter of the campus, one mile long. The team was to run around the trail five times for a total of five miles.

"At a good pace, you should complete your circuit in forty minutes." Mr. Parker said. He glanced at Desta. "Some of you could do it in thirty-five or less."

Desta translated the distance into a more familiar measure. "That's eight kilometers," he said under his breath. Even as a kid in the country, he never ran even a quarter of that. Jake seemed dubious about completing the course too.

Mr. Parker appeared to have read the mood of his team. "I don't expect all of you to finish the course on your first attempt," he said, "but at least try half of the rounds. And let's meet at Lincoln Courtyard afterward."

Jake seemed to relax. Desta hoped he could finish the circuit.

"Okay fellas . . . Ready?"

The team bunched up, some still doing their run-in-place warm-ups.

"One . . . Two . . . Three . . . Go!"

"See you all in forty minutes!" Mr. Parker said.

Hands curled into fists; forearms bent and moved from side to side in rhythm with kicking feet. Two runners got out in front. Desta and Jake were in the middle of the pack and struggled to keep pace with those ahead. They moved on, long hair whipped in the wind, feet crunching grass and gravel, chests rising and falling like brisk ocean waves, lungs working hard like bellows.

Their sound and movement grew as the front runners pushed ahead. After the first mile, a few students began to fall back.

To Desta, these youths, with all their grunting and exertion, seemed like troops training for duty, to no clear end. But he reminded himself that the point of these runs was to condition their bodies to compete.

Long before they reached the halfway point, more runners fell behind. Except for half a dozen students who kept up the pace, the team was already strung out; some walked to catch their breath and then ran or jogged. The early leaders continued, with Desta and Jake behind them. At around three-quarters of the circuits, Jake had a wheezing cough. He stopped and said he wanted to go in. Desta patted his back and encouraged him to complete the remaining rounds. Desta's father's words came to him. *If you begin something, you must finish it!*

After they rested a bit, they jogged and walked, vigor alternating with fatigue, and finally reached the end of the route, where they found themselves alone. After they caught their breath, they went directly to the Lincoln Courtyard, where many of the runners sat gathered on benches, talking with Mr. Parker.

"Did you make it to the end?" the coach asked when he saw the late arrivals.

Jake acknowledged they did.

"I'm proud of all of you," Mr. Parker said.

Desta shook his head, disappointed by their performance.

"Those who didn't finish, don't worry about it. You'll get better with practice. The key to being part of the team is to stay motivated and strive to improve. Early on, we'll run every other day, to give your bodies a day to recover. Later, when you're in good condition, we'll do it four days a week. Those who miss a session can make it up on weekends." Mr. Parker picked up his clipboard and rose, and the team members followed him to the gate.

"See you Friday," Mr. Parker said and waved.

"See you then, coach," Jake said. The rest waved back.

THAT EVENING, as Desta looked out his bedroom window, his vision looked blurry. He blamed it on his unprecedent physical workout that day. For the rest of the hours both before and after dinner, Desta continued with his reading of Conrad. It has been slow going, feeling as though he was plodding through a deeply furrowed farm field. He stumbled at times with sentences spanning several lines, and words and phrases joined by "at," "and," "between," "for," "from," with dashes joining them to asides, and festooned with commas, semicolons, and colons. He needed to finish reading the book before class the following day.

Big words sat on the page, immovable as a rock. Ideas piled on ideas, and Desta lost the author's train of thought by the end of the sentence. There were turns of phrase and expressions Desta had never seen before. He marked the words he didn't know with a checkmark and underlined the sentences and phrases he liked or needed to revisit.

Between the ponderous storytelling and lengthy descriptions were beautiful passages and vivid images that redeemed the writing and kept Desta reading to midnight, to the end of his assignment.

He grasped the essence of the narrative: Five men on the deck of a ship at the mouth of the River Thames, enjoying the view and the setting sun, reminiscing about bygone sailing adventures. Reflecting on great mariners who shipped out of the same estuary, some never to return, and others who came home to tell their stories, as these men did.

One man gave a bright account of piloting a steamship up the Congo River, and described what he saw and experienced, hinting at the meaning of the story's title. Desta was eager to read on and discover where the tale led.

Desta could feel the nostalgia and yearnings of those men in the story as they gazed at the buffeting waves, the vanishing sun, the evening's growing gloom. The stories and images touched him profoundly, traveling far from home into an unknown world, risking everything.

He put the book face down, the open pages pressed on his desk. He yearned for the day when he would find that coin, return home, and tell stories of his adventures. He did not fear for his own life, as much as dying without seeing that second coin.

He picked up the text and copied into his notebook the words he had marked. He looked up their meaning in Webster's Dictionary and wrote them down, then closed his books and put them in his backpack. He changed into pajamas, peeled back the bed cover, and lay down. He put out the light and closed his eyes, still thinking of future adventures as he drifted off.

DESTA NEEDED TO SOLVE one more dilemma. What the Johnsons would want from him for the accommodation he had gotten for the full year.

As he rode home with Jake after his two o'clock class, Desta told his host brother what had troubled him. Jake chuckled and replied, "My parents didn't strike a deal with David's folks to make you work for your room and board," he said. "They think that your presence in our house benefits the whole family. For them, hosting you is like all of us traveling to Ethiopia without leaving home," Jake said. He turned to Desta and grinned.

"As for housework, there is very little for you to do. We have house-keepers who cook and care for the house—Elsa Alberti during the week, and Mindy Kovacs on weekends. Twice a week, two other ladies deep clean the house. And a company takes care of the yardwork and gardening.

"I already told my parents about the cross-country team, and they were pleased. But if it makes you feel better, we can ask Mother what chores you could do at home. She's always finding things that need doing."

Desta sighed under his breath. "That would be fine," he replied. "I'm just not used to going to school without working for it."

Jake eyed Desta obliquely. "You're in America," he said, "and you'll get used to living as we do."

Jake's words got to Desta. "You can say that again," he said. "I suppose you're right. I probably will get used to it. Thanks for the reassurance."

When Jake and Desta arrived home, Mrs. Johnson was sitting at the kitchen table with a cup of tea and a wedge-shaped, layered sweet—which Jake called a *banoffee* pie, his mother's favorite tea treat. She stared at three stapled sheets of paper, the top flipped over, drawings on its reverse side. A beautiful gold pen lay next to her papers.

Mrs. Johnson wore a two-piece Prussian blue suit as if she had just come from her office in town. Her tousled brown bangs set off her dry demeanor. Mrs. Johnson looked up from her papers and gazed at Jake as she ate her pie.

"Mother," Jake said, "Desta wants to help around the house. What can he do?"

Mrs. Johnson's brow knotted; she seemed surprised by the question as much as Jake's urgency, Desta thought.

"We didn't intend for Desta to be a domestic worker," she said. If he insists on doing something, why don't you two work out what that should be."

"Thank you, Mom," Jake said, with lightness in his voice. "I just wanted to run it by you first. I will think of something."

"Let's put away our schoolbags and meet by the pool," Jake said as he and Desta went upstairs.

Outside, Jake explained his routine tasks: walking Kooper, skimming the pool, tidying the patio, and watering the potted plants by the front and back entrances.

Jake and Desta arranged for Desta to walk Kooper in the morning and Jake would cover evenings. Each would take care of the pool, patio, and plants on alternate weeks.

Jake showed Desta how to clean up after Kooper. He took Desta over to the large clay pot on the patio, containing the dog's leash and toys, and a roll of small green bags. Jake peeled off the top layer from the roll, inserted his fist into the bottom of the bag, and then opened it to use to pick up the animal's waste.

Then they walked to the side of the driveway; Jake pointed to a large gray bin where they disposed of the used bags after Kooper's walks. The idea of picking up the dog's waste and transporting it in a bag had surprised Desta.

"Thank you," he said. "This has been quite interesting." With that, Desta and Jake went to their rooms.

In his room, Desta sat elbow anchored on the desk, chin resting on the heel of his hand. His stomach roiled to think of handling Kooper's doings every day. Yes, he remembered cleaning cow stalls as a boy, but he couldn't answer why picking a dog's dropping was so different or re-pulsive to him. Just then, he recalled that the Great Mystery had said Kooper was Kooli reincarnated.

If it were Kooli, would Desta pick up after him? His answer was yes. His qualms slowly faded like morning mist.

He drummed his fingers on his desk as his mind leapfrogged to the days he spent roaming the fields below his home with Kooli in tow. He felt as if his life had come full circle. He covered his face and wept. He lay on his bed, eyes on the ceiling, washed by memories.

Then he got up and went to his desk, took out a notebook from his backpack, opened it in the middle, and drew grids for a calendar. Then he listed all the important things he must accomplish during the year. He listed them by priority: search for the coin, his education, running cross-country. He put down the days for his housework and marked the calendar as he'd agreed with Jake. He also noted that he would send messages to Tsadok as needed.

Even though Desta saw the cross-country workout benefited no one—himself or the Johnsons, he now would feel less guilty having these chores to do around the house. All the responsibilities he had to himself and others clearly were listed and Desta was happy when he lay in bed, it was as if a cloud of something lifted from his shoulders and he could fall asleep in peace.

FIFTEEN

Friday—on their second day of practice, Desta and Jake swapped their school clothes for running outfits and met their coach and teammates outside, chatting on the newly cut grass.

It struck Desta that all the other guys were bigger than him. Jake, for example, was tall and thickly muscled from his long, stout legs to his shoulders. Desta was spare and lean with little extra padding.

How can I possibly compete with them? I'll need two strides for every one of theirs. And that would tire him out twice as fast. On second blush, it seemed ridiculous that he'd agreed to join the team.

Mr. Parker smiled at Desta and Jake, quelling Desta's misgivings. "You two did well at first practice," the coach said, a silver whistle hanging from his neck.

"We barely made it to the end," Jake said, with an echo of disappointment.

"The most important thing is you completed the course," Mr. Parker said. "This is an endurance sport. I've no doubt you'll do well in time. The key is to practice, and we'll do a lot of it."

Desta thought the coach was expecting a miracle, but he would do his best to do better, without using the coin's magic to give him any advantage. He would succeed by sheer strength of will, as he had with all of his life's challenges.

Mr. Parker blew the whistle. "Let's do warmups for twenty minutes," he said. He had the team do stretches and then run in place to increase heart rate and oxygen uptake, he explained. The coach glanced at his watch and blew the whistle. "Enough! Let's see what you can do today."

Then, all took off at a good, steady pace. Feet thumping on the dry, even path of the trail and making thrashing noises through the dry leaves that covered the ground beneath the canopy of trees, they went. Some huffed and puffed, and others ran as if breathless.

Desta tried to control his breathing, but the run got more demanding as they advanced. His throat felt scalded, his mouth dry. His legs stiffened, and his ankles ached. He strained to keep pace with the lead runners as he passed the midpoint of the course.

"Jake," he hollered, "I'm going to rest for a bit."

Jake stopped and came toward Desta. "Can't you keep up?"

"My body is not cooperating." He leaned on a fence post to catch his breath.

Jake studied Desta. "Sorry to see you're having a problem," he said regretfully. "It seems to me that you may have to wait till you build more muscles and gain strength. You need a lot of energy for this sport. Your body can't give what it doesn't have."

"Let me just rest a bit," Desta said and crumpled. "You go, and I'll walk. . . . please," Desta begged.

"We'll walk together. . . . Come on!" Jake gave Desta his hand.

Like the day before, Desta and Jake walked and jogged the rest of the course, picking up speed as they approached the starting point, where the coach and the other runners waited, some sitting on the grass.

"Well, well," Mr. Parker said as Jake and Desta arrived. "You did better today. Keep it up."

"Thank you," Jake said, stiff-lipped.

"Jake would have done much better if he hadn't stopped for me," Desta said. "I'll work on my speed, Mr. Parker."

"Ok, fellas," the coach said, raising his hand for the team's attention. "Monday, meet here again at 3:30. Go home, and get some rest."

Jake and Desta headed for Jake's car and drove home. Desta felt miserable in body and spirit. "What a shame!" he said and sighed.

"Don't worry about it," Jake said. "It's not the end of your running career. After you gain weight and condition your body, you can try again for the team next year. We should have thought more about your physical fitness."

Desta considered his father's warning and Coach Parker's encouragement before warmups. Through all the challenges in his life, he'd learned that if he worked hard, he could succeed. He would not be defeated now. "I've never been a quitter," Desta said. "I'm going to run every day in the backyard."

Jake turned and squinted at Desta. "You're *really* determined," he said. "Go ahead and give it a try."

When they got to the house, Desta ached all over. But he was upbeat, almost giddy. He went upstairs and showered. The warm water soothed his body and settled his mind. *I will eat well and practice and become a better runner.*

THE NEXT DAY, Desta woke at four, as usual. He studied and did his homework till six-thirty. Then he put on his Lincoln College sweatshirt and pants, crept down to the mudroom, laced up his running shoes, and went out. He jogged the quarter-mile perimeter of the yard four times. The gray, crushed stone walkway was noisy and difficult to run on. When he finished, he was sweaty but not out of breath. His ankles and calves bothered him, but he was unwavering.

He went to the kennel by the mudroom and leashed Kooper, all excited to see him. They strolled the yard together, flooding Desta with the same happiness he'd felt in his boyhood walks with Kooli. After a time, Desta sat down on a bench.

"Kooper," Desta said, gazing into the dog's eyes. "Are you Kooli?"

The dog wagged his tail. Desta then reached out his hand. "Give me a paw!"

The dog lifted his paw and rested it on Desta's palm. Still holding his eyes, Desta asked, "Are you really my old friend?"

The dog pressed Desta's hand.

"Okay. Are you Kooper?"

The dog gazed at Desta.

"Kooli?"

The dog wagged his tail.

"Okaaayy," Desta said, baffled. "I never dreamt we would meet again in this life."

The dog tossed his head up and down as if to say *I know*.

Speechless, Desta hugged his friend and smiled. They rose and finished their walk, and Desta returned Kooli to his kennel. Desta went up, showered, and dressed. He felt strong and happy, though Kooper's connection to Kooli still mystified him.

As he gazed at his image in the closet mirror, he renewed his resolve to succeed in school, find the coin, and not let either overwhelm him. And he would somehow have to overcome the challenges he faced with his cross-country practices. Now that he was in it, Desta realized cross-country coud help him more than just competing in the field. Confidence spread from head to heart.

After a meal with the family, Desta came to his room to read and do his homework. Before that, however, he wanted to hang the painting of the two coins. He brought it from the closet and left it on the floor, leaning against the wall near his desk until he decided on a good spot.

He would have hung it to the right of the window near his desk, but that space was already occupied by a 12-by-16-inch picture. In it, a couple stood on a path that curved through pink, purple, blue, and white flowers. A tall, handsome tree, unfamiliar to Desta, and several bushes were in the background.

On the golden frame at the bottom, it read "Gone with the Wind" in large bold letters. Desta didn't know what that referred to. He liked the picture and all the sentiments it displayed. But he wanted the symbol of his quest to hang right where this picture was so that when he looked up from his desk it would remind him of his purpose here in America.

He figured the image on the wall must be important to Jake's sister Shae. He would ask permission to swap it for his artwork. He went downstairs to look for Jake and found him washing Kooper in a big aluminum basin, which touched Desta.

Desta asked Jake about the picture on his wall. "That's a poster of Shae's all-time favorite movie, but it's your room now," he said. "You can replace any of her pictures with yours."

"Thank you," Desta said and returned to his room, excited. He grasped the sides of the movie poster and brought it down. He held it before him and studied the couple's intimate image, wondering what it felt like to hold and be held by a woman.

After his father warned him six years ago about the urgings of his heart and body, Desta had kept his desire for girls to himself ever since. Now he remembered his father's words like it was yesterday.

If you give in to these feelings, you could end up losing yourself, your dreams, and your aspirations, as well as destroying the dreams and as-pirations of someone else.

He stowed the poster face down on the top shelf of his closet and then carefully mounted the painting of the coins where the poster had been. Above the trees beyond his window, the setting sun splashed bright rays on the painted scene of the gold coins, buffeting ocean, and white sands, which dazzled in the light.

Desta stared at the painting for a long time. He remembered how he and his benefactor, Dr. Kal Petrov, had found it hanging on the living room wall of the doctor's rented home in Bahir Dar. He recalled the art-work had been brought from Romania by the American artist Roman Burkhardt, but Desta never learned who had painted it or entrusted it to Burkhardt, who'd taped a letter to the back of the frame.

Desta was hunched over his desk doing his homework when Jake came to his door with some shirts, and Desta invited him in. Jake said, "Three years ago, when my parents took me on a college tour, I bought a bunch of shirts that I never wore, and now they're too small for me. Would you be interested in them?"

He picked up a T-shirt that said Princeton in orange on a black back-ground. The next displayed Yale in white on a field of blue, and the third had the name Harvard on a crimson red field. There were matching hooded sweatshirts. Blue was Desta's color, and he liked the Yale shirts and Princeton's; orange and black were the hues of sunset and impend-ing night. The Harvard shirts didn't appeal to Desta.

"Thank you very much," Desta said, smiling at his host.

"You're welcome," Jake said. "You could wear one for the cross-country practice on Monday. Keep the hooded shirts for the fall when the weather is cooler."

"I appreciate that," Desta said. He couldn't wait to ferret out his thoughts about the Princeton colors.

Jake glanced toward Desta's desk and noticed the new painting he'd hung.

"Oh wow! That's the picture you swapped with Shae's?" Jake took two steps toward the image. "This is beautiful!" He drew closer, search-ing for something. "Who did it?"

"Nobody knows," Desta said. "It came to me in a cryptic path. I've been curious to know the artist who produced this masterpiece." He tightened his lips and stared at the painting.

"Love the colors: orange, yellow, and gold," Jake said. "Like our house."

"You're right."

"Are these coins the same as the one you're looking for?" Jake asked, his face bent toward Desta.

"No," Desta replied. He clamped his lips and sighed.

"I hope you'll unravel this mystery soon."

"Appreciate that, Jake," Desta said cheerily.

"See you at dinner," Jake said, and left.

Desta spread the Princeton shirt on his desk, sat down, and studied it. He absently ran his hand across its smooth fabric, his mind elsewhere.

What might the colors of this shirt portend? Like the fruit, orange suggests something sweet, and black corresponds to somber or gloomy, equivalent to sour—like Sweet and Sour, the keeper of the Second Coin of Magic and Fortune. The association struck Desta. *Was he reading too much into this?*

In his world, everything that happened to him was, by design, part of the ancient prophecy controlling his journey. He exhaled, open-mouthed. He crossed his arms over his chest, re-crossed them, and wondered where his insight would lead him.

It was all too confusing. Desta gathered the shirts, put them in drawers, and lay down on his bed, face up. Sleep was his redeemer. He closed his eyes and vanished into peace and comfort.

THE NEXT DAY, after Desta's walk with Kooper early morning, the enticing aroma of baking bread drew him to the kitchen. A batch of puffy, fist-sized rolls, a staple of the family's Sunday brunch, was already in a basket on the kitchen counter.

"Good morning, Mindy," Desta said. "I love how the house smells when you're making brunch."

"Mrs. Johnson has me bake bread first thing in the morning so the whole family wakes up to the scent of it," Mindy said.

"It's a treat," Desta said.

"Take a seat," Mindy said. "Have some with tea if you like. Brunch won't be for a few hours."

Desta sat on a tall chair at the island. Mindy brought him tea and two shiny rolls on a plate. "Enjoy!"

"Thank you," Desta said, and picked up a roll. "You have a passion for these things."

"Yes," Mindy said. "My dream is to open a bakery one day."

"Then why don't you?" Desta asked.

"Money stands between me and my dreams," Mindy said. "But I'm working on it." Her hazel eyes twinkled.

"Is this weekend job all you have?"

"Yes," Mindy said. "My husband Rick and I have a five-year-old son, and I look after him during the week. Rick's insurance job barely covers our expenses, so I decided to take this job to save up for my bakery business."

"That's admirable," Desta said.

"You do what you can to work toward your goal," Mindy said.

"That's right," Desta replied soberly. "Life isn't much without a dream."

He ate the bread and dipped a morsel in his tea. "If your rolls are any indication, your bakery should be a success."

"Thank you," Mindy said. "They're nothing special. I also make cakes, pastries, and pies. I took this job because the family wanted the kind of bread and pastries that I make. Baking bread at the Johnson home on Sundays is a family tradition that goes back several generations. My family is originally from Byelorussia, and my specialty is Russian pastry, which Mr. and Mrs. Johnson love."

"I'm impressed," Desta said, "What time do you come in?"

"Around seven, but I make the dough at home the night before."

"As you probably know, I'm from Ethiopia. We make different kinds of bread, but in my family, my mother made loaves mostly from rye, my favorite."

"How funny that you came to a town called Rye," Mindy said. Her plump cheeks pulled up into a smile.

"One of the many mysteries of my life," Desta said, tightening his lips. He brought his cup and plate to the sink. "Thank you so much for the lovely rolls, the tea, and the chat."

"You're welcome!" Mindy said, "If the family wasn't allergic to rye, I'd make that kind of bread."

"Don't worry about it," Desta said, "but thanks just the same." He rinsed his plate and cup and loaded them in the dishwasher. "I'll see you later."

"See you soon."

AFTER BRUNCH, Desta sat at his desk doing homework when Mindy knocked on his door. "Someone wants to talk to you," she said.

"Talk to me?" Desta asked. "Let me put my slippers on."

"Yes, on the phone," Mindy replied. "Come."

Desta followed her to a gray telephone, next to a stack of magazines on a coffee table bracketed by two leather chairs, near a good-sized window with the same backyard view Desta saw from his room.

Desta had never sat here or browsed the magazines. He still sought the family's permission for everything he did in their home. Desta hadn't heard the phone ring, and he wasn't sure it even worked.

"The man is on the line. I left the phone in the kitchen off the hook. When you pick up here, I will hang up the downstairs phone."

Desta marveled that in America calls came directly to the house, even right outside your bedroom door. He remembered in his old hometown, he'd be summoned by appointment to the telephone station, a half-hour walk from home, and receive a phone call standing in a narrow booth.

As Mindy instructed, Desta picked up the phone and said, "Hello!" Then came a click on the line, confirming that Mindy had hung up.

"Desta?"

"It's me," Desta said, happy to hear the familiar voice. Desta and David exchanged greetings, and David apologized for not calling earlier.

"The courses I'm teaching take a lot of my time," David said. "Last night, I had this dream again involving you, and I wanted to see how you're doing."

"Dream? . . . What about?"

"Something I'll tell you when we see each other. Would next weekend work for you?"

Desta said he'd call David back once he cleared it with his host family.

"Everything is well?"

Desta updated David on his progress since he started school.

"It sounds like you've settled into your courses, and I'm glad to hear you're also doing sports. Call me once you confirm with the Johnsons."

"I will," Desta said. "And I've something to share as well."

"Hopefully see you soon," David said, and hung up.

Desta strolled back to his desk. *What was David's dream about that he has to tell me in person?*

In the evening, Desta told Mrs. Johnson about David's call and asked if Desta could visit with him the following Saturday. Mrs. Johnson checked the family calendar and said that was fine. Desta then asked Mrs. Johnson's permission to call back David, and he confirmed their date for next Saturday—the seventh.

For the next week, Desta was preoccupied with thoughts of David and his dream.

SIXTEEN

Coming out of the locker room on their third day of practice, Desta and Jake ran into Mr. Parker. "I had a phone call from your father," he told Jake.

"What about?" Jake asked, knitting his brow.

The coach turned to Jake's companion. "About your training, Desta. We discussed it, and he's right. For the first month, you run at an easy pace with the slower runners. After you gain weight and stamina, you can run competitively."

Turning to Jake, the coach said, "You, on the other hand, can run with the rest of the runners."

Jake looked at Desta, who stayed quiet, face hardened. In his first two practices, he'd been a liability to Jake, and kept him from running the entire course. Desta had no good reason to challenge the coach's decision. He'd come to the team unprepared, mentally and physically. But he also hated being seen as less capable than his teammates. He knew that it was up to him to prove himself.

"That's fine, Mr. Parker," Desta said. "I appreciate that you'll give me a chance."

"You come from a country of runners," the coach said. "You just need time, good nutrition, conditioning, and practice."

Desta and Jake joined the team for their stretches on the grass. Desta noticed there were twelve runners, down from the initial sixteen. Mr. Parker blew his whistle, and the team took to their feet. Jake and Desta ran behind the pack at a moderate pace.

"Jake, please keep up with the others," Desta said. "Let me go at my own pace until I feel comfortable."

"I prefer we run together and keep each other company," Jake said.

Desta said, "I will be fine. But it's up to you."

Jake and Desta continued together, mostly jogging, sometimes running as fast as they could, and completed the five loops with the last two team members.

Mr. Parker clapped his hands and shouted, "Bravo!" when Jake and Desta came running to the start line at top speed.

"Thank you, Coach," Jake said. "We hope we'll earn that praise in the coming months." He smiled.

"You still did better than the last two times."

"Desta did much better this time," Jake said, "I'm proud of him."

"Way better," Mr. Parker said. "You got here in under an hour— fifty-five minutes to be exact."

The eight who had finished sat sprawled on the grass and chatted.

Mr. Parker got the team's attention. "Okay, men, we'll only be running the campus course two more times. After that, we'll do real cross-country runs off campus. You all did great today. Now take a shower, go home and get some rest."

Everyone rose. "Thank you, Mr. Parker," Pete Campbell said. "I look forward to those off-campus runs."

"Will be a nice change," Steve Hauser added.

All waved at the coach and left.

FOR THE NEXT WEEK, Desta was preoccupied with thoughts of David and his dream.

Desta continued to run with his cross-country team, at a slower pace, to honor the coach's suggestion.

Now the team also began to practice around the Rye Country Golf Course which, according to Jake, was arranged by his father, as Mr. Johnson's family was one of the founders of the golf club.

This week his biology and chemistry labs started on Tuesday and Thursday, one for each. He also kept thinking about David Hartman's meeting on Saturday, the 5th of September.

Wednesday, September 2nd. Shortly after lunch, before Desta's fourth day of cross-country practice, Jake drove Desta to an optometrist in town, recommended by the school clinician. After a battery of tests, the eye doctor determined that Desta was nearsighted and prescribed corrective eyeglasses for him.

Returning to campus, they changed at the locker room and went out to find Mr. Parker addressing the team on the lawn.

"As part of your training, you need to understand how your muscles work, and how to condition them to become top athletes. Let's go inside so I can explain this."

The team followed the coach into the gym to a classroom. Standing at the blackboard, Mr. Parker said, "In sports, just like everyday life, we rely on muscles and bones for physical activity. It's crucial to know the mechanics of our bodies.

"Cross country is a sport of speed and endurance, and each aspect relies on its own muscle group, which we train differently for maximum efficiency and success."

Mr. Parker's words piqued Desta's interest. *Efficiency* and *success* were what he strove for in his life: success in school, finding the coin, and now, becoming a top athlete. He scooted to the edge of his seat, rested elbows on the desk, and his chin on the heel of his hand.

Mr. Parker drew what he referred to as slow-twitch, fast-twitch, and intermediate fast-twitch muscle fibers on the board—a flaccid, tube-like segment for the first, a fatter, ball-in-a-tube illustration for the second, and something inbetween for the last. He filled all three with lateral lines corresponding to the fibers.

He explained that slow-twitch fibers use oxygen to produce the energy the body needs from the food we eat, also called an aerobic process. These fibers do not fatigue quickly.

"On the other hand, fast-twitch fibers use the muscles' stored fuel, called glycogen, to produce the energy that propels us when running," the coach explained. "This process doesn't use oxygen and is called an anaerobic process. The supply of glycogen is limited, and these fibers can tire quickly. Intermediate fibers share many of the characteristics of slow-twitch fibers, but they can contract faster and with more potency."

Mr. Parker continued. "As cross-country athletes, you'll need to train and condition all three types of fibers in your legs, thighs, buttocks, and other body parts to achieve your best. We will do many uphill repeat runs—short ones for speed and strength, and long ones for endurance.

"The courses you run to train and compete are often uneven. You will likely run up and down hills, around curves, and across flat courses of grass or dirt. All these features make you change your speed and running patterns, how you use your muscles, and the way you expend your different energy sources. This activity is what we refer to as muscular efficiency and running economy. Once you understand these basic principles, you'll know how to train your body for maximum performance," Coach Parker concluded.

Desta mused at the duality of his own body: some muscles for speed, others for endurance; just as the world contained light and dark, love and hate, the head and tail of a coin. He felt destined to run cross-country.

Lastly, Mr. Parker said they could collect their team rosters after today's run. The coach took his students back outside for warm-ups. Once they'd finished, he blew his whistle for practice, and on the second blow, the team set off. Jake and Desta ran from behind at a leisurely pace.

Jake and Desta got their rosters and headed for the locker room. On their way home, Desta kept pulling on his hair as he thought about his athletic endeavors in America and what it all meant in the long run; would he compromise his education and search for the coin? It was then that Desta realized his hair had gotten too long and that he needed a haircut. When he mentioned this to Jake, he said he'd arrange it with a barber and take him there one Saturday.

Back at home, Jake and Desta ate sandwiches Elsa had prepared. "Let's see who's on our team," Jake said. He pulled the roster from his backpack, and set it down between them.

"I'm curious who the front runners are," Desta said. "I envy them."

There was Luke Collins, the captain, and winner of the New York State high school championship. The Callahan brothers, Tim and Sam, Steve Hauser, Pete Campbell, and Ben Miller were all cross-country lettered runners in high school.

Pete Campbell, Ben Miller, and Derek Walker had run cross-country for at least two years, and were also high school lettered runners.

Jake and Desta, along with Dominic Spencer, Ken Corrado, and Jack Murphy, were newbies.

"So is there a state championship for junior colleges, too?" Desta asked.

"Yes, national as well."

"And do they give scholarships for being a good athlete?"

"Yes. And cross-country runners have a better chance if they're state or national champions."

Desta's heart sank. David had told him he could earn a scholarship if he did well in sports, but now it seemed Desta had to be a champion, too.

"You know, Jake," Desta said. "I was hoping for an athletic scholarship, but with my running so far, it seems like a mere fantasy. But I will do my utmost, out of respect for all that your dad, Mr. Parker, and David have done for me, and to honor my father."

"Don't be so hard on yourself," Jake said. "You have three months to get there." He smiled.

They cleaned up after their snacks and retreated to their rooms.

Desta looked forward to seeing his friend David Hartman the following Saturday.

At night, as Desta was about to go to bed, he noticed a shimmering light over the journal. He pulled it out and opened it at the page containing the last entry.

Dear Desta,

Now you're fully involved in your running sport, you need a daily prayer regimen. These prayers are suitable for your spiritual development, but the words themselves can help reinforce your daily struggles to succeed in your running and academics. They are all in the twenty-one legends found in the Coin of Magic. To simplify your daily recital and prayer, I've split them into three categories, each containing seven words. You decide which groups you want to incorporate into your daily prayer. I suggest you recite one set every day. That way, you'll have the benefit of all the twenty-one legends.

The 21 Coin Legends

Heavenly Virtues	Coin Virtues	Life Virtues
Honour	Magic	Love
Humility	Justice	Wealth
Diligence	Loyalty	Courage
Prudence	Integrity	Wisdom
Spritualty	Equanimity	Excellence
Temperance	Magnanimity	Leadership
Benevolence	Guardianship	Scholarship

Of these words, be mindful of wealth. It's a vessel of blessings and curses, a prerequisite of virtue and an embodiment of vice, as an expression of merit and fault—the dualities of your life.

Good luck to you, son.

SEVENTEEN

Saturday–September the 5th. The first thing that hit Desta as he came downstairs for brunch was the smell of frying bacon, overtaking Mindy's fresh-baking bread he enjoyed when he came down to take Kooper for a walk and jog around the property.

Weekends were the only time the Johnson family ate meals together; the rest of the week, school and work kept the parents and children on separate schedules.

He found a warm, leisurely atmosphere in the family room. Mr. Johnson and Jake sat across from each other, faces buried in newspapers, father with the front section of the *New York Times* in big, bold letters and Jake with the sports.

Mrs. Johnson sat nearby at the square table by the window that overlooked the patio and pool, *the perfect spot for quiet conversation, tea, and pie*, Desta thought. She wore a floral, lime-and-white housedress that reached her ankles. She read her *Architecture Digest* magazine; a cup of tea sat before her.

Aida was in the kitchen with Mindy Kovacs. Desta had just come down, and shared a couch with Jake.

Except for the plates, the dining table adjacent to the kitchen was set and held with enough food for an army. There were platters of scrambled eggs, sausages, bacon on a silver tray, a basket of bread rolls and toast, and a pitcher of orange juice. Mindy brought warmed plates and placed them before each chair, and poured the juice into each glass. Then she went to tell the family breakfast was ready.

They all sat down to eat. Mrs. Johnson shot her small, brilliant eyes at the two young men to her left. "Desta, we have been shortchanging you at our brunches. You don't eat bacon and sausage, and it would help you to have more protein than just scrambled eggs.

"Jake said that you need to build yourself up to be a competitive athlete. From here on, we'll ensure you eat protein-rich meals. This morning, you'll eat your first New York steak."

Mindy approached the table with a plate of beef, set it in front of Desta, and left. He gazed at the succulent brown meat in disbelief and wondered what New York had to do with it.

Mrs. Johnson said a prayer, and then "Let's eat!" to a clatter of forks and knives on plates. They all ate silently.

Desta enjoyed the food and company and thought of all he had lacked growing up in Ethiopia. Once they finished, Mrs. Johnson rang a bell under the table, summoning Mindy.

"We're ready for the banana pie, please," Mrs. Johnson said.

In two trips, Mindy cleared the table. Then she fetched dessert on small plates, two at a time, and passed them around. The pie was cloying for Desta, but he cleaned his plate to be polite. Mindy then brought coffee for the parents and tea for the youngsters. Mr. Johnson sipped his coffee and addressed Desta.

"After talking with Mr. Parker, we thought you should take it easy on your runs until you get sufficient training and become stronger. More importantly, it's better this first semester for you to focus on your studies, because they will determine your future chances."

"I think I'll be fine, Mr. Johnson," said Desta, trying to sound confident. "I can do both if I discipline myself. Besides running with the team, I'm practicing on my own."

"Try it for a couple of weeks and see how you do," Mr. Johnson said. "We'll make sure your meals at home support your training. . . . And we'll be happy to know your time at Lincoln College was worthwhile."

"I plan to do my best," Desta said. "It's my life's mission."

Mindy collected the cups, and the family rose from the table.

Desta addressed his hosts. "Thank you both for your kindness. My steak was wonderful," he said and headed to his room.

IN THE AFTERNOON, Desta awaited David outside by the main gate, playing with Kooper and occasionally peeking at the long drive.

David arrived at two p.m. sharp in a new, blood-red two-door car that introduced itself as Chevelle in cursive lettering on the trunk.

David got out and warmly hugged Desta. He wore jeans and a short-sleeved burgundy shirt. He asked, "How was your week?" Before Desta could answer, he added, "And are you getting along well here?"

"School is good, and so is my situation here," Desta said. "Come, everybody is by the pool."

Desta and David found Mr. and Mrs. Johnson sitting on the patio under an umbrella having drinks, keeping out of the intense sun.

Mr. Johnson stood to greet David, and the two men shook hands cordially. Mrs. Johnson put down her cup and did the same. Her husband pulled out two chairs and invited David and Desta to sit.

Aida and her two girlfriends were in the pool, and Jake in the house. Mrs. Johnson offered David a cold drink and something to eat, but he declined and said he and Desta would eat later in town.

Desta played with the dog, within earshot of the three adults.

"He is an easy-going young man—rather studious," Mr. Johnson said. "And he gets up way too early for most of us."

"We're trying to fatten him up," Mrs. Johnson said. "Desta's joining Jake on the school's cross-country team, and he needs to gain weight."

"I found that Ethiopians have lean bodies because their diet is mostly grains and legumes," David said. "But with our rich food, he's bound to gain weight in no time."

Jake appeared out of thin air, and David rose to shake his hand. David asked his advice for a good place to eat.

Jake didn't hesitate. "For good, simple food, Willy's," he said. "The best hamburger joint in town!" He gave David the driving directions.

David thanked Jake and his parents, and he left with Desta. He looked around the black leather interior of David's new car.

"It's very nice," Desta said.

"Thanks," David said. "A gift from my parents for my Ph.D."

"That's even nicer," Desta teased.

"My parents are generous people."

Desta clamped his lips to hold back his emotions. In school back home, he remembered begging his relatives for 1 *birr*—the lowest Ethiopian paper currency—to buy a pen or a pencil, while American families bought their kids cars that cost thousands of dollars.

"I've also ridden in Jake's new car, called Alpha Romeo, but it's smaller than yours," Desta said, and tried to make himself feel better.

"Jake drives an Alpha Romeo?" David asked, sounding surprised. "That's very expensive," he said, his voice rising a notch. "His parents can afford just about anything."

Willy's was in a nondescript three-story building that looked like a house more than a restaurant. The curtained windows on the upper floors suggested people lived there. Desta and David noticed a long row of parked cars up and down Midland Avenue.

"It certainly looks popular," David said. Luckily, they parked where a car was just leaving near the dining room window.

Above the entrance, weathered letters on a brown plaque announced, Willy's Five Points Tavern, the establishment's full name.

David and Desta waited by the door to be seated. The interior, save for the first long room whose curtained windows overlooked Midland Ave, was dark, smoke-filled, and cavernous. To the right, a rotund, bald man attended the bar. He seemed spirited as he moved from one end of the packed bar to the other, serving his customers.

The bright light above the counter in this dim back room shone on the barman, making him the focal point of the tavern. Left of the bar and in the back, more people sat with plates layered with loaves of bread like miniature hills. Voices bounced off the ceiling, back onto the crowd.

A large woman of about forty with a painted face and dark hair asked David and Desta if they would like to sit in the back.

"We'll wait a bit," David said. He pointed to the corner table by the front window. "Looks like that's coming available. Thanks."

David turned to Desta. "Had I known it would be this crowded and smoky, I would have taken you somewhere else," he said regretfully. "My interest in the food overrode my intuition." He smiled.

They finally got the table David sought. The woman with dark hair brought them two long cardboard menus. David scanned his, front and back. Desta read everything carefully, but the descriptions of the dishes conveyed little to him.

"What would you like?" David asked.

"To be safe," Desta said, "I think I will order whatever you get, so long as it doesn't contain pig meat or sausage."

David smiled. "I'll get an all-beef burger with vegetables."

"Thank you," Desta said, relieved.

The orders came packed with two thick discs of charred, pounded meat on a bed of lettuce. The juice from the meat and tomato collected on the plate like raindrops. On the side were French Fries. Their server also brought two knives and forks and bottles of Coca-Cola.

David passed the knife through the middle of his burgers, cutting them into halves. He took two bites and said, "This is very good. Willy's lives up to its reputation."

"This is my first burger and I like it, too," Desta said, and took a sip of his drink.

The two took their time eating, hoping the clamor would eventually die down so they could comfortably speak. By the time they finished their meals, the crowd and the noise had diminished.

"Glad to hear you have joined the cross-country team," David said, eyes on Desta. "That gives you another way to excel in school and improve your chances for a better college. I know you didn't have time for afterschool activities in Ethiopia.

"Now, by doing well in your studies *and* sports, you'll improve your chances to transfer to a good university. It's really important that you get off to a good start this semester with your American education, and that you already think about what schools you want to transfer to. Start gathering information about them now, to see which suit you."

"Jake wants to go to Yale. I don't know about it, but I'm drawn to these colors—blue and white. He's given me shirts from Harvard, Yale, and Princeton."

"Look, you have the whole year to learn about each school and decide."

"I don't want to wait the whole year. I'm planning to start processing my college application over the Christmas break. I'd like to earn most of my higher education at a four-year university."

"That is fine," David said. "I'm partial to Princeton because of my family connections there. It's where my dad got his undergrad and graduate degrees, and my mother her master's; they both met there. And I also understand the Johnsons' older daughter, Shae, goes there.

"My family's Princeton connections aside, your ticket to any of these top schools is your grades, school activities, and recommendations from teachers and the Johnsons."

"Interesting that you mention Princeton," Desta said, looking at David warily. "Jake gave me shirts from these schools he had gotten a few years ago that were too small for him. It seems I'm fated to consider Princeton. Their school colors are orange and black, which is like Sweet and Sour, the meaning of the name for the owner of the second coin. There may be a reason."

Desta watched for David's reaction.

"I don't know what to say about that, but my intuition tells me you should seriously consider that school."

"These things are no coincidence, David," Desta said. "I like what orange represents, but not the darkness that goes with it—and not getting caught up in the identity of the person I'm looking for. But I have no control over my destiny."

"Of course you do," David said. "Ancient prophecies are just roadmaps. You're the driver who navigates the route."

Desta knew better than to argue with his friend.

"Apropos of which," David said, "is anything ailing you?"

"Like what?"

"Whatever hinders your progress."

"I don't think so," Desta said. "I've some pain in my head, but I still function okay."

"Well, I had a recurring dream where you were in this hazy white light, surrounded by a black circle. You struggled to break free over and over, but each time you collapsed from exhaustion."

Desta sighed. "It may be the Sweet and Sour you were seeing—the duality of my life, our life, our world. . . . If you believe in such a thing, our spiritual guides may play a part."

"I don't generally give credence to dreams, but after having the same dream three times, I'm inclined to think that it's a message from someone somewhere. I still believe there is a reason why we came into each other's lives."

"That's very clear. It may have all to do with the coin. Speaking of which, with sports and my schoolwork, I'm not going to have time to go out and search for it."

"That is a project by itself. Don't rush it now. You need the time to do this methodically."

"I know," Desta said. "It's the work I can do when school's out."

"I'm doing some work for you to that end. Through NYU where I teach, I do research at the Brooklyn Museum's Ancient Egyptian Department, and I'm in contact with a few Jewish organizations. We'll see what develops."

"You took me by surprise," Desta said. "I've no words for this. As you know, I'm so limited on what I can do about that coin."

"That's why I want to help."

David signaled to the waitress to bring the bill. Once paid, David Hartman and Desta left Willy's.

David stopped the car at the Johnson's gate, and they both got out. they shook hands and hugged. "Just focus on schoolwork and your running for now. Don't worry about the coin," David said.

Desta's friend and mentor drove off. Desta unlocked the side gate and headed to the house. Desta didn't know what to make of David's dream. He'd been given a life path that he had little control over. He would have to wait for his future to unfold in this new land. He crossed his hand over his chest and pressed. The edges of his spirit softened and his nerves soothed. Back in his room, he lay down and his heart grew tranquil.

JAKE AND DESTA RAN with the team three times a week for all of the second week of September, still at their own pace, finishing the runs with improved speeds. Desta religiously ran seven laps around the Johnsons' property every morning.

During this time Desta received his new prescription glasses which helped greatly with his distance vision.

Starting witht the end of the second week of September, the team extended their practice runs along trails, parks, open fields, and old carriage roads, sometimes sharing them with pedestrians and cyclists. Often, they encountered deer, turkeys, squirrels, and all types of birds. They ran along the wetlands near Long Island Sound, and took in the salty marine air.

Desta's training came with pain and sore muscles all over. His throat, mouth, and lips still grew hot and dry. On occasion, he had abdominal cramps, nausea, and vomiting. But none of it stopped him. He pushed himself to do his best, and despite all the hardship, he felt euphoric after each run, taking a hot shower and finding deep, blissful sleep at night.

His high-protein diet brought many noticeable changes to his well-being. In a little over two months, he felt fit and agile. His cheeks plumped up, his skin smoothed, and his eyes shone brighter. Lean, strong muscles layered his legs, thighs, and shoulders. He had not expected the speed of his transformation, which seemed nearly-miraculous to Desta and the people around him.

Even though he was eating more, he'd added only fifteen pounds. But he had grown strong, running long distances with greater ease and speed than most of his teammates. Even Jake was surprised that Desta, considerably smaller and leaner, now outperformed him at practice.

"I knew you had it in you," Mr. Parker told Desta when he finished second in a recent run. "Your talent was simply undeveloped." He clapped Desta's shoulder admiringly.

"Thank you," Desta said. "It came from days and weeks of practice."

EIGHTEEN

Desta had paused his search for the coin and was adjusting well to college and his cross-country team. But still he needed to learn more about his host family—their values, beliefs, and expectations—to feel like he was on solid footing with them.

Desta felt he had become a good student of human nature after living with so many families, including his own. He'd never taken his relationships for granted, no matter how nice his past hosts had first seemed. Experience had taught him that those relationships could sour over minor misunderstandings. Without the goodwill of his hosts, repairing their broken trust almost never worked.

Over the years, he'd learned that the people at the lower end of the family hierarchy—domestics, guards, gardeners, even close friends— were the most important to get along with to have good relations with the rest of the household.

Now, Desta had to navigate yet another unfamiliar family, with its own quirks and dynamics. In the past, he'd found that his hosts' housekeepers had been most amenable to tutoring him about their employers.

One afternoon when he saw Elsa Alberti carrying a big basket of laundry from Aida and Jake's rooms, he seized the opportunity.

"That's a big load, can I give you a hand?" Desta asked. Elsa jerked her head in surprise. "I can manage," she said, "but if it gives you pleasure, sure.

Desta carried the big basket on his head, the custom in the Ethiopian countryside. He set the basket on the long folding table in the laundry room.

"Thank you so much," Elsa said, smiling brightly. "The thought is as important as the deed."

"You're welcome," Desta said. "I'm used to helping people around the house. Don't hesitate to ask if there's anything I can do for you."

"That's kind of you," Elsa said.

LATE ONE SATURDAY, Desta sat on a bench far from the house along the perimeter path, after a game of Frisbee with Kooper. A book and the red disk sat by his side, while the dog lay on the grass across from the white sand border, cooling off. Desta drank in the foliage and the red, yellow, and gold roses and hibiscuses around him.

Earlier, the gardeners had worked the whole grounds. One cut the lawn with a giant machine; the second trimmed the hedges with clippers, and the dead growth with scissors. A third used a blowing machine to remove every fallen leaf and twig from the backyard.

Now the sun tipped west, every standing object casting shadows, and tranquility settled over the compound. The Johnsons and their children had gone to New York City for an event. Desta, Elsa, and Kooper were alone on the premises.

As usual, Elsa strolled the footpath after finishing her work, and seemed pleased to find Desta and Kooper on her route.

"Is it just us three in this huge place?" Elsa asked. She stopped and surveyed their surroundings.

"It's ours for this brief time," Desta said, "if our presence counts as an entitlement." He smiled.

"I do enjoy my quiet walks here. But I wouldn't want to manage a place this big. She glanced at Desta, her plump face brightening.

"Have a seat," Desta said. "We rarely get this chance."

"Leisure is a luxury in our world," Elsa said.

Desta wondered if she was referring to America in general. "Have you lived in another world?" he asked.

"Yes, Italy!" she said. "I was five, too young to remember much, but my parents tell me how much slower life was in the old country."

Desta was intrigued. "Tell me. . . how did you come here?"

"You see, in 1935, my father was a soldier in our national army. When his oldest brother in America learned that Italy was about to invade Ethiopia, he urged my father to join him in the United States. My father thought the invasion of Ethiopia was unjust and cruel. Two of my uncles on my father's side died in that war. Later, when the world came to its senses in 1945, my father returned to Italy and brought all of us here–me, my mother, and my two siblings."

"That's very interesting," Desta said. "Do you know I come from Ethiopia?"

"I do," Elsa said. "I'm curious to know what Ethiopians think of Italians now. It was a shameful war that should never have happened, and it benefited no one."

"I don't think the new generation of Ethiopians hold grudges against Italy. The older folks do resent the country's unprovoked aggression. So, how did you end up working for the Johnsons?"

The corners of Elsa's mouth pulled up in irony. She looked into the distance. "To tell you the story," Elsa began. "This used to be my mother's job. She needed to work when my father died of cancer fourteen years ago. It was her first job, and her English wasn't great.

"Mr. and Mrs. Johnson had young children then, and needed a housekeeper, and they found my mother through an acquaintance. They speak fluent Italian, which made it convenient for my mother. All of us children were grown and out of the house by then, and the job saved my mother from sitting at home alone, doing nothing.

"Exactly fourteen years later, she quit. She couldn't handle the work anymore, it was too hard on her, you know. As fate would have it, I found myself living alone six months ago, after my husband left me. Our children were grown, and I was free. To keep my sanity, I took Mother's job when she left." She smiled. She shifted her ample form, crossed her arms on her chest and looked down thoughtfully. Her wedding band shone in flakes of gold in the afternoon light.

"Our lives are not our own," Desta said. "An invisible hand charts our course, and we merely follow."

Elsa briefly regarded Desta. "It sometimes feels that way, doesn't it?" she said. "But I'm happy here. They are good people."

"I've no reason to think otherwise," Desta said. "Thanks for sharing your story."

"You couldn't ask for a better family to live with. Strict, yes, but you have to be, when your children must go out into a turbulent world." She smiled matter-of-factly. "It's a new world, you know. And the Johnsons try their best to prepare their children for it. Sooner or later the kids will have to live in it without the people who raised them. After a certain point, all of us parents live on borrowed time."

"Have they always lived on this beautiful estate?"

"They are an old family," Elsa said. "Mr. Johnson's ancestors were among the original English settlers of Rye. This house sits on the location of a former manor, once surrounded by big fields worked by tenant farmers. So sometimes your hosts' values and attitudes about things are as ancient as their heritage."

"Interesting," Desta said, filling the silence. "It's wonderful to walk the land your ancestors owned and feel your connection to them."

"Indeed," Elsa said, rising. "I need to continue my walk. I've unfinished work."

"Please go on," Desta said. "Thank you for sharing your impressions with me, so I'm no longer in the dark about this place."

After Elsa left, he tried to read his book awhile, but couldn't concentrate. Elsa's stories drifted in and out of his thoughts like aimless clouds. He folded his book and called out to Kooper, and they walked around the path to the house, passing the mound of hydrangeas, and a family of daisies along the fence in groups separated by evergreen hedges. But strangely, as he went, Desta began seeing double each time he looked far away.

When he mentioned the problem to Jake at dinner, his host brother suggested he see a doctor at the school clinic.

That evening as Desta got into bed, he worried if his vision problem might be connected with the pain in his head. He put his hand on his chest and went to sleep.

NINETEEN

Lincoln College's cross-country team took shape. They began regional competitions in early October. In the first three meets, Desta and Jake finished in the top ten percent, then the top five percent in the next four. Desta sat out the state championship on Saturday, November 7th, because of a sprained ankle, but Jake finished 5th.

Although the team dropped to nine members after the state meet, Mr. Parker was encouraged at how well his remaining runners had performed. The intense training he had put them through had started to pay off. And surprisingly, his head problem has been less frequent and less severe when he had it.

Fresh from their accomplishments, Desta and Jake planned to compete in the National Junior College Athletic Association or NJCAA, as Desta had seen it written, on November 21 in Utica, New York.

In the lead-up, Coach Parker drove the team to Rock Ridge Public Golf Course for an intense workout. He called for their attention as they piled out of the school's white minibus. "Hey, fellas, first, I want to tell you that I'm very proud of you. If we continue to improve, we can be top-ranked at nationals."

"We did okay last year," Luke Collins said. "And we have an even better chance this time."

"Yeah, with our top runners, Jake and Desta, why not?" Ben Miller said. He glanced at them and smiled.

"But we all need to do well," Pete Campbell said.

"That's right!" Mr. Parker said. "That's why these crush repeats are important. Let's go!"

As they entered the golf course, the team was like a wound spring. Desta sensed their energy and determination, the bounce in their step, the excitement in their voices.

"Today, we'll do ten intense repeats on a marked one-kilometer course. You'll get one-minute breaks," Mr. Parker said, and scribbled something on his clipboard. A golf cart stood a few yards away.

"Since I'm not fit enough to run with you, I'll pace you in the cart," Mr. Parker said, smiling. "Do the first run at an easy pace. The other nine, alternate easy and fast, taking your breaks in between. Got it?"

"Yes, coach!" the runners said as they huddled, ready to take off.

"Relax on this one. . . . it's your warm-up!"

The runners leaned forward, some with hand on knee.

Mr. Parker looked at the silver stopwatch in hand and called, "Reeeadyy . . . Go!"

Desta and his teammates took off. They moved in a rhythmic cadence. Their arms swung through the air while their feet did the same on the ground.

"Looks good, Looks good," Mr. Parker said, keeping up with his runners. "Nice, nice—group it up."

Mr. Parker drove ahead to the half-kilometer mark. "One-thirty-three," he counted out to his three lead runners, and then for the next three, "one-thirty-six . . . one-thirty-seven . . . perfect, perfect! Good job, Desta!"

The coach called out encouragement for the last half kilometer. "Good . . . good . . . nice Desta," Desta heard Mr. Parker say.

As the runners finished the full 1k course, Mr. Parker kept up a steady commentary on his athletes' performance. "Three-O-two. Perfect, guys. Three- O-five. . . good separation. Perfect guys, but don't be too far apart."

They all stopped to take their first break.

"How did that feel, guys?" Mr. Parker asked.

He came to Desta. "If you need to, you can run a couple extra repeats at the end of the first ten. If you want to hold back a little during the 1K, that's fine."

The group again lined up at the start line for their second kilometer run.

Coach Parker gave the command. The team took off, but Desta stayed with them this time. Coach Parker again followed them, and called out their names, their time, and added compliments for each as they came in.

"Nice . . . Nice . . . Good . . . way to finish!"

"Go ahead take a five-minute break," the coach said, after their 5th repeat 1K run.

Like everyone else, Desta welcomed the respite, and they all thanked the coach and caught their breath. The runners took off again after the short hiatus with the coach's whistle and command.

"You're looking good . . . looking good . . . Keep it up . . ."

"Hey, three-o-five . . . three-o-six . . . three-o-eight . . . hey, that's money . . . that's money," he said when the last of the runners came in at the end of the ten 1K repeats.

Everyone was drenched, breathing hard, and looked exhausted. Desta drank from a proffered bottle of water, which only made him thirstier. As he hopped into the van, Desta invisioned a nice hot shower and a cool glass of water. He couldn't wait to get home.

TWENTY

Saturday, November 14th was to be the cross-country team's last hill workout before the nationals at Utica the following weekend. The runs promised to be intense, focusing on endurance, speed, and strength. Desta wasn't looking forward to them. These hill repeats pushed Desta to his limits. He aways felt like his throat was on fire, his lungs might burst into pieces, and his heart pop out of his chest. After Desta recovered from his sprained ankle, he had joined the team the previous week on three seven-mile endurance runs, and Desta had been encouraged by his performance. He had paced his teammates, and even led the group in two runs.

But the team had lost Ben Miller and Derek to shin injuries, leaving just seven runners—Jake and Desta, and five veterans—to compete in the nationals.

Desta remained focused. Every morning and evening, he recited the seven heavenly virtues from *The Record,* one of the three sets Tsadok had recreated from the twenty-one coin legends. The recital of these virtues restored Desta's confidence and strengthened his spirit.

THAT MORNING, Desta and Jake got to the athletic field shortly before the rest of the team arrived at 8:00. Mr. Parker ushered them into his white van, and they headed to Castle Rock Hills Park. Desta was also thinking about his haircut at 2:30 that afternoon.

"Hopefully, there won't be many sightseers this early," Mr. Parker said, surveying the road.

"It's too cold for visitors anyway," Jake said.

At Castle Rock Hills, Mr. Parker stationed the car at the end of the empty parking lot, near the trail that paralleled the road, and they all got out. The sun was above Long Island Sound, draped in a silver-gray cloud. A distant, gauzy haze spread over the pewter water in the east, and the cities and towns far to the south.

The team filed out onto the gravel paving, eyes tense, breathing frosty clouds of air.

"You won't need your jackets; you'll warm up soon enough," Mr. Parker said.

They slowly peeled off their jackets with misgiving and tossed them into the van. In only a T-shirt, shorts, and shoes, Desta thought his blood would congeal in the chilly morning air. He rubbed his hands together and blew on them.

Some runners crouched and stretched, shifting their weight from one leg to the other. Others placed hands on hips and gyrated their torsos and necks. Desta just ran in place, his arms and hands flailing to keep the blood flowing.

"Let's do a one-mile warm-up first," Mr. Parker said. "Run alongside the road, and I'll wait for you in the van at the next lot.

The runners jogged at a leisurely pace up a hill.

"You're looking good. . . . looking good," Mr. Parker said when the runners reached him. It seemed to Desta that they'd hardly broken a sweat.

"The first hill is always easy," one teammate responded. He looked up at the landmass sharply rising before them. "It's this next one that's tough."

Mr. Parker looked up the hill and said, "The repeats on that hill will be critical for next Saturday's race."

Desta sighed. For an instant, he was gripped by the fear that all his weeks of training might not be enough to succeed at the nationals.

Some runners stared at the slope with the intensity of a fighter who was trying to psych out his opponent. Others paced, eyes penetrating and thoughtful, steeling themselves for what they knew would be their most challenging workout yet.

With clipboard and pen in hand, Mr. Parker approached the group and laid out the morning's regimen: ten 90-second repeats with two minutes' rest.

Afterward, they would drive back to the first parking lot, and the team would rest for fifteen minutes and then do seven repeats to the top of the second hill, each time returning downhill with long strides.

"Start light and keep your pace easy. Don't go overboard. Running harder than necessary won't give us a better workout. Ease off your up-hill training and lengthen your recovery time."

"These repeats could be pivotal to your success at the nationals. Don't run or jog during recovery. Just walk two to three minutes for short runs, four or five for longer. Right now, we're focusing on speed and strength training, not endurance."

The team and Mr. Parker walked toward the bottom of the hill.

"I will blow my whistle when the time is up. You stop and walk down."

The runners lined up before an imaginary line.

"Readyyy . . . three, two, one, go!" The team took off like spooked birds.

"Easy . . . easy . . . ," Desta heard Mr. Parker say in their wake.

Arms moving back and forth in rhythm with his feet, Desta climbed the slope ahead of his teammates with surprising speed.

Mr. Parker blew the whistle at the end of ninety seconds and every-body stopped. Desta turned and looked to find his teammates several feet behind and staggering on the graveled terrain.

They walked back down and took their four minutes' rest.

"Desta, you're way too fast," Mr. Parker said. "This is not a race. Re-member, you have nine more repeats."

"I didn't mean to," Desta said. "My feet went ahead of me." Desta smiled.

Mr. Parker gathered the team. "Don't let your feet run away from you. He smiled. "Start slow but increase your pace with each run. That way, you'll finish the last nine short repeats and conserve your energy for the long hill repeats after a fifteen-minute break. The finish is what counts; that's what you're training your body for."

Desta stuck with the group for the next series of runs, despite his im-pulse to run ahead of them. He felt better and stronger after each race, while he saw other teammates flagging.

Desta had his difficulties by the final three repeats. His lower back and the front of his thighs were sore, and he strained to keep an even ca-dence. Others, too, seemed to struggle.

"I know," Mr. Parker said with sympathy. "This was your most in-tense hill repeat, and a rather steep slope."

"Let's hope we don't have to run a hill like this next Saturday," Jake said.

"Indeed," the coach said. "Come, let's replenish your sugars with orange juice." The team followed the coach to the car like soldiers behind their captain.

Mr. Parker opened the trunk, handed off a stack of plastic cups, took from an ice-filled Styrofoam bucket the cold juice, and poured some for each of his athletes.

"Ahhhaaa," just about everyone uttered like someone from a Coca-Cola commercial.

"Thank you, coach," Jake said. "This is unexpected."

"Anytime, Jake," Mr. Parker said. "After your refueling break, you guys should comfortably complete the season's last seven long-hill runs."

Mr. Parker packed up the juice and made for the driver's seat.

"Hop in," he told the team. Desta hobbled, and the rest hurried into the rear doors.

"We'll park at the bottom lot," Mr. Parker said, briefly glancing back. "You'll run the mile, and then jog back to the car. Do this five times."

From the searing pain in his hamstrings, Desta didn't think he could do the long-hill runs, but just the same, he recited the seven heavenly virtues under his breath, while his teammates idly chattered.

Everyone spilled out into the parking lot. Mr. Parker glanced at his watch. "I want you to finish each of your repeats in fifty-six seconds, with a four-minute break in between." He led the team to where they had first began.

Desta was determined. He clenched his teeth and tried to block out the discomfort in his thigh.

The team lined up and crouched in position.

"Readyyy. . . go!" To Desta, the coach's command felt like a sudden gust of wind at Desta's back. He tore up the hill with his teammates, enduring the pain. Halfway up, the discomfort grew so unbearable he began to lag. Jake urged him on, but help came only when Desta recited the seven heavenly virtues again. Miraculously, the pain vanished, and he reached the top of the hill.

"Feeling better?" Jake asked as they jogged back.

"I am," Desta said. "Incidentally, how are we doing with time? I'm thinking of my haircut at 2:30."

Jake peeked at his watch. "We're good."

After they completed their repeats, Mr. Parker drove the team back to campus, and Desta and Jake went home. Jake parked in the open garage. They were hungry, and Jake went to the kitchen to ask Mindy to make them something to eat.

TWENTY-ONE

"I bet you're famished," Mindy said. She brought two towering sandwiches on plates to the narrow end of the table. Desta and Jake followed behind and sat down before their food. Mindy had layered them with tomato slices atop a bed of lettuce, covered with cheese, and nickel-sized pickles. On the side was a salad of apples, pears, and cucumbers sprinkled with pecans and doused with white cream. Desta and Jake eyed their plates ravenously.

Mindy returned with tall glasses of cranberry juice. "Enjoy!" she said.

Desta and Jake ate their meal like starved travelers and emptied their glasses in three chugs.

Mindy returned. "Want more?" she said. "I know how you get after your workouts, so I made extra."

"That's enough for now. We need to get going for Desta's haircut," Jake said. Desta and Jake thanked her and rose.

"Let's wash up and meet in the kitchen," Jake said to Desta. "Wear something warm, it's going to cool off later."

"Okay," Desta said happily. He was eager to visit a new place and have his first American haircut.

Desta wore his Lincoln sweatshirt, a blue jacket, and jeans. He found Jake downstairs standing at the kitchen island in jeans, a hooded pullover, and a dark gray jacket. Jake chatted with Mindy.

Mindy took her car keys from her purse and handed them to Jake. "Drive carefully," she said.

They walked to the mudroom. Desta was mystified at why they were taking Mindy's car instead of Jake's beautiful Alpha Romeo.

They exchanged slippers for tennis shoes. From a rack of hats on the wall near the entrance, Jake took a black Yankees baseball cap and put it on his head. In the mirror on the opposite wall, he fussed with it until it sat evenly, tipped slightly forward. He moved his head one way and the other until he was satisfied.

Desta looked in the mirror and tugged on a few strands of hair, to see how long it had gotten.

"We'll be driving Mindy's Ford Torino," Jake said, and stepped outside. Desta imagined the Bronx wasn't a good place to drive in a fancy car.

"I guess a bigger car is safer on the highway," Desta said.

"There's a different reason why I'm driving this car," Jake replied. "The Bronx, like much of New York City, has gone through hard times lately, and it can be dangerous to park a fancy foreign car on the street in some neighborhoods.

"Dangerous? Does that mean we could get hurt?"

"No, I don't think so," Jake replied. He seemed to equivocate.

"I saw some bad parts of New York when David and I went there," Desta said. "I wouldn't be shocked."

"That's good then," Jake said, sounding relieved.

They hopped into Mindy's car and headed to Interstate 95. The afternoon traffic flowed like a rushing river. Desta couldn't imagine what the barbershop would be like or who would cut his hair. His heart stirred with anticipation as his mind cogitated over Jake's concerns.

As they drove, Jake cranked up the music on the radio. Desta enjoyed the roomy interior and its pleasant scent. Jake tapped the wheel in rhythm to the "I Think I Love You" song, his earlier concerns seemingly forgotten. He swayed his shoulders and head, and then rocked back and forth when the music changed tempo.

"Glad to see you so happy," Desta said when the song finished.

Jake's face glowed. "I had a crush on a girl last year," Jake said, wistfully. "This song brought back those memories."

What's it like to feel that way? Desta wondered, but he said, "How nice!" Throughout his life, Desta had been so focused on his education and finding the coin, he'd buried his feelings for girls.

The beat and the tune still echoed in Desta's ears. Jake glanced at the map spread on the dash, and abruptly swung the car into the exit lane, apologizing for jolting Desta in his seat. They continued to the Bronx and Pelham Parkway to local streets, finally arriving at East 187th Street near Webster Avenue.

"Here we are," Jake said, studying a plaque above the entrance to Delroy's Caribbean Barber shop, on the bottom floor of a tall brick building.

Jake looked around uneasily. "The question is . . . where can we park?"

Both sides of the one-way road were lined with mostly dented and faded old cars, some so big they seemed to take up enough space for a school bus. Jake wheeled down the street slowly as he scanned for a vacant spot. Ahead, near the corner of East 187th Street and Park Ave, he noticed a white Lincoln with shiny hubcaps about to leave, and he waited for the man to clear out. He wore white clothes, a black bowtie that complemented his dark skin and a massive halo of hair. Desta wondered if the man had come from their barber shop, and if he was going to a wedding.

After they parked, Jake looked up and down the street and said, "This area doesn't look so bad."

He put his hands in his pockets and looked left for oncoming traffic. "Let's cross," he said.

They headed toward the barbershop. Desta looked around at the tall brick-and-cement buildings framing the street, and the wind-blown trash in the gutters. He inhaled deeply and said, "The air is a bit acrid. It's not much like downtown Rye."

"That wasn't what I meant," Jake said. "The Bronx has its share of problems: gangs, drugs, thieves, prostitutes."

Desta was too absorbed with the sights around him to worry about the city's troubles. Dense clouds camouflaged the westward sun, darkening the forest of old five-to-seven-story buildings.

DELROY'S CARIBBEAN BARBERSHOP was between Marion's Pharmacy and a rusted gate that joined with a tall building.

Red, white, and blue stripes framed its two large windows and wrapped around a pole to the right of the entrance, which Desta found curious. On the sidewalk by the door, a hinged whiteboard listed the barber's services and prices.

Jake pulled the screen door open and stepped in, Desta behind him. The air smelled of disinfectant, strong and piercing, and Desta held his breath.

"Good afternoon," a young man with a large spherical hair said in a deep voice and strange accent. In Ethiopia they called this kind of hair

goferay. Desta remembered in American magazines they call it "Afro."
The man sat at an old, mottled wooden desk with a calendar, many papers, and a blue cup filled with pens and pencils.

Jake returned the greeting. "I'm sorry we're late. I made a two-thirty
appointment."

The man glanced at Jake's neatly trimmed hair and looked puzzled.

"Not for me," Jake clarified. "It's for this fellow here. His name is Desta."

"My name's Sedrick," the man said. He shook hands with the visitors. "Nice to meet you both. Have a seat," Sedrick said, gesturing to the
bench near the window, opposite where two men and a boy sat.

Three barber's chairs, each facing a sink and a tall mirror, sat evenly
spaced along one wall of the room.

Three barbers with Afros stood behind their chairs and sculpted the
hair of three men into a sphere as big as the moon. One customer was so
fair, he reminded Desta of the deity on church walls in Ethiopia.

In Desta's homeland, young Ethiopian men in big cities had adopted
the American name and were often seen wearing the hairstyle. In Ethiopia's past, the haircut was associated with *fanos*—a militia group—
but the American version had not caught favor in the small towns
where Desta lived.

Desta saw Afro hair in photos on the shop's walls. Two pictures of a
woman with a huge Afro straddled the large mirror before the middle
chair. WANTED BY THE FBI it said above the pictures in bold print.
Desta stared at the massive hair that had swallowed the woman's ears
and temples and encroached on her cheeks. His gaze moved between the
two images, as if at any moment he expected the woman's hair to swal-
low the rest of her face or crush her neck. Her eyes were intense and
disdainful, her lips stiff and resolute, her hair an emblem of power and
rebellion.

The image on the right was a profile view. Someone had scribbled
Black is Beautiful! in bold black ink on the white of the poster below the
image. Here, too, her hair dominated the photograph, surrounded by an
arc of light, mimicking a solar eclipse. The woman in the photo was
beautiful: parted lips, delicate nose, birdlike eyes, and her forest of hair.

Desta watched the customers having their Afros trimmed and shaped.
The middle man's Afro was stunning. Desta liked that his face and ears

were below the hairline, nicely setting off his high cheekbones, straight nose, and big eyes.

Desta hadn't imagined getting an Afro before, but he was tempted after studying the customers in the shop.

The middle chair was now free, and the barber gestured to him. "C'mon, brother."

Desta winced. He searched the man's eyes for a hint of warmth behind the term of endearment, which some of his siblings had never called him. To have a stranger claim him as a brother was beyond peculiar. He resented the presumption, and being reminded of the blood relations, many of whom he'd never been close to and had long since severed ties. The coin and its tattoo on his chest were now his only relatives.

The man introduced himself as James Thomas, and Desta told the barber his name. "Sit. . . Be right back," James said and left.

Desta waited for the attendant to sweep around the chair, and then sat. In the mirror, he saw James's last customer, a young man, checking himself in the glass to the right of the door. The man turned his face and patted down the errant strands of his massive hair. He tightened his lips in a smile and left.

James returned with towels and a white plastic cape, which he draped and secured around Desta. The barber pressed a lever near the floor and lowered the chair, swiveling it a little toward the sink, and dropped the back so Desta could rest his neck in the notch in the rim of the basin. He turned on the faucet, picked up a hose attached to the spout, and doused Desta's hair while massaging it.

James shampooed, conditioned, and rinsed Desta's hair, before dab-drying it with the towel. He lifted Desta's seatback, and randomly pinched and pulled Desta's hair. "Your hair is way long, brother. Why did you let it grow so much?"

Desta was defiant. He wanted to tell James he wouldn't answer him unless he addressed him by his name but thought better of it.

"This would make a beautiful Afro, bro. . . . but I charge double the regular haircut. He pointed to the woman's photo on the facing wall. "This hair of yours can be as beautiful as hers."

Desta held back his frustration as he thought of how to get the man to stop calling him brother without offending him, at least not before his haircut.

For the time being, James kept pulling on his hair, like he was untangling tree roots.

"I don't want an Afro," Desta said.

Glancing at James and Desta, the barber to their right said, "Hair that long and thick would outdo Angela's."

"With a big Afro, a good-looking fellow like him would be a hit with the ladies," the middle-aged barber on the left said.

This last remark was curious to Desta. He scratched his temple, and for the first time seriously considered having an Afro, like "Angela." But before he decided, he wanted to know more about the woman he might fashion himself after.

Desta looked again at the wanted poster and now focused on the smaller black words below the large white lettering. They said Angela Yvonne Davis.

He had heard about the woman on the radio one evening while Jake and he rode home from their cross-country workout. She'd been arrested in a New York City hotel a month ago, supposedly for a crime in California, but Desta had never seen her photo.

"Make up your mind, bro," James said, "I have a customer coming soon."

Desta looked James in the eye. "My name is Desta," he said. "Let me think for a second."

Desta wanted to look presentable for the national meets that Saturday. There would be scouts from major universities. If he was a top finisher, he hoped to have a good chance to be recruited. Desta certainly didn't want to go there looking like Angela Davis, a criminal.

"I need it cut very short, with a bit more hair on the top," he said.

James shook his head and asked, "You want a crewcut?"

"If that's what you call it . . . then, yes," Desta said.

James inserted the tips of his scissors along the right side of Desta's head and began Shaering his hair like a sheep's fleece. Balls of it slid down his cape and rolled on the floor like tumbleweeds.

"Where you from?" James asked, and Desta told him.

"Ras Tafari!" Desta was at a loss.

"Your king! "Helleselassie!" the barber on the right said, mispronouncing the name.

"Reggae!" the middle-aged barber on the left said, chuckling.

"Bob Marley!" the barber on the right said, and laughed.

Desta was bewildered. James explained.

Desta said he had never heard of the Rastafarians, reggae music, or Bob Marley. And *no*, people in Ethiopia didn't think Haile Selassie was a prophet.

After a chatter of snips, a drone of buzzes, which sounded like bees coming and going at different pitches, James was finally done.

As a finishing touch, the man turned Desta's head one way and the other, making sure the cut, done in a gradient, was even all around. James then took a can from the counter and gunned it over Desta's head, covering him in a mist with a strange but pleasant scent.

James handed Desta a hand mirror, and he inspected James's work at all angles. Desta handed the mirror back, and James removed the cape and tossed it in a bin under the sink.

Desta bent and brushed the hair from his pant legs, stood up and double-checked his new American haircut in the big mirror for the last time.

"Thank you very much," Desta said, handing James eight dollars.

James thanked Desta. "Come see me again," he said.

Jake put down the magazine he was reading and approached Desta, assessing his haircut. "Looks good," he said.

As they drove home, Jake turned to Desta. "I'm glad you resisted the temptation to get an Afro," he said. "As you might have noticed, our school is pretty conservative. The few black students have short hair. You would have stood out."

"After seeing all those Afros in the shop, I was tempted. But Afros look like a helmet. I never liked long hair anyway," Desta said.

LATER IN THE EVENING Desta lay on his bed and considered his trip to the Bronx, which had affected him in many ways. He thought his haircut had been only a pretext for something more fundamental. He thought God was either mocking him or reminding him never to take his comfortable life for granted.

Outside his home and school, America was proving to be far less affluent and monolithic than he'd imagined before coming here. These past three-and- a half months, he'd sometimes felt like his problems were behind him. But Desta knew better. His life beyond this school year was still uncertain; he was merely a guest of the Johnsons.

His nomadic life had followed him. He'd made it here through the generosity and goodwill of others. But to be an adult, he would have to fend for himself. The Bronx awakened questions he must ask to find the truth about himself. If life was hard for those born and raised here, who probably had a home and a family to fall back on, then Desta, without such privileges, would find his life here still more challenging.

He writhed. Moments later, he drifted into sleep.

TWENTY-TWO

On Sunday, Desta intended to rest and recover from the previous day's intense workout. He slept until nine.

The way Desta now felt didn't bode well. The soles of his feet felt like he had walked all night on a bed of coals. Yet they were normal to the touch; the fire appeared to be in his flesh and bones. Desta feared that all the months of hard training might be in peril if the pain didn't heal soon. And he still had two more intense runs with the team before next Saturday's competition.

He sat up, splayed and folded his legs, soles facing each other, and massaged his feet, which relieved the pain only until he stopped. Then he reached his hand over his heart, imploring the coin to intercede, but the burning only worsened. What was this, that even his magical coin couldn't heal?

Someone knocked on his door, and Desta hesitated. Fingers drummed the door, and he called, "Come in!"

"I came to see how you're doing," Jake said. "You're usually up much earlier."

Desta told Jake his situation.

"You overdid it yesterday," Jake said, looking worried. "All of us did. You may have damaged the nerves in your feet, so rest may be best for you today. You can see the doctors at the clinic tomorrow, but they're not specialists; you may need to get a referral to see one. Can you walk?"

"The pain doesn't interfere with walking."

"Come down for breakfast, then," Jake said. "I'll ask Mindy for Epsom salts and a special cream to help soothe your feet."

After breakfast, Jake brought a box of Epson salts, a jar of cream labeled *Cool-A-Ped Foot Lotion*, and an aluminum basin. In the bathroom, Desta soaked his feet in the warm, salty water for twenty minutes. Afterward, he dried, applied the cream, and massaged his soles, and returned to his room. The treatment relieved his feet, like ice on a burn, but only for so long.

He sat at his desk and studied for two midterm exams. When he finished, the problem with his feet lingered with him like a bad dream. He thought over and over about its implications.

Desta needed answers that seemed beyond the powers of the coin. He thought of his spiritual guide, Tsadok; they'd been out of touch for some time. Desta got up, retrieved the blue journal from the shelf, and flipped through to the last entry to see if there were any messages from the ancient spirit. He found none. He closed the tome, placed it on the shelf, and returned to bed.

Damaged nerves . . . rest may be the only solution. The more Desta thought about Jake's words, the more disturbed he became. Would this mean dropping out of the nationals? How long would he need to rest?

Desta couldn't spend the rest of his day worrying about this. He felt a sudden urge to leave his room and go somewhere, near water.

As if they'd heard his thoughts, Jake and Aida came by Desta's room.

"We are thinking of going to the boardwalk," Jake said. "I'd suggested you rest to deal with your feet problem. We came to see if you feel okay and want to come with us."

"I do," Desta said. "I'll get dressed. Be down there shortly."

The three of them piled into the family station wagon with Kooper and drove to Playland. They parked and headed to the boardwalk, accompanied by Kooper on his leash.

They first strolled the 700-foot sun-bleached boardwalk. Jake and Aida discussed the upcoming Thanksgiving holiday, and which relatives were coming for dinner.

Desta walked with Kooper behind the siblings, enjoying the open space, the sound of the surf, and the calls of the gulls. After the round trip on this spacious walkway, Jake and Aida turned toward the damp shore along the water's edge.

"Kooper loves playing in the water and romping in the sand with the other dogs," Jake said, and gestured for Desta to join them.

Awkwardly but politely, Desta declined, explaining that any rocks or pebbles they walk on would be hard on his feet.

Jake studied Desta. "Are you sure?"

Aida stepped closer, "Your feet hurt that much?"

"Yes," Desta said. "As much as I'd love to come with you, I should rest my feet. I'll sit here on a bench and spend some time with my thoughts. He passed Kooper's leash to Jake.

"Okay," Aida said, her puzzled countenance inclined toward the water. "Hope you find some comfort for whatever bothers you." She grabbed her long hair like a tuft of grass, twisted and knotted it, and tucked it under her purple knitted hat, which made her head seem to swell. "I don't like the damp feel of my hair after the beach walk," she said, turning to Desta. "See you in a bit." She descended the stairs to the beach with Kooper.

Jake paused on the steps and said to Desta, "Take care, and don't concern yourself too much."

"I'll be okay."

"I'm not worried you would be kidnapped," Jake said, smiling. "But it's so deserted now, it's a dreary place to be alone." Jake joined his sister and Kooper waiting for him on the sand.

That is the beauty of it, Desta thought. Playland Amusement Park and the nearby beach seemed completely different from his first visit with David this past summer. He remembered the grounds swarming with cars and people, the air filled with loud music, screaming kids, and the clanking of mechanical rides. The beach was packed with skimpily clad folk strolling or lying on the sand like basking seals.

Desta pushed his chin up and sniffed the air. Absent were the acrid smell of cigarettes and the lush aroma of sizzling meat, popcorn, and French fries.

Now the boardwalk was quiet as a graveyard, the only sounds the seagulls, surf, and owners calling to their dogs on the beach. The swirling wind brought the familiar scent of the sea: salt, plankton, and fish.

Left on his own, Desta attended to his gnawing feelings and thoughts, above all the mysterious problem with his feet. He hadn't felt a thing yesterday while running or afterward, right up to his bedtime.

As his mind reeled at the possible causes of his problem, his sights slipped through the railings, edging the boardwalk and onto the frothing water. Absently, he watched the gently rolling waves break on the rocks and sandy shore, their sound mollifying his senses. He stared at the water as if it might contain the answer to his problem.

"Damaged nerves," he verbalized inaudibly, recalling Jake's words. It sounded severe enough. He leaned forward, hands gripping the bench, his legs tucked under, and thought.

Desta had given so much of his time and energy to his athletics in hopes of a scholarship to a good school. The challenge to excel at the NJCAA Cross-Country championships had come to symbolize every hurdle and hardship he hoped to overcome in his education and the search for the Second Coin of Magic and Fortune. His success at the nationals would validate the strength of mind that had gotten him through all the trials of his childhood.

Desta had to do his best to beat his woes. He rose and paced the deck, as if it might assuage his worries. Finally, he walked up to the railing and stood facing the water, one arm resting on the bar.

Two seagulls crossed his sights, disrupting his thoughts. He watched them sweep through the air, wings banking and flashing in the dull gray hour. They screeched and squawked as they dove to pluck their meal from the water, seemingly happy. Desta wished he was like them. *The beauty of being airborne*, he thought.

From the corner of his eye, Desta noticed a blurred form on the boardwalk. He turned toward it, to find that the figure was now standing next to him. Desta instantly flinched and put space between them.

"Calm down, calm down," the figure whispered.

"Who are you?" Desta asked. His past encounters with phantoms softened the edges of his fears.

"I'm a resident ghost of the Haunted House at Playland," the specter said. "I couldn't help but notice that you're disturbed about something. You're here all alone with nobody to talk to. You know, people who keep problems to themselves suffer the most. Care to share what's bothering you?"

Desta studied the shadowy form for a moment. He felt so desperate over his present concerns, he'd gladly have shared them with the devil himself, if he had a solution.

After hearing Desta out, the ghost said, "Why torment yourself about a future that may not occur? What matters is this moment, this very second, not the one yet to be. You can't own the future. No one does! But each of us can claim the present. It belongs to all of us."

"If I don't plan my future, I won't fulfill the purpose that brought me to this country. This moment does not stand alone, it's part of my future. I cannot afford to leave things to chance."

"It seems you fail to remember one thing," the spirit said. "Whoever charted your course to this point would not abandon you. Have faith!"

Not blind faith, thought Desta. But the ghost's reminder gave him some small comfort, like passing his burden to someone else. He said nothing.

"I know what's going on in your head, son," the spirit said. "In a situation with no clear outcome, acceptance can be your comfort and strength. Acceptance is freedom. Let things be."

Desta looked into the gray, chilled air as if in a trance. He considered the advice of the ghost of Playland. His chest was packed with emotions, yet his heart and mind were clear and calm. With a hiss, he breathed out everything pent up inside, and serenity descended upon him. Again, he slowly inhaled and released air with equanimity. He turned to the specter, who patiently watched Desta.

"Thank you!" Desta said. "More than anything else, your last words hit me the hardest. All my life, unless I'm in control, I'm scared."

"Yes," the ghost affirmed, "acceptance not only brings you peace of mind, but the clarity to deal effectively with the problem at hand."

Desta's fingers moved absently over the railing as he pondered this advice.

"Leave it to the air, the universe, God, or whatever you choose to name it. Sometimes there is a reason why difficulties arise in our lives. We need to be patient until they pass. Good luck!" The specter vanished.

Desta started at the sudden departure of the ghost of Playland. He shook his head, as if to wake from a dream. He turned and gazed at the waves again as he struggled to make sense of this strange encounter. The evening grew darker, and the wind whistled.

"There you are!" Jake shouted, startling Desta.

Desta said, "You make it sound like I was lost, and you just found me."

Aida came from behind her brother with Kooper. "Yes," she said. "We came by twice, and we couldn't see you.

"We walked the entire grounds and asked the groundskeepers if there were spirits in the haunted house that abduct visitors," Jake said, smiling.

"One nearly did," Desta said, forcing a grin. "I barely escaped."

"Yeah, right!" Aida laughed and fixed her gray eyes on Desta. "But really, where were you?"

Desta hesitated, and the said, "Here the whole time." He realized that he probably wouldn't be believed if he said he'd been visited by a ghost. Instead, he said, "I needed time and space alone to think through some things. Thank you for that."

"Our pleasure! But this whole incident is rather mysterious," Jake said. "You are making us question our sanity.

Aida shook her head. "I don't know what to say either," she exclaimed.

"It's gotten cold. Let's go home," Jake said.

They headed to the car, Desta behind the siblings, mulling over what the Playland ghost had done to hide him from view.

It occurred to Desta as he returned to his room that evening after dinner that he should send a message to Tsadok about his problem.

After everyone had gone to bed, Desta retrieved the magic wand from the closet and sat on his bed cross-legged with the device before him.

Desta gave the invocation to accept and transmit his message, and the green light glowed on the big nine at the center of the wand.

> *Dear Honorable Tsadok, High Priest of the Ark:*
>
> *I'm sorry I have not been in touch lately. I need your help with an urgent matter, if you don't know about it already. Lately, I've had a painful, sensation in my feet. My host brother thinks I might have nerve damage. Would you know of any other cause of this problem?*

Desta anxiously waited for his spiritual guide's reply. Several minutes later the ancient priest's response came.

> *Dear Desta,*
>
> *I've wondered about you. That gentle spirit at the beach has already answered your question. Follow his advice. The sensation in your feet is for your protection.*

Desta clamped his lips, a bit disappointed. He rose and returned the wand to his suitcase. He undressed and got under the covers. The warm sensation in his feet was still on his mind as he finally fell asleep.

When he woke Monday morning, Desta's feet had not improved. His soles were still warm, and now they also felt like needles and pins if he stood for very long.

He had to go to school for his midterm exam. He showered and dressed, slung his backpack on his shoulders, and went down for breakfast with Jake.

Mrs. Johnson inquired about Desta's foot problem and suggested seeing a podiatrist, but that Desta first would need a letter from the school clinic. Meantime, she would ask her assistant to make an appointment for him.

Desta and Jake left for school. Mr. Parker was disappointed that Desta couldn't take part in the team's first of two final workouts before their competition Saturday.

"It sounds like bruised skin or muscle fatigue," Mr. Parker said dismissively. "I knew something like that could happen, Desta. You pushed the hardest at last Saturday's workout. After classes, go home and rest instead of working out. Wednesday, too, if you must. I know you have it in you to do well next Saturday."

Desta resented that the coach seemed to expect Desta to compete despite his aching feet. *"Why does he single me out like this? Does he think I'm superhuman?"*

At noon, Jake and Desta went to the campus clinic and got the slip Desta needed to see a foot specialist. Afterward, his host brother drove Desta home, stopped at his mother's second office next door, and asked Mary to call the podiatrist's office and make an appointment for Desta. Then Jake returned to campus alone for the afternoon workout.

After lunch, Desta found a note taped to his door from Mary confirming his podiatrist appointment at 3:30 pm the next day. Desta went into his room, did his homework, studied for two more exams, and took a nap.

TWENTY-THREE

Desta woke at 6 pm to find Jake at the door looking haggard and sad.

"You will not believe what happened," Jake said, voice breaking.

"Tell me," Desta said, lifting his head and looking eagerly at his teammate.

"Steve, Peter, and Tim were struck by a car."

"What?"

"We were running up the hill on the footpath by the side of the road, and this woman swerved to avoid hitting a stray dog, lost control of the car and struck our teammates."

"Oh, my God! Those three always ran together like they were triplets."

"And you ran with them a lot," Jake said.

"Especially early on, when Mr. Parker had me keep pace with the slower runners. So, how bad are they hurt?"

"Steve and Tim have broken legs. Peter broke his left hand and ribs and is in serious condition."

"Oh, wow!" Desta pressed the tips of his fingers on his forehead and imagined these proud athletes, their bodies, spirits, and dreams crushed.

"I'm sorry to hear this," Desta said. "What a terrible blow for everybody involved. They were so looking forward to Saturday."

"I know," Jake said. "Luke and I were ahead by a few yards, and Sam, about the same distance behind them; otherwise, we'd have been hit too.

"You were lucky," Desta said.

"I can say the same for you.

"I second that."

"How are you feeling?"

"My feet are much better, thank you." Desta thought about his good fortune. *Am I lucky that my feet played sick, or because someone is looking out for me?*

"I hope you recover soon," Jake said, and left.

Desta felt the heat in his feet, and the tragic news only brought him more worry about missing the contest next Saturday.

And then it struck him that he was obsessing about bad luck that hadn't even happened to him, while his broken teammates had no chance to compete.

Desta covered his face with his hands and thought about the Playland ghost's advice. *How right he was*, Desta thought. *I don't own the future. But I am entitled to the present.* He vowed never to worry over future events that he couldn't control. With that, a kind of sacred tranquility seized Desta. He felt free and happy.

ON TUESDAY, Jake and Desta went to the hospital to visit their team-mates. All three shared a room and were in casts. Steve and Tim, beds close to the entrance, were awake and talking. At the far end of the room, Peter was sound asleep. The nurse said his two fractured ribs had punctured his lungs, and he had been awake all night in severe pain.

Desta and Jake sat at the foot of each bed and asked their teammates how they felt and how long they would be in.

"It's unfortunate, but it's a miracle that worse didn't happen," Jake said.

Desta thought how fate—bad or good—visited all of us. A woman drives up a country road; a dog crosses in front of her; she veers to avoid it and smacks into three runners. How could it be a coincidence that the three victims just happened to be at the same place and time as the dog and the driver?

Desta believed what happened was predetermined, its purpose to offer whatever lessons the people affected could draw from them. Desta took that simple insight as his life lesson.

Desta slipped his hand under his shirt and spoke. "I want to do some-thing to help each of you, but I'm not sure if it will work. I have the image of an ancient object with healing powers. Please allow me." Desta pressed the tattoo above his heart and called out, "I command you to heal Steve and Tim's legs" seven times." Then he rose and, with each man's permission, suspended his hand over their damaged legs and whispered his mantra again.

Everyone watched, mesmerized. Then Desta went to Pete's bed and whispered the same for him. The room was so quiet that they could hear their breathing.

"I hope all of you get better soon," Desta said.

"Are you a shaman?" Tim asked, propping himself on his elbows. "It seems like you lifted a dark cloud over us. Thank you."

"I feel the same way. . . . What you did was so cool," Steve said.

"Sometimes it does not work. But I called upon the power of healing because your injuries are so serious."

"Very cool!" Jake said, his eyes brightening.

"If it works, it will be a miracle," Steve said, glancing at Desta, "and we're certainly grateful."

"You can call it a miracle, voodoo, witchcraft, or anything you like, so long as I can have my leg back," Tim Callahan said, sounding skeptical.

Desta looked at Jake. "I think we better go. I still have homework to do."

The pair wished their teammates a speedy recovery and left.

"When do you think we can see them again?" Desta asked Jake as they drove home.

"Probably not until next week," Jake replied thoughtfully. He shook his head and added, "It's a shame. Tomorrow, we go to our final workout. Thursday, we get ready for our trip to Utica on Friday and Saturday."

"It will be just four of us then," Desta said. "It's such a disappointment! But as hard as it will be, we must try our best."

"What's a bummer is that you couldn't go on yesterday's workout," Jake said. "And Luke and I had to stop the run because of the accident. We went straight home after the ambulance drove them to the hospital."

"We shouldn't dwell on our setbacks since we can't change the past," Desta said. "But we can do something about the future. . . . Regardless of our circumstances," Desta continued, "We need a good strategy for Saturday's event, including what we eat—from Thursday to the day of the race—and the prayer and visualization exercises we need to do before it. I've got some ideas from a sports magazine, and I'll share them with you when we get home."

They sat across from each other in Desta's bedroom on the long window seat, and from his notebook, Desta shared what he called the crucial strategies for success for their race.

Two days before the race, they would eat whole wheat bread, rice and pasta, lean meat, and fruit. On race day, meals should be white bread, pasta, or rice, starchy fruit like bananas and potatoes. They could also eat two to three eggs, at least three hours before the race. They would drink juice every day, and plenty of water before and at intervals during the race.

Before the race, they should stretch and warm up and do visualization exercises: see the course, their run, winning, and getting their awards on the podium. And they should pray at bedtime and before the race asking God to give them strength and stamina to win the competition.

For the run, they would position themselves on the front line, stay with the lead group, run evenly, and at the finish line, kick with all their energy to beat the front runners. Desta loaned his notebook to Jake so he could practice on his own.

That night before Desta slept, he visualized the run, his victory, and his cross-country award.

THE TEAM'S SOUR mood was hard to stomach. The four runners and their coach sat in a conference room at the Castle to discuss the trip to the JC cross-country championship in Utica on Saturday.

Mr. Parker's eyes were red, as if he had been reading too much. He seemed lethargic, his brittle smile fracturing from effort, his words flat and hollow, like a reluctant messenger. His tense audience appeared at a loss for words. *What could they say*, Desta thought, *that would change the tough spot we're in?*

"Tim and Steve left the hospital yesterday to recuperate at home. We don't know when Pete will be released," Mr. Parker said. "None of them will be coming with us to the meet."

"It's heartbreaking," Jake said. He turned to his housemate. "But the last thing we would want is to let this setback affect our performances."

"Yes, we need to set it aside and focus on what we need to do," Desta said. He clamped his lips and nodded at Jake, as did Luke and Sam.

"How are your feet, Desta?" Mr. Parker asked.

"Good enough to race Saturday," Desta said. He grinned through his tightened lips.

Mr. Parker advised them to bring a first aid kit, snacks and drinks, and extra warm clothes, socks, and hats for the competition, against the prospect of rain or snow. He referred to a written schedule and reviewed the course of events.

The next day at 7 a.m., they would leave the school for the four-hour trip to their hotel in Utica. They would check out the running route at the Valley View Golf course in the afternoon.

Registration on Saturday was from 9 to 9:30. The five-mile race would start at ten and end around 11, depending on the contestants' running time. The event then was to conclude with awards and speeches at 1 p.m.

"See you tomorrow at seven sharp," Mr. Parker said, and dismissed his runners.

THAT AFTERNOON as Jake and Desta drove home, Desta confronted the grim fact that the Abraham Lincoln Cross Country team was a mere skeleton now. Sam always finished last; Luke and Jake were their most promising runners. Desta hoped to do well.

Desta verbalized his thoughts. "After all our hard work, it's sad that the team fell apart like this!"

"I can't tell you how much it hurts," Jake said.

"I bet Mr. Parker feels worse," Desta said. "He wanted to put the school's name on the map."

"I think he did," Jake said with a sad note in his voice. "And that's why he put us through the hard workouts."

"And he probably feels responsible for the accident and for Derek's and Ben's shin splints at last Saturday's training," Desta said. "He meant well. . . . but then sometimes we can't escape predetermined events."

Jake turned toward Desta. "Predetermined?"

"It's complicated," Desta said. "I had a premonition of sorts."

TWENTY-FOUR

Early Friday morning in the school lot, Desta and Jake got out of their car and zipped up their jackets from the biting cold. Just then Desta saw from the corner of his eye a vision that might as well have come from the sky.

Desta exclaimed "ERRA!", his father's call of surprise.

"Is this real?" Jake added, eyes adjusting to the feeble gray hour. Their convalescing teammates stood before them like apparitions.

"We are!" Pete said. "You look as shocked as our doctors were when they examined us the day after your hospital visit."

Jake looked at Desta, and then the three men standing before them in their running suits.

"Does this mean you're coming with us?" Jake asked.

"Of course!" Pete said, smiling confidently, like a soldier ready for battle.

Mr. Parker and the Callahan brothers soon arrived as the day brightened and the sun slowly rose from the distant haze, its rays filtering through the boughs of naked trees. Desta half expected the coach to shout out loud, but he merely stared at the three former patients, seemingly unsure if his eyes deceived him.

Luke approached his teammates. "But you should be in bed recovering from your broken bones," he squeaked, his thin lips quivering.

Coach Parker hung on the response to Luke's remark.

"We should have been," Pete said, surveying the stunned group. "But when we woke up Wednesday morning, we were completely healed, as if nothing had happened. So, we decided to surprise you this morning."

Face drawn, eyes pinned, Luke and Sam looked skeptical. "This is like a story from the Bible," Luke said, finding his voice. "Magic isn't science, or spiritual."

Mr. Parker appeared equally mystified by his runners' testimonials. He glanced at his watch. "I don't know much about faith healing, but this seems like a miracle!" he finally said. "Let's get going, and you can fill us in on your . . . recovery."

All quickly boarded the white minibus. Mr. Parker navigated the sleepy neighborhood to I-87 North and then to I-90 West. For some time, they rode in silence. Some dozed off, and Desta sensed no one knew what to say about their teammates' miraculous healing.

After a time, Mr. Parker shot a look to his charges and said, "Could someone please explain how exactly your injuries healed?"

Steve described Desta's dream-like ritual at the hospital on Tuesday, and how he felt the changes in his body begin shortly after Desta and Jake left.

"I didn't feel anything until midnight, after my pain medicine wore off," Tim said.

"I slept through Jake and Desta's visit," Pete added.

The other runners were quiet and seemed to doubt their teammates' story. Some looked to Desta for an explanation.

"This all sounds like voodoo," Sam said, and eyed Desta with a devilish grin.

Desta gazed back at him, expecting more cutting remarks.

Mr. Parker shot a quick glance at Desta. "Can you explain this, since it seems you had something to do with it?"

Desta fidgeted. "I don't know how exactly it works, but when I pray using a . . . special charm I possess, I often get the outcome I seek."

The other runners looked at Desta with awe. Desta needed to end the discussion or risk making public his most intimate secrets. Fear rose in his chest.

Looking around at his teammates, Desta said, "I can't say more, because it's all a mystery to me too."

A murmur passed through the group. Tim opened his mouth to speak, but then clammed up.

"It's all right," Mr. Parker said, "I don't know what you did, Desta, but I'm sure glad you did it."

"Thank you so much," Pete said. Desta could almost feel Tim and Steve nodding behind him, their eyes on his cropped hair.

The air inside the van thickened, as if conspiring to stifle any more talk of miracles. Desta sighed silently.

For a long time, no one talked. The three healed athletes dozed in the back. Jake took out a book and read; Desta thought to do the same, but found himself absorbed with the open, peaceful country passing by his window. His eyes glided from far-off, white-barked birch trees to furry spruces and red pines, standing aloof from the shrubbery that hugged the road's shoulders. Farm silos and homesteads stood resolute in the distance. The minibus sped smoothly on the straight, even road, banked on the curves, and tumbled gently over bumps and rough spots.

They made just one stop at a gas station in a little town, where they refueled and then ate at the adjoining sandwich shop. Back on the road, the van pulsed with energy. The team chatted volubly, while Desta kept his eyes on the fleeting scene outside, and his mind on his goal: to finish the meet in the top ten.

His question remained unanswered as they reached the outskirts of Utica. They had been back on the road for ninety minutes, but it felt like thirty.

Mr. Parker pointed out the tall, solitary structure in the middle of town. "That's where we're heading," he said.

It looked like it had emerged from the earth, like a tree or stone outcropping. It reminded Desta of a tall rock his father had remarked about on their way to a remote village. He'd said, "When Gragne Mohammed's army invaded Ethiopia in 1500, he threw that rock like a javelin, and planted it in the earth."

Desta had been incredulous; the rock was much too large to lift. He'd concluded his father's story was a fable to convey the power of the Muslim warrior.

When the cross-country team reached the center of Utica, Desta saw that the mirage of his earlier observation was actually a building—brick, stone, and mortar. Mr. Parker pulled to the curb, and all got out. While his teammates unloaded their bags, Desta paused for a long moment and fixed his eyes on the ten-story, brown-and-gray structure before him. He ran his eyes across the front of the hotel. Its height, age, and facade reminded him of the buildings he'd seen near the barbershop in the Bronx.

He pulled his things from the minibus and walked behind his contingent to the entrance to the Hotel Utica. A mustachioed, middle-aged man, pale as a ghost, greeted them at the door. He offered to carry Mr. Parker's luggage, but the coach declined and headed straight for the registration desk, his athletes behind him.

The lobby bustled with students milling around in their school jerseys. At the counter, a young woman with luxuriant brown hair efficiently recorded each guest in a big open register. Then she pulled keys with numbered fobs from drawers, placed them in sets on the counter, and pushed them toward the waiting coaches. They, in turn, passed out the keys to their team members.

Mr. Parker and his athletes were assigned rooms on the fourth floor. As they all headed to the elevator, Desta noticed that most of them seemed tense, and from their bloodshot eyes, sleep deprived.

Mr. Parker looked at his weary team. "Aren't we lucky we didn't have to travel far? Most of these fellas probably came across the country without much sleep."

The doors opened as they reached the elevator, and a nervous, chattering group spilled out. The Lincoln College team stepped aside to let them pass, and then filed into the elevator.

The doors closed, and the elevator climbed. "That group of guys looked worried about the race," Tim said, flashing a chipped tooth.

Mr. Parker eyed him critically. "Never give in to fear," he said. "You should be like a soldier who goes into battle determined to win. Right, fellas?"

Everyone nodded except Sam.

At the fourth floor, the coach glanced at his watch and said, "See you in the lobby, 1:30 sharp. We need to check out the venue for tomorrow."

Jake and Desta got a north-facing room with double beds. The view from the curtained window arrested Desta the moment they entered.

They stowed their bags in the closet and their knapsacks by their beds. Jake pressed the edge of the nearest mattress. "This is really inviting," he said. Desta surveyed the brown wool blankets layered with white sheets and topped with plump white pillows.

"Let's stretch out before we meet up with the team," Jake said. He took off his shoes and dropped on the bedcovers like a fallen tree.

On the nightstand, a Bible and blue brochure with the hotel's building on the cover caught Desta's eye. The Bible instantly brought painful memories of childhood—his mother's excessive piety, the way the priests had used the holy book to punish him or compel his obedience, and the long hours he'd spent standing in church pews.

He picked up the brochure, sat on the chair, and skimmed it. He learned that the tower they occupied was built in 1912, four years before his father was born. And that Utica's valley and river were named Mohawk, which sounded Biblical to Desta, like Moab, the ancient kingdom of Israel.

Desta headed to the window and slowly pulled back the curtains to better admire the splendid view. The town sat on rolling terrain, filled with low, whitewashed businesses and homes, reminding him of ancient Middle Eastern towns pictured in his grade school history book.

He spoke the word *Mohawk* out loud. It echoed agreeably, as if his mouth were a cave. It seemed like he had known it long ago. "Weird," he said, a word he'd lately picked up from his schoolmates.

Momentarily his eyes were drawn to a green trench farther toward the edge of town, which Desta thought must be the Mohawk River. The tufts of bush and grass edging the riverbed somehow reminded him of the Kilty River that bordered his grandparents' old estate.

The Mohawk's winding course intrigued Desta. The region didn't appear mountainous, yet the river had carved a serpentine path, as if rocks and rising land masses had hindered its journey and forced it to take time charting its course. Had the effort been painful, as with the Blue Nile River, or Desta's own life path? No matter, Desta had found another reason to like the Mohawk River.

Jake was now snoring. He gnashed his teeth and turned to his side, bending his body in an *S*, like the meandering Mohawk. Desta caught himself daydreaming, and reminded himself he was here to prepare for tomorrow's race. He needed to face the worry pulsating through his heart.

He lay down on his back, rested his right hand on his chest, closed his eyes, and eased into a trance-like state.

A half hour later, Desta and Jake woke. At Desta's suggestion, they each soaked a washcloth in hot water and washed their faces, necks, and underarms. They changed into their sports uniforms and went downstairs.

"You're the first to show," Mr. Parker said. "Thank you."

"Desta doesn't waste time," Jake said, and winked at his teammate. "He's been so anxious about this event."

"It's okay to have butterflies in your stomach at a competition," Mr. Parker said. "It means you desperately want to win."

"As much as I would like that, just to be among the top JC runners in the country is a privilege," Desta said, trying to project confidence to the man who had invested so much effort in his success.

When all had arrived, they drove to Mohawk Valley Golf Course, eight miles from the hotel. They parked across from the clubhouse in a sizeable lot with elm trees and a row of cypresses on a grassy island at its center. Many runners and coaches from other schools were already coming and going from the course. All seemed tense and focused and spoke very little.

Desta found the atmosphere off-putting. The clubhouse, a large rectangular structure with a low-pitched roof and a long porch in front, looked more like a roadhouse than a playground for the wealthy. There were few houses nearby, and the golf course was closed for the season, which made the grounds seem strangely abandoned despite the crowds.

Mr. Parker and his team surveyed the venue and approached the clubhouse. A middle-aged man came from the building and introduced himself as Hank Greenfield, the golf club's assistant manager.

"You probably want to see where tomorrow's collegiate event will be held. . . . Let me show you," Mr. Greenfield said.

They walked left of the clubhouse to a flat, open field with bushes and trees on the left. To the right, near the end of the parking lot, were rows of chairs, folding tables, and a big sign on posts that announced NJCAA 1970 Championship in white letters on a blue field.

A few yards farther left, bracketed with corded, movable posts and fifteen feet wide, was the finish chute. Several yards from the parking lot, on the expansive field was a pre-marked white line where the runners would start their race.

Mr. Greenfield glanced at Mr. Parker's team. "If you fellas want a test run, go ahead. Just follow the markers," he said.

"That's the plan," Mr. Parker said. "Thank you."

They followed the other runners on a paved path from the parking lot to the field. Before them, about a hundred yards from the clubhouse, a small structure denoted a restroom. In front of it, on a large, paved area, two rows of golf carts sat like ducks. Beyond the building, an American flag hung limp atop a silver pole. On the grass, a dozen coaches stood in clusters talking among themselves. Mr. Parker introduced himself and his team to one of the groups.

"What part of Illinois are you from?" one coach asked.

"We're from New York," Mr. Parker replied.

"Ohh, with the insignia on your jacket, I thought . . ." the man began, then stopped.

"You think Illinoisans are the only ones with a claim on Lincoln?" the man next to the first inquisitor said with a chuckle. He wore a jacket that said Monroe Community College, Rochester, NY.

Some of Mr. Parker's team dropped on the grass and started stretching; Desta joined the others running in place. He remained standing so he could focus on the tableau before him to ease his nerves: Deep purple woods, trailing evergreens, a quilt of brown and yellow on the terrain below, and a web of roads on the sloping earth across the valley.

Farther off to the right and below, the whitewashed buildings of a small town lay in bright patches, like the stars in Desta's astronomy books.

Once everybody was done with warm-ups, they took off their heavy clothes and piled them on a table. In Lincoln sweatshirts and shorts, they lined up for the coach's start command.

Mr. Parker stepped forward. "You guys go see what fun we'll have tomorrow," he said with a smile. "Remember, don't race. . . . Just jog it." Then he called out, "Readyyy! One, two, three. . . Go!"

The team returned fifty minutes later, winded but not exhausted.

"What do you think? Piece of cake, huh?" Mr. Parker teased.

"The course is soft and muddy in some spots, rocky or grassy at others, with a few steep hills and sharp turns," Luke said. "We've run similar courses before.

"It all depends on the weather and the competition tomorrow," Pete said.

"The course is only five miles. You should do okay," Mr. Parker said, "Now, get a good night's sleep. Let's go to our hotel, eat, and get to bed early."

They all gathered their clothes, headed to the bus, and drove back to the hotel. The team ate an early dinner—pasta, bread, and steak with fruits and vegetables, and headed for their rooms.

As Jake and Desta rode the elevator, Desta reflected on all the athletes he'd seen today in the lobby and at the golf course, every one of them fit, lean, and much taller than him. His butterflies returned. *What am I doing here?*

Winning the championships had become a symbol of every hurdle to be overcome, every hardship he would face, and every sorrow he would bear during his years in America. It could be a testament to who he was, a validation of all the challenges he'd conquered to be here, an affirmation of his future.

He must do his absolute best to achieve his dream and have no regrets.

TWENTY-FIVE

The next day Desta rose at 6 a.m. Jake was sound asleep. Desta covered the lamp on his nightstand with his jacket and turned it on. He fished out the scroll from his backpack and went to the bathroom. He sat on the toilet lid and began reciting the twenty-one legends, stopping to feel the words of each, particularly those that called for personal achievement: courage, excellence, diligence.

But he didn't call out the magic entry in the legend. He knew that fair play meant he must rely on his efforts alone for this race, with no help from the coin's power, and so he merely looked at the entry to complete the count of seven. But he recited the call for personal achievement, which he felt God had given to all humanity.

After studying the twenty-one words seven times, he returned to bed. He put away the scroll, turned the light off, and lay down, hoping for a few more hours of sleep. But it refused to come, no matter how hard Desta tried; these were his usual hours for schoolwork, and he found it futile to reset his internal clock.

He kept thinking about the race. He rose, took out his notebook, and reviewed the strategy that Desta and Jake had formulated a few days ago and recited his heavenly virtues.

At seven, Desta woke to Jake's alarm. They showered and dressed. Jake scanned their plan for the meet. Then they went to the hotel restaurant to find it packed with athletes. They ate the foods that were a part of their race strategy.

They returned to their room, and put on their Lincoln College running shorts, T-shirts, long pants, jackets, and running shoes. With school sweatpants and tops over their running outfits, they headed to the lobby to join their team, and by nine o'clock, they'd arrived at the Mohawk Valley Golf Course.

The grounds swarmed with runners, event officials, and local folk. Some participants registered and collected their numbers. Others milled about, waiting for the start. Mr. Parker distributed his teams' tags, and Desta got number 147.

He wondered if his number was a good omen. There were *three* sevens in this tag—two times in the number fourteen, plus the number seven itself—and in the date of today's championship, November 21st. If he then added to these six sevens the seven in 1970, that made for *seven* sevens, and that sum—forty-nine—was his birth year in the Western calendar. In Ethiopia's calendar, he'd been born in 1942; forty-two was the sum of six sevens. Every way he looked at it, the numbers seemed to bode well.

But he was not going to jump the gun. *I'll have to wait and see.* He hoped there would be plenty of water stands along the course.

It was forecast to be forty degrees Fahrenheit at start time, but it felt colder. A raw wind from the west grazed their faces and drove leaves and debris from the parking lot; people pulled their hats down and zipped up their jackets. Clouds masked the sun and sky, some silver-gray, others dark, tattered, and ominous.

Mr. Parker said, "It looks like rain's coming early."

"We just got our first taste of it," another coach said. His navy-blue jacket said Brookdale Community College. "I feel the dampness on my face."

Once everyone had their tag numbers, the event's director, a tall man with fierce eyes, had the runners assemble behind the pre-marked white line on the golf course. Desta looked around at the hundreds of fit competitors and thought it was a wild dream that he could be among the top finishers. But like everything he had done in his life, he could only follow the plan and do his best.

Desta motioned to Jake, and they scuttled to the start line and stood right behind it. Soon all the runners congregated along the hundred-foot-long line, two and three deep.

An official stood off to the right, gun pointed to the sky. Desta glanced both ways. Somehow these pale runners reminded him of the underside of a giant bird's wings, wide open and poised to take off. He hoped that he and Jake would be the head of that bird.

The man fired the shot, and the athletes took off like a massive gale, with legs and arms working like swimmers through water. After a short distance, the runners bunched, and then spread out in knots behind a dozen athletes, Desta and Jake among them, pressing ahead. A few minutes into the race, Desta turned to see all those strapping athletes struggling to catch up with him. Many people with umbrellas and rain-coats cheered them along the path, and it buoyed his spirits. The pace setters forced those behind them to keep up.

The weather bore out Coach's prediction. Shortly after the first mile, it began to drizzle, cold and biting. The athletes ignored it and kept pace, focused on victory.

Sprinkles quickly became steady rain. The ground turned soggy, the hills and curves slippery and dangerous. Yet everyone did their best to keep their rhythm. Desta adjusted his muscles and his pace to sprint uphill and kept an even stride on flat terrain.

As intended, he and Jake remained behind the leaders. The rain now fell in buckets, cutting their visibility and speed. Desta tasted a brack-ish mix of rain and sweat, his mouth no longer dry. The earth smelled like mildew.

The spectators dwindled as the rain intensified. A din rose from around Desta, as a few brave souls cheered on the runners. Desta could barely see through the water streaming down his face, and no amount of swiping helped. He might never finish this race, let alone win it, but he was determined to keep up.

Desta's group reached a steep curve when a runner ahead tripped and fell, bringing Desta down with him. Jake staggered and tried to help Desta, who waved him on. Desta took a moment to check himself for in-juries; a few runners passed him. He quickly got to his feet and continued running. Desta noticed his group was already gone; it now seemed impossible to catch up with them, but rather than give up, he ran faster. His group now came into sight. He kept running, and counted six runners ahead of him, including Jake. If nobody else overtook him, he would finish seventh, and he was okay with that.

Just as they passed the last mile mark, the rain stopped, and the day brightened. Desta's clothes clung to his skin, making progress harder. He bit his lip and pushed hard for the front runners. Within minutes, he

closed on them. The two tall, thin athletes were still in the lead, Jake and
the other three strung behind them. Desta passed these four and waved
for his host brother to come along as the lead pair picked up speed.

Desta saw the finish chute; this was his chance. He took off as if
driven by a raging wind, and glanced back to see if the tall runners were
speeding to overtake him. They had fallen back, but he was buoyed to
see Jake right behind him. Many onlookers applauded Desta and clicked
their cameras as he crossed the finish line.

Desta and Jake smiled and hugged, barely standing. Mr. Parker ran
up to them, bent his bulky frame, and engulfed Desta and then Jake,
calling out, "Bravo! Bravo!" Desta's victory had yet to sink in; he was
still absorbing the fact that he had finished the race. It seemed like a
miracle.

Many runners now arrived and crowded around the finish line. When
the rest of the Lincoln team learned Desta and Jake were the top finishers, they pumped fists and hugged one another. Mr. Parker passed them
towels to dry off, but Desta preferred to change his wet outfit, and the
coach led the team to the small building's bathroom to change.

Paper and pen in hand, reporters approached Desta, but Mr. Parker
waved them off. When the team finally emerged from the building,
the coach was chatting with several reporters, who turned their attention to Desta.

"Is it true that you only trained for two and a half months?" one reporter asked.

"Yes," Desta said.

"You must have been a runner before you came to the United States,"
a second asked.

"No."

"But your countrymen are born runners," said a third. "Abebe Bikila
won the Marathon in Rome six years ago running barefoot. Do all runners in your country compete barefoot?" He looked down at Desta's feet.

He turned and looked at the man, and found no malice in his big
green eyes, which bore a child's innocence and a monk's sincerity.

"I really don't know, but most probably wear shoes," Desta said. He
recalled what his oldest sister Saba had said when he told her to wear

shoes. *If God thought we needed shoes, we would have been born with them.* He lighted up.

Mr. Parker sensed Desta's unease with the reporters' questions. "That's enough," he said. "This young man needs to rest. You may ask more questions later." The coach led his team to the crowded parking lot, reporters tagging along.

Mr. Parker took them to the platform on the grass alongside the paved lot. "They'll have the awards ceremony for the top three finishers here now," he said.

The head of the NJCAA gave a short talk, honoring all the participants and the crowd for braving the rain and cold. Then he gave out three team awards, Abraham Lincoln College among them, followed by awards for the top three individual competitors. He counted down the winners, starting with third place. All three got plaques and certificates. In addition, Desta and Jake received navy blue sweaters with the NJCAA shield in white over the breast. "Cross-Country Champion 1970" appeared in white below it, and three white bands circled the left arm below the shoulder.

After the ceremony, Desta looked in vain for university recruiters who might want to talk to him. He shook hands with the runners and the coaches he met and told them it was an honor to compete with them at a national event. Then he joined his team and headed to the minibus. He felt a fleeting sting of disappointment that no college scouts had seen him run. But then the electrifying moment at the finish line and the cheering of the crowd came back to him, and he brimmed with unbridled joy and wonder at his achievement today, against every obstacle put in his path, with no help from the coin's magic. His victory was his, and his alone.

Desta's host family was elated at the news when Jake and Desta arrived home in the evening and embraced them both. Desta had craved such praise and recognition all his life, and now he savored it. As he crawled into bed that night, he was tired and sore all over, but the memory of his win and the adulation he received among many washed over him once again, lulling him into a deep sleep.

TWENTY-SIX

Desta awoke Sunday morning after his NJCAA championship victory
with his senses thrumming, as if a million needles pricked him with
happiness. He'd felt this way when he first began earning his own
money in high school, and when he'd flown the aircraft he built himself. Then, Eleni, the spirit guide of Washaa Umera, had seen a warm
glow and sparkle in him, and called it *bliss*—the same complete contentment that now flooded his senses.

His victory had brought him unexpected accolades: pats on the shoulder, handshakes and hugs, the smiles and admiring eyes of strangers to
whom he must have seemed so alien. All of that was intoxicating, but
the win was what ultimately mattered to Desta.

Desta slept until nearly nine o'clock, and then went downstairs for a
snack to tide him over until brunch at 11.

Mr. Johnson sat on the couch in the family room and looked up from his
newspaper. "You're written up in the *Rye Record*, Desta," he said. "We are
so proud of you!"

"What did they say?" Desta asked and came closer.

"Take a look." Mr. Johnson handed the paper to Desta, and he took it
with him to the kitchen to get his cereal and tea before returning to his
room. He sat on the window seat and began to read the newspaper article.

*Lincoln Exchange Student Wins Solo Men's Title at NJCAA Cross-
Country Meet*, announced the headline. The half-page article described
Desta's stunning win at his first meet, in a record time of 13 minutes and
21 seconds for a 5K run, and noted that Jake Johnson finished second,
20 seconds behind Desta. It reported that the school took third place in
the team competition, their first-ever national championship. Desta was
pleased they'd gotten his name right, and mentioned he was Ethiopian.

After finishing the article, Desta refocused on the *headline*. Why did they call him an exchange student?

The answer was a mere echo in Desta's head. He studied his grainy black-and-white photo near the finish line, frozen in time, gaping, rain-drenched, and near collapse.

Yesterday, as he and Jake approached the crowded parking lot after the race, his victory had not yet sunk in. But when his teammates, competitors, and other coaches gave him their hearty congratulations, it registered that he had done something special. And however transient, the contest had connected him to strangers in a way he had never experienced before.

In the warm, sun-splashed room, he stared at his miserable image in the paper. Happy though he was to be celebrated for his victory, the real prize for him was that in so doing, he'd improved his prospects of a scholarship at a top college.

A knock on the door took Desta from his reverie, and Jake walked in.

"David Hartman just called," Jake said, smiling some. "He had gotten wind of your win and wants to talk to you. I told him to call back in a couple of hours."

"Thank you," Desta said and drew Jake's attention to the newspaper headline about the race, in particular the word "exchange."

Jake seemed at a loss, too. "I don't know where they got that from. Last year, we had an exchange student at Rye High, but not from Ethiopia." He smiled. He explained that a student exchange program was a reciprocal arrangement between schools or countries where high school seniors spend a year studying in a host country.

"I know what that program is, but . . . Desta trailed off.

"Maybe they called you an exchange student to make a subtle insinuation about our school."

"Why?"

Jake passed his hand over his forehead. "You see, the City of Rye has always resented our school because it sits on the largest piece of real estate in town, tax-free.

"Tax free?" Desta asked.

"Yes," Jake replied. "As an education institution, the school is exempted from paying taxes."

Jake paused and then continued. "I've heard that some locals and newspapers refer to Lincoln College as a glorified high school. Maybe people in Rye City are jealous that this championship puts us in the national limelight."

Desta's brow knotted. "Glorified high school?" he asked. "Is that how other schools see us?" He wondered how this might affect his college prospects.

"Of course not," Jake replied. "Our school has a top academic program and is one of the best transfer schools in the area. Jake gazed at Desta. "Don't worry," he said. "As a national champion, you'll get into the school of your choice. C'mon, let's go down for brunch."

"HOW MARVELOUS!" David Hartman said, "You never told me you were such a good athlete."

"That's because I never was," Desta said, smiling.

"I won't ask for all the details now, but this is terrific!" David added.

"Thank you, David," Desta said. "But it's terrific only if it helps me get into a top university."

"It should," David said. Desta thought he caught a hint of doubt in David's voice. Then he quickly added, "Now you have to make your studies match your achievement on the field!"

"It's my goal in the next few weeks."

"I'll see if I can arrange with the Johnsons to come see you after Thanksgiving," David said.

"That would be great!" Desta said. They exchanged best wishes for the holiday and ended the call.

Desta went down for brunch. The table overflowed with food in a beautiful display, and zesty aromas filled the house. After the meal, over coffee and tea, Desta and Jake related their experiences—the trip to Utica, the event venue, and the competition. Desta found words inadequate to capture all his thoughts and feelings. He cherished this moment as much as the race.

His host parents went to visit city friends, the siblings left to do their own things, and Desta to his room to study hard until the end of the semester.

A couple of hours later, after Desta finished studying for his classes, he decided to share his recent accomplishments with his ancient mentor.

After he went through the routine of setting up his magic wand, and invoked the green light from it, Desta began:

Dear Honorable Tsadok, High Priest of the Ark,

> *In case you have not heard the news from the wind, I'm now a national junior college cross-country championship winner. I've never dreamt I could do this, particularly knowing I had little athletic experience in Ethiopia. What saddened me was what I came to realize afterward. I was lucky enough to achieve this unexpected win and recognition. Still, there are thousands of young Ethiopian boys and girls there who live and die without realizing their full potential. I hope our country develops enough economically so its young get to excel in whatever talent they possess. My life would have been inconsequential if not for the prophecy and the coin's legends that inspired my leaving home. I'm grateful to the two entities and you for guiding me tirelessly to be where I am today.*

Several hours after dinner and more studying, Desta noticed the usual shimmering light over the Record. He pulled it to his desk and opened it at the last entry.

Dear Desta,

> *I'm aware of your win. Congratulations! As to the challenges your country's youth faces, you hold their freedom. The union of the two coins is the panacea of all the economic and social ills of the world. For now, focus on your goals.*
>
> *Good luck with your efforts, son!*

TWENTY-SEVEN

The Sunday afternoon before Thanksgiving, the day after the NJCCAA championship, Jake had shown Desta a framed proclamation by President Abraham Lincoln, establishing Thanksgiving as a national holiday. It was dated October 3, 1863, and contained these words, highlighted in bold: "I do therefore invite my fellow citizens . . . to set apart and observe the last Thursday of November next, as a day of Thanksgiving and Praise to our beneficent Father. . . ." This document clarified to Desta why the Johnsons and classmates had eagerly awaited this food and family event.

While scanning Lincoln's message, Desta's eyes stopped at the numerical entries. They intrigued him. He detected clues as to why Desta was chosen to live with the family. The two pairs of digits in 1863 each added up to 9, as did the sum of the 9s, 18. Nine was a key digit entwined with Desta's life and the magic wand that navigated his life path. And 9 plus 3, the date of Abraham Lincoln's proclamation, added to twelve, representing the number of hours in a day and months in a year, a life cycle, round as the coin.

According to Tsadok, twelve was a magical and sacred number associated with personal goals, hopes, and ideas. Finding all this in Lincoln's document seemed no coincidence to Desta. He put the framed image down thoughtfully.

"He was a great man!" Jake said. "He paved the way for this country to be what it is today."

"I can see that from what you said and read about him," Desta remarked.

"I've things to do in my room," Jake said, rose, and walked off with the framed document.

Desta had found his host family's veneration of Lincoln puzzling. He thought that such devotion to anyone made it harder to see the shortcomings in heroic people and their great ideas. *Blind faith can be perilous for the naive and uninformed,* Desta thought. He'd imagined if the whole country felt the same as the Johnsons about Mr. Lincoln, he might one day be canonized into sainthood.

Moments later, Desta had walked off to his bedroom, his mind occupied with Thanksgiving and the people he would meet.

ON MONDAY AFTERNOON of Thanksgiving week, after Jake and Desta returned from school, Elsa took Desta to the back of the house, where she unlocked a storage room that greeted them with stale air. She switched on the light to reveal a sea of disparate objects covering the floor, tables, and shelves.

"This is the family's catchall storehouse," Elsa said, stating the obvious. "When we change the wall décor or the dining sets, we come here." She dashed across the room and opened the window.

To the right, old leather-bound books, some with spines cracked and edges frayed, lined half the wall from ceiling to floor on large shelves. Yellowed paperbacks and miscellaneous artifacts filled the rest of the shelving. On the facing wall and floor were several framed paintings—a sunset over red, hazy earth; a couple walking along a beach, hands locked, wind whipping their hair, leaving fresh tracks on the white sand; another, a dream-like vision of water lilies and pastel-blue sky.

Desta had the impulse to pour over the paintings, but Elsa directed his attention to yet another set of shelves to the left of the bookcases. But these shelves were wide and deep.

"These are the Thanksgiving dishes and glasses we must bring to the kitchen and wash. You'll bring them to the house, and Aida will run them through the dishwasher."

Desta thought the many serving dishes, plates, and glasses of all shapes and sizes would be enough for a hundred guests.

Next, Elsa unlocked and opened a large mahogany cupboard near the dishes and glasses. Its shelves were filled with gleaming utensils, some with golden handles in open metal boxes, and two large wooden containers on the bottom.

"Some of this serving ware and cutlery is over two hundred years old. For this holiday, we'll use the settings in this wood chest," she said. She opened it to reveal a flannel, fabric-lined chamber stacked high with forks, knives, and spoons in three slotted rows alongside utensils unfamiliar to Desta.

Elsa emptied half of the chest's contents onto the shelf; she asked Desta to take the rest in the chest to the house, empty it in a basket, and return with the chest to collect the second batch. Upon his return, she took a plastic bag from the corner and said, "Let's go back to the house."

In the house, Elsa put the plastic bag on the island counter. She then opened one of the cabinets, brought out two large, folded cloths, grabbed the plastic bag, and had Desta follow her to the formal dining room with the silverware chest and had him put it down on a section of the long dining table.

On a second trip to the kitchen, he brought the remaining silverware and placed it on the table next to the chest. Elsa spread both cloths on the table, flipped open the chest, picked out the stacked silverware from their slots, and placed them on one cloth: a six-piece set for each one of sixteen diners. Most pieces were lustrous; others showed a dull patina.

Then from the plastic bag, Elsa brought out a small wooden spatula, a soft, stained cloth, and a round jar labeled "Wright's Silver Cream," with an image of a knife, fork, and spoon. She opened the container, scooped a gray paste with the spatula, and applied it to the cloth.

Elsa picked up one of the knives. "To remove the discoloring," she said, "we need to clean them with the paste and this polishing rag." She gently rubbed the knife blade on both sides with the cream-smeared rag. Once the utensil shone like new, she set it on a large, clean section of the cloth. Then she put down the rag, moved the box to one side, and said, "Now continue with the rest. Any questions?"

"Why so many? You said there would be sixteen people," Desta said. "Aren't a fork, knife, and spoon enough?"

Elsa's dimples on her cheeks turned into dots. "This is nothing," she said, "In the old days, guests were served meals with ten to fifteen courses, and there would be that many utensils for each guest—butter knives, cutting knives, three or more different forks and spoons . . . In those days, people also spent five to six hours at mealtime."

"Once you're done polishing, bring all the silver to the kitchen and rinse it with water. . . . no soap," Elsa said and walked away.

For the next two hours, Desta rubbed and polished ninety-six forks, knives, and spoons with Wright's Silver Cream with the utmost thoroughness, even between the tines of each fork.

It was tedious work, but Desta had to be mindful of all the details. *Bev Johnson sees flaws where they don't exist*, he thought. His pile of polished tableware dazzled like diamonds. He then brought it to the kitchen and rinsed and dried all the pieces with a towel. Finally, he transferred them to a large cloth-lined basket and left them on one side of the long credenza in the dining room.

IT APPEARED THANKSGIVING was not just about family, food, and merriment, but also showcasing one's home. In the dining room, laundered cream curtains looked translucent in the daylight, and the hardwood floors shone like a sea of mirrors.

A horn-shaped wicker basket sat on folds of straw-colored fabric at the center of the long table. The gifts of harvest, corn, gourds, apples, plums, pears, and acorns spilled from its mouth. Dried brown-and-gold maple leaves adorned the borders.

Rows of long-stemmed wine glasses dazzled in the sunlight while the tinted tumblers gave off little of the light that reached them. The wine glasses stood above the napkins and the tumblers above the forks, and from a distance resembled a ranked marching army.

The kitchen bustled with activity as Mrs. Johnson in her casual floral print dress, Elsa, and Aida prepared the food. The air was thick with the aroma of strange, appetizing spices.

In the family room, Mr. Johnson and Jake watched a televised football game between teams they called Green Bay Packers and Dallas Cowboys. The guests were expected anytime.

The first to arrive were Dick and Emma Johnson. Desta stood by the stairs and watched Shae, Jake, and Aida rush to their grandparents and hug and kiss them one by one. Grandpa Johnson looked toward Desta over the shoulders of the man's grandchildren as they hugged him. Skip and Beverly Johnson embraced the elder Johnsons next.

"Come, Desta," the head of the house said with a wave of his hand.

"This is the young man from Ethiopia we have told you about," Mr. Johnson said to his parents, with one hand on Desta's shoulder.

"How do you do?" Grandma Johnson said. She extended her hand, her clouded blue eyes fixing his.

"Very well, thank you," Desta said. He shook hands with her and her husband.

"How do you like it here?" Grandpa Johnson asked.

"I like it very much, thank you," Desta said.

Mr. Johnson took his mother's dark wool coat and white shawl and hung them in the big coat closet while Jake did the same for grandpa.

The couple was a revelation in their finery. Grandma Johnson wore an ocher dress, cream cardigan, and a brooch of maple leaves with a pearl at the center that echoed her pearl earrings and a double-looped necklace worn over her sweater. Grandpa Johnson was dressed in a black suit, white shirt, and a tie that crookedly rested on his chest, with the hint of harvest colors in his orange-and-brown paisley pocket square.

"I have learned from Skip that you and my grandson won the cross-country national championship. Congratulations!"

"We did. Thank you, Mr. Johnson."

"That's marvelous," Grandpa Johnson said, his gray eyes full of happiness.

"I hear that they are good pals," Grandma Johnson said, steadying her gaze on Desta.

"Jake, Aida, and Kooper couldn't have asked for a better buddy," Mr. Johnson said. He wore a light-yellow button-down shirt and peanut color pants to complement polished brown loafers.

"Not only in sports but Jake and Desta are also good study partners," Mrs. Johnson said.

"That's good," Shae piped in. "Jake's never been good at managing his time." She smiled at her brother.

"That's not true," Jake challenged, "But it's been good having Desta here." He winked at his housemate.

"Come to the family room," Mrs. Johnson said, leading her in-laws through the double doors. All the children and Mr. Johnson followed. An exuberant fire in the hearth across the room made the atmosphere warm and cheerful.

"How about cocktails?" Mrs. Johnson asked.

"Isn't it too early for happy hour?" Grandpa Johnson said, chuckling.

"All the hours are happy on Thanksgiving, Dad," Mrs. Johnson said.

"Please sit," Mr. Johnson said from behind his wife. "I'll make us drinks."

He went to the kitchen and returned with a tray, a martini for his mother, whiskey on the rocks for his father, and two gin and tonics for his wife and himself.

Mrs. Johnson declined, saying, "Not at the moment, honey." She sat on the sofa opposite the parents, across the platter of cheese, crackers, and slices of smoked meat on the coffee table between them. The husband put the tray next to the appetizers, collected his drink, and sat beside his wife.

"Have some snacks," Mrs. Johnson suggested, picking up the platter and offering it to the parents first, then her husband, and then setting it down. After chatting awhile with the grandparents, she excused herself and came to the siblings and Desta, who stood conversing at the edge of the room. "Why don't you all go get dressed for the meal," Mrs. Johnson whispered. "I'll do the same soon." She then went to the kitchen, and the four youngsters went to their rooms.

Aida returned with a knee-length long-sleeve dress with the fall's hues: reds, yellows, and russets, all complementing nicely her sandy brown hair, her freckled skin, and light blue eyes.

Shae Johnson wore a sleeveless dress with curling leaves, pumpkins, and grapes. Jake donned his tan herringbone jacket with a white shirt, dark pants, and shoes. Desta sported his blue coat, khaki pants, brown shoes, and socks.

They found the house humming with still more guests—Eric and Denise Johnson, brother and sister-in-law, with their two teenage girls; Trover and Martha Clark, sister, and brother-in-law, with their two grown boys and Shae's boyfriend, Nash Carver. The children moved gracefully through the guests, as they offered their hands, smiles, and welcomes.

All were fabulously dressed except Nash Carver, who wore stylish jeans and a pressed beige flannel shirt. Women wore browns, beiges, and blacks in their dresses or shoes, silver or gold earrings, and matching necklaces.

Denise Johnson, slim, tall, and refined, carried herself as someone who knew she had wealth, looks, and intelligence. She gave Desta more than a cursory acknowledgment when his host introduced them.

Mr. Johnson's older sister Martha Clark had striking looks—big brown eyes, delicate nose, and a face shaped like a heart—but time had diminished her beauty. She shook hands with Desta with the respect she showed the others. She asked a few questions about his family back home and how he was getting along with her brother's family.

The men wore jackets, button-down shirts, and ties in the season's colors.

With all these handsomely dressed people around him, Desta couldn't help reflecting on his remarkable transformation. He had adjusted to America's upper-class dress code in four short months. In that time, his smooth, hairless skin had become softer and more translucent, allowing his rich heritage to show through. In recent months, students stared at him on campus, and people in town and stores often asked about his origins or said, "You're not from here."

"Why not?" he would tease.

"Because you don't act or talk like us," they'd say with a touch of condescension.

"I hope that's not anything bad," he would say.

"Oh, no—your accent and regal bearing make you different and interesting."

The more he absorbed the American—or perhaps it was the Johnsons'—way of life, the more it smoothed out the rough edges of his upbringing. Yet strangely, as he grew more comfortable in his adopted home, his Ethiopian identity and the values and standards he was raised with slowly surfaced. His spare diet and financial hardships in the past had made it difficult to realize any of the qualities the people here now identified in him.

With those struggles behind him, he could be more fully himself and tap into the traits of his heritage: reserve, dignity, self-respect, graciousness, composure, and speaking softly. In a remote Ethiopian village, where most people couldn't read or write, he'd been raised to be responsible and kind, to respect others no matter who they were, conduct himself properly at home and in public, and live the ten commandments. To his surprise, he had discovered that those standards equaled those in the Johnson home. For all these reasons, his transition to America had been easier than he'd expected.

Mr. Johnson came to the group as they sat before the fire. "Let's feast," he said.

Mrs. Johnson gathered the others from throughout the house, and everyone came to the formal dining room where the table had been set the night before. The walnut table and matching chairs were cleaned and polished to the same luster as the silverware Desta had spent hours polishing early in the week. The two dining room chandeliers with their thousand diamond pendants shone brightly in the afternoon light.

"Your seats are assigned by name," Mrs. Johnson said. "Now, please form a line for the food at the kitchen island and serve yourselves."

"Seniority is an earned privilege," Mrs. Johnson said, smiling. "Mom and Dad, you go first."

A line quickly formed by age for the older adults, with the young people behind them in no definite order. Desta, Jake, and Aida were last. Desta noted that he was to sit between Martha Clark and Grandpa Johnson.

As Desta watched the adults fill their plates, he wondered what turkey tasted like; he'd never heard of this animal before the holiday. The previous night he'd watched Elsa and Mrs. Johnson put two giant birds in the oven, and then a short while ago, he's seen them on racks atop wooden boards. Now they were puffed up, brown, and glistening. He had never seen birds that big. Where he grew up, his older brothers would trap a wild bird they called *Kok*, no bigger than an ordinary hen, whose meat was tasty.

At the table, Desta followed everyone else's lead. He took a few slices of turkey and a scoop of stuffing and doused both with the brown sauce, a couple of spoonfuls of doughy potato, green beans, the crimson sauce they called cranberry, and a bread roll. He sat down in his assigned seat and put a napkin on his lap. Like the others, he sat erect and waited for the hosts to sit down with their meals.

The light pumpkin-colored napkins displayed "Thanksgiving" in large italic letters, followed by "family," "thankful," and "blessed" in smaller letters, shown haphazardly like fallen leaves. "November" in large letters appeared at the bottom.

"Got enough?" Grandpa Johnson asked, glancing at Desta's plate.

"Yes, thanks."

"Do you have turkey in your country?" Martha Clark asked Desta.

"No," Desta said, "This is my first."

Once all had taken their seats, Bev Johnson said a prayer.

Heavenly Father, thank you for keeping us healthy through the year.
Thank you for enabling us to come together again on this special day to
give gratitude for the blessings you give us and the food and drinks we
are about to share with our families.

We seek your love, mercy, and grace as we pass another of life's
milestones into the future. Thank you again for our families celebrating
the moment and for what we have. Amen!

"Amen!" The celebrants gripped their filled goblets, raised them, and
declared: "Happy Thanksgiving!" Then they tilted and clinked them
with their nearest neighbors, said "to your health," and took a sip. The
guests gazed at the food with warm, happy faces as hands reached for
gleaming silverware to feast on the heaping plates before them.

Desta studied his neighbors, Martha Clark and Grandpa Johnson, to
glean how to eat this feast. The brown turkey meat with the gray sauce
tasted delectable. So did the mashed potatoes, the crimson cranberry
sauce, and the moist bread cubes with minced apples and raisins. The
only sounds were the occasional clearing of throats, the din of metal on
porcelain, and the hum of energy around the table. At one point,
Grandma Johnson signaled Elsa to bring her a quarter martini on the
rocks. Everyone enjoyed their red wine or water.

After the plates were collected, Elsa served pumpkin and pecan pie.
Some stayed at the table after dessert and drank wine; others left for the
living room, where a magnificent fire was going.

Desta and Aida went to the kitchen to help Elsa with the dishes.
Shortly after ten o'clock, all the guests left, except for Grandpa and
Grandma Johnson, who had come from Florida and would be staying.
Once Desta finished helping Elsa, he said goodnight to everyone and
went upstairs.

TWENTY-EIGHT

Family members, students, and teachers prepared for what was coming with the end of the warm days of summer, past the autumnal equinox in the last week of September.

During his intense cross-country workouts and efforts to adjust to his academic career in the new country, Desta noticed the changes around him like objects one sees through peripheral vision. The changing hues in the trees. The cooler days. And the shortening of the daylight hours.

It was like traveling through rapidly transforming scenes, a shifting palette. From the end of September through the end of November, in the backyard trees and those along his cross-country running route, Desta observed hues of yellow, orange, gold, copper, russet, carmine, and scarlet until this final coloring assumed the earth's deep brown and burnt sienna, all dropping to the ground at their different stages of transformation.

Once, when he walked Kooper in the yard among the fallen yellow leaves, Desta brought seven small ones to his room, arranging them in a circle on the corner of his desk.

The weather swung back and forth from calm and warm to nippy and breezy as the days and weeks advanced.

The blossoms from the bushes withered and fell in great numbers too. All the fallen dry flowers and leaves tossed in the wind and trampled underfoot finally turned to dirt.

With the loss of their foliage, the trees grew stark and naked as if they had died too, but no one mourned them. It saddened Desta; it was as if those beautiful hues had somehow evaporated into thin air.

Now, here he was sitting in his room thinking about all those past events and having never made the association of the season Americans call *fall* to the *autumn, which* Desta remembered it being called. Seeking clarification, he sought his American Heritage Dictionary. It listed

twenty-six definitions for fall, but none was for a season. He wasn't
about to ask anyone about this and appear ridiculous. He realized that
term must have been derived by association for the beautiful leaves
flowers that dropped from the trees. He wondered why people used the
name *fall* more than *autumn*. He thought *fall* better described the natural
events of this season.

The other seasonal changes that came along: The *Snow and cold were
obvious enough*, Desta thought.

He had experienced cold and *baredo*—hail—what people at home
thought of as snow—as a shepherd in the Ethiopian highlands. During
the rainy season, the air sometimes made his teeth chatter uncontrollably,
and the baredo could be relentless, as it tore up the earth and stung his
fingers when he scooped it up. Desta thought no cold or snow in America
could surpass those childhood experiences. But he was in for a surprise.

First, the snow was different from what he was used to. It didn't
come from the sky as hail, but harmless, cottony flakes. One early December morning Desta looked out his window to find the entire
backyard had turned completely white. The family had discussed the
possibility of snow the day before, but Desta had not imagined it to be
a bright, enveloping blanket.

Desta couldn't contain his excitement. He ran downstairs in his pajamas, put on tennis shoes, and stepped from the mudroom into the
snow outside.

He scooped some with his bare hand and put it in the palm of the
other. He pinched and rolled it between his fingers to find that it wasn't
the solid hail of childhood, but a soft and fluffy substance that melted
into water. Soon, his fingers began to numb, and the rest of him felt as if
he were wrapped in a cold banket. He brushed off the melting snow
from his hands, and dashed back into the house, but he still hadn't gotten his fill of the snow. He returned to his bedroom window and gazed
out at what had been a vast lawn just the night before.

As Desta stood thinking about the wonders of nature, Roman
Burkhardt's letter came to him, with its account of the hooded, bearded
man who came to Burkhardt in a snowstorm and gave him the painting
of the coin that now hung on Desta's wall. Did the snow hold any significance for the coins? Desta thought it couldn't be a coincidence.

"YOU NEED TO BUNDLE UP," Jake said one morning, seeing Desta in his usual jacket and tie for school. He handed him gloves and one of his heavy jackets. Before they left the house, they needed to shovel the snow and clear a track for Jake's little Alpha Romeo. Desta could see their breath, gray, curly, and transient. Even in all his layers of clothes and gloves, the cold penetrated deep into his body. In the car, Desta hugged himself to keep warm while they waited for the motor to heat up. When they finally drove off, Desta looked around and said, "Is this how it's going to be all winter?"

"Pretty much," Jake assured, "but this isn't so bad. Gets a lot colder later in the month, and all through winter."

Desta's brow pinched. He shook his head and glanced to either side of the road. Dirty snow piled along the boundaries of the road. The pavement ahead was slushy and mounds of snow appeared on cars parked at the curb and in driveways.

By late afternoon, the snow appeared in discrete mounds. When they went for cross-country practice, the ground was wet and slippery in places, and compact and rigid at others, and their pace faltered.

Back at the Johnsons, their beautiful compound suddenly seemed bleak, all of nature hunkered down and hibernating. Desta could see for miles from his window through the bare branches of trees, to the roof-tops of houses and buildings. He noted for the first time how much bigger the world around him seemed with all the foliage gone. As he studied it further, Desta also found beauty in the melancholic view.

He thought how short life was, and the endless cycle of birth, growth, decline, and death made him wonder about life's meaning and purpose. He reasoned it had to be found in the mark that life leaves behind. As for his life, that would be finding the Second Coin of Magic and For-tune. He cleared his head and brought his attention back to what had stirred him up, the beauty before him, the silence, the memory of the magnificent snow.

From that day on, each time it snowed, every outing was a produc-tion. Over his regular clothes, Desta wore a padded jacket and hood, a hat, gloves, and scarf. He slowly got used to this new way of living like everybody else had.

The snow wasn't all dull routine. Desta, Jake, and Aida would play in the backyard on weekends and holidays. His host siblings taught him how to make snowballs—the objects of a game. Jake scooped a clump of snow with cupped hands, then pressed and patted it to make a tight, compact ball. "This can be nearly as deadly as a rock," Jake said, holding the finished ammunition in his palm.

"Who would you fight with it?" Desta asked.

"You!"

"Hope you're kidding," Desta said, eyeing the ball.

"Nope! I'm serious."

Desta studied Jake. "I'm afraid I may have to opt out then." He gave a small, nervous laugh.

"On second thought," Jake said. "Since you seem uncomfortable, let's wait until Christmas break when we're both more relaxed."

With this advice, Jake and Desta went inside to their rooms.

AS HE'D PROMISED HIMSELF, Desta buckled down to his studies after Thanksgiving. He had kept up with his courses and consistently done well in math and science. With English, however, he continued to labor on his essays. With so much of his time devoted to running, he'd kept falling behind on his reading assignments, and he had a hard time writing compelling essays about stories and characters so far removed from the world he knew. He needed to immerse himself more in the language to think in English. But he was still determined to do well.

He was also mindful of Jake's success. Desta knew it meant a lot to Jake and his grandfather that Jake attend Yale University. Desta continued to make sure that they studied together at home and in the school library. Like Desta, his host brother also planned to transfer to a four-year college, hopefully Yale, in the fall. Both had sent postcards to several schools requesting admission applications.

They began final exams on Monday, December 14th, and finished a week later. Desta was not sure how well he did, and their grades would not be released until they returned to classes in January. For the time being, Jake and Desta were relieved that the first semester was behind them.

When they came home, they learned they would spend Christmas in their winter cabin in Deer Meadow, Vermont, instead of their summer vacation home at Hyannis Port on the Atlantic coast of Massachusetts. Desta was disappointed because he had heard so much about this home and little about the mountain cabin.

TWENTY-NINE

Monday evening, Jake and Desta set up the Christmas tree in the living room, with Aida hovering about, trying to help with the decoration. A fire burned in the hearth as Mr. Johnson read the Wall Street Journal on the couch. Mrs. Johnson had just walked in from the family room when someone knocked on the front door. Jake dropped what he was doing and dashed to open it. It was his sister Shae with a suitcase in tow.

"Guess who's here?" Mr. Johnson announced, dropping his newspaper on the couch. He rose and stepped toward his daughter. Jake and Shae hugged and kissed, and then he took her suitcase and watched Shae wrap her arms around her father, who bent forward and kissed her.

"Glad you arrived earlier than your mother said you would," Mr. Johnson said. "Was the traffic light?"

"As you can imagine, holiday traffic . . . . It wasn't too bad," Shae said. "I did the best thing; I left two hours early and took Route One to I-95 via the George Washington Bridge and then the Hutchinson River Parkway to Rye. Interstate 95 would've taken me till midnight." She smiled, then greeted her mother and Aida.

As Desta watched these displays of affection, he realized the meaning of family and belonging. In contrast, how meagerly his family acknowledged him on his rare holiday visits, making him feel more like a guest than one of them. During these encounters, Desta always felt lonely and homeless.

Shae had been away from home for only three months and they often talked with her family on the phone; yet now they treated her as if she had been gone for years. As he stood there lost in thought and battling his emotions, Desta felt no envy or ire for what he'd lacked at home; as so often before, he accepted the fate that dictated his lifepath, just like when he'd say "that's okay," when okay really meant he had no choice but to live the life he had been allotted.

"I've been so looking forward to meeting you!" Shae said, extending her hand to Desta.

"Me too," Desta said, shaking hers. He found himself wishing Shae had hugged and kissed him instead. Despite being content living with the Johnsons, he once again felt like an outsider in this family. He smiled with clamped lips and reined in his feelings.

Shae smiled from her even, white teeth to her eyes, and *probably with her heart too,* Desta thought. He liked Shae; she was natural and unpretentious.

"I heard that you're quite a runner and won the nationals," Shae said. Her eyes held Desta's with reverence.

"No, not really," Desta said. "I just lucked out."

"He is too modest," Jake said, giving Desta a devilish grin.

"Can I take your suitcase to your new sleeping quarters?" Jake said. "Desta is now the proud occupant of your old room." He smiled.

"I'm glad somebody put it to good use," Shae said, her face still radiant. "I spent many good years there."

"Go ahead," Mrs. Johnson said to Jake. "I think she won't mind having a warm meal, too."

"The fire looks heavenly," Shae said, glancing at the golden flames. She took off her coat and gloves and asked if her brother minded hanging it in the coat closet. Jake complied and returned to the room.

Mrs. Johnson's eyes brightened. "I have a better idea. Leave Shae's luggage for now. Jake and Aida, please bring here the long folding table and six chairs, and let's have hot soup by the fire."

"I can help," Desta said.

"That's all right, Desta," Mrs. Johnson said. "Aida knows the door code, and which chairs to bring."

The two siblings headed off, leaving the four others standing at the ready near the plush leather sofas.

Mrs. Johnson regarded her daughter. "You look very fit, darling,"

Shae tossed her head, whipped her long sandy hair, and said, "Just five pounds, mother."

"It's becoming."

"Do you exercise, or is it the rigor of academics?" Mr. Johnson asked, taking in his daughter from head to toe.

"I work out at the gym."

Jake and Aida set down the table and chairs between a sofa and the Christmas tree, across from the righthand wall. Jake and Aida chuckled, humored by the unexpected activity. Mr. Johnson and Shae seemed keen for the improvised arrangement.

"This is rather crazy," Mr. Johnson said, not hiding his enthusiasm. "We could have made a fire in the family room and eaten at the table in the adjoining kitchen."

"Skip," Mrs. Johnson sang, her face turning to her husband. "It's fun to seize the moment. Sometimes, the nicest experiences in life are those we don't plan."

"Like our first kiss," Mr. Johnson said, almost in a whisper. He grinned broadly.

Busy popping the table legs, Jake said, "Let's find out how much fun this will be."

"Mr. Cynic!" Aida interjected. "I think mother's right."

Elsa stood at the door, surveying the commotion in the living room. On seeing her, Mrs. Johnson said, "Elsa dear, please bring in the soup, but first fetch a tablecloth and six napkins."

Desta grabbed the end of the open table opposite Jake and helped him center it on the floor. Elsa returned with the tablecloth, snapped it, spread it across the table, and the boys then positioned the six folding chairs around it.

"Well!" Shae said, "I feel like a statue. Can I do something?"

"You have steady hands," Mrs. Johnson said. "Help Elsa with the soup bowls."

Shae and Elsa hugged, kissed, and had warm words before heading to the kitchen. They soon returned with steaming bowls of lentil soup on trays, with napkins, spoons, and a basket of crackers.

They set them down one at a time at each place setting. Shae stood with the others, waiting for a signal from her parents. The aroma of curry and cumin filled the air and brought Desta memories of home.

"Smells very good . . . Let's sit," Mr. Johnson said, pulling a chair from the end of the long table, and everyone else sat down around him.

"This is the soup our Indian housekeeper prepared when we lived in India," Mrs. Johnson said wistfully.

"Let's see how it tastes," Jake said, dipping the tip of his spoon into the rich, yellow-brown liquid.

Shae beat Jake to it. "This is delicious," she said. "Good and hot, and spicy hot, too," she said. "The kind I like."

"Good choice for a cold day," Mr. Johnson said. He looked at Desta. "Are your foods spicy?"

"Very much," Desta replied. "Ours can be spicier than this."

"What's in it, Mom?" Shae asked. "I don't think you ever made this before."

"I got it from my old English cookbook," Mrs. Johnson replied. "The main ingredients are brown lentils, white onion, garlic cloves, and carrots. The enhancers: ground cumin, curry powder, thyme, and olive oil. I'll give you the recipe."

Everyone seemed ravenous. Hands shuttled effortlessly between bowl and mouth, faces masks of contentment. Metal and porcelain occasionally clinked. The younger siblings and Desta sprinkled crackers in their soup and ate the mushy mixture, while Shae and her parents crunched the crackers in their mouths before chasing them with soup.

Mrs. Johnson glanced at Jake's empty bowl. "Save room for the second course. We're having smoked salmon and cream cheese sandwiches and, of course, English tea."

"Oh, good," Jake blurted, his eyes lighting up. "One of my favorites."

Others, mouths still occupied, acknowledged the news with nods.

Moments later, Elsa came to ask if she should bring the sandwiches.

"Give us ten minutes," Mrs. Johnson said.

Aida finished and rose, collected the bowls and spoons in two stacks, and brought them to the kitchen.

In a few minutes, Elsa came with a big tray of six white plates containing open sandwiches on each—rye bread covered with cream cheese and dill, topped with slices of blushing pink meat.

Aida distributed the plates to the diners and went back to the kitchen, returning with six glass cups brimming with hot tea on a tray and passed them around.

Desta, unsure of the type of meat atop his sandwich, stared at it.

"Is that all?" Mrs. Johnson asked Desta. "This is our last meal of the day."

He wondered if the meat might be bacon, but it didn't smell like it. He gathered his courage and asked, "What kind of meat is this?"

"That's fish—called salmon," Mrs. Johnson said.

This looked nothing like the fish Desta knew, which was gray, with lots of bones. He felt better. "Thank you, I can eat fish," Desta told his host mother, and then had a bite. The fish's smoky flavor reminded him of *quanta*—smoked beef jerky he used to eat at home.

Everyone else tucked into their sandwiches too. Observing Mrs. Johnson's cardinal rule, everyone ate quietly, glancing at one another or looking away as thoughts filtered through their heads. They sipped tea occasionally, although Desta found it odd to drink it with a fish sandwich, being used to biscuits and bread with his tea.

When the group had nearly finished, Elsa came in, and Mrs. Johnson asked her to clear the table. Elsa gathered the remains of dinner while the group continued sitting and chatted.

Shae gave news of the success of her college women's lacrosse team. She also spoke of a Mr. Reed, his wife, and their son Jason, family friends who had come to Princeton the previous weekend to check out the school for their son. Everyone but Desta chipped into the conversation; he felt shy to speak on an unfamiliar subject.

"Shae, are you still thinking of driving to Vermont with your boyfriend?" Mrs. Johnson asked.

"The plan is," Shae began, "Nash will pick me up tomorrow, drive to the city to visit his aunt, and on Wednesday we'll head to his parents' winter place in Belleayre Mountain. Then Thursday we'll drive to our cabin in Deer Meadows."

Aida groaned. Jake stiffened his lips. The parents were expressionless.

"Sorry," Shae said. "Aunt Bella really wants to meet me, and Nash had promised to bring me this Christmas break—only for a couple of days."

"That's fine darling," Mrs. Johnson said. "Honor the woman's wishes."

The flames in the fireplace had long gone. Only the butts of two logs remained. White ash crusted like fallen snow protruded from the burnt end of one. A tendril of gray smoke rose from the other and vanished through the chimney flue.

Jake must have noticed it, too. He got up and stoked the fire with more logs from the side pile.

Afterward, Mr. Johnson thanked his wife for the meal, got up and went to his couch and newspaper. Mrs. Johnson retreated to the kitchen, and Jake and Aida to their Christmas tree.

"How are you doing in school?" Shae asked Desta. "Being on a competitive sports team and taking a full course load is not easy."

"No, it's not," Desta rejoined. "I've maintained good grades in most of my courses. I'm hopeful I will do better in finals now that I've extra time to study."

"What do you want to become?"

"After I meet my personal goals, I'd like to be a medical doctor."

"Yes," Shae said rather thoughtfully. "I heard from Jake about your aborted plans in Bulgaria. It sounds like you have the aptitude to become a doctor here."

"It's one of my goals."

"Jake said that you'd like to transfer to Princeton," Shae said. "I don't know all the rules for transferring, but it might be a good idea for you and Jake to come to Princeton and talk to people at the admissions office."

"I'll talk to him," Desta said. "Thanks for your suggestion."

"I need to go up to my room," Shae said, rising. "You and I can talk more about it."

Desta thanked Shae, rose and walked over to where Jake and Aida were busy decorating the Christmas tree with what looked like a thousand glittering trinkets and a network of vines, turning the green fir into a gaudy display of those objects.

"What next?" Desta asked, seeing both admiring their project. They gathered the unused decorations into three boxes and set them aside.

"You'll see in a minute," Aida said, with a bright smile.

Jake drew out an electrical cord from under the tree and fingered the switch along the cord. He looked at his sister and Desta and said, "Readyyy?"

Aida's eyes fixed on the tree for the thrilling moment.

"Yesss," Desta said. "Let's see it."

"Trrruuum!" Jake sang and pressed the switch. In an instant, the excitement evaporated from his face. "What happened?"

"I don't know," Aida said. "Let's check all the connections." She got up and looked around the tree, starting from the top, for any missed links, but everything was properly attached.

"See if it's plugged in," Jake said, baffled.

"Yaaaa," Aida cried. "It was not put in all the way."

With Jake's second attempt, the tree instantly glowed as if studded with diamonds. Aida clapped, and so did Jake and Desta.

"Hurray!" all shouted.

Mr. Johnson lifted his face from his newspaper and glanced at the children. He put down his *Wall Street Journal,* came over, and said, "I'm glad to see you three having a good time," he said.

"Fixing up the tree is always fun," Jake said.

"It's too bad we don't open our Christmas gifts here by the fire, under this tree every year. Of course, we'll do that at the cabin in Vermont, as usual." Mr. Johnson said.

"I know," Jake said. "But we'll still have this tree to enjoy for the rest of the month after we return next weekend. I'm sure Joe will have a tree set up for us at the cabin, although it won't be as grand as this one."

"We should plan to leave early tomorrow morning," Mr. Johnson added. He asked Desta if his family put up a tree for Christmas. Desta replied that they don't celebrate the holiday with trees, and that pine trees don't grow in Ethiopia. The father said goodnight and left. Desta thanked Jake and Aida for letting him help set up the tree, and then followed suit.

That evening, as he lay in bed, Desta reflected on the different Christmas rituals at home and in America. In Ethiopia, people kill cows; here, people cut down and decorate pine trees with glittering ornaments. On the holiday, Americans exchanged gifts. He hoped no one would give him any, as he had no money to buy presents for them, and he wouldn't know what to buy for this family, even if he could. He sighed deeply. He covered his face and let sleep free him from his disquiet.

THIRTY

It was Tuesday, the day after college exams ended, three days before Christmas, and the start of the family's holiday vacation. Desta slept deeply until 8 a.m. He was content with the few weeks of freedom he'd now have.

Desta looked forward to his first American Christmas—the first Christmas he'd be happy to celebrate. At home, his family had marked Coptic Christian Christmas on January 7th, the day Desta was born. But they had never celebrated his birthday, and Desta had always felt left out.

The Johnson family had debated where to spend Christmas—at home, their summer place at Hyannis Port on the Atlantic Coast of Massachusetts, or their winter cabin in Deer Meadow, Vermont. Aida and Jake had described the Hyannis home's grand ocean views from all over the house, and Desta had his sights set on going there. But the night before their departure he learned, to his disappointment, the family would be in Vermont instead.

The Johnsons said the drive took four hours, and that they wanted to leave at ten a.m. to beat a forecasted late-day snowstorm.

"What's wrong?" Aida asked when she saw Desta.

"I was so looking forward to seeing the Hyannis house."

"The Deer Meadow cabin will be lots more fun," Aida said, her face sunny with happiness. "We can go skiing, tobogganing, and snowboarding, and of course, have snowball fights." Desta knew only about snowball fights, and he was resigned to discover the others for himself.

In two separate trips, Jake and Desta brought out boxes full of groceries Elsa and Mrs. Johnson had purchased the day before, and two large cartons of Christmas gifts, and set them down near the garage. Returning, they lugged suitcases, and Desta brought out a new pair of boots.

When all were ready to depart, Mr. Johnson backed the beautiful maroon Jeep Super Wagoneer out of the garage. Jake said it was a year old, but it looked brand new. Mr. Johnson unlocked the station wagon, revealing a leather-clad maroon interior with gold trim.

The seatbacks shined. Jake and Desta loaded the trunk, layering suitcases and duffle bags on one side and the cartons on the other. Jake flattened the duffle bags so Mr. Johnson could see out of his rear-view mirror.

Desta walked around the immaculate machine, admiring it. Although this car sat higher, the front reminded him of the Volga, a Russian car Desta knew from his town in Ethiopia. That car galloped down the drive. Desta could sense the contained energy in the Wagoneer too. And he was eager to feel its thrust once they hit the highway.

They all hugged Elsa, who was spending Christmas with her family in the Bronx. Then all boarded the Wagoneer, parents in the front and the three youngsters in the back, Aida in the middle.

Desta couldn't believe his eyes. The car was spotless; Desta recalled Jake saying it had sat in the garage since they bought it. Mr. Johnson brought the engine to life and let it warm for a few minutes. It purred with Mr. Johnson's foot on the brake. Once they exited, the gate closed and locked, but Jake had to get out of the car and put the padlock on the side entrance.

Mr. Johnson eased the vehicle down the driveway and to the street. He turned right at Boston Post Road, and soon got onto highway I-95. The Wagoneer now came to life and seemed to gallop like a bridled horse.

The three in the back were quiet and observant. Desta, hand gently caressing the leather seat, kept his eyes on the snow-washed world outside. He thought about the mysterious journey that had brought him from Ethiopia to Rye to live with the Johnson family, and now on a journey to spend his first Christmas in a remote, mountainous place. He tightened his lips and gazed out as he thought about the ironies and mysteries of his life.

"Easy, darling, easy," Mrs. Johnson said to her husband.

"That's okay, Mom," Jake said. "Let's see how much this car can put out." He chuckled.

"Do you want him to get a ticket and ruin our day?" Mrs. Johnson replied. "This is the time the police are out, and they say red vehicles are pulled over the most."

In his dark glasses, Mr. Johnson looked at the dials on the panel before him and scanned the car's mirrors. "I'm watching out for them, sweetheart," he said. "I'm only going seventy-five miles an hour." He glanced and grinned at his wife.

"This is a fun car," Aida said.

"Why red, anyway?" Jake asked.

"Ask your mom," Mr. Johnson said. The morning sunlight brightened his face.

"Mom's reliving her romantic youth every time she gets in this car," Aida said.

Mrs. Johnson turned her head toward her daughter. "Look at the brood we got from those beginnings," she said, smiling. "But really, red is a cheerful, lively color that I've always loved."

"Cheerful and lively?" Aida asked. "I'll remember that." She chuckled.

"Me, too," Jake chimed in and smiled.

"And she leaves all the responsibilities of this car to me," Mr. Johnson said, "including getting a speeding ticket. I drive it more than she does." He didn't smile.

He pressed a button and a staticky, low voice came through the car speakers. "Did you hear that?" Mr. Johnson asked. "The North Tower of the World Trade Center is now the tallest building in the world."

"What else are we famous for?" Mrs. Johnson said indifferently.

"Making red cars," Aida said, snickering.

Mr. Johnson cranked the volume. "Another record," the man on the radio said. "Agatha Christie's Mousetrap is now in its 7,511th performance."

Desta turned to Jake. "Who is Agatha Christie?"

"A famous author."

The idea of being recognized for one's accomplishments appealed to Desta; he loved it when the crowd came to watch him when he flew on his self-built craft seven year ago, and when he won the national cross-country championship last month.

"Maybe," he said, "after I find that second coin and become a doctor, I will be a writer."

It seemed like a crazy notion when he couldn't write a decent term paper. He looked out of the window. Road signs rushed away, and the white world moved like windswept clouds. Desta was enjoying himself, new ideas in his head, bright warm sunlight tickling his back, and a car that rocked him gently like a cradle.

After nearly an hour, they left I-95 for I-91 North. The radio continued its chatter, but nobody was listening. Mrs. Johnson occasionally said, "Watch it, darling."

"Since we'll be on this road for a while, let's have some music," Mrs. Johnson said.

"Let's listen to one of our 8-track tapes," the driver suggested.

A few scratchy sounds ushered in a melodic guitar, and smooth, liquid voices poured out, the instruments pausing slightly at the transitions. And then the song's lines, cryptic and layered with meaning about teaching one's children and doing the same to one's parents too.

Desta felt he was one with the guitar, the voices, and the lyrics, floating on air. He turned to Jake. "Who are the singers?"

"Crosby, Stills, Nash, & Young," he said. "They are famous anti-establishment artists who are unhappy about the social and political situation in America."

Desta didn't immediately grasp the messages in the words or even Jake's response, but the music's allusions to family and journeys and farewells sent ripples of emotion through him. He gazed out the car window, thinking about those lines and references to father and son.

Desta remembered the beatings he had endured from his father and brother. He bit his lip and clenched his teeth, eyes glazed with feeling. The lyric about dreams and choices one can make helped ease his pent-up sentiments.

His father had dreamt of a son who would make him proud as an accomplished farmer, but his grandfather's spirit had tasked him to find the second coin, sending him on this worldwide adventure.

When the song ended everyone was quiet, as if the music had entranced them. Jake and Aida sat back and closed their eyes. Desta crossed his arms and legs and stared into space out his window. He thought about the unpredictable consequences of a life in motion. From hardship and constantly moving forward, he'd found opportunities that brought him thousands of miles from home, traveling with the Johnsons to celebrate Christmas in Vermont.

A weather forecast came over the radio. "Looks like we beat the snowstorm by a couple of hours," Mr. Johnson said. "They're expecting two feet of snow tonight and three tomorrow." They had just passed the village of Deer Meadow and were climbing the hill toward the cabin.

"That was the plan, wasn't it?" Mrs. Johnson said.

"Weather forecasters don't always get it right," Mr. Johnson replied.

THE CABIN WAS NOT the pigeonhole Desta imagined, but a three-bedroom, two-bath house built from stained logs that covered the walls and ceiling. It sat on a hill overlooking the snow-swathed town of Deer Meadow. A garage had been converted into a recreation room and guest quarters. They unloaded the Wagoneer and brought their belongings into the recreation room, and Desta and Jake carried the food to the kitchen. The cabin was cold, and Desta warmed his hands with his breath as he walked around checking it out.

The spacious living room had wood paneling, and housed a chimney and fireplace on one side, and three tall, expansive windows on the other. Farther to the right stood a walnut dining table with eight chairs. A five-foot tall, freshly cut tree stood, anchored to a circular metal pedestal that sat on a square green cloth, all done by the caretaker, Jake said. The kitchen and dining nook were behind the facing wall. A staircase near the recreation room entrance led to sleeping quarters above.

Mr. Johnson turned up the heat and lit the logs and kindling already laid in the fireplace. Mrs. Johnson and Aida opened the curtains, and they made hot chocolate and toast while Desta and Jake hauled the rest of their things in from the recreation room.

The house was spotless and smelled of lemon and bleach, but soon enough, Desta detected the pleasing scent of burning wood, and food in the kitchen. He peered through the large windows at the hilltop setting and felt the fire's warmth. Anticipation, ease, and joy for the holiday filled him.

"Everybody ready for hot drinks, toast with marmalade, and crackers and cheese?" Mrs. Johnson called out from the kitchen. For a moment, Desta was back in eighth grade, hearing a swarthy, frog-eyed classmate in fancy clothes tell the class about the marmalade on toast and black tea he'd been served at an elite British school in Addis Ababa when he went to take an entrance exam.

They drank and ate around the long walnut table as they chattered, breaking Mrs. Johnson's cardinal rule against talking and eating. Afterward, they all rose and cleared the table. Mrs. Johnson and Aida started preparing dinner. Desta and Jake brought boxes of Christmas decorations from the recreation room to the living room. They hung all the ornaments on the tree and arranged the gifts around it. Mr. Johnson got more firewood from the reaction room and piled it neatly on the granite slab fronting the hearth, and then went upstairs. Jake got his suitcase and went upstairs with it.

Desta stood at the window and took in the view. The air looked pale above the patches of snow where the feeble rays of sun lingered on the eastern hills, above a sickle-shaped river. Desta recalled as a little boy he'd stay outside at sunset, enveloped by the shadow of the mountain above his home, and watched the sun's golden drape climb the facing mountain until it vanished from his world. A wave of melancholy passed through him. He blinked and tossed his head to hold back tears.

The first words from Mrs. Johnson's tape played in Desta's head: about the journey, rules families play by, and becoming one's true self as one breaks with the past.

His eyes brimmed, remembering those precious moments of boyhood. He wiped his tears with the back of his hand and panned his eyes over the lovely, sleepy village that spread over the valley floor like a patch grain field, studying places he couldn't quite make out.

"Enjoying the view?" Mr. Johnson asked, startling Desta.

"I am," Desta said, stiffening his shoulders. Mr. Johnson stood next to him.

"What is that river called?" Desta asked. "It reminds me of the one below my parents' property. And it's shaped like a tool my family used during the harvest."

"Aha, the scythe!" Mr. Johnson said his family had once been farmers and knew about such things. "That river is called Ottauquechee."

Desta squinted. "Pardon?"

"Awtah . . . KWEE . . . chee! An American Indian name."

"Interesting!" Desta repeated the name slowly to emphasize the right part of the word. "This area is rather mountainous. Why the name 'Deer Meadow?'" he asked.

"When our English ancestors came, the valley was covered in meadows full of white-tailed deer. So, they called it 'Deer Meadow.' Lawrence Feldman Stone, the grandson of a prominent American family, invested a lot of money to make it look as we see it today."

A strange, meaningless, warm sensation passed through Desta.

"One of my classmates is a Stone," Desta said.

Desta had never heard of the man and didn't know what to make of him. He paused to think of a reply more sensible than *that was interesting* or *how nice of him.*

Mr. Johnson grabbed the binoculars from the credenza near the window and looked through them as he adjusted the focusing dial.

"Here," Mr. Johnson said, handing them to Desta. "Look through the lenses and see if you can find a large white building on the left edge of town."

Desta played with the dial for a bit and found it.

"That's the Stones' Hotel," Mr. Johnson said, and took the device from Desta. When we go to town on Thursday, we'll stop there and see Mr. and Mrs. Stone. They want to meet you."

The revelation jolted Desta. *Interested in meeting me?* He held his breath. Mr. Johnson scanned the valley with the binoculars as if trying to locate something he had just remembered.

"Who are they?" Desta asked finally.

"Old family friends who read about your championship in the papers." Mr. Johnson replied. "With our busy schedule back home, there was no time to meet before this week."

"I see," Desta said, mind spinning. Questions filled his head. *Did someone mention to them something about coins?* As much as he wanted to ask more about the Stones and their invitation, he held his tongue.

"They also live in New York, but have homes all over the place," Mr. Johnson added, as if answering Desta's unspoken question.

"I have nothing to say just now, Mr. Johnson," Desta said, "but I certainly look forward to meeting and learning more about your friends."

"*That* you will," Mr. Johnson said, heightening Desta's curiosity even more.

Jake saved him from any more talk of the matter. "Desta, do you want to come upstairs?" he said, standing at the top landing.

"Well, Mr. Johnson," Desta said, rubbing his chin. "I guess we can talk more another time."

"We will!" he said, still looking through the binoculars.

"See you later," Desta said, and ran up the stairs.

Jake led Desta through an open door. "This is our room," he said. Two beds sat on opposite sides of the room, with a nightstand and window between them. The space was unconventional; the ceiling dropped sharply, making the outside wall considerably shorter than the others.

"I just hung all my clothes in the closet," Jake said. "We need to wear our nice shirts and trousers for dinner on Christmas day. You might want to do the same with yours to get the wrinkles out."

"Okay," Desta said.

He retrieved his suitcase from downstairs and hung his clothes alongside Jake's. Soon, they went down for dinner: chicken, rice, salad with croutons, and sliced bread and cream cheese. "It's a simple meal, but there's plenty," Mrs. Johnson said apologetically.

"Considering we just arrived," Mr. Johnson said, "this is fine. Thank you, honey." He grinned.

After dinner, Aida cleared and cleaned the table. Desta and Jake rinsed and loaded dishes into the dishwasher and cleaned up the counter. Mrs. Johnson made tea, and her daughter served it in white cups with sugar and milk.

Jake sipped his tea and asked, "How about a card game?"

"Let's play pinochle!" Aida said.

"No, darling," Mrs. Johnson said. "We have a lot to do in the kitchen."

Mr. Johnson glanced at his watch, "Ohh!" he said suddenly. "My show starts in five minutes." He walked to the living room, turned on the TV, and sat down on the sofa.

"Desta, would you like to see the show with me?" Mr. Johnson said. "I've never seen you watch TV." On the screen, staticky zig-zag lines gave way to a blurry scene that slowly grew clearer.

"I know," Desta said, coming to the living room. "With school and cross-country practice, I never had time."

"This is your vacation. . . . relax and enjoy yourself. Before you sit, please stoke the fire with a few more logs," Mr. Johnson said.

Desta did as requested and sat on a chair next to his host before the screen of the big, boxy TV.

"The reception is not great here," Mr. Johnson said apologetically. "But you can still appreciate the program."

A dark-haired young man was training to become an insurance salesman. As the story unfolded, Desta learned that the man had epilepsy, and had once aspired to be a teacher. But he'd had seizures and collapsed at his first high school class, terrifying his students, and he'd abandoned his career.

Outside of school, the man had befriended a black student-athlete who hoped to become a sportswriter. The dark-haired man had helped the athlete with his English and continued to tutor him after he'd left teaching.

Dr. Welby had referred the salesman to a specialist, but he'd refused to go, fearing his condition would be reported to the authorities, and he would lose his driver's license. The man had hidden his condition from everyone, including his wife and the student-athlete. But the disease affected his new job, and then one day he collapsed in front of the student and other people, who showed empathy for his situation. This finally motivated him to get medical help, and he was able to control his disease and return to teaching.

"Did you like it?" Mr. Johnson asked, expectantly.

"It's a touching story," Desta said, "particularly the people's relationships."

"Yes," Mr. Johnson said. "The kind we all should have in our daily lives. . . . It's a popular show that addresses many interesting medical cases."

"You know," Desta paused, "As you may be aware I dream of becoming a doctor one day, and I liked the medical aspect of the story."

"I know what you mean," Mr. Johnson said. "I once aspired to become a doctor myself, but somehow, I became a banker instead."

"You know," Desta began, "I kept wondering if Dr. Welby might be your twin. You have identical white patches around your temples, kind faces and warm smiles."

"Well, Desta!" Mr. Johnson said, smiling broadly. "That means I missed my calling as an actor!" He chuckled. "Now, what would you like as a Christmas gift?"

"I have no ulterior motives," Desta said, and grinned. "I'm just stating the facts."

"All right," Mr. Johnson said, getting up. "Thank you. We need to go to bed now. . . . try to watch the show when you get a chance. It's on this time every week." Mr. Johnson checked on his wife and daughter, still busy in the kitchen, and Desta went upstairs to bed.

THIRTY-ONE

By the time Desta hit the bottom of the bumpy slope, he was out of breath as if he had just stopped running at top speed. He sat on a platform made of three joined, parallel boards atop a pair of runners, and held a rope tied to the front. But he couldn't control where he was going, and the sled turned, spinning Desta out like a discus. Aida, Jake, and Kooper rushed toward him.

"Are you all right?" Jake asked. Kooper sniffed him.

"The ride knocked the wind out of me," Desta said. "I'm otherwise OK." He rose and brushed the snow off his clothes.

"That's part of the thrill," Jake said. "You got to get used to it."

"Let's go up again," Aida suggested, and led the way up the hill, shuffling and dragging her red sled behind her, Jake following.

Desta liked sledding, but he also found it scary. Was it because he might crash, break a bone, or worse? He had watched Jake and Aida fly downhill and land safely on their sleds at the bottom, snug against the snow pile. When Desta had gone, gravity was in control, not him, which he realized was part of the scare *and* thrill.

He needed to give it a second chance. He followed Jake and his sister to the top of the hill. Jake laid on his belly on his green sled. He spread his arms like wings, and glided downhill with such force that when he folded his arms right before the bottom, his head shot through the snow pile like a torpedo, raising a plume of snow dust. Aida went next, but rode sitting. Desta was tempted to copy Jake, but he'd first need to know that his friend came out unhurt. Desta's second seated run was more fun, and the bumps less noticeable, but he had not expected Aida to pelt him with snowballs, which she clearly enjoyed, giggling merrily.

Jake came to Desta's defense and a snowball war broke out between the siblings while Desta stood by and caught his breath. Kooper, agitated and deferential to Jake, barked at Aida every time she threw a ball at him. The siblings finally called a truce, and all three, accompanied by Kooper, walked up the hill. This time, Desta went down the hill on his belly, and ended up slamming his forehead into the hardened snow, bruising himself.

Again, Kooper ran behind them and rolled in the snow like his human mates. They did two more runs before heading home, exhausted and hungry, but promising each other a snowball fight in the afternoon.

During lunch, the three of them decided that Desta and Jake would fight, and Aida would be the judge. The contest would be at two pm on the plateau behind the house, and the opponents would make their snowballs ahead of the game.

"First, the rules," Jake said. "Each of us makes ten balls in advance, and we use them until none are left. The guy who takes the most hits loses. There will be a twenty-five-yard no-man's-land between us. No hitting if one of us falls, or when we need to go get more balls from our bags."

"In other words," Aida interjected, eying Desta. "Suppose you hit Jake while he's on the ground or getting more balls—you lose a point for breaking the rule."

Jake said, "Also, you lose a point when you step on the boundary line or enter the neutral zone; one point on the first offense, and two on the second."

Aida continued. "When you get hit, you miss your turn. The other guy keeps throwing snowballs until he misses."

Jake and Desta each went outside with a plastic bag to make snowballs, while Aida retreated to the kitchen to help her mother.

Desta made his snowballs the size of an apple, digging them up from deep in the snow to make them more compact, Jake had advised. After Desta finished, he put his stash in his bag and buried it in the snow, marking the spot with a stick. Jake did his own.

Lastly, the two returned to the recreation room, collected strings and four sticks, and went to the plateau. They planted the two sticks fifty yards apart, east-west direction on the playing field, and strung a line between them, low to the ground. Twenty-five yards beyond this line, they planted the next pair of sticks parallel to the first, and spanned them with a string, too. They then went into their room to rest.

At two o'clock, the rivals with their bags of snowballs appeared on the battlefield before their judge. Jake brought a small aluminum folding ladder for Aida to stand on to referee the game.

Jake took the south side of the first marked line and Desta the north side of the second. Aida set up the ladder halfway down the edge of the twenty-five-yard neutral zone. Each player emptied their bag, flattened it, and placed their snowballs on top.

At Aida's count of three, the fight began. Jake's volley shot toward Desta, but he ducked, and it missed his head by inches, landing on the mound behind him nearly intact. When his turn came, Desta danced around and shot his ball at Jake, missing him by several feet. Jake had watched Desta's eyes and swiftly gotten out of the targeted spot, a lesson for Desta. When his opponent's turn came, Desta watched Jake's eyes and dodged his throw too fast, tripping and falling, drawing a hearty laugh from Aida.

Desta rose quickly and positioned himself near his ammunition. He picked up the second ball and stood, one foot forward, body leaning back; he moved the hand that held the ball three times in a fake attempt. Then he threw the ball and grazed Jake's arm, but it wasn't judged a hit.

Jake's third try was a success; he got Desta squarely on his back.

"You violated the line rule, Jake," Aida said, coming over to check. Jake had stepped on the line to the neutral zone, and Desta, by default, got the point. In the fourth round, both missed their shots, and in the fifth, Desta hit Jake on the arm as he shielded his face. On the sixth volley, Jake scored, and then again on the seventh because Desta was out of bounds. For the last three rounds, each scored a point, finishing in a tie, which was good enough for both.

Aida shook each player's hand. "You guys were a lot of fun to watch," she said. "What a way to spend an afternoon!"

"Desta, you impressed me," Jake said. "For your first time, you did great."

Desta didn't know if Jake's comment was the truth or mere flattery, but he thanked him, and said, "I appreciate that." All three went inside to the kitchen.

"Your father and I were watching you through our bedroom window," Mrs. Johnson said. "Desta is quite an athlete."

"Thank you, Mrs. Johnson," Desta said. "I had fun."

Mrs. Johnson brought them hot chocolate and a tray of cookies from a box that said *Bahlsen Leibniz Butter Biscuits*. The drink and cookies tasted heavenly.

"When is Shae coming?" Jake asked his mother.

"She said she would arrive tomorrow afternoon. She wanted to spend some time with her boyfriend and family for a few days. Nash was going to Europe for the rest of Christmas break."

"I just wish she'd seen our snowball fight," Jake said, turning to Desta with a smile.

"You'll have plenty of time this Christmas break to showcase your talent." Mrs. Johnson grinned and went to the kitchen.

Desta went upstairs and took a shower. The hot water was the most fabulous balm for his body, mind, and spirit. That night as he lay in bed, he reflected on his first snowball fight, and how well he was adapting to his American life.

He wished he could write to his family about this and so many things he'd experienced in America. But his family lived far from a post office, and he knew no one who could convey a letter to them. Desta decided he would share his thoughts with the only one who could receive his messages: his guardian and guide, the High Priest of the Ark. Desta pressed a hand over his chest, and soon after, he fell asleep.

As usual, at 4 o'clock, he woke up and remembered what he must do. He brought out the magic wand from the closet and sat on his bed with his legs folded and crossed, the device in the cavity before him, all the 9s facing up.

Dear Honorable Tsadok, High Priest of the Ark,

I apologize that you have not had tidings from me lately. Here are the things I've seen and done since my last message to you.

Near the end of November, I celebrated a Thanksgiving holiday— a family and food affair—where the main course was a large bird they call a turkey, the size of three chickens. The meat was delectable. The people, mainly family, were genial and accepting of me. I had a rather pleasant time at this dinner.

After the holiday, I focused on my studies and my science projects, which concluded with my final exams on Monday this week.

We arrived three days ago at the Johnsons' vacation home in northeastern America, in the state of Vermont. The area is mountainous, just like my birthplace, and being winter, it's covered with snow. We are here to relax for a week. Today we children slid on boards in the snow and compacted it into balls that we threw at each other in a mock fight.

I still need to begin searching for the second coin. I plan to do so during my long summer break.

Please send a reassuring message somehow to my family about my situation so they will know that all is okay with me.

By the way, have you seen or heard from Eleni?

Hope to hear from you soon.

Yours, Desta Abraham.

After Desta sent the message, he went to sleep and woke at 7 a.m. to find Tsadok's response.

Dear Desta,

I'm pleased to hear you have continued to adapt and do well in America. Because of your challenging upbringing here, I worried that it might be hard for you to open up to strangers. It appears my worries were for nothing.

You wondered whether I know what's going on with you from where I am. Yes, sometimes I get clear messages; other times, it's vague and chaotic, so I had to wait until I heard from you to learn how you are.

Regarding your search for that coin, do it when time allows. For now, focus on securing your future studies and living situation. Watch for signs from your shekel and the magic wand when to start looking for the missing coin.

No, I've not heard from or seen Eleni for some time. It appears that she and her faction's interest in you was only for your coin. Now that you and your shekel are out of reach, she disappeared.

Let me hear from you again when you can.

The best to you in all your endeavors.

Yours, Tsadok.

THIRTY-TWO

No one had expected what awaited them when they woke on Thursday morning. Except for Desta, nearly all slept in until mid-morning. Mrs. Johnson and Aida had stayed up until the wee hours preparing for Christmas.

When the family finally stirred, they flipped switches, turned knobs, and plugged in appliances, and all were dead, as if they had used up all the electricity and now had to wait for fresh supplies. Since they couldn't cook breakfast, the Johnsons decided to go to town instead.

They washed up and dressed—wool hats, heavy jackets, scarves, and gloves— and readied to go to town to eat and sightsee and shop for last-minute Christmas gifts.

All followed Mr. Johnson to the door. He had barely a foot across the threshold when he halted, as if barred by an invisible hand. Last night, they had watched the snow come down in violent gusts of wind. Now serene and lifeless, it was piled in dunes on the walk to the Jeep and the driveway. They'd need to shovel their way to the station wagon if they were going to get anywhere.

Jake dashed to the recreation room and returned with shovels and two pairs of boots. Father and son laced up, and shovels in hand, stepped outside and began scooping and tossing the white abundance into the yard, as the others watched from the living room window. Jake and his dad huffed and puffed, brows sweaty, and breathed clouds of steam like chimneys. Desta had never seen such a thing before.

Aida said, "It must be freezing out."

Mrs. Johnson scanned the tableau before them. "At least the sun is out," she said, "and it should warm up soon."

"I hope you're right, Mom," Aida said. "Once we get to town, we'll be walking the streets."

"I'll be in the kitchen," Mrs. Johnson said. "Let me know when they finish."

Desta and Aida stepped out and walked toward father and son, who had already cleared the walk, and were starting on the driveway.

"Can we help?" Desta asked.

Mr. Johnson stopped and regarded Desta hesitantly. "Sure," the man said, handing him the shovel. "Give it a try."

His host father's apprehension surprised Desta.

"But you need to wear the spare boots in the recreation room," Mr. Johnson said.

Desta went in and came out wearing boots. The father was back inside to change into warmer gloves. Jake continued to labor.

Holding his shovel, Desta stuck a hand inside his jacket and pressed the coin's image on his chest, quietly repeating: "Give me the power I need to do this job quickly."

Desta began to scoop and toss the snow. Mr. Johnson returned and began to clear the snow from the Jeep, and Aida relieved Jake and shoveled the driveway with Desta, while Jake scraped ice from the car's windshield.

To their astonishment, Desta and Aida had cleared the remaining driveway in fifteen minutes. Jake and Desta stowed the tools in the recreation room while Aida went in to fetch her mother. Mr. Johnson stomped the snow from his boots, started the Jeep, and let it warm. Once everyone else had boarded, they drove off.

Mr. Johnson stopped at the bottom of the hill and said, "Ahaa! There's the culprit for our power outage!" A giant tree had fallen across the power cable. The emergency crew was working furiously, some up on the pole, a few on the ground; one stood in a metal basket in the air where the cables were attached.

As the family drove along, they noticed more poles leaning, some on the verge of falling. More trees lay across wires, and a man was cutting the branches of one that had fallen on his driveway, his saw pulverizing the air with a whine.

"The problem is, there are way too many wires and poles in this town," Jake said.

"You've only just noticed?" Mrs. Johnson said, sounding surprised.

Jake said, "I didn't really notice them until today, if you know what I mean."

"That's the problem," Mr. Johnson said. "We're not in tune with our environment until we have a problem."

Aida was not going to be left out of this banter. She looked around and said, "There are so many wires and cables across poles and criss-crossing the sky, a spider couldn't spin a better web." She chuckled.

"What a vivid analogy, darling," Mrs. Johnson said. "The thing is, history dies hard in this town. People here like to leave things the way they are. That is the charm and beauty of it."

Desta turned to Jake. "What else could they have done with these wires?" he asked.

"Bury them underground, like in bigger towns."

"Speaking of history, charm, and beauty, if you're not too hungry, let's drive to some landmarks while we are still on the road," Mr. Johnson said.

"Good idea," all said.

"Let's see the covered bridges," Jake said. "They're Vermont's claim to fame."

After connecting to Deer Meadow Road, they drove along a route that followed the river's meandering course, passing homes all along the river. Desta couldn't help but think of the ancient Egyptians and Meso-potamians who settled along the banks of the Nile and Tigris and Euphrates rivers and made history.

"The people here built covered bridges to connect the population from one side of the river with the other," Mr. Johnson said.

They turned right and then swung slightly left, and came to Madi-sonville Covered Bridge Road, which passed right through a long wooden shed open at both ends. After clearing the one-lane deck, they parked, got out, and examined the old bridge.

A Christmas wreath with a red bow hung at the entrance. Dirty snow had piled on the edges of the road, and a fresh, white layer spread be-yond it. The sun brightened the snow, and the air paled in comparison.

They got in the Jeep and drove farther north for five minutes, then cut east and came to another open structure whose entrance gaped like a gi-ant fish. They parked near the entrance.

Slippery When Wet, a sign warned. The family watched their steps on the bridge.

The air was thick with the rush of a river and waterfall. They stopped to admire the bridge.

Joined upright boards, black and weathered, formed a tunnel. Inside, a pair of wooden post-and-beam trusses supported the roof that sheltered the long, solid planks of the wooden road under it.

"It's over a hundred thirty years old, and still standing," Mrs. Johnson said, coming close to Desta, who craned his neck and swiveled his head to admire the structure and watch for passing cars. The sibilance of the river, swollen with melting snow, competed with their conversation. Along the riverbanks and beyond, leafless trees like sticks made a beautiful, austere tableau.

"It's amazing that this simple structure has lasted so long," Desta said.

"Not all have made it," Mr. Johnson said. "There used to be hundreds of them. Many were washed away by floods or destroyed by other calamities."

Desta looked up at the sky over the long roof and saw cloud formations like those he'd seen at home. A white figure perched on a snowy horse in the clouds. Desta watched it, wondering if it might come down any moment or fly away. The same azure blue sky of his childhood framed the image. His eyes lingered as he made sense of the vision, and for a moment, he was back in the field below his childhood home, where he'd seen many images in the sky while shepherding his family's animals.

"Let's take some pictures," Mr. Johnson said, bringing Desta back to the moment. The man took his camera from its case, and they all gathered for several shots before the covered bridge.

They all got into the Jeep and headed to Deer Meadow town to see more covered bridges spanning the same Ottauquechee River.

They came to the Lincoln Covered Bridge. They had to park some distance away from it and walk. Steady traffic flowed through the wooden tunnel. An American flag hung high above the entrance.

To Desta, this structure, too, looked old with its weathered exterior and modesty.

"Its ingenious technology paved the way for modern steel bridges," Mr. Johnson said. "It has stood intact here since 1836."

"Are you enjoying yourself?" Mrs. Johnson said, glancing at Desta.

"I'm fascinated," Desta said.

"Let's go to the town center," the mother said. "We'll get something to eat, then walk around a bit to see more of the town before we go shopping."

"That sounds good, honey," Mr. Johnson said.

They returned to the Jeep and drove into the town.

"Breakfast has come and gone. Where are we going for lunch?" Aida asked.

The family debated their favorite eateries and settled on Bella's: lentil soup, salad, and pastrami sandwiches. They finished at quarter to two, and Mr. Johnson paid the bill and after agreeing with the mother and siblings to meet at four, he and Desta rose to go to their appointment with the Stones in their hotel.

Mrs. Johnson and the siblings would shop up the street from Bella's, while Desta and Mr. Johnson went to their friends' hotel two blocks away.

The hotel lobby enveloped guests in comfort and warmth. Flames from the hearth at the back wall and the cozy sofa chairs nearby were a welcome change from the cold outdoors.

Mr. Johnson greeted a young man at the reception desk. "We're here to see Lawrence and Meredith Stone," he said. "Could you please let them know?"

"We'll call them now," the man said, and left.

"You should know something," Mr. Johnson said to Desta. "The Stones funded your college expenses through the Catholic charity. Mrs. Stone is an active member."

"Is that so?" Desta said. "I can't wait to meet them."

"Yes!" Mr. Johnson said. He gazed at the fire, hands in his pockets.

Moments later, Desta looked up to find Lawrence and Meredith Stone had suddenly appeared before them like ghosts. Mr. Johnson took a step back.

"You didn't see us coming?" Mr. Stone asked. The couple knit their brows.

"No, at least I didn't," Mr. Johnson said, turning to Desta. "No matter— how are you?" Mr. Johnson shook hands with the Stones.

"And you're Desta, of course," Mr. Stone said, bending and offering his hand. "Pleasure to meet you finally."

"Me, too," Desta said, briefly regarding the man, surprised at his enthusiasm.

"How do you do?" Mrs. Stone asked, smiling warmly.

Desta smiled back. "I'm doing fine, thank you," Desta said.

"We've so looked forward to meeting you," she said.

"Me, too," Desta said, and studied her face. Her eyes, a darker shade of her gray hair, held Desta's. Her face, serene as a sleeping baby's, was fresh and glowing. She wore a tight-fitting red top, a beige calf-length skirt, and low-cut brown boots.

Desta had the strange feeling he'd met the Stones before, but he couldn't recall the time or place. He shook his head. This mystery and their sudden arrival made Desta wonder if the couple might indeed be ghosts.

But of course not. What was Desta thinking? It was just one of those occurrences he couldn't explain.

"Let's go sit at the hotel restaurant," Mrs. Stone said, gesturing toward the dining room. "We can hear more about Desta there."

"Most of the lunch crowd should be out shopping," Mr. Stone said. He wore a peach-colored wool V-neck sweater, a cream shirt. His slacks and shoes were the color of creamed coffee.

They entered the restaurant directly from the lobby, opposite the reception desk and past the hearth. The large dining room was nearly deserted. They walked to the far corner near a window, and sat, the Stones across from their visitors, the two men facing each other.

A woman of about thirty with shoulder-length blonde hair appeared and offered them menus, but Mr. Johnson quickly put out his hand and said, "We just ate lunch, thank you."

"A light one, Skip," Mrs. Stone insisted.

"I've no room even for a snack. Appreciate it just the same, Meredith. But order yours, and we'll keep you company."

"We ate not long ago too. We'll just have coffee," she said.

"I as well," Mr. Johnson said. Desta asked for tea. The young woman took their orders and left.

Mr. Stone appeared keen to speak with Desta. "We've heard about your accomplishments and are proud to play a small part in it. We read

about your national cross-country win in the *New York Times*. Congratulations!"

"Despite the torrential rain and taking a spill during the race. What a
marvelous story!" Mrs. Stone said.

"Thank you both," Desta said. "I was just lucky that day. I know
many better athletes than I."

"No matter, you still won the race," Mr. Johnson said. "Desta is an
extremely modest fellow. He doesn't take credit for all the hard work he
put his body through."

"Thank you, Mr. Johnson," Desta said and turned to the couple."
Mr. and Mrs. Stone, I recently learned that you had a key role getting
me here for college," he said. "I want to thank you so very much."

"We did very little," Mrs. Stone said, seemingly believing her words.
"Mr. and Mrs. Johnson take the lion's share of the credit." She looked
up and smiled at Desta's host.

"But your support made the Hartman's idea a reality," Mr. Johnson said.

"From all accounts, you were a deserving young man," Mr. Stone
said. "And from what you've done so far, you merited our help."

The waitress brought their hot drinks, and they all took a sip.

Mr. Johnson looked around and said, "You have done a beautiful job
with the remodeling."

"It's a historic hotel, and it needed some modernizing," Mr. Stone
said. "Places like this need to be preserved."

"It took a year after we purchased it," Mrs. Stone said.

The couple talked about similar projects they had done in the area
and elsewhere, to benefit local residents and visitors.

Desta studied the Stones for clues to where he might have met
them. But he got no hints from their smiles, eyes, the way they spoke,
or their presence.

He gave thought to why he had instantly liked them or had a warm
sensation in his heart when Mr. Jonson mentioned their name to him a
couple of days ago. The Stones appeared to be in their late fifties, and
had similar features, though Mrs. Stone was daintier. Their eyes were
soft and active as they talked, their noses sharp and similar, complemented by smooth, tapering faces framed by thick, dark brown hair.

Desta's eyes rested on Mrs. Stone, face and eyes steady as she listened to her husband and Mr. Johnson converse.

Desta didn't know what the Stones did for a living. Their clothes and demeanor did not show their work or wealth, nor was it clear from how they spoke or acted. They put on no airs, like some important people he'd encountered in America and Ethiopia.

By nature or intention, the Stones seemed not to define themselves by material success, or let it influence how they related to others.

Mr. Stone struck Desta as down-to-earth and a deep thinker. He revealed little of his emotions; his thoughts registered in contemplative, distant eyes. Sometimes he narrowed them as if not to reveal too much of his soul. When he finished talking, he clamped his lips like a lid on a pan, as if nothing should escape that he didn't want people to know. When charmed, the corners of his mouth pulled up, turning his face into a bemused Mona Lisa smile.

When others spoke, his head tilted slightly, which Desta took as humility. Mr. Stone struck him as a complex man—someone he'd like to get to know. Desta concluded that the couple's unaffected nature didn't reside in outward appearances, but someplace much deeper.

"What schools will you apply to after Lincoln?" Mr. Stone asked.

Desta named five, and finished by saying, "My first choice is Princeton."

"That's a great school," Mr. Stone said, smiling. "Just make sure you have good grades."

Mr. Stone asked if Desta had siblings and if they also aspired to come to America.

Desta explained that he had four brothers and two sisters, all married and living as farmers in the countryside. He said he would have done the same, but somehow his good fortune and timing had brought him to America.

"We have heard from David Hartman about your life journey," Mrs. Stone said. "What kept you going?"

Her direct, personal question caught Desta up short, and he struggled for an answer. "Well, Mrs. Stone," Desta began. "I myself don't know. It seems I was called to my journey to America so that our paths might cross and I would be here speaking with you now.

"How else to explain how the path here could start out from a remote valley of shadows? I was a shepherd boy, groomed to be a farmer. People call it fate or coincidence; some might say I'm a castaway, carried on the wind to a better country. You have made possible one more step forward in my life, and I'm grateful for the opportunity you and Mr. Stone have given me to be here."

"It's our mission to help individuals with a promising future. We are equally grateful that you trust us unquestioningly and have come into our circle of people who have enriched our lives.

"And I want to be clear that while we are proud of your cross-country success, we expect nothing in return for our help with your education," Mr. Stone said.

"Let's hope you do well in your courses so you can get into the school of your choice," Mrs. Stone said.

I've done the best I could. I will see what the future holds, Desta thought to say, but it seemed inadequate. Instead, he said, "Thank you so much. I plan to apply to a few schools that offer athletic scholarships. That's one reason I took up running."

Deep down, Desta still had difficulty believing that universities paid students to attend just because they were good athletes, particularly foreigners. But without other options, he needed to believe that his championship gave him that chance.

"We need to meet up with the family," Mr. Johnson said, turning to Desta.

"It was so wonderful to see you," Mrs. Stone said.

"Don't mention it," Mr. Johnson said, "I'm glad you could fit us into your busy holiday schedule."

All rose. They shook hands and wished each other a Merry Christmas and a Happy New Year.

As Desta and his host father headed to their car, Mr. Johnson said, "As I mentioned the other day, the Stones are old family friends. We go back three generations. They are big philanthropists in this country for religious charities, and for Black institutions. The family founded one of the earliest black colleges in the country. They are good people, and I'm glad they agreed to help you when David and I raised the idea to them last summer."

"They strike me as some of the kindest people I've met," Desta said.
I'm honored that you brought me here to meet them."

"There you are!" Mr. Johnson said.

Aida and Jake stood on Main Street near the Jeep. "We just stowed
our Christmas loot and were coming to the hotel for you."

"Well," Mr. Johnson said, a smile gathering on his lips. "We found
you instead."

"Let's show Desta how the town decks out for Christmas," Mrs.
Johnson said.

They walked south on Center Street between a snow barrier and a
row of old brown, grey, and white brick stores and houses. Christmas
lights were strung all along the way, twinkling like jewels in a crown.

Desta padded along with the group, taking it all in. The parents
looked at him expectantly, as if to ask, *Are you enjoying yourself?*

The genteel ease and coziness of the town were growing on Desta.
All through the day, he couldn't shake the sense that time had stopped
here. Rather than diminish it, time seemed to have only made this place
more vibrant and charming.

Their stroll brought them to the courthouse, which Mrs. Johnson said
was historic and fascinating. They walked around it, entered an old library, and browsed its books. Afterward, they listened to a choir in a
small white chapel behind a church that Mrs. Johnson likened to a doll-
house. From there they headed for the Jeep and drove home.

That evening, a young man came to the door with a large package
and handed it to Desta, which he said was sent by Mr. and Mrs. Stone to
wish the family a Merry Christmas. The man left, and Desta put the gift
under the tree.

Later that evening, Shae arrived, looking weary and haggard. Everyone hugged and kissed her, happy she'd arrived without any trouble on
the road.

"As it turned out we didn't leave the city until this morning," Shae
said, "Aunt Bella wouldn't let us leave yesterday. She had a wonderful
dinner and Christmas gifts for us, and we felt obliged to stay overnight.
We drove to Belleayre this morning where we spent a few hours with
his parents. Afterward, I drove Nash's car here."

"Glad to hear you had a good time with Nash's aunt and made it to these mountains without a hitch, Darling," Mrs. Johnson said.

Shae thanked her mother.

After dinner Mr. Johnson said, "With Shae in our fold, our family is now complete. Let's all look forward to a great Christmas celebration tomorrow."

THIRTY-THREE

At noon on Christmas day, Jake and Desta went to town and bought the family dinner from a caterer who prepared elaborate meals for wealthy vacationers. Beef was one thing on the menu that Desta knew from his own family tradition. On Christmas day in Ethiopia, his father brought home meat from a cow he and the neighbors had purchased and slaughtered.

Desta and Jake brought home three rib bones of roasted cow meat wrapped in aluminum foil and placed it like a crown on a large white plate. The rest of the feast comprised two large plastic jars of onion soup, sauteed mushrooms and minced onions in separate containers, and two bags of sliced sourdough bread.

Mrs. Johnson, Shae, and Aida excitedly examined the holiday bounty and put it in the oven to keep warm.

Desta and Jake found the table set and curtains drawn, daylight dazzling the glass and silverware on the table. Red wine in two dark green bottles stood at either end of the long log table. A pitcher of apple juice also sat on the table.

The aroma of baking dinner rolls filled the air, and holiday music welled up from the brown wood cabinet between the dining room and kitchen nook.

Mrs. Johnson and Shae came out of the kitchen. "Let's go change," the mother said to Shae and Aida, and all the three celebrants went upstairs, returning shortly in their holiday clothes. All wore clothes in hues of red, light green, beige and gold.

Everyone beamed, happy and eager. Jake stoked the fire, brought more wood from the recreation room and piled it neatly on the flagstone near the hearth.

Shae brought the foil-covered roasted meat and placed it in the middle of the table. Aida fetched the onion soup and baked rolls. Returning to the kitchen, Shae brought the sauteed mushrooms and sourdough bread and put them alongside the rest of the food.

The fire bristled fiercely, making the room warm as a summer's day, while outside was a sea of frosty white. To Desta, it all felt too good to be real.

Mrs. Johnson removed the aluminum shroud to reveal glistening, puffed-up meat attached to the ribs like standing racks. She sliced the beef with a slender knife and piled it on a large oval red platter, then covered the ribs again and set them aside.

Aida served the hot onion soup in green earthenware bowls, and the warm sourdough slices on separate plates. The basket of rolls was set aside for the main meal.

Everyone sat down. After Mrs. Johnson said the Lord's prayer, her husband said, "Let's have some Nat King Cole!" He went to the music cabinet and started up the record player, and then returned to the table. Soon the room rang with song.

The intimate melody was about roasting chestnuts, Christmas carols, and people dressed to resemble the Eskimos. The man's voice, deep and resonant, moved Desta with happiness.

"You can't have Christmas without that man!" Mr. Johnson said.

"He is Christmas music!" Mrs. Johnson said.

Bright yellow fire waved and lapped in the hearth. The man's liquid voice and the musical accompaniment transported Desta; the whole house felt like one colossal capsule flying to another world. He was so happy it seemed he would gush with tears of joy at any moment. He pressed the spot above his heart, whispered, "Stop it," and felt normal again.

Next came the main course: prime rib, sauteed mushrooms, onions, and baked potato. After Nat King Cole's wondrous song ended, Mrs. Johnson asked Jake to play more holiday music on the radio. Mr. Johnson opened a bottle and poured everyone half a glass of wine. Desta took less, as alcohol didn't agree with him.

He sat at the great table in this house, in the company of people so far removed from his origins, enjoying his first American holiday dinner, and for a moment it seemed he had been here all his life. As he reflected on this, his thoughts turned to how his family celebrated Ethiopian Christmas.

Plush cowhides spread over freshly cut *ketema*—pulpy green grass in the living room. Two to three *mosebs*—skirt-shaped colorful baskets—with layers of *injera*—flat bread. Stews of meat from a cow slaughtered for the holiday, *tibs*—sauteed meat cubes—with onions, garlic, and spice-laced clarified butter, with *doro wat—chicken sauce* to supplement the meat, and *tej*—honey wine in clay or horn goblets. Family members surrounding the moseb enjoying their food and wine; fires burned in two separate hearths. The house was redolent with the aromas of the feast.

"Who wants more?" Aida asked, after refilling the serving plate with meat. Everyone said they were saving room for dessert.

Aida collected the dinner dishes, and all the family waited for the last course: sliced logs on beautiful green plates. On closer examination, Desta could see the dessert was a layer cake covered in chocolate, fashioned into a log and garnished with real twigs and plums. Shae called it a *buche de noel* cake.

Aida declared it her favorite Christmas dessert. Desta had already become a fan of American confections, and this one tasted terrific. He wondered if the Johnsons had intended for their dessert to look like the logs in the walls.

After dessert, they all left the table and sat around the fireplace, poised for the next ritual: Christmas gift-giving. From Jake and Aida, Desta received gloves, socks, two shirts, and a wool hat. From Shae, a Princeton University hooded jersey. A box of homemade chocolate chip cookies for each of them came from Elsa Alberti.

Mr. and Mrs. Johnson gave Desta five hundred dollars, and Grandpa and Grandma Johnson four hundred, the same amount they gave to their grandchildren. Each gift was tucked in a long, stiff envelope with a circular window revealing the face of the man on the hundred-dollar bill.

For the deserving young man you are. You're an inspiration to all of us. Thank you for being a good friend and teammate to our grandson, Grandpa Johnson had written in squiggly letters. Desta recalled how his hands shook.

This was the first Christmas Desta had ever gotten a gift, let alone many. It felt like the first time anyone had fully valued him and made him feel as worthy as anyone else. The childhood scars that so often had

made him feel undeserving had never fully surfaced until now. The
more he regarded his gifts, the pile of torn wrappings, and the chatter of
the family, the more urgently he wanted to run upstairs and cry.

He could no longer feign good cheer. He gathered his windfall in a
shopping bag, thanked everyone again, and rose.

Mr. Johnson got up and handed Desta an envelope. "Sorry, I forgot
this," he said.

"Oh, thank you," Desta replied matter-of-factly, dropped the envelope in the bag, and hurried upstairs.

He put the bag on the floor outside his bedroom. Then he got a bath
towel, spread it over his pillow, and lay face down. He cried until his
eyes ached and all his surging emotions had been purged.

He felt cleansed and happy. He was grateful that this holiday had
given him such joy—through his tears. He blotted his face with the
towel and wiped his nose. He lay on his back and stared at the sloped
ceiling, his mind whirling. Why had he cried so much?

He'd experienced what family and acceptance really meant. For so
long, he had yearned for this kind of belonging with his own family.
The Johnsons' unexpected generosity and love had opened him up and
bathed him in tears.

When he returned from his room, Mrs. Johnson and Shae were in the
kitchen, and Jake and Aida at the table playing cards. Mr. Johnson sat in
front of the TV set. A few smoking logs were all that remained of the
fire. Desta pushed them to the center, added some kindling and firewood, and blew into them. Once the kindling began to flame, he sat in
an armchair before it.

Desta again thought about his outpouring of emotions, and the pain of
being denied the love of family and pride in himself that he had so desperately wanted his whole life. The revelation felt like a bump in the
road on the life's journey he had long since accepted. It now became
one more thing he had to accept and take more seriously.

He remembered something else. *Celebrating Christmas in December
means I'll have my birthday to myself in January,* he thought.

Why had he needed to go through so much to finally find a home
where he was welcome? He knew he might never answer his own

questions; he had no control over his destiny. His fate was to follow the path laid out for him, however rough it might be.

With some resignation, Desta raised his hand, scooped the air and all his own dark feelings, and tossed them over his left shoulder.

Jake pulled a chair from the dining room and sat next to Desta. "Where did you go?"

"I went upstairs to reflect in private on the wonderful gifts all of you gave me," Desta said, smiling. "What time do we go skiing tomorrow?" he asked, surprising himself with his casual air; he knew little about skiing.

"We should leave around nine. The ski slopes are close, and we'll need to rent skis for you."

What Jake said didn't make any sense. *Desta needs a ski to ski.* He repeated the phrase in his head.

"I'm looking forward to it," Desta said.

"You'll have fun," Jake said and went upstairs.

Desta said good night to Mr. Johnson first, then to his host mother and the sisters, and followed Jake moments later.

In their room, face up on the bed, Desta remained awake while Jake began snoring. He wondered how the number seven might have played in his fortune for him to be living with the family. Right off the bat, the Johnsons have seven characters. Then, with a pen and paper, he listed the family members' first names and counted the letters in each. Skip had four, Beverly had seven, Jake had four, Aida had four, Shae had four, and Desta had five. When all are added, the total was 28. This number is seven times the four faces of the coin. Seven plus four is eleven—the image of the two coins when they rest side by side. And in Abraham Lincoln, there are seven letters in each name. The seven's magic power may have indeed, played a vital role in Desta's living with the Johnsons. He turned off his bedside lamp and covered his face for a journey through the night to tomorrow.

THIRTY-FOUR

Desta looked west from the brown clubhouse building and thought it miraculous that he saw no mangled bodies, splayed legs, or crushed bones on the wide, trampled snow at the foot of the mountain. Mr. Johnson unloaded the group's skis and boots near the building's entrance and went to park the Wagoneer. While the group gathered their ski gear, Desta observed his surroundings. In the wide expanse beyond the building, people sheathed head to toe like Eskimos lumbered toward the lift cars. Others flew down the mountain like daredevils, tracing serpentine paths. When they reached the bottom, they swerved and stopped as if they had powerful brakes underfoot. Like Desta's family, the newly arrived came and went from the store.

Desta already had second thoughts. If the Johnsons expected him to fly down the slopes like the skiers he saw, he would have to consider his options before they rented skis and boots for him. He had no intention of risking his life over something as frivolous as skiing when he had yet to find the magic coin.

Desta tapped Jake's arm. "Tell me, do you think I can learn to ski downhill with just an hour or two of practice?"

"Of course," Jake said, showing his even white teeth. "You're a national champion. Skiing should be a piece of cake."

"Seriously," Desta said, imploring Jake with his eyes. "I don't generally like heights. Then the whole idea of speeding downhill on those slender skis seems dangerous to me without good training."

Jake grew serious. "Okay," he said. "You're a great long-distance runner; why don't you go cross-country skiing with Mom? She won't ski downhill, with her knee problems. Cross-country is easy; it's almost like walking."

"Now that sounds like a good plan," Desta said, smiling broadly. "I've been walking all my life."

After gathering the rented boots and skis, they exited the building. Desta sat on a bench under the eaves, and Jake helped him put on his shoes first and then his skis. Next, Jake held a pole in each hand and moved them back and forth in rhythm, telling Desta to do the same with his feet in tandem with his arm motions. "Just follow what Mother is doing," Jake said. "She's a good skier."

Desta was in for a surprise. He thought of *Lesim*, a girl who once offered Desta her father's old, gnarled shoes to protect his feet from thorny shrubs while he was building a fence. When he declined, she put them on and went romping, but quickly tripped and fell, and Desta had laughed heartily. He didn't want to hear people laughing at him today.

He waited till Shae finished helping her mother with her boots and skis. Mrs. Johnson wound her burgundy scarf around her neck and pulled her purple hat down to her brow. Then she grabbed her poles from her daughter and stood up straight. She looked toward Desta. "Ready?"

"Long time ago," Desta replied, smiling. "I'll follow you."

Mrs. Johnson moved like a sidewinder at first. Once she had enough room, she aligned her skis and began to slide forward, hands and feet moving in rhythm, left-right, left-right, like a marching soldier.

Mrs. Johnson made it look easy. Desta glanced around to see if anyone was watching him. There were two skiers close enough to have overheard Desta speaking with Jake.

His skis felt glued to the ground. He feared not just falling, but how he would get back up. He had to stay upright. He planted the pole in his right hand and pushed forward with his right ski. Next, he did the same with his left hand and foot.

"Doing good . . . doing good," Jake and Shae said.

Desta repeated those steps again and again. Mrs. Johnson, several yards ahead of Desta, turned and said, "Yes, he's doing well!"

In his head, Desta followed the rhythm of the skis and felt surefooted with the help of the two poles, which served like an extra set of legs. Mr. Johnson and Aida came out of the store and watched Desta and Mrs. Johnson. "Have fun!" they said in one voice.

Jake ran up and said, "We'll see you at noon."

"See you then . . . you four have a good time!"

The land was flat along the foothills, and previous skiers had already compacted a long stretch of snow. There were quite a few people ahead. Some strode silhouetted in profile against the snow and reminded Desta of ancient Egyptian wall drawings.

Mrs. Johnson turned and asked, "How do you feel, Desta?"

"Good, thank you," he said, glancing at his host.

Desta, indeed, was doing fine. He rapidly gained confidence as his skis glided effortlessly through the white dust, and he felt he could do it all day. "This is better than walking," Desta told his companion.

"Among downhill skiers, it's not highly regarded," Mrs. Johnson said, "For people who want a leisurely excursion in the snow, cross-country skiing is a wonderful activity."

"I see that."

"Desta," Mrs. Johnson said, her voice abruptly urgent. "With all these holidays and family gatherings, I've not had the chance to ask you something."

Desta never liked these pregnant questions. In the past, they had always brought bad tidings. On edge, he paused slightly and looked at Mrs. Johnson.

"Do you ever write to your family?"

He paused longer this time—such a delicate and personal matter that had gradually faded from his memory.

Unknowingly, he had shut down his feelings and thoughts of those times, as if sealed behind a stone in his head: his painful childhood, fractured family relationships, and all that had happened to him through-out his young life. But he knew the residue of that was still deep in his mind, bringing him confusion and pain. Only the other day, at Christmas dinner, he'd had unhappy memories of home.

He held no grudges or ill feelings for anyone in his family. He had forgiven them all. Once he'd let the coin guide his life, the world had become his family, and he now believed in its limitless possibilities for love and happiness.

He spared Mrs. Johnson this half of the truth, and said, "I'm not sure you know this, Mrs. Johnson," Desta began. "I've no direct communica-tion with my family, as they live far from towns with postal services."

"You haven't heard from them, or they from you? Even about your running championship?"

Mrs. Johnson's last question surprised Desta. Why would his win be more important than he was?

"No. Not even that."

Mrs. Johnson shook her head. "We knew something was wrong because we didn't see any letters for you in our mailbox. We were all so busy, we didn't think to ask you about it. So, when do you think you might hear from them?"

His orphan's life stood before him like an apparition. "I really don't know, Mrs. Johnson," Desta said, his voice cracking. He felt a great pain inside. *Probably never* was his first thought. He said instead, "Probably not soon." Desta wanted to cry his eyes out. His own words made him feel like the loneliest person in the world. He imagined himself alone in a vast open space where he could run and run and never reach the end. He could shout at the top of his lungs, but his voice had no echo, and vanished in thin air.

Mrs. Johnson shook her head and clucked her tongue. "That's not right." Desta needed to change the subject quickly, or he might break down in front of her.

"By the way, Mrs. Johnson," he said. "Thanks for everything you have done for me—your happy and comfortable home, the generous gifts yesterday—I was deeply touched. I can't return your favors in kind, but God will. . . . I'm sure."

"Don't mention it, Desta," Mrs. Johnson said. "You are a great addition to our household. It is a blessing to have you with us."

"Thank you for your kind words, Mrs. Johnson. . . . How is your knee?"

"It's causing me a bit of discomfort, and we may have to turn back soon," she said.

"I will tell you a personal story," Mrs. Johnson began. "My mother and father divorced when I was twelve, and I grew up with my mother in England. During the Second World War, I was in Calcutta, India. My father, who remarried, was a president of a successful British company there. During the eight months the Nazis bombed London, correspondence with my mother was terrible. Sometimes I didn't hear from her for months. It is one of my darkest memories. So, I empathize with your situation. You must get connected somehow. I'm sure your family is very concerned too. And you live so far."

"I know, Mrs. Johnson," Desta said. "Sometimes we have no control over our fate."

A laughing couple zipped past them but not before the man's pole tangled with Mrs. Johnson's, nearly knocking her over. They barely apologized and left a cloud of frozen breath in their wake.

Mrs. Johnson stopped. "I think we better go back," she said. "My knee is not feeling well. . . . and there are dangers out here."

"Do you want to?" Desta asked, surprised. They had skied barely twenty minutes.

"I know you would rather continue. You can ski some nearby while I'm having coffee at the clubhouse," she said. They returned to the clubhouse together.

An attendant helped with her skis and brought them inside. Mrs. Johnson glanced at her watch. "We have a little over hour before we meet the rest of the household. If you do ski, don't go too far."

"Okay," Desta said, excited to continue. With the coin's protection on him, he wasn't worried about anything. This time Desta went in the opposite direction. The terrain was still flat, but with fewer skiers, which was fine by Desta; he preferred untrodden, quiet places, where he was more in touch with his spirit, and better able to communicate with other spirits.

He was pleased about his personal exchange with Mrs. Johnson. She had been the most inscrutable person in the household. She often said little to him and projected a tough exterior. He now realized that deep inside she was sweet and compassionate, and it made him want to skip and hop along the snow-covered path, but for his bulky, awkward footwear.

Sometimes, unexpectedly, difficult moments brought people closer. He thought of the time when his father was sick with a contagious disease. After school, Desta had found his mother alone in a makeshift shack to keep herself safe from Abraham's disease. During the night, Desta and Ayénat for the first time had shared personal, intimate stories.

He was happy to experience alone the snow's pristine serenity and spirit-like evanescence, and in its holy whiteness a symbol of purity. God!

Desta glanced at his watch. He had already been skiing for half an hour. He needed to get back precisely at noon, as Mrs. Johnson had asked. As he turned, he saw a man sitting on a high horse, covered in snow. Desta steadied his gaze, wondering if this was a statue.

"Welcome to our neck of the woods," the figure said, frightening Desta. He and his horse were white even under his arms and on the horse's belly, where the snow couldn't reach.

"Are you the Great Mystery?"

"That I am," the figure said. "Did you have a good Christmas?"

"Yes, it was great," Desta said. "How about you?"

"My people and I do not celebrate Christmas," the Great Mystery said, turning his face away indifferently. He shook his head as if to chase away something that bothered him.

"Let me first say congratulations on your victory last month."

"Thank you," Desta said, surprised.

"I know everything that takes place in my land. I was there on the day of your contest."

"You were?!" Desta asked. "Is that why I had strange premonitions as I ran the course?"

"Considering the bad weather, I wanted to give you moral support."

Desta stared at the ghost, but he said no more.

"Too bad we didn't meet then. I'm supremely grateful for the outcome."

"That's all that matters," the Great Mystery said. His horse impatiently stomped his feet and whooshed his tail.

"What ultimately matters to me is that the win helps me get a college scholarship."

"Yes, that . . . You're quite a forgetful fellow, aren't you?"

"I can be . . . . but what about it?"

"You didn't open the envelope you were given on Christmas day."

Desta had to think through all the gifts he received, including the monies. He remembered being overtaken by his emotions and going upstairs to relieve his pain. He'd put all the money away, but his gifts were still in the bag.

"Yeah, I remember Mr. Johnson gave me a plain envelope that I forgot to open. I didn't think much of it."

"Don't think it's trash and throw it away."

"Of course, I won't. I just forgot."

"It is from someone who will play a crucial role in the fate of the two coins."

Desta had to rein in his impulses. "Any more advice for me?"

"Nothing else for now. Just remember what I said."

"This mystery is beyond intriguing. I hope to know more. . . ."

"Go back to your family now. . . ." With that, the Great Spirit and his horse disappeared.

Desta flew to the clubhouse. Everyone was back, holding warm coffee in Styrofoam cups.

"Did you have fun?" they asked.

"I did," Desta said. "Lots."

They finished their coffee and headed to the Jeep, with the family's skis harnessed to its roof rack.

Arriving home, Desta helped Jake collect all the ski equipment and brought it to the recreation room. The mysterious envelope was at the top of his mind. Once he knew that the family wouldn't miss him before dinner, he hurried upstairs. He retrieved the envelope from his gift bag, opened it, and found a letter inside.

Dear Desta,

Meredith and I were moved by your story when David Hartman and his father shared it with us last July. They told us of your urgent need to secure a place at college for the fall, after abandoning plans to study medicine. They thought you could contribute to society if you were able to attend a good American college.

"My wife and I have long been involved in philanthropic work. We are pleased with all your achievements in academics and sports so far, as your instructors have attested. Your coach, Mr. Parker, tells us you have exemplary discipline and dedication to achieving your goals.

We know you're anxious and uncertain about completing your college education. My wife and I are happy to pay your tuition, room and board for the next three years at the college of your choice. Let's hope that this arrangement will also make it easier for you to gain admission.

We feel honored to be a part of your academic career in America. Let us know if you have any questions about the arrangements we are making on your behalf.

With best wishes,

Larry and Meredith Stone

Desta read the letter five times, tears surging. He felt enormously grateful. "Thank you, God! Thank you, Mr. and Mrs. Stone!" He scooted off the bed and kneeled on the floor. He anchored his elbow on the side of the bed, placed his face in his in his hands, and thought.

The emotions he'd held back earlier now found meaning and purpose to express themselves, and they flowed. After all the pain and struggle of his cross-country training, and the sense of incompleteness he he'd felt when he received the paper and plaque of recognition, the reward of his dreams had arrived a month later. *God has a way of teasing and surprising people*, he thought.

He'd overcome one major obstacle, and now he must find a good university to transfer to. He prayed to God to complete his dreams. He rose and sat on the bed.

He noticed on the chair the black-and-orange Jersey that Shae had given him for Christmas, the symbol of Sweet and Sour, associated with the coin and its owner, the beacon of his journey, dreams, and adventure. He folded the letter and put it back in the envelope, kissed it, and put it in his bag. He would keep this to himself for the time being. When the time was right, he would share it with Mr. and Mrs. Johnson and the family.

Desta thought how he should break the news. As happy as he was that a burden had been lifted from him, he also felt that this charity was a weight on his pride; it underscored that he hadn't paid for his education.

The happiest moments of his life were when he had first flown his flying craft, and when he decided to work to support himself his last two years of high school. Here in America, he could work part time to pay some of his basic expenses, but the cost of school was beyond his ability to earn it. He had to accept the way things were and be grateful for the good people who helped him.

Still conflicted, Desta resisted the impulse to run downstairs and share the news. He needed to wait until his heart said so. He would tell Mr. and Mrs. Johnson first, and their children later.

Jake was at the door. "What're you doing here by yourself?" he asked. "Everyone is asking for you. We're about to sit down for dinner."

"I'll be right there."

He rose, washed his face, and dab-dried it. *Strange,* he thought, why *have I been tearing up so much lately?* He had rarely cried through his painful experiences in Ethiopia, preferring to keep it all inside.

The family ate dinner quietly. Afterward, they sat by the fire and drank tea. They recounted the day's events; none of them had skied in a long time. Desta said how much he had enjoyed walking in skis.

They talked about returning here before winter ended. Mrs. Johnson went to her room because of her knee; Aida attended to her. Jake also went up. Mr. Johnson sat by the fire and read his newspapers, a glass of white wine on the round table between the sofa and the big armchair.

Desta went upstairs and returned with the Stones' envelope. "Sorry to interrupt, Mr. Johnson," Desta said. "May I sit with you? I've something important to share."

"Sure." Mr. Johnson folded the paper and set it aside. "Whatcha got?"

Desta handed him the envelope.

Mr. Johnson looked at it front and back, and proceeded to open it slowly, as if savoring the process. He opened the flap, pulled out the letter, and read it.

"This is marvelous!" he cried. "This should make your next three years at college so much easier."

"I'm hoping so," Desta said. Usually, he avoided the word *hope*; to him it meant weakness of purpose. But there were still many unknowns about the Stones' gift; what if for some reason they withdrew their offer? Desta hated to be at the mercy of others. His life path had been strewn with other people's broken promises, including his own family. To protect his heart and spirit, he needed to be guardedly optimistic.

"How come you're not excited?" Mr. Johnson asked, his brow pinched.

"I'm just overwhelmed by their generosity," Desta began. "And coming from people I only just met. If I got accepted at Princeton, this could mean fifteen thousand dollars or more for three years of education."

"Don't worry," Mr. Johnson said, fixing his big eyes on Desta. "Mr. and Mrs. Stone have much more in the bank than what they offered you." He smiled benignly, then added, "You don't know how much they do for you."

Desta set his left elbow on the arm of the chair, joined his hands, and stared at Mr. Johnson. This mystery reminded him of all the ghosts and spirits who had secretly helped him throughout his life.

"I will tell you more about the Stones later," Mr. Johnson said. "We need to rest now. It's a long drive tomorrow. But do you mind if I share this news with Bev? I'll return the letter tomorrow." He got up and went to his room.

Desta dropped his hand. With both hands holding the chair arms, he gazed into the fire, wondering if the Stones were also ghosts. *What's going on in my head?* he thought and went upstairs to bed.

THE NEXT MORNING, when Desta came down at seven-thirty, Mr. and Mrs. Johnson were already in the dining nook having coffee and croissants.

"Congratulations!" Mrs. Johnson said brightly.

"Thank you, Mrs. Johnson," Desta said, unsure if he merited the praise. But he tried to look genuinely happy. "How is your knee?"

"Much better, thank you."

Desta went to the kitchen, made himself a cup of tea, and sat down with the Johnsons.

"You won't have to worry about your college expenses anymore," Mrs. Johnson said. "God works in mysterious ways."

Desta thought Mrs. Johnson sounded just like his mother, Ayénat.

"We know how hard you trained for your cross-country meet to earn a scholarship," Mr. Johnson said. "Now, you can focus completely on your academics to get into the school of your choice."

"I'm doing my best, Mr. Johnson," Desta said, glancing up at him. He picked up a slice of toast.

"Another thing," Mrs. Johnson said. "'Mr. and Mrs. Johnson is a bit too formal. Would you please call us Bev and Skip?"

"No, Mrs. Johnson," Desta said. "Where I'm from, we never call an older person by their first name."

"You're not at home," Mr. Johnson said.

"But still . . . ," Desta replied.

A thumping sound upstairs soon became the shuffling of feet on the steps. Jake and Aida came to the dining nook, followed by Shae. They all asked about their mother's knee, gave words of encouragement, and went to the kitchen.

Shae and Aida offered to make scrambled eggs, sausage, bacon, and sauteed potatoes. Everyone except Desta said it was a good idea. Jake poured hot water into a cup, added two heaping spoons of sugar and a teabag, and came and sat down. He picked up a croissant and began enjoying his pastry and tea.

Mr. Johnson said, "I'll shower now." He detoured to the kitchen to kiss his daughters. "Thanks for making breakfast."

Mrs. Johnson chatted with Jake a little longer, and then said to her daughters, "We need to leave by twelve at the latest, girls," before going for her room.

After their tea, Jake and Desta went to their room to pack.

Everyone enjoyed their breakfast, including Desta who ate all served minus the bacon and sausages.

Afterward, everyone helped clean the house, packed their belongings in the Wagoneer, and prepared to leave. Mr. Johnson sat at the dining table and wrote a lengthy note on a yellow pad to the caretaker, placed it under the napkin holder on the table, and they left.

As they drove through town, past the Stones' hotel, Desta shook his head to think that after all the months of dreaming, worrying, and working himself into the ground for his education, his fate could be shaped by a couple he'd never met before. There had been a time when fifty cents or 1 birr was a precious thing to him, and now strangers were paying thousands of dollars for his college career.

The road twisted and turned with the river's course, through snowy hills and fields, finally flowing, like a tributary into the main highway that would bring them home. Desta reminded himself to send Mr. and Mrs. Stone a thank-you note.

THIRTY-FIVE

Desta confronted a more arduous task than the half semester he had spent preparing for the national cross-country competition. Filling out the transfer college applications and writing the essays were very demanding. The ones he had filled out for the Bulgarian medical school were much easier and shorter.

Yes, he has two remaining weeks of his Christmas break. Now he thought the Princeton application alone would take him that long. Then the question was, which school would be more accessible? He knew that some Ivy League colleges and public universities were more challenging than others. Even if he were to consider some of the easier ones, completing their application would still take a long time. Princeton was his first choice because the school's black and orange colors had a pull on him because of their association with the coin owner. Desta would apply to Princeton, one more Ivy League school, and two public universities. He still needed to find out if his cross-country championship would help him earn a three-year scholarship with any university.

He had just opened the folder containing the Princeton applications and reviewed the many pages, checking everything he needed to complete the application. The reference to his parents' degrees, the school(s) they earned them from, and the one on ethnicity stopped him.

Did it mean students from uneducated and farming parents would somehow be viewed unfavorably? What about his ethnicity? So long as he qualified academically, why would it matter who he was? Desta felt he was treading on unexplored American social and educational landscapes. Desta's life revolved mainly around his school and athletics. His trips to New York City and the Bronx gave him a glimpse of life very different from the one he has been leading since he had arrived six months ago. Those experiences had woken him to a different reality.

Although he has now lived in America for nearly six months, he had never thought of his skin tone or heritage. When Desta completed this application, he would label himself black. It made him feel like he had discovered himself for the first time. Or would it even affect him, something transitory as check marking a multiple-choice question on a test?

All those reviewing his file would also know who he was: black and African. What was the point of this ethnicity label? That he had a name, that he was a human, by all the attributes that define people, and that he was alive with reasonable intelligence. Wouldn't this have been enough?

How about his parents' educational level? His father, Abraham, was a brilliant man who never got the opportunity to learn how to read or write. His mother, Ayénat, would probably not get the chance as her expected role was to keep the house and raise children. Would this affect his chances of getting into the school? Then, the section where he had to list any awards, honors, or books he had written. This awareness made him feel better because he was the cross-country national champion. For all that had happened to him, it felt so good to feel somebody important, a winner.

With this positive feeling, Desta proceeded to write his essay. He knew this would take the longest time.

From his suitcase in the closet he brought out his notebook where he had written the essay for the Bulgaria medical school. He needed to update this document and a variety of subtopics the Princeton application required him to write.

Desta wrote eight pages from Sunday afternoon to Tuesday noon, revising them several times. He needed to reduce these to one page.

Later in the afternoon, Mr. Johnson, who had come from work early, came to Desta's bedroom. This moment was the first time the man had come here, and Desta was a bit nervous. Luckily, he had cleaned his room and his desk was uncluttered. Mr. Johnson sat at the window seat.

"I saw Mr. Stone today," Mr. Johnson said. "He said he spoke with someone from Princeton, and they had told him that the essay is a significant part of the application. He needs to tell the admission committee not just about a list of things you have done but who you are, what your background is like."

"Thank you for that information, Mr. Johnson," Desta said. "I've been working on it for three days. I've substantially cut from the original length to two pages but still need to reduce it to one."

"Good," Mr. Jonson said and paused. "Mr. Stone graduated from Princeton and is very well-connected with the people there. He can help some, but you would bear much of the weight by getting top grades and writing a compelling essay."

"I will know how I did when school opens in two weeks," Desta said, steady on his benefactor's face. "Regarding the application and the personal essay, I'll continue to work on it."

"Excellent!" Mr. Johnson paused again, his eyes studying Desta. ". . . What's this that you've not heard from your family since you came here last August?"

"This is not the first time I have not heard from my family for months, Mr. Johnson," Desta said. "That's how it has been since I left home as a ten-year-old. . . . Coming so far has made connecting with them more difficult because there is no mail service in the area they live."

Mr. Johnson caressed his chin, thoughts playing on his face. "I understand you lived with relatives and strangers as you were going through school in Ethiopia. . . ." The man trailed off and appeared to struggle with something.

"Yes," Desta said. "Some of the families I didn't know before we met but adopt me as a family through what we call the Fathers-of-the-Breast ceremony."

Mr. Johnson's chin jerked. "What?"

Desta explained that these men Desta adopted as his fathers after suckling their thumbs.

Mr. Johnson fixed Desta with a sharp gaze. "How?"

"It happened through a ceremony when I lived with two separate families where I suckled the right thumbs of the men after they dipped them three times each in milk and honey."

"Fascinating!" Mr. Johnson said. The surprise in his eyes had not gone out when the light from the spring sun took over his face. "Only the men?"

Desta tightened his lips and looked away. He batted his eyes, turned to Mr. Johnson, and said, "Their wives didn't want to."

"Very interesting," Mr. Johnson said, rising to go. "I'll let you continue with your essay."

"Thanks for Mr. Stone's information."

Desta placed his elbow on his desk, pressed the inner corners of his eyes between his thumb and index fingers, and sighed deeply. Before him were the images of the two women who refused to accept him as their son, juxtaposed by their husbands and the priests who came to conduct the ceremony. The cups of milk and honey were on the table before them.

And then, when he thought of the fractured relationship with his mother, he broke down. Desta, let it be. Once finished, he went to the bathroom, washed and dried his face, and came to his essay.

The next day, he got up early and wrote his "Thank you" letter to Mr. and Mrs. Stone. When he showed it to Mrs. Johnson, "This is beautiful," she said, "Let's send them on a nice card. When I go to the office later, I will stop at a store and get you one."

Desta thanked her and went upstairs.

That evening, David Hartman called to see if they could get together on Saturday. Thrilled, Desta said, "Why don't you come to the house? I've something to show you."

Mrs. Johnson gave Desta the *Thank You* card and a stamp the following day.

It was a simple but lovely cream-colored card with three rows of frost blue mountain peaks on the front bottom section, lined with a row of evergreen trees near the edge. "Thank you" in cursive lettering was tucked in the right corner, above the trees.

The inside was plain, and the envelope was mustard color. Desta studied the front a little, his eyes on the peaks signifying Vermont's mountains, below which they met. He thanked Mrs. Johnson and went to his room with it.

Carefully, he copied the letter's content onto the card, covering nearly a page and a half of it with his slanting hand. Afterward, he folded and inserted it into the envelope and closed it. He affixed the stamp at the top right corner and placed it on his desk to go out with the family's morning mail.

SATURDAY, before David Hartman arrived, Desta had boiled water in a kettle and left it warming on the stove. He brought the four-seater folding card table from the garage and set it up in front of the window seat in his room.

Then he went downstairs to the kitchen and brought two cups, a plate, a bowl of sugar, and two black tea bags on a tray and put them on the table.

He placed half a dozen of Elsa's Christmas chocolate cookies on the plate and waited for his guest. Right around 2 p.m., he began to peek out of the window. When he saw David's red car driving up the driveway, he dashed out of his room and raced downstairs. He pressed the gate's remote opening button on the wall by the front entrance.

With a neatly trimmed beard, a leaner frame, and glasses, David looked more like a seasoned professor than the casual and carefree graduate student he used to be. His carefully cropped head of hair looked good too.

"I wouldn't have recognized you if I had seen you in the street," Desta said, grinning.

"Is that so? How about that—" David said cheerily. He studied Desta. "You've filled out quite a bit," he said. "The Johnsons must have been feeding you well."

"Thank you," Desta said. "You can say that, but you should have seen me in November when I was on the cross-country team. I was a lot thinner then. . . . Let's go in." The visitor took off his shoes first at the entrance and followed Desta upstairs.

"What a beautiful room you have!" David said after he stepped in." He walked to the window facing the backyard. "And you have this fantastic view."

"You should have seen it when it was all green," Desta said. "Yes, I feel fortunate to be living with the Johnsons. Sometimes, things work out in ways you could have never imagined. And thanks for all you did to make this arrangement possible for us."

"I know you had wanted to be at the medical school in Bulgaria, but, yes, there are things we have no control over, indeed." David strode to the opposite window. He leaned over the seat and looked out. "I bet those rose bushes are lovely when they blossom in spring," he said.

"Sit down," Desta said. "I'm looking forward to the days when this place turns green again."

"In another three months—" David's eyes panned around the room, first over the landscape painting on the wall above the headboard, another on the wall between the entrance and closet, of a couple walking through a path in the forest surrounded by a blue mist, and finally of the two coins painting on the left of Desta's desk.

David turned toward Desta. "Oh, yes, to continue with what I was saying, no matter how we dream or plan, sometimes things work out in surprising ways. This situation is particularly true in your case. I feel there is something or someone involved, however."

"I've long been convinced about that," Desta said, "But no matter who is involved, for me, some higher power chose you as a vehicle for bringing me into this good country. I'm thankful."

Desta excused himself and went downstairs. He returned with two cups of tea, a bowl of sugar with a spoon, and a plate of cookies on a tray and placed it on all the card table.

"Please sit down," Desta said, serving one of the cups to David.

Desta pulled his chair from under his desk and moved it to the card table facing David. Each scooped their sugar, poured it into the tea, and mixed thoroughly. In between their sips and bites of the cookies, they talked. David referred to his teaching job at New York University as challenging enough to keep him interested in his work but missed his travels as he searched for material for his Ph.D.

Desta shared his challenges as a cross-country runner, balancing them with his courses, the fun he'd at the sight of the first snow, and his recent family trip to Vermont. And then he stunned David when he told him about the Stones' offer to pay Desta's three more years of college education.

"That's marvelous," David said. "Who would have guessed six-seven months ago the trajectory of your journey in America would go in the way it has."

"I agree," Desta said, "but as much as I'm an optimist, the caveat is nothing is guaranteed, and I'm not clear if there would be any conditions. I will let you know when I know more. For now, I consider it as manna from heaven."

David smiled. "All I can say is I'm happy for you."

"To segue into something related," Desta began. "I'm applying to Princeton. I've written the biographical essay but needed someone like yourself to read it. Afterward, we can go out if you have that in mind."

David Hartman was happy to look over Desta's essay. After they finished their tea and cookies, they moved to Desta's long desk. David Hartman began reading the essay while Desta continued to fill out the rest of the application.

"This is terrific," David said. "The only thing is it's long."

With Desta's permission, David was willing to help reduce it to one page.

The young professor excised extraneous words and phrases and deleted or truncated long sentences. Afterward, he read it several times, fixing things here and there during each round. David thought the finished version was concise enough to fit on a page. After carefully reading it, Desta was pleased and thanked David for his time and willingness to help him.

When they finally looked out the window, it was dark, and snow was falling. They decided to postpone going to town for a meal for another time. Desta put on his heavy jacket and prepared to escort David to his car, his home custom. Downstairs, Desta put on his boots David his shoes and they went out. At the car, Desta extended his gratitude with a warm hug to his friend and they parted.

Desta spent two more days on the application and had his essay professionally typed by Mary, Mrs. Johnson's secretary. On Monday, he stuffed the application and essay into the return envelope and mailed it to Princeton.

THIRTY-SIX

The second semester began on Monday, February 1st. Like all winter long, snow ruled the land. Desta and Jake put on heavy jackets, gloves, and boots and shoveled the driveway, brushed off the mounds on Jake's car, and scraped ice from its windshield.

The compound was dead quiet; no bird sang or wind stirred the naked branches, as if all life had ceased.

"Things will change," his family had told him as they went through the seasons. How much, Desta could only guess from the exuberance of last summer, when he'd arrived from Ethiopia.

He was looking forward to spring—when, he presumed, like back home, much of nature awakened. In Ethiopia, most trees kept their leaves through the changing seasons. The grass remained relatively green, particularly in the highlands, when 'winter,' the rainy season, ended in August, and spring arrived the following month. Then the gray, seeded farm lots began to sprout grain. The hills, fields, and yards dazzled with bright yellows, reds, and shades of pink and purple flowers.

Desta eagerly awaited the end of the snow. Would it depart by degrees, or instantly liquefy on the first day of spring? He imagined the former, but when he thought of winter and spring in turn departing and starting on March 21st, it seemed that all the snow should vanish, so the miracle of life could begin.

Desta hoped to see leaves grow, grass sprout, the insects and birds return. At school, he looked forward to walking Lincoln's rose-lined pathways, and to the sculpture garden, to commune with the spirit of the place.

He had many things to accomplish in the coming semester. To give himself more time to search for the coin, he planned to take four courses, one less than last semester, and drop sports. He would become

more skilled in the different aspects of the magic wand. It had been Tsadok's gift to him, and he felt obliged to put it to good use. And he
intended to take more time to study the inscriptions on the ancient stone
tablet. He counted on returning to New York City to talk to Robert
Krause for any leads he might have about the owner of the second coin.

Desta and Jake went to campus to register, wearing nice clothes and
ties under their coats. But Mr. Parker wasn't at the gate, and no one was
there to police the dress code. Perhaps the school only enforced the rules
in September, *for the benefit of new students*, Desta thought. Both were
relieved they hadn't been collared by Coach Parker about the team.

Desta had put his fall courses out of mind as he planned the new semester's activities, but three days after classes resumed, the registrar
issued the grades for the last semester.

Desta received his humiliation and disappointment. He got a B in
English, the subject he loved and prided himself on, *not the kind of
grade a school like Princeton wants to see*. Desta blamed himself. He
hadn't written good essays; he didn't write like American kids. His papers read like Amharic texts translated into English—stiff, awkward,
and mediocre. He blamed his high school in Ethiopia for a lack of
books, and not emphasizing English reading and writing.

He hoped his 3.8 overall GPA would still be good enough for the
schools he had applied to. But he was determined to do better in English. To read and write more was the only way, he thought, that he could
improve his proficiency.

After he'd returned from Vermont, Desta had grown more open and
trusting toward his family, and people in general, albeit still guarded
about his private things. Outwardly calm, he strode more confidently,
and met people with a sure, steady gaze. He enjoyed his meals and spent
more time with family members. He played with Kooper on their walks
in the snow.

But inwardly he struggled. He knew Mrs. Johnson was deeply religious, and he feared she'd disapprove of him practicing with Tsadok's
wand. But much of his future was bound up with the magic of the wand
and the coin. Now he wanted to do more with them, maybe summoning
the Great Mystery and through him learning about the spirits of crucial
figures in American history.

In the meantime, he settled into a daily routine of classes, assignments, and household chores—and every morning, reciting his legends.

On the second Saturday in February, Desta got a letter from the
famed university in New Jersey, Princeton, inviting him for an interview
on Monday, March 1st, at two o'clock. The news thrilled Desta. But he
soon grew uneasy. What if he couldn't answer their questions, or words
failed him, or he had nothing to say about anything? He'd not only ruin
his chances to study there, but also to explore the missing coin's connection to that school. Desta shook his head at these strange thoughts.
He knew fear and doubt were part and parcel of his life. He had overcome so much to be here; he couldn't let fear sabotage his dreams.

He realized that his doubts probably stemmed from knowing too little
about the school. He wanted to study there primarily for its academic
reputation. The magic wand had even confirmed that Princeton was the
best choice. But that wouldn't be enough to convince his interviewer.
Desta wanted Shae's advice, and Jake arranged a telephone appointment
with his sister.

On Friday evening, Shae called and gave Desta a list of questions that
a college interviewer might ask. She suggested Desta have mock ses-
sions with Jake on the weekend, and read *The History and Culture of
Princeton*, which was on her old bookshelf.

When Desta told Shae he had already read the book, she said,
"You're ahead of the game." Shae added, "Don't be nervous, and
be yourself."

"Thank you so much, Shae," Desta said, but the "be yourself" remark
puzzled him. "Who else does she think I could be?" Desta asked himself. *An intriguing American saying*, he thought.

Using Shae's list, Desta and Jake did two-hour mock interviews on
Saturday and Sunday. Desta also browsed through the Princeton book.
By Sunday evening, Desta felt confident about his meeting at Princeton.

On Monday, Mrs. Johnson and Desta left at ten o'clock to allow time
to have lunch with Shae and tour the Princeton campus before Desta's
appointment. The roads were clear, and they drove straight through
without any delays. On the way, they talked about their lives. Mrs. Johnson spoke about growing up in England without her father; Desta

described how he put himself through school with little financial support
from his family.

They listened to news and music on the radio, and some classical music on an eight-track tape. Desta would have liked to have heard *Teach
Your Children* just once.

After driving leisurely and stopping for gas, they reached Princeton at
noon. They shared a pizza at Valentino's on Nassau Street with Shae,
left the car there, and entered a side gate to the main entrance.

"Good luck!" Shae said. "I'm sure you will do fine."

"Thank you, Shae," Desta said. "I appreciate your confidence in me."

Shae ran for her next class and Desta and Mrs. Johnson walked the
campus grounds and ogled the striking spires, gargoyles, and wall reliefs
of the buildings. They visited the Firestone Library and the Princeton
Chapel. The sun reflected the snow and the air glowed, making their
walk more enjoyable.

Inside the admissions office, a fair-skinned woman with a short Afro
rose from behind her desk and introduced herself as Angie Watson. She
shook hands with Mrs. Johnson first. "You must be Desta," she said,
and offered her hand.

"That he is," Mrs. Johnson said, turning to her charge, her face
brightening.

"Nice to meet you both," Angie said. "Please have a seat."

The woman made a call, picked up a cream-colored folder, and approached the two visitors. "Mrs. Johnson, feel free to wait here and
peruse our magazines and newspapers while Desta is interviewed," Angie said, smiling.

"Come, Desta," Angie gestured, and pushed a door opening into a
short hallway. "There's been a change of plan," Angie said. "The Director of Admissions will see you himself."

"Director!" the word echoed in Desta's head. Directors were powerful and intimidating, like the officials who ran his schools in Ethiopia.
Frenzied butterflies suddenly invaded his stomach. Just before Angie
knocked on a door halfway down the hall, Desta pressed hand over
heart, and whispered "stop it!" His stomach calmed again.

"Desta, this is Mr. Stephen Gray," Angie said.

"Good afternoon, Desta," Mr. Gray said, extending his hand and a practiced, threadbare smile—*from too many student interviews,* Desta thought. He shook the man's hand. Angie handed the folder to Mr. Gray, who thanked her, and she left.

"Sit down, please," Mr. Gray said, motioning to a U-shaped chair across a desk that looked much older than the man. Mr. Gray tilted his eyes to the tab on the folder, then leaned back in his chair.

"You're from Ethiopia?" the director asked, sounding curious. "How long have you been in this country?"

"Six months."

Desta briefly scanned the director's face, hoping to read his heart through the pale hazel eyes.

Desta gave Mr. Gray the same unaffected smile that had disarmed his foes and won him friends over the years. Whether it made a difference or not, at least he would be himself. The air was tense, and Desta felt no amount of good cheer would improve it.

"You came to finish high school here, then?"

"No. I'm a first-year college student."

Mr. Gray seemed perplexed, as if Desta had replied in Amharic.

Mr. Gray opened the folder and one by one turned its pages. "You're applying as a transfer student then," he said, neither query nor statement, his face growing more baffled with each page he scanned. Mr. Gray picked up the last sheet in the folder, a handwritten letter. It seemed he had found the object of his search. His edgy, stumped look gave way to concentration on solving the mystery.

He seemed to read the letter word for word, then placed it on his desk. He reviewed the rest of the file, more carefully this time. The *New York Times* article about Desta's championship drew the lion's share of Mr. Gray's interest.

He leaned back and read it. "That's quite an accomplishment," he said, smiling genuinely this time. "You fellows are talented runners. I watched your countryman, Abebe Bikila win the marathon in Rome seven years ago. Running barefoot! Imagine!" He shook his head. "I read about him with great interest."

Next, Mr. Gray pulled out Desta's grade report. "You don't like English, eh?" Mr. Gray said teasingly. He returned to the handwritten letter, which Desta assumed was a recommendation. The man handled it with reverence and set aside everything else in Desta's application. Desta knew at least five people had written letters of support: his three instructors, Coach Parker, and Mr. Johnson. Desta was dying to find out whose had captured the attention of the Director of Admissions.

Mr. Gray looked up at Desta and said, "How do you know Mr. and Mrs. Lawrence Stone?"

The revelation startled Desta. "I don't really know them well," Desta said. "They are friends of my host family, the Johnsons."

"I see," Mr. Gray said. "As a rule, Princeton doesn't accept transfer students, even from Lincoln College." He grinned. "I was not aware of your situation. Right now, we are processing the Early Decision applicants." He turned and waved toward stacks of cream-colored folders on tables to his left and behind him. "All of these."

The phone rang. "Your next appointment is here."

Mr. Gray returned Desta's papers to the folder. "You seem like an interesting young man. I would like to chat more, but I must see the next applicant. Thank you for your interest in Princeton." The two shook hands, and Desta walked out conflicted, confused, and disappointed. He hadn't gotten to share anything that he and Jake had spent hours rehearsing. Mr. Johnson had advised Desta to make a positive impression, but Desta hadn't said anything memorable to Mr. Gray. Everything seemed as bleak as a winter sky.

He made sure not to show his feelings to Mrs. Johnson, who had taken the day off from work to support him today.

A dark-haired young man with glasses sat across from Desta's host mother, reading *The Daily Princetonian* draped over his right arm.

"How did it go?" she asked the moment he returned to the sitting area.

"It was an interesting interview," Desta said. He looked out of the window thoughtfully.

"That doesn't say much." Her brow knitted.

"Let's go out, and I'll tell you."

Mrs. Johnson coiled her scarf around her neck, Desta zipped his jacket, tugged the ends of its collar, and buttoned them. They thanked Angie and left.

Mrs. Johnson glanced at her watch. "It's twenty to three. If we leave now, we should get home around four-thirty, good enough to beat most of the rush-hour traffic." They hurried through the snow-covered campus past Nassau Hall and exited the same side gate. Desta opened the front of his jacket and got into the car.

Mrs. Johnson pulled her vehicle onto the two-lane street, and in a few short turns entered I-95 for Rye.

"So, what exactly happened at your interview?" Mrs. Johnson asked, as if the question had been burning in her.

Desta told her exactly what had happened.

"That's strange," Mrs. Johnson said. "It sounds like somebody dropped the ball."

Desta quietly digested this new American expression. He guessed that she meant a mistake.

"I don't know who erred exactly, but the director should have explained what was happening." Desta shook his head. "That letter from the Stones and the article about my cross-country got him a little more interested. If not for that, I think he would have dismissed me right away; he even said that they don't accept transfer students."

"Hmmm. . ." Mrs. Johnson paused. "I don't know, Desta. It seems we've been on a wild goose chase."

Desta had to think about that turn of phrase, too. She probably meant their trip had been for nothing.

"Wild or tame, hopefully, the goose will come home to roost sooner or later," Desta said, smiling at Mrs. Johnson.

"We need to solve the mystery of the Stones' letter first, and then we'll have a clearer idea of what's happening. You must talk to Skip, particularly regarding our friends' connection to Princeton."

Desta nodded. "Okay," he said. "I still have three more schools to hear from. And I don't think this trip was in vain. I had a great time, learned a lot, and enjoyed our lunch with Shae."

"Not at all," Mrs. Johnson said. "I enjoyed the day we spent together too. And it was nice to get away from the office."

"I need to close my eyes briefly," Desta said. "The glare from the snow is bothering me."

"Go ahead," Mrs. Johnson said. "And take your mind off the interview." He glanced at her to see if she was joking. In her sunglasses, he couldn't tell.

Desta thanked her, leaned back, and closed his eyes. Soon he was gone.

Desta woke as the garage door at the house opened. He rubbed his eyes and shook his head. "I slept the whole time?" he asked. "I'm sorry, I meant to keep you company."

"Not a problem, Desta," Mrs. Johnson said. "You had a long, stressful weekend. You needed the rest. And I kept busy with my thoughts."

They changed their shoes in the mudroom. "Thank you so much again, Mrs. Johnson," Desta said and went to his room. Once again, he felt like when he had won the national championship and discovered no college scouts had come to talk to him: there, *but not there. Ambivalent. Gray.*

"Things take time," a voice said. He looked around the room, but there was no one. *Was it Tsadok?*

THIRTY-SEVEN

On Sunday afternoon, March 7th, Desta was doing homework when a knock came at his door.

"C'mon in," he said.

"Excuse me, Desta," Mindy Kovacs said, leaning on the door jamb. "Mr. and Mrs. Johnson would like you to join them for tea in the library."

The unaccustomed formality of the invitation mystified Desta. *Why the library?* Desta rarely stepped foot in that room; he thought of it as Mr. Johnson's private domain, where he often sat on its leather sofa, reading his papers and magazines, or did paperwork at his sunny desk by the south window.

Much as Desta would have loved to browse the library's floor-to-ceiling bookshelves, he didn't have privilege to do that. There was an unspoken division between the family's common areas and personal spaces, so Desta respected that.

"I'll be there in five minutes," Desta said. He washed the fatigue from his face in the bathroom sink, combed his hair, and put on a clean shirt and pants.

As Desta walked down the stairs, he sensed something unusual was in the making. He wondered how his hosts would receive him; would they rise as he entered the room, in a formal gesture of respect?

Desta entered the library and found the couple sitting on the sofa. Two white cups of tea, a sugar bowl, spoons, and a plate of chocolate chip cookies sat on a large silver tray on the table before them.

"Good that you could come see us now, Desta," Mr. Johnson said, smiling genially.

"Indeed," Mrs. Johnson added. She gestured for Desta to sit on the small sofa across from them. Mindy came with a cup and saucer of tea and set them before Desta. Mrs. Johnson thanked her and Mindy acknowledged her boss with a "welcome," and left.

"Do people in Ethiopia have four o'clock tea?" Mrs. Johnson inquired. *Was this leading to something bigger?* Desta wondered.

"Most people back home don't take an afternoon tea break," Desta said. Each sipped their tea and nibbled a cookie.

"The reason we asked you here is…" Mr. Johnson hesitated and gazed at Desta. The air grew tense. Desta glanced at Mrs. Johnson, who seemed nervous.

"Mr. Johnson," Desta said, smiling, "I'm happy to hear whatever's on your mind."

"Bev and I and the children would like to formally adopt you as our son." Now Desta was at a loss for words.

"Look," Mrs. Johnson said. "You don't have to say yes now. This is just a proposal. We know you're making friends, but in many ways you're still on your own in this country. We think it's important for a young man like you to have family to rely on, but your own family is so far away. And we all love you as one of our own."

Desta's throat prickled with emotion. He reached over and pressed his heart.

"I'm touched beyond words," he said, and wiped the wetness from his eyes. "I'm honored you think I'm worthy of this generous and kind gesture."

"We wanted you to know how we feel, and we'd like you to think about it," Mrs. Johnson added.

"I thank you," Desta said. "I'd like to consider what this would mean for all of us."

"For this to work," Mr. Johnson said, fixing Desta with kind eyes, "we also need to think about *how*. Since you're above sixteen, the legal limit for adopting international children, we must find an alternative way of doing this. Bev, I, and the children are intrigued by your country's tradition of "Parents-of-the-Breast" adoption. We thought we might pursue it that way; it's not unlike having a church perform a baptism or a wedding ceremony. We know a minister who would officiate."

Mrs. Johnson said, "We might schedule it for Sunday, March 21. It's the beginning of spring, and new life. And also Shae's last day of spring break from Princeton, so she could join us. I know that in your country, the family slaughters a lamb for the occasion. That's not practical for us, but we could make arrangements with our local butcher."

"Again, thank you for your kind consideration," Desta said. "I will let you know soon."

"Very good," Mr. Johnson said. "Please go back to your studies."

Desta drained his tea and left. He counted the stairsteps to his room, sixteen in all, but his mind was elsewhere. He should have been happy about his hosts' idea, but he felt unsure about it. His two previous Parents-of-the-Breast adoptions hadn't entirely succeeded. And he reminded himself that the coin was meant to be his only family. He needed to pray on the matter. He would share the news with Tsadok, David, and the Great Mystery.

Using the magic wand, he sent a message to Tsadok and the Great Mystery. He called David on the phone, who thought it was a great idea.

Desta determined that the moon would become full on Friday, March 12, at two-thirty a.m., and asked the Great Mystery to meet him then, near the giant evergreen tree at the far corner of the Johnsons' compound. The full moon was Desta's most favorite phase of the lunar cycle, and as such represented the end of one life and beginning of another.

Tsadok replied, you *should consider anything that feels right to your heart and can help advance your mission, but first consult the coin.*

ON FRIDAY, March 12, at 2:15 a.m., Desta arrived at the appointed spot. The compound was draped with the beguiling silvery light the full moon dispensed and that Desta loved. The Great Spirit and his horse appeared, looking like a snow-covered mountain, the evergreen's silhouette behind him.

"What is it you need?" the Great One asked.

"You're way up there," Desta replied. "Can you come down from your horse to talk? I'd like to share something important."

The Great Spirit grunted. "I usually don't dismount so early in the morning, but I'll do it for you." He slid toward the horse's rear and landed on the ground. To Desta's surprise, the steed remained standing like a statue.

"Please sit on the bench with me and see what you think of this idea," Desta said.

"I'm a spiritual guide to the Stones, so I know about the Johnsons' offer. What do you lose by accepting it?"

"It's complicated," Desta said, "I made similar arrangements before, and they didn't work out. I'm hesitant to chance it again."

"Life itself is a chance, an evolving experiment," the Great Spirit said. "Would you stop living and experimenting because of bad past experiences? You've gotten this far in your life because you were willing to take chances."

"I hadn't thought of it that way before," Desta said.

"What are your other concerns?"

"Committing to a relationship I would be obliged to maintain. Right now, I'm obligated to school, and the coin that will be with me the rest of my life."

"Life is not a free ride. All good relationships require commitment. You've got to give to receive. You must put effort into a relationship to benefit from it. Is there anything else?"

"I think it has to do with love; I've always sought it but haven't found it. Even with my siblings, our love fizzled out once we were apart."

"Aha!" the Great One cried. "First, you must accept and love yourself, but your problem is more fundamental: You have been seeking the parental love denied you as a boy. You looked for it in the families you lived with. Sadly, that love is long gone. You must accept this and move on. You are in a new land, living with new people; you must give yourself and them a chance. . . . Accept the offer with gratitude and move ahead with the ceremony."

Desta stared into the pale world, thinking about the Great Mystery's words. He pressed his index finger on his lips and thought about the spirit's advice. Desta let go of his hand and said "You're right. Trying to reclaim lost love may be like trying to reclaim a spilt fluid. Thank you for your counsel."

"You're welcome!" the Great Mystery said. "Remember, you're not stuck in the past; you're starting anew, okay? I've got to go now."

Wakan Tanka rose, and with a starting run, jumped onto his white steed.

He waved to Desta as he turned the horse. Moments later, he dissolved into the moonlight.

Desta returned to his room. Then he fetched his magic wand and, setting it before him, asked it to respond to the idea he had in mind. Shortly after, Desta saw with delight that a green light glowed from deep within the curlicue of the big 9 at the center, then spun and vanished at the base of the shaft. Now Desta felt he could wholeheartedly accept the Johnsons' proposal.

THIRTY-EIGHT

Desta had anxiously awaited the news that arrived in a thick white envelope from Princeton University. He opened the letter, fingers shaky, eyes tense. The first word said it all. Congratulations! He didn't fall out of his chair because he was standing in front of Mrs. Johnson. His eyes filled with tears as he handed the letter to her to finish reading it.

"This is terrific," she said. "How wonderful!" They hugged. "You deserve it."

Desta didn't hear her words. "Thank you," he finally said as he collected the letter and went to his room to cry for joy into his pillow.

Two days later, Jake received his acceptance letter from Yale. "I've never heard Grandpa so happy before," Mrs. Johnson said of the news. The combined good fortune of the two boys was such that Mr. Johnson took the whole family to dinner at his Rye Country Club to celebrate. Celebratory as it was over lamb roast, which to Desta tasted gamey, different from the zesty and succulent kind he used to eat at home.

Desta hadn't been taken out to dinner before, much less in such an exclusive setting. People stared at him as if he had just walked into the room from Mars. Their eyes and faces held no malice but seemed inquisitive to Desta. Some were subtle; others, particularly an older, lurching woman with ruby and gold necklaces and a hat crowned with flowers appeared painfully uncomfortable.

After the family finished their main meal, a portly man across from the bejeweled woman rose and walked to the Johnsons' table and shook hands affably with the parents. Then, eying Desta, he asked, "Whatcha got here?"

"We're celebrating our young men's admission to college," Mr. Johnson said casually, sidestepping the man's affront. Then he introduced Desta, noted his heritage, and the schools the visitor and Jake would be attending in the fall.

The man sidled toward Jake and shook his hand. "Congratulations!" Then he turned to Desta and said, "You too," as he withdrew his hand.

The family quickly ate their cheesecake, finished their drinks, and left, flanking Desta protectively as they walked out of the restaurant.

On the ride home, Desta couldn't make sense of his experience at the club. He didn't feel hurt but baffled and confused. That night before he lay in bed, he imagined what happened to him that evening was a handful of dirt, which he tossed over his left shoulder. He felt at ease as he drifted into sleep.

IT WAS MARCH 21ST, the first day of spring, a date ripe with meaning. It echoed the twenty-one legends in King Solomon's Coin of Magic and Fortune and was the day of the ceremony for Desta's third Father-of-the-Breast, and, he hoped, for his first such mother.

The ritual was to be held in the living room at noon, officiated by Reverend Conrad Lewis Dates of Abyssinian Baptist Church in Harlem, a pastor Mr. Lawrence Stone had recommended. The three Johnson children and David and his parents would serve as witnesses.

Jake and Desta rearranged the two living room sofas into a single row. Afterward, they brought four chairs from the dining room and organized them in a line behind the sofas. Before the first row sat a table covered with a green herringbone tablecloth. On it, a round silver tray held green and gold cups of honey and milk. Flanking the table stood two armchairs facing the audience.

Some ten feet away, a fire burned in the hearth. In the yard, sunbeams tickled new life from the earth.

Dr. Dates and the Hartmans—Hal, Jean, and David—sat in the front row. The three children and Desta sat on the back chairs. Mr. and Mrs. Johnson perched on the armed seats.

The room bustled with tension, excitement, and happiness. Once all was ready, Mr. Johnson stood before the table, and began. "Before we proceed, let me give some background about today's ceremony. When our family was in Vermont over Christmas, Bev and Desta went cross-country skiing together. She discovered then that Desta had no way to

communicate with his family in Ethiopia. Desta also shared that during
his education there, his family couldn't support him, and that he lived
with families who adopted him.

"To adopt someone past childhood, Ethiopia has an interesting custom called the Parents-of-the-Breast ceremony. How this works, you
will see soon.

"Desta has been a great addition to our family and his school. His
drive to excel in everything he does inspires us all. He has clear goals
for what he intends to accomplish, and we want to see him succeed.

"But no matter how much ambition and drive a person has, one needs
the support and encouragement of others. Although the law in our country doesn't recognize today's ceremony, we choose it to formalize our
intentions toward Desta."

Mr. Johnson gestured to the green-and-gold cups. "Milk and honey
will be the bridge to our relationship." He smiled his seraphic smile. "I
won't spoil the rest. Now I'll ask Doctor Dates to come up and say a
word and conduct the ceremony."

Dr. Dates rose, and Mr. Johnson sat down.

Desta's palms perspired and his stomach tightened. Would Mrs.
Johnson refuse to adopt him in the end, as two other women had? Pressing hand over heart, he calmed himself.

Dr. Dates cleared his throat and stood straighter. "I'm honored to be
chosen for this occasion. . . . When Mr. Johnson described what we
would do today, I was intrigued and challenged. How could I contribute
meaningfully to this ceremony? We don't do this in our country. However, I realized that this adoption ritual was not so different from our
baptism or a wedding ceremony, and it is fundamentally about family
relationships and commitment. So, I accepted the request, and here I
am . . . Let's start with a prayer."

All stood. Dr. Dates lowered his head and said, "Lord, gathered here
in your presence are the family and friends of Skip and Beverly Johnson. The Johnsons have opened their home and hearts to Desta
Abraham, the young man from Ethiopia who is so far from his natural
family. Mr. and Mrs. Johnson wish to adopt the young man, and to love
and support him in his life's pursuits. We seek your blessings for the
family and Desta in this endeavor.

"We thank you for the love and friendship you have put in their hearts. May you enrich their relationship so they will continue caring for and loving one another.

"Thank you, Lord! Amen. You may all be seated."

Next, Dr. Dates read verses from the Bible, and then invited Desta and Mr. Johnson to the table. Following Desta's instruction, the reverend asked Mr. Johnson to dip his thumb in the milk and let Desta suckle it. They did this three times, and then repeated the ritual with the honey. Mr. Johnson sat down; it was Mrs. Johnson's turn. Desta watched anxiously as she first seemed to hesitate, then joined Dr. Dates, and completed the ceremony.

Everyone rose. The three siblings rushed to Desta and hugged him one by one. "You're now our official brother!" Jake said, smiling.

"How neat is that?" Aida added, beaming.

"I think this whole idea of adopting a new family member is cool!" Shae said. "I'm so glad we could do it."

The other witnesses gave the parents and Desta handshakes, hugs, and congratulations. The room seemed to sparkle with happiness.

Elsa had set the dining table before the ceremony, and now lunch was ready. The lamb was served with vegetables, and pasta with peppercorn sauce, complemented by red wine. Dessert was tiramisu.

After the meal, Elsa Alberti came over to Desta and said, "I'm so happy for you!" Desta rose, and they hugged. He helped her clear the table and take everything to the kitchen.

When Desta returned, he found Dr. Dates standing with Mr. and Mrs. Johnson, ready to leave. Soon, the man shook hands with the parents and Desta, waved to the rest, and left. All went to the family room, sat, and chatted while having hot tea for an hour longer.

In the meantime, Desta thought about searching for the Second Magic Coin before he hoped to find a summer job. So, when the Hartmans prepared to leave, Desta pulled David aside and said, "I meant to ask you a favor. Would you please ask Robert Krause if he has time to see me toward the end of May?"

David said he would ask his friend and let Desta know. Shortly after the Hartmans departed, Mr. Johson came to Desta and said, "One privilege of adoption is that you can always call us Mom and Dad instead of Mr. and Mrs. Johnson."

"Thank you," Desta said and went upstairs, filled with happiness.

THIRTY-NINE

Spring in America was as rich and vibrant as in Ethiopia. A great number of flowers budded, unfurled, and opened wide as bursting into laughter. Roses in red, white, and yellow sprouted from the bushes that bordered the fence in the compound. Around the house and near the gate, daisies and daffodils showed off their orange, yellow and red hues. And there were delicate sweet alyssums in violet, blue forget-me-nots, and the bright, cheerful colors of pansies and violets.

Everywhere, green gushed from the once-frozen earth and naked trees. It amazed Desta that so many leaves could grow to fill those once bare branches, and that the grass sprouted so fast that the gardener had to cut it twice a week.

Desta enjoyed his walk along the path to the sculpture garden on campus. He even jogged on his old cross-country route to see the wildflowers covering the fields and their enclosing fences. In nature's generosity of spirit, spring indeed felt like home to Desta, although the man-made gardens here were more vivid and colorful than in Ethiopia.

Desta felt reborn with the season. Jake and Aida now introduced him as their brother to other people, some of whom looked confused, while others took it as a joke, or thought that his parents must trace their roots to Africa. At first, Desta was dubious of Jake and Aida when they spoke of Desta as their sibling, but they said it with such sincerity, he had no reason to doubt them.

One Saturday afternoon in May, Desta, Jake, Aida and Kooper went to the boardwalk and took a stroll on the beach with the dog on a leash. Afterward, they sat on a bench and watched the setting sun turn the waves on Long Island Sound golden. The three sat side by side, Desta in between the siblings, with Kooper resting on the decking, feet parallel, snout flat on the boards.

Desta conversing with the spirt of President Lincoln at the
Abraham Lincoln Junior College sculpture garden.

Jake turned to Desta and said, "I always wanted a brother. . . . just like Aida has her sister Shae. Now I do." In that quiet, sacred moment, Desta believed him. Desta had four brothers, most of whom he hadn't been close to. But he couldn't imagine *not* having a brother. "I'm glad you got your wish. I'm happy to find a brother far from home."

Desta felt at ease with his new family. Nothing really had changed in their day-to-day interactions; he wasn't quite unreserved with his adopted siblings and didn't take their goodwill for granted. No, the change for him was internal, a sense that he had settled in with a family that accepted him as their own, which comforted him.

IN THE SECOND SEMESTER, his lighter course load helped him focus on improving his English reading and writing. He finished his classes by two, and on the days Jake had no later subjects, they went to the library or the sculpture garden to study and do their assignments.

Desta loved to do his schoolwork at the sculpture garden. It reminded him of the serene, scented eucalyptus groves where he once studied for school finals.

At Lincoln's sculpture garden, he loved the scent of blossoming bushes, and the company of the twenty-nine figures—Lincoln at the center, bound by a circle, and seven on each of the earth's four quadrant lines—portraying people who fought to preserve the country or wanted to change it, those who made history, and others who fought for their very existence.

Mr. Lincoln was considerably taller than the others. His angular face, inward eyes, and the weight of the air around him made Desta linger a bit longer. These groupings of men and women weren't random; there was purpose behind it.

A plaque stood at the start of each coordinate line outside of the Lincoln circle. The one going north said, "Union Generals." The southern line indicated "Confederate Generals." The eastern branch declared, "Freedom Fighters," and the westerly line said, "Die-hard Defenders." None of this meant anything to Desta, but what he saw intrigued him. He knew it was about American history.

He inspected the Die-hard Defenders, admiring their distinct features—the smooth, restrained faces and pained almond-shaped eyes, as if fixed on a distant enemy. All had straight hair, some tied in a ponytail.

Those figures that aligned north-south had high brows, strong jaws, and aquiline noses, assertive and purposeful gazes, and neatly cropped, soft hair.

The sculptures oriented in the eastern direction looked authentic and original—rugged bones, less defined faces, sorrowful eyes, and fine curly hair.

After observing the details, Desta realized that beyond just artistic expression, the sculptures and their arrangement had symbolic meaning. But now Desta was taken with a foreboding in the air. It held sadness and hurt, and he didn't know what to make of it. He gathered his things and left to find Jake in the library.

Desta found his host brother and they left for home. That night after Desta crawled into bed, a message came in a dream that he must return to the sculpture garden the following day at 4 p.m. with the magic wand.

The next day, after his 2:30 class finished, Desta went to the statues. To his astonishment, they all had turned into ghosts, still standing but insubstantial as a cloud. He wasn't afraid; he'd seen many spirits in his life. When he stepped into the garden, Desta could feel a troubled, sorrowful energy thick in the air around them. He walked down one of the alleys to the base circle, lost in thought. Why had the statues become ghosts? He approached the first figure in the eastward line.

"Why do you all look so sad?"

"Because we were enslaved Africans who died with our sorrows still within us."

Desta shook his head. He moved to the next quadrant, the southerly line. "Why are you unhappy?" Desta asked the first ghost.

"My group is more angry than sad."

"Why?"

"We lost a war we should have won."

"Sorry to hear it," Desta said and headed to the next group, facing west.

"What pains you?"

"Dispossession. . . . We're American Indians who lost our precious Mother Earth."

"And you took your pain to your grave?"

"Not by choice."

"So sorry," Desta said and moved to the last group, facing north.

"Why are you sad?" Desta asked the first spirit.

"I'm more sorry than unhappy," the ghost said. "That I didn't have the power to avert the civil war or save the many lives we lost unnecessarily."

Desta finally turned to the towering ghost at the center and asked," Mr. President, what is it that ails you?"

"That I can't turn back the clock to fix the mistakes my country made."

"Knowing the immutability of such things, Mr. President," Desta said, "your soul's only redemption is to accept what is. Forgive your country, forgive yourself, and pray that your citizens and their leaders do good by the people in the future."

Desta then turned toward the line of ghosts before him. "I'm sorry all of you have taken the pain of your life to the grave," Desta said. "Your sure first step to find peace is to forgive others, accept what can't be changed, and move on."

Desta took his magic wand out of his knapsack. He stood before each group, held up the staff, and said three times, "Heal these spirits. . . . Heal these spirits. . . . and all who they represent." Lastly, to President Lincoln, he said, "Heal this man. . . . Heal this man. . . . and all the past and present presidents who have erred."

When Desta turned away from President Lincoln, all the ghosts were bathed in a beautiful white light. The dark, somber cloud had lifted. Peace and happiness had descended. The first spirit of each group shouted, "Thank you!" one after another.

"You're welcome!" Desta said. "May you live happily from now on." He waved and left the park. When he turned one last time, all the ghosts had turned back into sculptures.

He felt he had just accomplished an important mission, as if he'd long been needed for this task. Joy and serenity came over him as he strolled to the library to look for Jake. He said, "Thank you, God!"

Desta kept coming to the sculpture garden twice a week on the days Jake had classes until five.

As spring advanced, Desta noticed the days grew longer and warmer. Some flowers along the campus walkway began to wither; first, the edges of their petals curled as if scorched by fire, then the colors dulled, until eventually the bloom dried up and fell to the ground.

Many of the wildflowers along the cross-country trail and the adjoining field had long fizzled. The sculpture garden was once again a peaceful, happy place. As he sat before its statues, Desta felt the tranquil presence of the spirits he had talked to.

When the garden grew too warm or bright to read in, Desta retreated to the shade of the maple trees nearby. When he tired of reading or grew distracted, he put down his book and followed wherever his thoughts and senses took him.

Desta thought about the coming months before his sophomore—*what a word*, he thought—year at Princeton. He continued to do his best in his studies, mainly in English. He didn't know what he might do for the summer, but he would like to spend it in New York City searching for the owner of the second coin.

Spring galloped on like ocean waves before a strong wind. By mid-May, Desta was done with classes, and looked forward to the arrival of summer. Jake got a full-time job at Chase Manhattan Bank, where his father worked. Aida went to Europe with a friend's family for two months. With her new economics degree, Shae got a position with the Department of Commerce, and would be heading to Washington, D.C. after a two-week visit to the grandparents in Florida. Mary Winslow, Mrs. Johnson's home secretary, was on maternity leave for eight weeks.

Desta didn't have a job or someplace to go. But his host mother offered him a filing job three days a week at her office in town and at home.

He thought he would go on his own to New York City on his days off, to look for the owner of the second coin.

Then a call came in from Grandma Johnson, asking if Jake and Desta could spend part of the summer attending to the collection in their former mansion and the second house next door. "I don't want hired hands touching these things," she'd said, according to Mrs. Johnson.

Jake could only help on weekends; Desta could commit to four hours a week. Grandma said he'd be paid ten dollars an hour, which would help with his daily expenses.

Desta didn't know where the mansion was, or what they had to do there, but he was intrigued by the mysterious offer, while Jake had a mixed response. On Saturday of the third weekend in June, Jake and Desta put on old jeans, shirts, and shoes, like field workers, and readied to go to the old mansion. Desta tempered his expectations and kept mum, not wanting to ruin the suspense.

They took the walkway from the beautifully manicured yard on their right to the gate in the back fence directly opposite the main house, a straight line from Desta's window. Jake released the double lock, and they stepped in.

"This mansion," Jake volunteered, pointing to the enormous edifice before them, "was built in 1771. My grandparents lived here before they moved to Florida. If you're lucky, the coin you're looking for might be in this building." He smiled at Desta.

Desta halted in his tracks and searched Jake's eyes for a shred of truth beyond his banter, but his brother merely walked on.

The stately old mansion was clad in grey brick, with a row of tall French windows at the bottom and a series of dormers on top. Vines climbed the walls and clung like moss, edging the windows like thick eyebrows over the white-trimmed frames. The branches of trees extended over the roof, shading the house and pathways, and giving the compound an otherworldly feel.

Jake led Desta to the side entrance and had him wait while he quickly stepped in, turned on the light, and disabled the alarm. He asked Desta to leave the door open and come in. Jake walked around and opened the windows in the reception room. A large gold-rimmed mirror sat above a glossy credenza.

"Jake," Desta called out. "In Ethiopia, before you enter a building that's been shut up a long time, you cross yourself or have it blessed by a priest. People believe that evil spirits dwell there and will smite the first person who enters."

"Not in America," Jake replied indifferently, preoccupied with Shaeves of yellowed notes on the credenza.

"According to this," Jake said, staring at the stack of papers, "we are supposed to start in the guesthouse, and then work in this building. Grandma Johnson must have left these instructions when she was here for Christmas."

They walked through the huge living room with dark wood paneling covered with impressive paintings of all sizes. Leather sofas and chairs, large mirrors, elegant antique furniture, and patterned, woven rugs filled the room. Then to the library, its books lining opposite walls, and in between, old sepia photographs of women with hourglass figures wearing roses and peacock-feathered hats, their busts floating over voluminous dresses; finely clad men with top hats, and black suits or great coats—couples, families, and individuals, looking happy before famous places.

A sofa, chairs, and coffee table sat in the center of the room on a brown, gold, and purple rug over a rust-hued, glossy hardwood floor. A mahogany roll-top desk with cubbyholes and many drawers sat opposite the entrance like a sentinel.

"This place is like a museum," Jake said. "Much of the art on the walls will be donated to the Metropolitan Museum of Art. In September, they'll come to collect them. Sometime in August, we'll take them down, dust them, and get them ready for pick up. But now let's go to the second house."

The guesthouse had cream-colored wood siding, and a pitched shingle roof. Alongside the mansion, it seemed like something of an afterthought. Unlike the main house, time hadn't left its mark here. It seemed this modest home had not witnessed the comings and goings of many people, or too many cycles of the seasons and rhythms of the heavens.

They walked from the flagstone path to the cement-bound guesthouse. Jake unlocked the front door, reached up and flipped the light switch, and stepped in without hesitating. Desta lingered a bit, and walked into what would be the living room, but looked more like a storage room. Spiders had draped their handiwork everywhere.

On the walls and floor, there were more art, artifacts, figurines, sculptures, and portraits of dignified people in fine clothes, with stoic faces and sad eyes that pierced Desta. Others were rendered in tattered garments, looking dazed and forlorn, with ashen skin, as if they had just emerged from prison. Many objects sat in open cardboard boxes and paper bags.

Desta needed to think about the coin collection that was supposed to be somewhere in these two buildings, and what boded for his search for the magic shekel. But for now, the scene before him captured his attention.

"Uncle James amassed all the things in this house," Jake said, his voice tinged with reverence. "He was probably one of the few white Americans who loved collecting art and artifacts about American Blacks. He died seven years ago, and he stipulated in his will that his collection be sold, and the money given to his chosen charity. We haven't shown it to many people since he passed, and no one was interested. Now the museum is, but they want to see the pieces cleaned up and better organized before they come again. That's our job." Jake smiled. "And we're getting paid six times the minimum wage."

Desta was glad his pay was so much better here than in a store downtown.

Whoever had brought the collection from storage and dumped it in the living room had left a path through it, like a trail through the woods. Jake and Desta made their way, bending down and inspecting boxes, surveying pictures on the wall, personal effects, and the reminders of the home's late occupant.

When they reached the middle of the room, Jake looked at a sizeable painting above the mantel and said, "That's Uncle Jim."

A thirtyish, broad-chested man with a mischievous smile gazed out at Desta, and he smiled back, as if they were already acquainted. Behind the standing figure were the blurred figures of musicians.

"Uncle Jim started as an opera singer, but somehow that didn't work out, and he began giving private music lessons to children of wealthy families in the area. Later he went into the jewelry business. He traveled all over the world procuring diamonds and other precious stones for a big store in New York. . . ." Jake trailed off, his eyes still on the man. "He lived in this house for twenty years with Madame Tata, his Russian housekeeper. Seven years ago, she moved, and it was around that time he fell ill with cancer.

"At Grandma's request, he moved in with my grandparents. He had his own private space, and their housekeeper cared for his needs. He was the youngest child, and her favorite. Uncle Jim knew that the end was near, and he had all these things taken out of storage and brought here so he could go through them. But within a few months he died, and my grandparents moved to Florida. Nobody knew what to do with all his stuff, and the house has been unoccupied since."

They followed the meandering path through Uncle Jim's possessions, careful not to step on them as they made their way to the other side of the room. On the right, atop two long tables, were piles of old books of different sizes, and folding, ornamental picture display cases. The sheer mass of objects on the tables reminded Desta of the funerary goods he had seen in burial chambers of the mummies in the Washaa Umera caves of Ethiopia several years ago.

On the wall above the table, a large, signed poster of Abraham Lincoln with the slogan "Don't Swap Horses in Midstream" intrigued Desta. The meaning could have been more precise, and the idea seemed impractical. Who in their right mind would turn such advice into a campaign slogan? Gazing at Lincoln's signature at the bottom made Desta feel closer to the great man.

Jake picked up a worn photo case and brought it close for Desta to see. "Look," he said, "a young Black boy—five or six years old— perched on a small wooden cart pulled by a pair of scruffy goats."

Desta burst into laughter when he saw it. Jake laughed, too, as if he had just realized the ridiculousness of the image. The boy wore a charcoal gray turned-up hat, with matching coat and pants. He held the harness line, appearing as serious as an adult. Desta knew about goats; he used to look after them. He'd never known that they could be trained to pull a carriage like a horse. The picture was dated 1895.

They proceeded down the hallway, passing two rooms on either side, each containing more boxes. In the master bedroom, piles of royal regalia sat under plastic sheets on the bed: robes, coats, and hats, along with neck and hand adornments.

Inside the seven-by-seven-foot walk-in closet, new shirts of many colors still wrapped in cellophane arrayed the slanting top three shelves. Sweaters, socks, and scarves also in their packages occupied the lower two shelves. On the right and against the facing wall hung various dress suits, jackets, ties, and trousers. Desta admired their hues and textures and ran his fingers along the delicate garments.

"Now I know why Grandma wanted us to start in this house," Jake said. "This project can't be done in just two months."

Desta had to ask what was on his mind. "Do you think we might find a coin collection somewhere in here?"

"I'm sure there is," Jake said. "I remember going with him to specialty coin shops in Manhattan before he got sick, where he bought and traded coins."

"I hope we can find them," Desta said. "I'd like to try, however remote the chances."

"We are bound to find something. . . . Right now, we should plan for this project. Let's go home and discuss this."

They turned back, Desta leading the way. Jake locked the door, and they went home. They sat on the couch in Jake's room and discussed their strategy. They decided to first sort and separate the good from the junk; the latter would go out on the porch. That would give them more room to work with what was left. Then they would classify the rest by type—paintings, photos and related items, artifacts, books, jewelry, and statues. Once they'd grouped these items, they would number them, and then record everything in notebooks. With the plan set, they went to town to purchase notebooks.

After they returned, Jake called his grandmother and told her their plan, which she endorsed.

Back in his room, Desta was a bit flustered. He had already agreed to the filing job for his mother, and he had planned to spend part of his summer searching for the coin owner. Instead, he'd be cleaning, categorizing, and documenting objects of art from America's past.

Later that night, he brought out his magic wand and sent a message to Tsadok about his frustration.

At midnight Desta woke to Tsadok's reply in *The Record*:

"Don't question things that come up unexpectedly. There might be a reason why. The money you earn is more important than the coin right now. And it may have something to do with your mission."

Desta sighed deeply. He closed *The Record* and trudged back to bed, eyes open, fixed on the ceiling. Desta thought, of course, he would do this job diligently. *But how does it relate to my mission?* Of course, he had no answer. As so often was true, Tsadok will reveal what that is, he said to himself. He covered his face, turned to his side, and slept.

FORTY

On Sunday, Desta and Jake worked in the oppressive heat and humidity of the guesthouse. Bathed in sweat, they opened all the windows to let in the fresh, damp air and felt slightly better.

For several hours, they reorganized the scattered boxes, grouped similar items, removed trash, and consolidated what remained. They put things of less interest on the porch.

In the afternoon, Mrs. Johnson dropped in to see how things were progressing. It was the first time she had seen the collection, and she seemed stunned.

She picked up a figurine of a Black woman from a box and examined it. "I never knew James had such a passion for Americana," she said. She couldn't stop herself from going through the photos, documents, and artifacts in bags and boxes on the tables and shelves.

"You fellows are going to have fun with this," Mrs. Johnson said, glancing at Desta and Jake, who stood nearby, watching her. "Certainly educational. This record of our past isn't everyday knowledge in this country."

"You're quite right, Mom," Jake said. "But it should be, especially now. My generation, and probably yours, wouldn't even know about these things unless they'd studied history. Even then, we mostly learned about white people. Our history books say little about what these objects represent."

Jake continued. "Desta, you should enjoy this incredible collection while I'm at my job all week."

"That reminds me," Mrs. Johnson interjected. "Desta, you won't have time to work for me this summer. It's best if you spend all your days here. We must finish this project before you fellows return to school in September."

Jake's face stiffened. "I don't think we could finish if we worked every day for the next six months."

"I will do the best I can," Desta said. "I'm glad to work here the rest of the summer." The supposed coin stash in the home was in the back of his mind.

"I suppose I could ask Grandma if we can hire an extra hand, but she says she doesn't want strangers here."

"Particularly one who may hold an antipathy toward black people," Jake said and chuckled.

"You don't know who you're dealing with when you involve the public," Mrs. Johnson said. "I'll leave you to it. . . . Do your best." She turned toward the door and left.

Something had been on Desta's mind to ask his brother. "Jake, I'm curious about your uncle. Did he have children? They should be working on this collection."

Desta looked up at the row of men's photos on the wall he had seen the first day they came here.

"No, he didn't," Jake said and paused. "Mother called him a confirmed bachelor."

Desta thought about those last two words. They were another turn of phrase whose meaning he'd have to find out for himself.

Desta and Jake resumed their work, battling the heat. At some point, Desta suggested that they clear the living room floor on either side of the entrance to set aside the boxes for the Met.

By the end of the day, Desta and his host brother had arrived at a plan. Desta would spend the days sorting and organizing, and Jake would leave flattened boxes on the porch every evening after work. In the morning, Desta would fill these new boxes with all the things he had organized the previous day.

They followed the plan for the first week. The challenge for Desta was sorting and gathering such a wide variety of artifacts: art, photographs, books, and personal effects, large and small. They were jumbled together in cartons and wooden crates or scattered on the floor. It took a lot of work, and Desta struggled to judge what objects were valuable or ordinary.

The packing itself was a challenge. He had to carefully fill the boxes in such a way that the Met people could quickly discern the contents.

Some days, Desta began at seven or eight a.m. and worked until six or seven in the evening.

By the end of the first week, Desta realized he needed help from a higher source to lighten his work and make quicker progress. At night, he placed his hand over the coin on his chest and sought its magical power to help him do the job.

On Monday, he prayed over his parchment, asking God for a productive day, and to guide him to Uncle James' coin collection in the house. He had breakfast and set out for work.

"How are you doing?" Mrs. Johnson asked, startling Desta one afternoon in the second week of his work. Desta said he was doing fine.

She walked around the house. "It looks like you're making excellent progress." Her eyes and smile said more. "You're not expected to work like a slave," she added. "That was not meant as a pun. Outside of your lunch hour, you need to take twenty-minute breaks in the morning and afternoon."

"Good to know," Desta said, smiling. "Your lighthearted comment reminds me of the history I'm immersed in all day."

"Well," she said, and paused. "You understand what I meant. Taking time for yourself makes you more productive." She continued walking. "At this rate, you'll complete the bulk of the work by the end of August."

"We'll see," Desta said to please her. Uncle James's journal had noted some nine thousand objects; Desta doubted he could sort through them all so quickly.

"See you later," she said and left.

Desta thought about his breaks. Instead of wasting that time, he would use it to read some of the documents and study the artifacts that captivated his fancy.

He returned to the box he was working on. He pulled out different kinds of images—some folded or meant for display shelves, duplicates on stiff cards, and picture frames for hanging, and put them into empty boxes by type. As he moved a stack of pictures, one fell to the floor. He put the rest in a box and picked up the stray card.

He gazed inside an orange border at identical images separated by a vertical white line. Frozen time. Frozen history. The portraits of young and old Black women, heads wrapped in white fabric, some balancing large baskets of cotton on their heads, others bending and picking more of the white pods. Location: Savannah, Georgia, in the year 1871. *Precisely a hundred years ago,* Desta thought.

The images seemed merely some old pictures that anyone would toss in the trash. But to James van Hook Johnson, they had historical value. Desta carefully added the card to a stack of similar ones in the box.

Desta labored on the project like clockwork through the second week of July. The packages grew high and wide on either side of the door and deep into the living room, which came to resemble a warehouse waiting for a freight train.

Occasionally, Desta walked around the house to assess how much was still left to pack. Even after a fortnight of work, he was daunted by the vast number of Black American artifacts, pictures, and memorabilia still to gather, sort, and pack. Jake's pronouncement rang in his head: *I don't think we could finish if we worked every day for the next six months.*

No matter, Desta labored diligently. During his breaks, he continued to study images of people and read documents that caught his interest. He had not come across the purported coin collection, but he hoped to stumble upon it in the coming days and weeks.

ONE DAY, during his twenty-minute respite, he examined a photograph of a shoeshine boy sitting on a bench. The year was 1869. The boy propped his right arm on an armrest, fingers drooping, his left hand clutching the handle of his wooden box, the visor of his round hat turned left, its shadow swallowing nearly all of one ear. He gazed detachedly, wearily, at the camera. His eyes were puffy, and one knee of his baggy, worn pants was streaked with dirt. An oversized coat closed against his neck, as if to hold in his last vestige of dignity. Pressed lips seemed to hold in pain and disdain for the world he lived in.

There was so much darkness in the youth's expression and the mood surrounding him that Desta wondered if he ever saw sunlight. Desta had known those days in his youth; perhaps that was why he was drawn to the picture. The determination to pursue his education and the second coin, no matter his circumstances, had saved him from permanent gloom, he thought.

At five, Desta locked the door and went home, head brimming with the images he'd handled all day.

Before bedtime, he brought out his magic wand and sat cross-legged on the bed, the device before him. "Please help me finish my project before school starts," he repeated earnestly. Desta also reached for the coin image on his chest and implored it. Then he put away the device, recited his legends, and slept.

When Desta went to work in the morning, there were no boxes on the porch, and inside the house, he discovered that all of the things he had sorted and left unpacked the night before were now in boxes. His brow creased, wondering if Jake might have done this after Desta left for the night.

As he worked that day, this unexplained anomaly passed through his mind like a dream. Desta's host brother appeared in the late afternoon. "You've worked like a horse," Jake said. "I came here this morning to see how many more boxes I should get you tonight and was surprised to see that all of those I got yesterday were gone."

"So, you . . . you didn't come here last night and pack more boxes?" Desta asked, studying the man intently.

"Nope," Jake replied. "If I had, I wouldn't have made it to work today."

"I don't know what to think then," Desta said. He shook his head.

"I need to go eat," Jake said. "Then I'll get more boxes and leave them on the porch tonight."

"Thank you," Desta said absently, frozen in place, feeling like he'd lost his mind. He soon came to his senses and resumed his work.

As he walked home from Uncle James' house that evening, Desta wondered if the magic of the coin image on his chest and his morning recitals might explain all the work done overnight. He felt an eddy of excitement; if his coin continued to help him, he might finish the work before school started in September.

At night, Desta prayed over the parchment and his shekel, soliciting their help with the packing this night.

FORTY-ONE

It was Friday, the eve of the last day of July. When Desta got to work, he found only half a dozen boxes on the porch. He wondered if his prayers and the magic power of his coin had once again done his packing for him.

When he unlocked the door and stepped inside, he was mystified to find all the lights on in the house. He thought perhaps he'd forgotten to turn them off last night.

He walked over to where he had left the sorted artifacts. As he suspected, all had been grouped and boxed by type and size. And to Desta's surprise, many more artifacts had been added to what he had set aside to study in his free time, as if whoever had done this knew what interested him.

That morning, Desta focused on the documents, paintings, and posters scattered throughout the house. He brought the leftover boxes from the porch, opened them and taped their bottoms, and began gathering records concerning enslaved people.

He found a folder marked "Plantation Records" that contained all manner of documents: estate liquidation notices with schedules of human property; court papers about the sale of enslaved people, with names and the prices they fetched; shipping logs, passage certificates; wanted and for-sale ads from newspapers and magazines. All these were mixed in with journals that recorded the daily activities of enslaved people at a plantation. Still more folders for his review concerned the auction, sale, and ownership of enslaved people.

Desta struggled to control his emotions and feelings about these records. Before leaving the house at the end of the day, he made sure to turn off the lights.

"I ordered a large supply of boxes to be delivered to Uncle James's tomorrow," Jake said when he ran into Desta outside with Kooper. "We can be at my grandparents' house to receive them."

"Great!" Desta said. "That will be less trouble for you."

"I wish I had thought of it sooner," Jake said.

Desta tossed and turned in bed for hours that night. The words and images about slavery he'd seen that day were too much. He couldn't quite fathom all of it, but somehow grasped that he'd been assigned this job to understand the realities of America's complicated past. He made himself sleep, knowing he would wake at four as usual.

ON SATURDAY, the last day of July, at noon, Jake and Desta went to the grandparents' compound. They opened the main gate and waited for the shipment. Shortly, a truck arrived, its cargo hold filled to the brim. Two men unloaded the flattened cartons and piled them on the porch, some spilling onto the flagstone walkway.

Jake thanked and tipped the two men, and they left.

"There you have it," Desta's host brother said, with a smile.

"Well," Desta piped up. "This means somebody has their work cut out for them," he said, grinning.

"Let's hope *they* can make a bigger dent in Uncle James' treasures with all these boxes," Jake said, a wry expression on his lips.

"We'll see," Desta said. "Let's go home now." He was not planning to work that day.

That night, to Desta, the coming day felt like an eternity, and Monday seemed to exist on the other side of the universe.

THE SECOND DAY of August finally arrived. Desta walked to work, nerves taut as a guitar string, heart pulsing with anxiety, and his mind in eager anticipation.

He had barely reached the threshold of James van Hook Johnson's verandah when Desta's jaw dropped and his eyes flared. Most of the truckload was gone. Hands shaking, he opened the door.

Desta's fingers flew to his mouth as he studied the well-lit scene, speechless. Nearly all of James van Hook Johnson's collection was packed and stacked high and deep in the living room. *Was this the work of his magic coin and morning prayers?* It looked like a huge crew had worked all weekend, and someone with a key to the house had forgotten again to turn the lights off when they left.

But who? Desta had no answer, but he was certainly glad for the help. He could spend the rest of August as he wished, and search for the Second Coin of Magic and Fortune. It meant he would earn less money, but he was willing to make that sacrifice to continue his quest for the coin.

Back at home that evening, Desta asked Jake, "Do you know if a crew worked at Uncle James's house over the weekend?"

"No," the host brother replied. "If that were the case, Mom would have mentioned it."

Desta approached his host mother in the kitchen. "How is the project coming along at Uncle James'?" she asked.

"Rather well," he said. "Have you, by any chance, heard from Grandma Johnson lately?"

"She called this weekend to ask how your work was going, and I told her that you were doing a great job."

Now Desta was utterly bewildered. If no one else had done the work, how could Desta explain to his host family that several months' worth of work was nearly finished after six weeks, and he himself had done only part of it?

The next day, Desta went to finish up at James' house. He walked down the hall to check the bedrooms for any stray articles or a store of coins. He found a few bags of posters, drawings, and postcards in one of the smaller bedroom closets.

He brought them to the living room and lined up all the large objects against the walls, and in front of them, smaller items, bags, and a few open mixed cartons.

With a broom from the porch, he swept the living room and hallway, stuffed the trash into empty boxes, and brought them to the verandah.

Desta checked the one-story house one last time, including every storage space.

He went back to the living room and abruptly sensed a bodily presence. He looked around but saw no one and proceeded to the door. He had just raised his hand to the doorknob when a voice from behind said, "Wait!"

Desta's hand jumped. He spun around to find a shrouded human form not far from him.

"I didn't mean to scare you," the figure said. "Thank you for your excellent work on my collection."

"Most of the credit goes to whoever worked here this weekend," Desta said. "I only helped."

"You are why my collection will finally find a home," the man said. "Otherwise, everything here would have languished for many more years."

"I'm not sure what to say," Desta said, "but I'm glad I could be of service."

"You are!" Several voices rang out behind the figure, and Desta's head jerked. "You will be of service in more ways than you can imagine."

Desta stepped to his left to see the entities who had spoken.

"You can't see them," the shrouded man said. "The voices belong to those who worked here for the last few nights and days. . . . They are the spirits of the slaves whose stories you gleaned from my collection."

Desta stilled himself.

"And you?" Desta asked, looking up at the tall figure.

"I'm James van Hook Johnson, who assembled everything in this house."

Desta raised his hand to his mouth, eyes fixed on the man, his mind whirring.

"Why did you collect all of it?" Desta asked.

"Generations of my ancestors fought for the freedom and fair treatment of Black and Native Americans, to little avail," the man said. "I thought I would do something more meaningful: preserve these people's histories to educate future generations of Americans."

Desta dropped his hand. "Well, you have done just that," he said. "Collecting nine thousand artifacts must have taken a lot of money, time, and energy."

"You're right in all that," James van Hook Johnson said. "It was a mission I was meant to fulfill on earth. . . . Nothing else mattered to me."

Desta nodded vigorously. He understood the importance of fulfilling one's mission.

"Thank you for being here," James van Hook Johnson said. "You have freed me from my quest. I wouldn't take my place in heaven without seeing my efforts bear fruit. Now, my work will go to a museum where the world can see it; that gives me great satisfaction."

"I'm grateful to you, sir, for the work," Desta said. "My time here has been incredibly educational."

"Perhaps you're disappointed the work finished sooner than you thought," the figure said. "Don't despair. My mother is a thoughtful woman. I'm sure she'll compensate you as you expected."

"Who did the work?" Desta asked.

"My helpers and me. But as far as anyone else is concerned, you did it. That's as it should be."

"I'm sorry, but I won't take credit for something I'm not entitled to," Desta said.

"Then there is something else you are entitled to, which is the other reason I've stuck around here. . . . You will find an envelope under folded T-shirts in the top drawer of the bedroom dresser. Fetch it before you leave. Now I know why someone gave it to me; it is for your good fortune.

"It was January 7, 1949. I was standing in front of Alexander's Department store in the Bronx at noon, watching the snow tumble down with impunity, when a hooded old man with a long white beard approached and handed me an envelope. He said, "Guard this with your life . . . you will know who to give it to when the time comes."

Cold sweat ran down Desta's back, knowing that this was his birthday and the old man in James van Hook Johnson's story seemed like the one who had entrusted the painting of the two coins to Roman Burkhardt in Romania on the same day. The thought gave Desta goosebumps.

"Mr. Johnson, I'm not new to strange connections in my life, but when someone seen in one place appears thousands of miles away on the same day, it's spooky, as you say in this country."

"I've not opened the envelope, and I don't even know what's in it. I thought I would be punished if I tampered with it. Allegedly, it was very important to its intended recipient. I wish you all the best in your schooling and reaching your goals.

"One more thing," the specter said, and paused. "My coin collection is in a vault in my bedroom closet. Behind my robes, you will see a gray metal box on the right. The key is in the same drawer as the envelope.

Open the vault and take out the wooden chest. Go through the collection and see if your coin might be there.

"I have several ancient coins wrapped in silk fabric. Take one that you like as a gift to you from me. It will be a token of my gratitude and a reminder of our meeting and the hard work you have spent your first summer doing in America. . . . And we'll call it *Your Coin of Good Luck.* You will know it when you open the chest." James van Hook Johnson's puffy face lit up, which Desta thought was a smile.

"Afterward, return the chest of coins to the vault, lock it up, and drop the key where you found it. The treasure is stipulated in my will to be auctioned off and the proceeds donated to the charities I listed."

Desta's heart fluttered with excitement. His lips quivered. "Oh my! I never thought I would come close to your coins," he said finally. "Thank you very much for your gift to me."

The door swung open. Moments later, the spirit of Mr. James van Hook Johnson slipped through and vanished. Desta imagined that the silent voices followed him like a flock of birds.

Desta remained in the doorway as if struck by lightning, unable to move or think.

He looked around for any remaining spirits. The room felt quiet and light. Desta walked down the hall to the master bedroom, to the beautiful mahogany dresser where the cryptic envelope lay. He opened the top drawer and groped under the neatly folded white shirts. He clasped the envelope and pulled it slowly as if it might disintegrate. He pressed it between his fingers; it felt ordinary.

He was not ready to open it. He wanted to savor the suspense. He pulled open his shirt and carefully pushed it over his breast. His hand returned to the drawer and groped for the vault key. Finding it, he took it out and examined the gold device with a large circular base and a long stem. He was eager to open the vault and search for his coin in Uncle James's collection, but he was more intrigued about the envelope's contents than the shekels, which would take time to sift through to find his own magical coin. He set the key back in its place with the plan to return tomorrow, closed the drawer, and headed out.

Back home in his room, he sat at his desk, pulled out the envelope, fingers shaking, and carefully peeled the flap. In some places, it tore cleanly; elsewhere, the flap broke into bits before he freed its contents. He drew out the folded, cream-colored paper, lifted the first fold, and then the second to reveal two one-thousand-dollar bills printed in 1861. A portrait of a clean-shaven bald man with a prominent nose sat at the center of each. The denomination was written in the top two corners and on either side of the man.

A note read: "Good luck with your missions!"

Desta planted one elbow on the edge of his desk and gazed at the floor as excitement, fear, and confusion took him over. How could he explain to Jake or the family where he had gotten these bills? Were they real? Could he even exchange them for smaller amounts?

He squinted into the distance. How could he adequately explain finishing this six-month project in six weeks?

Moreover, how could he tell the Johnsons that he had met the spirit of their relative James van Hook Johnson and that he and his assistants help Desta finish the project impossibly fast? And what of the mysterious old man who had given the envelope to James?

He put the money back in the envelope, got up, and brought out the suitcase that contained his precious objects. Opening it, he carefully slipped the envelope between the folds of the cotton cloth bedding.

Then Desta went to Jake and told him he'd finished their project. Jake blinked in disbelief, and his mouth twitched.

"How . . . how is that possible?"

"Miracles happen, you know," Desta said, smiling. "And this is one of them."

"I don't know what to make of you sometimes, Desta," Jake said. "You can't possibly sort and pack nine thousand artifacts alone in a month and a half!"

"I wasn't alone," Desta said. "A group of spirits took part in the project."

"A group of spirits?!"

"Yes," Desta said. "It's too complicated to get into right now."

Jake shook his head. "It sounds implausible, but I'm glad it worked out," he said finally. "It means the Met people can take the collection and pay us sooner." He walked away, still shaking his head.

The next day, Desta returned to James's house and went directly to the vault after retrieving its key. His hand shook, and he struggled to insert the key into the vault lock, and then align it to release the locking mechanism. When he finally opened the hefty door, he found a beautiful wooden chest sixteen inches wide, twenty inches long, and twelve high, lustrous and golden, Desta ran his fingers over it to ease his nerves. The chest had a yellow key in its hole, which Desta slowly turned. He opened the top, blinked, and then steadied his eyes.

Silver, gold, copper, and bronze coins teemed to the brim, some with a dusty film and greenish patina, evidently untouched since their owner's death many years ago.

Desta had a sudden reluctance to disturb them, or the coloring time had coated them with; it felt wrong, like disturbing the body of James van Hook Johnson. He stood inactive for several minutes, staring at the coins as a welter of unexpected feelings surged through him. Desta decided not to handle the shekels until he could think through what was happening. He would need to figure out how to go through the large collection.

He closed the chest, put it back in the vault, locked it, and went home, his head weighty with an unnamed burden.

He decided to share his feelings and thoughts with Tsadok. He retrieved the wand from his suitcase and proceeded with his message.

To the Honorable Tsadok, High Priest of the Ark,

I'm in a situation where I cannot determine what to do. The late owner of a home where I've been working for the last several weeks left a chest full of coins, some that go back thousands of years. I met his spirit yesterday, and it permitted me to go through them in search of the Coin of Magic and Fortune. This morning, I accessed the collection, but I resisted touching the coins. I don't know why, and I was hoping you could explain.

Desta returned the magic wand to the suitcase. He pulled *The Record* from the shelf, set it on his desk, and waited for Tsadok's reply. The ancient priest of the Ark did not send his answer right away. When Desta was about to go to bed at 10 p.m., light shimmered over the correspondence journal. He opened the page with the last entry.

My Dear Desta,

> *Your reluctance to touch the coins in that man's treasure chest
> stems partly from your heart's fear of disappointment if you do not find
> the second shekel. Also, there is a coin in the collection that's antago-
> nistic to your own, which makes you reluctant to handle any of them.
> You must neutralize this negative property by passing the magic wand
> over the treasure.*

Desta stared at the cryptic message, trying to make sense of it. He
hadn't thought he'd be disappointed not to find the coin of his mission.
For him, James' coin collection was just another stone he wished to turn
over. He folded the tome and placed it back on the shelf.

After lunch, he returned to James van Hook's house with the magic
wand. He realized the best way to sift through the coins would be to
spread them on a large, flat surface.

From the master bedroom closet, he took a bedsheet, folded it, and then
spread it over the kitchen table. Next, Desta nervously retrieved the hefty
treasure chest from the vault, staggered with it down the long hall to the
kitchen and set it on the covered table. Taking the magic wand out of his
backpack, he hovered it over the chest, reciting repeatedly, "Remove the
bad energy contained in this box." When serenity descended upon him, he
returned the magic device to his backpack and opened the box.

To his surprise, the coins were dust-free and shining, as if someone
had polished them. He tipped the box and poured its contents on the table, to find at the bottom a silk pouch, its mouth tied with a string,
which he felt and found to contain a handful of shekels.

He spread the mass of loose coins wide and thin to see them easily.
He placed the pouch aside and began scanning the main cache of coins,
hovering over them, occasionally picking up one that intrigued him, but
mostly looking for the image of seven channels fanning from the center
to its edge, same as on his shekel.

After nearly two fruitless hours, he returned to the pouch of coins.
Something about it drew him in. He untied the string and spilled its contents at one corner of the table. Desta was stunned by the odd and varied
antiquity of these coins, the size of a thumbnail or a silver dollar, some

with a man's head in relief, or letters, or animals; others smooth as if flattened with a hammer. They came in gold, silver, and bronze.

One of the flat, faceless gold shekels felt warm to the touch. When he picked it up, its surface transformed into a woman's head and letters around the edges on one side, and chariots on the other. Desta liked the coin's magical quality and its warmth in his hand. He would honor James's generosity to Desta with this coin. He thought it would indeed be the right memento of his summer job. He returned the other coins to the pouch, tied its mouth, and placed it at the bottom of the chest. Then he gathered the rest of the coins and poured them in, completely covering the pouch.

Afterward he brought the folded bedsheet and the chest to the master bedroom closet. He put away the sheet and placed the chest in its vault, which he locked, finally placing the key in the drawer. At last, he closed and locked the house and left. As he walked, he enjoyed the warmth and smooth feel of his gift from the man who had devoted his life to unique Americana. It would be a good companion to his Coin of Magic and Fortune.

GRANDMA JOHNSON was thrilled. She said she would still pay Desta for two months of work. A week later, he received a check for twelve hundred dollars, for which he was thankful. He left it in his drawer for a few days, feeling guilty to get this much money when he hadn't done most of the work.

When Desta told Jake about his ambivalence, his host brother said, "Just remember if not for you, Uncle James's stuff would still be collecting dust in that house. Let's open an account at Chase and deposit your money."

The next day Jake and Desta went to downtown Rye and put Grandma's check and his Christmas gift money in his new savings account. But much to Desta's disappointment, the two one-thousand-dollar bills were worthless as currency. He was excited, however, to learn that their antiquity made them worth a lot more than their face value.

They left the bank and were heading to their car when an older woman in a long floral dress with flowing dark hair and twinkling eyes stopped Desta. "May I offer my insights about the two old bills you possess?"

Desta stumbled to a halt. Jake was several feet ahead, speaking to an acquaintance, but briefly glanced back at Desta, having overheard the woman's remark.

Desta looked above the woman and saw a sign on the building that read "Fortune Teller."

"What is it?" he asked the strange woman.

"1861 was the beginning of America's civil war, and the beginning of the end of our nation's old order. Four years later, a new nation emerged that led to who we are today. 1861 is also an angel's number. It symbolizes new beginnings, the foretelling of the future, the manifestation of all you seek to achieve. It can be a source of positive energy and happiness for you. Rest assured, these bills are for your good. Please keep them in your possession. Good luck," the ancient seer said, and waved before slipping into her abode.

"She is our resident witch," Jake said. "Some people say she is a good seer."

"I don't know, Jake," Desta said. "I . . . don't know."

Unexpectedly left with extra time on his hands, Desta agreed to work for Mrs. Johnson as a filing clerk three days a week for the remaining two weeks of August. On his days off, he would continue to search for the second magic coin and read all the books he'd no time for during the school year.

He wanted time to think about the black American memorabilia he'd pored over for six weeks, and about his extraordinary encounter with the spirit of the man who had collected them.

And he needed to learn the purpose and meaning of the two one-thousand dollar civil-war era bills James van Hook Johnson had received from a mysterious old man at the moment of Desta's birth thousands of miles away in Ethiopia. This made Desta more convinced his journey to America was planned before his birth.

Desta was eager to resume his search for the second Coin of Magic and Fortune. He called David and asked if he could arrange a meeting for him with Robert Krause on the weekend.

FORTY-TWO

The THREE SISTERS PANCAKE HOUSE at the corner of Lexington and East 34th Street was packed on a Saturday morning. Patrons stood in a long line, waiting to be seated. Desta scanned the tables inside and out for a sign of Bob Krause. Had Desta gotten the place or time wrong? When they'd spoken a few days ago, Desta was sure he'd written down his instructions correctly. He glanced at his watch; it was fifteen minutes past their meeting time. He thought to approach the hostess at the door to ask if she'd seen his friend, but decided he'd only raise eyebrows from the people on line who'd think he was cutting ahead.

A tap on Desta's shoulder startled him. "Sorry I'm late," Bob said. "I made the mistake of driving. It was hard to park around here." He strode to the hostess and gave her his name for the reservation, a party of four. She scanned a list on her notepad.

"Yes," she said. "You're in the eastern dining room, our quieter, nicer section." A thin smile passed her lips. "Follow me." Desta was relieved to be seated right away.

The eastern wing of this eatery was indeed removed from the commotion of the crowd and the kitchen. It would be easier for Desta to have a conversation here. Bob wrote down the names of his friends on a napkin and handed it to the waiter, along with a request to let them know where to find his table.

Once they'd arrived, Desta saw a definite age disparity between Esther Winkel and Arie Brenner, which he hadn't expected when David first proposed to meet with them. As it turned out, they were aunt and nephew.

Bob introduced them to Desta, and they acknowledged one another with smiles and handshakes. With wispy white hair and wrinkled skin, Esther appeared to be in her late seventies. Arie, with his thick salt-and-

pepper hair, seemed in his mid-forties. Bob and Desta sat together, facing the guests.

Esther and Arie ordered omelets, Bob and Desta scrambled eggs. Except for Esther, each also got two pancakes that they doused with
honey-colored syrup from a glass pitcher. All ate with gusto and spoke
very little, their eyes wandering occasionally to the families with children on the patio outside the large glass window. After their meals, each
ordered coffee, and Desta his usual tea.

Bob cleared his throat. "Esther and Arie, it's so great to see you after
such a long time—even if this meeting is to solicit your help." Bob
grinned, eyes panning his friends' faces. "As I mentioned to you when
we spoke on the phone, Desta believes that a Solomonic magic coin he
has been searching for is in this country. The owner is supposed to be a
Karaite. I wondered if by any chance you've come across such a coin or
know someone in our Karaite community who has it."

Bob then turned to Desta. "For our benefit, would you please describe in detail the treasure you seek?"

Desta cleared his throat, crossed his arms, and said, "First, thank you,
Bob, for arranging a meeting with Mrs. Finkel and Mr. Brenner in this
wonderful place. The gold shekel I'm looking for has the portrait of a
man on the front and a curled horse on its back. It has seven reliefs that
fan from the center to its edges on both sides of the coin. The coin has
magical power and brings wealth and fortune to its owner. Also, the person who now holds the coin has a name that means Sweet and Sour."

Arie's face lit up, punctuated with a puzzled look. He glanced at Esther, who squinted as thoughts played on her face.

"An interesting meaning for a name," she said, smiling faintly.
"When my nephew here mentioned the coin you're looking for, I
thought hard and remembered an incident our neighbors experienced involving a coin of great importance. The Karaite population in New York
City then was about three dozen. We lived in the Bronx and knew one
another because we were family or had common roots. All of us came
from either Palestine or Crimea in the Soviet Union."

Desta's heart skipped a beat at the mention of the two places. From
the map he'd seen in the caves of Washaa Umera, he remembered the
coin had gone from Crimea to Israel, the last place it supposedly had

resided. Knowing that Israel came into existence after 1948, Desta wondered if the name on the map was later changed from Palestine to the
new or if the mapmaker was prophetic.

The waiter returned with their drinks. They took their sips.

Desta was anxious to hear more of Esther's story. He looked up at
her. "Please continue. What was this incident?" he asked.

"The coin was stolen from our neighbors, and they were devastated.
The woman said the shekel was the sole reason she could travel alone as a
teenager on a ship from Jaffa in Palestine to New York. The coin was her
chaperone and protector." Esther took another sip, then held her cup with
both hands and looked away thoughtfully. Desta took a deep, silent sigh.

"Do you know who stole the coin, and if your neighbors ever got it
back?" Bob asked.

"They implicated a young man who once worked for them and disappeared after the incident. We moved away shortly after, and lost contact
with them. I've wondered if they ever got it back."

"When did you last see them, and do you know of any relatives?"
Arie asked.

"This was in 1921. The couple had a handsome young boy, and they
were expecting a second child. My mother worried the shock might
cause her a miscarriage. The mother had an aunt or something, but I
don't know about her husband."

Bob turned to Desta. "Does Esther's story help identify the coin
you're looking for?"

"I don't know for sure, but some of these clues seem relevant," Desta
said. He glanced at Arie's aunt and said, "You wouldn't by any chance
remember their names?"

"Not really. The woman had an unusual first name."

"Did it sound like Russian or Hebrew?" Desta asked.

"Neither."

"You wouldn't recall who the thief was, or the names of his relatives
in the Bronx?" Bob asked.

"No, I don't," Esther replied. "But he was a trusted friend of the couple."

Desta didn't know what to do with this information, but it meant that
the coin was indispensable to its owner, as his own was to himself.

The two men were quiet and thoughtful. "Desta, you're not entirely in the dark now. You have these clues to work with," Bob said finally.

Desta fingered the underside of the table as he mulled the man's words.

"Aunt Esther," Arie said, turning to her. "Perhaps you can talk to our relatives and friends from that time who may know more about the young couple."

"Many people have passed on, but I'll ask the few still around."

Bob signaled their waiter. He paid the bill, and all rose.

"Thank you very much," Desta said to Esther. "You certainly heightened my curiosity."

Bob Krause thanked Esther and Arie for coming, and they expressed gratitude for their meal. They all shook hands, and the couple left.

"I'm sorry we didn't find better information," Bob said apologetically.

"It's okay," Desta said. "What Mrs. Winkel shared is still useful. I'll have to assume that the coin might not be with the person who brought it into this country."

"We'll keep talking to people," Bob said. "Sooner or later, there'll be a break in your search."

"Thank you for everything," Desta said, and shook the man's hand.

"You're welcome!"

Desta had a sinking feeling as he headed for home. If that coin was indeed the one he was looking for and it was stolen, did the owner ever get it back? Did they die trying to retrieve it, as his grandfather had when he pursued the thief? Who might possess it now?

He felt like screaming as he walked up Lexington Avenue toward Grand Central Station for the train home. He looked around as the urge surged through him. He quickly passed his hand over his chest and calmed himself. He staggered along, thoughts swirling, barely aware of the traffic's din and the hurrying throngs around him.

"Hello!" someone said, coming from behind Desta to where he stood at the red light. Desta turned and beheld the figure. He looked vaguely familiar, but Desta couldn't place him.

"You don't remember me?" the old man asked.

It finally dawned on Desta. It was the same man he and David had run into after visiting the Empire State Building.

"I didn't get a chance to introduce myself when we met," the man began. "My name is Willard Makari. I've long wanted a formal acquaintance with you. Today seems to be that time."

A young woman emerged from the crowd and approached Desta.

"This is my granddaughter Calliope MacDuff," Mr. Makari said. "She wants to meet you."

These strangers are interested in me. It meant they must know something about him. Desta felt uneasy, but as he studied the girl, he felt a warmth deep in his heart, while his mind still analyzed the situation.

"Who are you?"

"We are ordinary people who happen to be connected to the supernatural."

"That's pretty cryptic," Desta said. "And why are you interested to meet me?"

"Because we know your origin and why you came here. And we know where the coin is that you're looking for," the old man said.

Desta felt his heart harden. "Where is it?"

"Underground," the girl said. "In a building at the end of an abandoned subway tunnel."

Desta was incredulous. From his grandfather's account, the coin was supposed to be near a large body of water. The traffic signal was on its second cycle, and Desta moved to cross the street. The strangers followed him. For a time neither spoke, but when Desta glanced at the girl, the warm sensation in his heart renewed.

"We know who stole the coin and how it ended up in its current location," Mr. Makari said. "If you want to get it, we can help you. It's a bit tricky and needs your cooperation."

"My cooperation?" Desta continued walking toward the train station.

"The coin was bought from the person who stole it by members of a secret society devoted to building wealth. They know that the coin can aid their purposes. Since they procured it, they've kept it under lock and key, along with other treasures in the place Calliope mentioned."

"What do I have to do to get it?"

"You need to cast a spell using your wand."

Desta stopped and stared at the old man. "How do you know I have such a thing?"

"I won't go into that just yet. For now, follow my instructions if you wish to get hold of that coin."

Calliope smiled at Desta, stirring his heart even more. "And you must bring your Coin of Magic and Fortune for good luck," she said.

"My coin?"

"So," Mr. Makari interrupted. "Hold your wand by the end of the handle that makes the three nines along the axis appear as sixes. Appeal to the coin's possessors to admit you to the building and then the treasure collection."

Desta doubted that the coin resided underground. And Tsadok had warned him it was dangerous to hold the wand from the wrong end.

"Does the group's name mean Sweet and Sour?" Desta asked.

Calliope knotted her brow. Mr. Makari's face tightened. "They are a secret society, and much is unknown about them."

Desta walked on, mind spinning. The old man and girl followed.

"If you want to investigate further, we can arrange to meet next Saturday," Mr. Makari said. "As I said, Calliope wants to get to know you. If you return, you two can spend more time together."

Desta's heart leaped at the suggestion. "What is it you want from me?" he asked her.

"First let me say that I go by Callie, short for Calliope. I'm a cross-country runner, and I read about your championship victory last year. And I'll be a freshman at Princeton in the fall and I would like to know you," she said.

Desta stopped again. "You too?" he asked, warily, but pleased at the chance to take a closer look at her. Callie's soft brown eyes, long lashes, smooth skin, fine delicate features, and long pleated hair aroused feelings in him he couldn't ignore.

"Yes," Callie said, smiling sweetly.

"Come next Saturday, and you two can talk about many things," Mr. Makari said.

They continued along Lexington Avenue, Desta now seriously considering the invitation. At 42nd Street, they turned left and headed toward Grand Central Station.

"What time next Saturday?" Desta asked finally.

"Ten o'clock," Mr. Makari said. "Wear old clothes and shoes. Some of the way will be dirty and muddy."

"I can do that," Desta replied. Eddies of excitement swirled through him. To spend another day with the girl, he could put up with plenty of dirt and mud.

Calliope pointed to a statue on a pedestal. "To make it easy for Desta, let's meet in front of Mr. Vanderbilt."

"Good idea," Mr. Makari said.

Calliope glanced at Desta. "As I mentioned, do bring your coin of magic for good luck," she said.

"I'll think about it."

Their arrangements made, Desta thanked father and granddaughter and shook hands with Makari. His eyes lingered on Calliope's face as he shook her hand gently but firmly. Her smile charmed him. He waved them goodbye and walked toward the station's entrance with a sensation in his heart unlike any he'd experienced before.

Desta didn't remember the ride home. He was deep in thought about Calliope, the magic coin, and the secret society that had kept it underground. He questioned the story of the magic coin that Bob Krause's friends had told, and whether that same shekel could have ended up underground.

Back home in his room, he was resting on his bed with warm thoughts of Calliope, when Mindy Kovacs appeared at his door. "David Hartman is on the phone," she said, "You can pick up on the hallway receiver."

"I heard you had a good time with Bob and his friends at the Three Sisters," David said.

"We did," Desta replied. "Didn't learn anything tangible about the coin, but there appear to be credible clues that it has come to New York. Bob's friend Esther didn't remember the owner's name, but she did indicate a special coin was stolen from them. She couldn't say if it was recovered."

David was quiet for a moment. "Well. . . ," he continued, "the fact that you have a lead that it may be here is still progress. Eight months ago, you had only guesses."

Desta stirred with excitement. "If I'm lucky, I may come much closer to it next week."

"Ohh . . . How so?"

"Do you remember that old man we met coming back from the Empire State Building last August?"

"What about him?"

"I ran into him and his beautiful granddaughter as I was heading for the train after meeting Bob and his friends. He says he knows who stole the coin and where it currently resides. He said the people who stole it have kept it in a vault underground, near an abandoned subway tunnel."

"That sounds doubtful," David said. "Who is he, and how did he know all this?"

"His name is Mr. Makari. But I didn't ask him how he knew all these things. By the way, his granddaughter will be a freshman at Princeton in the fall."

"Is that so?" David asked. "That's an odd coincidence."

"She is so beautiful. Calliope is her name, and I rather like her."

"I can tell from your voice."

"They invited me to go underground with them next Saturday to plead with the owners to give me the coin," Desta said. "We're meeting outside Grand Central's main entrance."

"I think you should find out more about these people before you go anywhere with them," David said. "Did they give you a phone number or address?"

"No," Desta said. "Don't worry, David. This is a chance I can't miss." Calliope's beautiful image hovered before Desta.

"Well then, I look forward to hearing about your adventure," David said, sounding unconvinced.

"Talk to you soon."

As Desta returned to his room, Calliope's face returned to him, filling him with happiness. She seemed somehow more lovely in memory. He sat at his desk to compose a text he wanted to transmit to Tsadok about today's experience, when he heard a soft melody. He cocked his ears this way and that to find the source. He rose and looked out the window but saw no one. No matter its origin, Desta concentrated on the music and the vision of Calliope.

A picture unexpectedly loomed before him, of a couple sitting on a bench—he and Calliope—holding hands, talking about nothing but saying a lot with their eyes and feelings. He couldn't wait until next Saturday to see that charming girl again.

During the week, Calliope's image came to Desta three more times. He thought about the coin, too, wondering if the underground chamber he would soon see was anything like the Washaa Umera caves he'd visited in northern Ethiopia. He tried to imagine the people who owned the coin. He also debated Callie's request to bring his coin. If it would please the beautiful girl, he would take his Coin of Good Luck, though he was too emotional to trust the wisdom of such an idea.

The appointed day finally arrived, and Desta's stomach was full of butterflies. After breakfast, he put on his oldest jeans, tennis shoes, and Jake's hand-me-down red Izod shirt. He put in his backpack an extra long-sleeved shirt, a notebook and pen, and the folded magic wand, and his Coin of Good Luck in his front trousers pocket. Then he asked his host brother to drop him off at the Rye train station.

"Good luck, and have fun," Jake said.

Desta thanked him and stepped out of the Alfa Romeo. He waved at his host brother and headed to the southbound train platform. Desta knew if he didn't do something about his fluttering belly, it might paralyze his ability to say anything. He passed his hand over his chest and told himself to stop it. The thoughts of the magic coin and Calliope alternated in his head throughout the train ride. He had doubts and fears, too, but spending the whole day with the girl excited him.

Mr. Makari raised his hand in greeting when he saw Desta crossing the street at the traffic light. He and Calliope stood in the shadow of Mr. Vanderbilt's statue, evidently eager to see him. Desta waved as he walked toward them, taking care to control his feelings for the girl.

"Did you enjoy your ride?" the old man asked, extending his hand to Desta.

"I paid no attention to it," Desta replied, smiling, as he shook Mr. Makari's hand. "I thought only of the magic coin and the time I would spend with you and your granddaughter."

"Good morning," Calliope said, offering Desta her delicate hand to shake. Desta's feelings rose again as he held the girl's hand.

"We've been looking forward to this day too." She wore jeans, a beige tank top, and tennis shoes. She had rolled her hair into a ball pinned in the back. Mr. Makari was in his usual old baggy clothes.

"The tunnel and the underground chamber that holds the coin are north of here, near the Bronx. So, we'll take the train."

The mention of the Bronx gave Desta a small eddy of excitement. Esther Winkel had said it was the last place the coin owner had lived, giving him added hope that the shekel might reside in the chamber.

"Good thing it's the weekend," Calliope said. "We won't have to fight for a seat on the train."

Mr. Makari purchased the fare tokens and handed one to each of his companions to go through the turnstiles. Several flights of stairs down, they found a northbound train, and got on and sat down quickly. By happenstance, the old man wound up between the youngsters. Desta sighed, anxious over this trip underground, with no clear idea of what he would encounter or where he would end up.

"We'll ride for about forty minutes before our adventure begins," Mr. Makari said, as if he sensed Desta's anxiety.

"How long would it take to get to the coin's location?" Desta asked.

"It depends," the old man said. "Without any roadblocks, an hour. If we have to change course, or we stop to study things that catch our interest, up to two hours."

Desta had more questions but said only, "I see." It seemed like a long time to walk underground. On the other hand, he thought he wouldn't mind being there all day if he were holding Calliope's hand.

"I'm going on this journey for the first time too," Calliope said, leaning forward and turning her head to glimpse Desta. "We should have fun." She smiled radiantly.

Desta held his breath. The warm sensation he felt inside was precious.

"It's a bit unnerving to be underground that long, but it'll be fun with you two, I'm sure." Desta said, and smiled back at the sweet girl. His fingers played with the coin in his pocket.

At the next stop, a woman got on with a crying toddler and sat on the bench on the other side of the door. The boy wailed no matter what the mother did. People stopped their talk and stared at mother and son.

Desta thought the coin's image on his chest might help. He pressed his fingers to it and murmured repeatedly, "Quiet the boy." Soon after, the car got relief.

"Here we are!" Mr. Makari said at the train stop that announced 191ST STREET in white letters on blue tiles. The three of them got out, and Desta looked around. Graffiti was everywhere; the place looked old and neglected.

"We're in the city's deepest subway station," Calliope declared, stepping toward Desta. "We're standing eighteen stories below ground. Being here is an experience in itself, don't you think?"

"You can say that," Desta said. "I've never been this far beneath the earth."

"Let's go," the old man commanded. After climbing several flights of stairs, they came to a long, barrel-shaped, well-lit tunnel whose end appeared to reduce to a point. It was warm, and Desta and Calliope began to perspire. The walls were covered in scrawls, grotesque images, and cryptic messages. Trash and debris were strewn across the floor as if windblown.

At the end of the tunnel, instead of going left, where stairs led to the street, Mr. Makari took them around a barrier and then into a side gate which brought them to a dingy, abandoned train tunnel that smelled like rancid oil.

Desta hardened his lips and stared at the dim channel. He caressed the Good Luck shekel. Of course, he would cross a desert to find the Second Coin of Magic and Fortune. Calliope knitted her brow; she questioned the safety of the dank subway.

"Let me explain," the old man ventured. "The main passage to the treasure chamber is better, but it has been made inaccessible since the coin was brought there. Going this way, we bypass the restriction and come through the back entrance of the building."

The old man produced a flashlight from under his baggy coat and gunned the beam down the tunnel. They walked in single file along a ledge, Desta behind Calliope. A few feet below were rails strewn with trash, bottles, and even a few metal folding chairs. After walking for half an hour, they came to an abandoned station platform.

"We'll now go upstairs, where we should find an unlocked door to another shaft that goes directly to the treasure chamber," Mr. Makari said.

"I hope it's better lit than the one we just took," Calliope said.

"It is," the old man replied. "This is how the society's senior members enter the chamber."

But when they got to the entrance, they found it locked. The old man nearly threw the flashlight in anger. "How could they do this to us?!"

He thought for a long time. "I'm sorry, Desta," he said finally. "It looks like somebody got my request wrong." He bent his head down and thought again.

Pensive and disappointed, Calliope turned her gaze toward her grandpa and waited.

Mr. Makari lifted his face and said, "I have an idea. We'll have a complicated and messy journey, but there is another route that will surely bring us to the chamber."

"What is it?" Calliope asked.

"Follow me." Returning to the abandoned platform, they climbed the stairs to find the exit door closed and locked. The old man pushed and pushed, getting angrier and more frustrated with each attempt.

"Of course," he said finally, as if conceding to the futility of his effort. "It's an abandoned platform and the city would have sealed it shortly after they shut down the station. Now the question is how can we get to the street from here?"

Mr. Makari looked at his granddaughter first and then Desta is if soliciting their solution to the quandary.

Callie looked puzzled and thoughtful. "We can always go back, send a clear instruction to the people who guard these gates, and we can try next weekend."

Desta couldn't come the following week. His family could have plans, and he had to get ready for school. It must be this day, or else the indefinite future. Then he remembered that when he went with David Hartman to visit the vigilantly guarded chapel that housed the Ark of the Covenant in northern Ethiopia, he used the image of his magic coin to force open the gates and door of the chapel.

"Give me a moment," Desta said stepping to the gate. With his right hand over his heart, he whispered, "Open this gate." Then he stepped back and watched.

Within a few minutes, the gate began to open slowly, until it was wide enough for the lost party to pass through.

Mr. Makari and Callie looked at each other, and then at Desta. "What did you do?" Callie asked, stepping closer.

"Just some trick," he said casually. "We got lucky. It doesn't always work."

"I'm glad it did," Callie said, the cloud lifting from her face.

"That's marvelous, young man," the old man said. "Thank you!"

All walked out of the dungeon, happy to be in the bright open air. Mr. Makari strode hurriedly, Desta and Calliope trotting behind him. Some fifty yards ahead, the old man stopped on the sidewalk. He looked one way and then the other and dashed behind a row of bushes to a rectangular hole covered with a metal grill. Desta and Calliope stood next to him. He gestured toward the hole.

"The treasure chamber is right about at the bottom of that building," Mr. Makari said, pointing to it. "The second passage is between this sewer portal and the coin's chamber. What we need to do is go down this hole and search for an entrance to the passage."

The old man retrieved a metal bar with a hook on one end from the bushes. He inserted the hook into the grill, leaned back, and dragged it away from the opening.

"Desta, you and I will check the shaft. Callie, you stay here and shield the hole from onlookers."

Going down the shaft required them to face the slender metal steps that looked like grab handles. Desta could hear rushing water as he descended after Mr. Makari. At the bottom there was a good-sized river, which the old man said was clean water, its organic matter having been filtered at a plant elsewhere.

They could stoop and walk alongside the stream, but there were cobwebs everywhere that clung to their faces, hair, and clothes, and the place was malodorous. The old man threw light from his flashlight across the water, but there were no signs of an entrance on the other side of the watercourse that would lead them to the second passage.

Realizing the futility of their endeavor, they came back out. Mr. Makari replaced the cover, and they continued. In the next block, the old man saw someone in shabby clothes emerge from behind a barrier near a building in disrepair.

He scuttled ahead and queried the man, who told him about a tunnel used by the homeless.

Mr. Makari's face lit up for the first time. "I think we are near the passage I'm looking for."

Behind the barrier were stairs that went down to a cave-like settlement that ran along the left side of an abandoned train track. They walked parallel to the tracks, passing tents, shacks, sleeping people, and blue plastic cartons teeming with cans, bottles, and trash.

"Excuse us," Mr. Makari would say every so often. "We're not police, only here to explore."

Some stepped out of their tents and waved; others uncovered sleepy faces and squinted at the intruders. Desta's heart raced with each step.

Farther down, they found a catwalk and marched across it to the other side. They went up one flight of stairs and saw a hefty portal to the right. They came to it and struggled before pushing it open. It was dimly lit, and they could walk without a flashlight.

They passed through a series of seven high turnstiles, one after another, then cleared the last barrier and passed through an iron gate. Tall mahogany double doors faced them.

"Here we are!" Mr. Makari announced.

Desta sighed. Directly above the entrance was an eye in relief, its lid covered with grass, its brow a thick hedge. Its form was nearly identical to the one that appeared on the portal of the Washaa Umera caves, except this one was bound by a circle with three arrows and framed by three 6s that lay crosswise on the left, and a solid vertical line on the right. Above these images, three lines of text read:

The Brotherhood of the Fallen Angel
and
Guardians of the Eternities

"Well…" Mr. Makari said. "You have your magic wand, right?"
Desta nodded.

"Take it out, point its 6s directly to the same numbers above the entrance, recite your mantra, and let's see what happens."

Desta retrieved his magic wand and did as instructed.

To Desta's astonishment, the massive doors slowly opened inward, revealing a large anteroom furnished with two sets of gold sofas and chairs and coffee tables in the center of the room. At the back of the room to either side of the double doors were two large octagonal tables and chairs with glittering chandeliers above them.

The walls were adorned with black and white photos and paintings of men, some that seemed very old, and mysterious artifacts and human remains. On the right octagonal table lay a skull above crossed bones, with the numbers 3-2-2 attached to sticks below the bones. Desta immediately saw that the numbers added up to seven. Did the number mean anything to this mysterious group?

"There are a dozen college secret societies in this building, each with its own chamber in the back, but they all share this living space." Mr. Makari said. He pushed open the back door and they went down a long hallway to a room on the left filled with glittering things on shelves and two large tables. Desta was elated.

"Go on," Mr. Makari urged. "If you have brought your magic coin as we suggested, it should lead you to the location of the sister magic shekel."

Desta didn't bring his coin of magic believing that its image on his chest would suffice. He folded and put away his magic wand and slung his backpack on his shoulder. With his right hand over his chest, he cautiously strolled around tables heaped with jewelry, coins, and other strange, dazzling objects.

The old man and the girl followed, studying all these things.

"Did you see any coins that resemble yours?" Mr. Makari asked.

"No," Desta replied. He shook his head.

"Don't lose hope," the man said. "There are a lot more in the next room. Go ahead. Callie and I will wait for you in the living room."

The door closed as soon as his companions left, and the room turned pitch black. Desta cringed. He held tightly to the image on his chest.

"Calliope, Mr. Makari!" Desta shouted. "What happened? Why did you leave me behind?"

He reached for the magic wand in his bag. With the nines facing him, he asked it to give him light and passage out of the building.

Moments later, the green light emerged from the curlicue and became bright as candlelight. Relieved, Desta traced his footsteps back to the main entrance but found it locked. He held the wand from the sixes side and commanded the doors to open, but they did not. Holding the rod under his chin, he pulled as hard as he could, but the doors still wouldn't budge. Sweat trickled down his face as his mind and heart raced.

He turned to see if he could find another exit back down the hallway.

Just then, a tall, wispy man appeared. "Don't despair. You will be all right," he said. "We want to talk to you." A tag on the vaporous man's chest read Hardwick in large print.

"Talk to me?" Desta could barely discern the man's eyes. "What about?"

"We'll let you know," the man replied. "But first, put your wand in your bag and remove your hand from your chest."

Desta complied and followed him through wanly-lit rooms of books and many other things, and finally entered a conference room, where seven men of different ages sat around a large circular table near the entrance. A long, shiny rectangular table occupied much of the room beyond them.

"Good afternoon, Desta!" the men said.

Desta dipped his head, startled that they knew who he was. "Good afternoon," he replied.

"We know you had difficulty finding this place," said the white-haired man who introduced himself as Garth Denhart. "We invited you here for a very important reason. We have determined that our coin is not what you're looking for," the man said. "But we are interested in purchasing yours."

Desta's heart coiled; his cheeks felt hot, and his tongue tangled. This whole adventure suddenly seemed like a setup. He let out a deep sigh.

"We'll pay a good amount," Mr. Denhart said.

"That means twenty-five million dollars," a younger man to the right of Denhart added.

"If you become a member, we'll continue to give you money," a third person across from the white-haired man offered.

"Money is not the object of my mission," Desta said. He chose his words carefully so not to offend and ensure his safe departure from this strange place. "But I'll think about it and let you know."

"But you have the coin with you," Mr. Denhart said. "Unless you give it to us, we won't let you out of here."

Desta thought hard on this ultimatum. Should he reveal that what he has in his pocket is not the Coin of Magic, but something else? He saw that he would have to part ways with James van Hook Johnson's treasure to reclaim his freedom. Reluctantly and deliberately, Desta inserted his right hand into his trousers pocket, pulled out the Coin of Good Luck and handed it to his detainer.

The man's eyes bloomed. His lips quivered. His voice cracked. "This . . . This . . . is our long-lost treasure. Where did you get it?"

Desta groped for a bit. "It was gifted to me by a coin collector."

"There were several of them housed in a silk fabric pouch. Do you know the man's name or where he lives?"

"The name is James van Hook Johnson, but he passed away seven years ago."

Mr. Denhart's face darkened. "Perhaps you can do a bit of research on our behalf and let us know who owns the remaining coins in that pouch. Let us know through Calliope or Makari," Mr. Denhart said. He hesitated and then added, "For now, this precious piece is enough, and we'll let you go."

"Thank you," Desta said, his face lighting with relief.

They all rose and shook hands with Desta. He thanked them for the offer.

"Mr. Hardwick will show you a more direct route to the 191st Street train station," Mr. Denhart said. Desta thanked the man and followed his guide out of the room.

"This building has four identical entrances and an equal number of routes to reach it," Mr. Hardwick said. "Unless you're intimately familiar with the place, it's very easy to get lost, as Makari did this morning."

"Too bad he was not better informed," Desta said. "We could have arrived a lot earlier."

Above the double-door exit appeared a large image of the Devil with his horns. *Did I just visit with devil worshippers?* Desta shuddered.

Outside the short tunnel, Mr. Hardwick gave him directions, involving a couple of turns and then through the subway tunnels that would bring him to the 191st Street subway station.

Desta thanked the man, shook hands and left. He ran through the tunnels, checking behind to be sure no one was following him.

As he rode the trains to Grand Central and then Rye, Desta thought repeatedly about the day's events. Were Mr. Makari and Calliope ghosts, or real? Why did they vanish on him? Was the girl meant to lure Desta into trusting the old man enough to come to the Devil's house? Would he see her again? Was she really going to Princeton this fall? Or was it all a dream?

FORTY-THREE

Orange and black: these school colors had first drawn Desta's interest in Princeton University. Once he'd learned that they offered a quality education, he'd wanted to transfer there. He had worked hard to get in, and he was about to begin his sophomore year there tomorrow.

On the eve of his departure, Desta had emptied his closet and piled his clothes on the bed. He was now sitting at his desk, turning and staring at the heap, most of it Jake's hand-me-downs that he no longer needed, and would put back once he picked out his clothes for school. At that moment he couldn't help but reflect on his mental state exactly a year ago, in the days before he embarked upon his new life in America.

Then, the year ahead looked as bleak, dark, and forbidding as a moonless night. Hunger, deprivation, the hardships of living with strangers in his own country, and the pain in his head that he couldn't shake—all of it had frightened him more than anything he had experienced before. Desta thought his challenges would be insurmountable on new soil, with a new family, a new educational system, and an uncertain future.

Now he looked back on the year: his loving host family, athletic success, awards, and benefactors all seemed like a miracle.

Outside of school and sports, Desta fondly remembered his camping trip with David Hartman and his Deer Meadow Christmas vacation with his host family. The Thanksgiving family gatherings, his walks with Kooper, and the weekend family meals also held happy memories in Desta's heart.

In retrospect, how silly it looked to him to have worried that much about his impending year in America. This year, his heart still stirred with fear as he wondered how he would fit in at the new school and what threat his head pain would pose to his life at Princeton.

He asked, too, how much longer he could endure not hearing from his family, not eating Ethiopian food, and not seeing a friendly face from home. Nostalgia and yearning prickled up his throat, but Desta quickly reached over his chest and pressed above his heart, and he felt easier.

He rose and began sifting through the piled clothes for those that still fit him and would withstand everyday wear: three or four pairs of jeans, casual shirts, and a couple of his winter jackets and gloves, but none of Lincoln's mandatory jackets, shirts, jerseys, or ties. Desta had learned from Jake that dress codes were now a thing of the past. Students could wear whatever they liked, guided only by society's norms and their own sensibilities.

He stowed most of the past year's outfits back in the closet and put his folded school clothes in his large suitcase on the bed. Then he packed his English books on one side, and his tennis and black dress shoes, wrapped in paper, on the other. He closed the suitcase and set it against the wall by the door.

Before Desta could deal with the suitcase that contained his precious objects, he needed to acknowledge the string of images that filtered through his head to complete the portrait of his first-year American experience. He sat on his chair and propped his feet on the edge of his bed. Then he leaned back, holding the back of his head with interlocking fingers; he let the movie of his life from a year ago play out before him.

First, there was The Great Mystery, his stand-in spiritual guide, whose presence, like Tsadok, his ancestral counsel, soothed and comforted him. Desta could visualize the many places they'd met—from that first warm summer night by a pond in Vermont's Green Mountain National Forest, where David Hartman and Desta had camped, to their more recent encounter at the Johnsons' compound on a full moon night.

Desta's mind then rolled over the highlights of the year. The spirits of the prominent Americans and the oppressed native Indians and black people he'd met and conversed with at the Lincoln Sculpture Garden, including President Lincoln himself; the spirit from the Haunted House of Playland, who counseled Desta about his painful feet that afternoon on the boardwalk.

His devoted friend David Hartman, the main cog in Desta's American wheel, the Stones saved Desta from stressing over his financial sources for the remaining three years of college.

The ghost of Uncle James, who kept the two one-thousand-dollar bills, his Coin of Good Luck gift. The enslaved Black Americans who helped Desta finish packing the man's collection in a much shorter time than he had expected.

Desta was grateful to Coach Parker for believing in and encouraging him to excel in the cross-country running sport. He was thankful to Bob Krause for arranging the Saturday brunch at the Three Sisters Pancake House in New York City with his friends. They gave Desta valuable clues about the Second Coin of Magic and Fortune.

Desta also acknowledged his subway tunnel escapade chasing a fake lead that had nearly trapped him with a group of Satan worshipers intent on robbing him of his magic coin. His attraction for Calliope and his vulnerability had clouded his judgment of the situation. It had been a hard lesson for Desta.

He wished he'd made more progress in his search for the magic coin. He had done what he could within his time constraints. He realized the clues he'd gathered from Bob Kraus' friend were still helpful.

Bringing his attention to the moment, Desta rose and filled the second suitcase with the box containing the coin, the ancient stone tablet, the framed painting of the coins wrapped in his T-shirts, the two one-thousand-dollar notes, and *The Record*, the journal of his correspondence with Tsadok. He set aside the magic wand and the scroll; after dinner, he'd recite the legends on the parchment and send a message to Tsadok using the wand. He put some of his books and notebooks in his backpack. He set aside *The Mystery of Ancient Jewish Coins*, recently given to him by David, to read on the road. Finally, he brought down Shae's *Gone with the Wind* poster and hung it where his coin picture used to be.

After dinner, he sat on his bed with the wand propped between his crossed legs. He invoked the light and began the message to his mentor and spiritual guide.

Dear Honorable Tsadok, High Priest of the Ark:

I want to thank you beyond words for your wise counsel all my life, and especially this past year, from so far away. I couldn't have coped without your guidance and foresight.

Tomorrow, I go to Princeton University to start *my sophomore year. My first year in America has been more than I ever expected. I'm grateful for how things turned out.*

The Johnsons have been wonderful hosts. Along with their household staff, they provided me with the comfort and security I needed to do well in school and sports. I'm so thankful for their kindness, and for adopting me. Their dog, Kooper, has been my loyal companion, playing in the backyard just like Kooli and I once did in my childhood-- such precious memories.

Everyone at school was kind to me. I leave Lincoln College with happy and lasting memories of my year there. My first serious attempt to find the coin was frustrating and disappointing, but I've met people who gave me clues that the second shekel has come to America. I plan to search for it in earnest in the next few years.

I'll send you word once I settle in at the new school.
Many thanks.

Yours, Desta Abraham

Desta folded the magic wand and set it by his side. He then recited the life virtues from *The Record* seven times. Recrossing his legs, he sat back and covered his face with his hands. He contemplated each kind person he'd met in America these last twelve months, and their contribution to his happiness and welfare. He said, "Thank you!" to all, and added, "May your future be blessed."

Then he rose, put the magic wand and scroll in the suitcase, and set it alongside the things he would take to Princeton tomorrow.

He washed up, peeled back the covers, and slid into bed. He lay his head on the pillow and imagined his next three years at Princeton.

Acknowledgments

My wife, Rosario, has been an ardent supporter of my work. Her undying faith in the Desta stories and the value she feels they would have to the readers have kept me going even when my faith seemed to waver at times. They say writing is a lonely experience, and Rosario allowed me the quiet and secluded space I needed to write these books.

I'm eternally grateful to my father, at whose knee I learned all the fundamentals of life, and to my mother, who taught me I can do anything I want if I apply myself, including becoming a writer.

I thank Vincent Cusenza, who edited and proofread this book, my fact checker and consultant, and Mr. James Oliveri, who proofread the final manuscript. I'm indebted to Philip Howe for his artistic magic with all the Desta covers and for his patience and understanding of my need to make the illustrations as authentic as possible, even when the reproduced images were flights of my fancy. I'm thankful to Greg Brown, who cleverly converted the loose manuscript into this handsome volume.

Last, but not least, I am grateful to the Creator, who gave me healthy faculties to record what I saw, read, heard, and experienced to use as material for this and the first four novels.

The painting of the two coins was given by a mysterious man to an American artist named Roman Burkhardt while living in Romania. The piece somehow ended up in Desta's hands and became one of his proud possessions. Based on the account of Desta's grandfather's spirit, he suspects that the image may be of the place where the two shekels were supposed to unite ultimately.

The record of correspondence between Desta and his
spiritual guide, Tsadok, the High Priest of King Solomon's Temple

DESTA 5 CHARACTERS

Abraham – Desta's father

Alberti, Elsa – weekday housekeeper at the Johnsons'

Aunt Bella – Nash Carver's aunt who lives in New York City

Ayénat – Desta's mother

Berry, Chuck – American singer and guitarist

Brenner, Arie – friend of Bob Krause who came as consort with Aunt Esther Winkel who was claims to have clues about the owner of the second coin.

Brown, Stu – Trig teacher at Abraham Lincoln college

Burkhardt, Roman – the American artist who was once entrusted with the painting of the coins.

Carver, Nash – Shae Johnson's boyfriend

Clark, Martha – Skip Johnson's older sister

Clark, Trover – Skip Johnson's brother-in-law

Dates, Conrad Lewis – the minister who conducted Desta's adoption ceremony at the Johnsons.

Davis, Angela – a black American Civil rights activist who was on a wanted list for a crime.

Dawson, Timmy – college bookstore clerk

Denhart, Garth – one of the underground secret society men who offered to purchase Desta Coin of Magic and Fortune

Donovan, Quinn – English instructor at Abraham Lincoln college

Fernsby, Chuck – Physics instructor at Abe Lincoln college

Eleni – the ghost/witch of Washaa Umeraa (in Ethiopia) who served as an agent to spirits who want to steal Desta's coin.

Gabriel, Juan – Chemistry teacher at Abe Lincoln college

Gardner, Benjamin – Tor's twin brother who attends Princeton University.

Gardner, Tor – Desta's school friend who attends Yale University

Gray, Stephen – Princeton Director of Admissions

Greenfield, Hank – Assistant manager at Mohawk Valley Country Club, Utica, NY

Hardwick, Stan – One of the underground secret society members who helped lost Desta find his way out of the underground building.

Hartman, David – Desta's friend and mentor

Hartman, Dr. Halford – David Hartman's father

Hartman, Jean – David Hartman's mother

Haile Selassie – former Emperor of Ethiopia, formerly known as Ras Tafari

Joe – the Johnsons' vacation cabin caretaker in Deer Meadows, Vermont

Johnson, Aida – Desta's youngest host sibling

Johonson, Beverly – Desta's host mother

Johnson, Denise – Skip's sister-in-law

Johnson, Dick, aka Grandpa – Skip's father

Johnson, Emma, aka Grandma – Skip's mother

Johnson, Eric – Skip's brother

Johnson, Jake – Desta's host brother

Johnson, James van Hook – Skip's brother

Johnson, Shae – Desta's oldest host sibling

Johnson, Skip – Desta's host father

Kaplan, Seth – Abraham Lincoln college student reporter

Kooper – the Johnson family dog

Kooli – Desta's former dog

Kovacs, Mindy – weekend housekeeper at the Johnsons

Kovac, Rick – Midy's husband

Krause, Robert – a friend of David Hartman who tried to help Desta with the search for the coin.

Lesim – Desta's relative daughter who encouraged Desta to wear her father's gnarled, old shoes.

Linda – David Hartman's girlfriend

MacDuff, Calliope – the mysterious girl who, along with her grandfather, tries to help Desta locate the second missing coin in a New York abandoned subway tunnel.

Makari, Willard – The mysterious old man who lured Desta to the underground secret society Devil worshipers.

Marley, Bob – a Jamaican Rhagae musician

Mulugeta, Colonel – one of Desta's former benefactors

Nelson, Bent – Biology teacher at Abe Lincoln college.

Parker, Keith – Cross-country coach at Abraham Lincoln college, dress code enforcer

Petrov, Dr. – Desta's former benefactor who encouraged him to go to medical school.

Presley, Elvis – American singer and actor

Saba – Desta's oldest sister

Sedrick – Desk attendant at Delroy barber shop in the Bronx

Shaw, Trent – the foreign students' advisor at Lincoln Junior College

Stone, Lawrence – Desta's benefactor

Stone, Meredith – Desta's benefactor, wife of Lawrence

The Great Mystery, aka Wakan Tanka – American Indian main resident spirit

Thomas, James – the barber who gave Desta his first American hair cut at Delroy shop.

Tsadok – Desta's ancestral spirit guide, high priest of King Solomon's temple

Watson, Angie – Princeton Admissions Office receptionist

Winkel, Esther – friend of Bob Krause who claims to have clues about the missing second coin.

Winslow, Mary – Mrs. Beverly Johnson's home secretary

Wakan Tanka, aka The Great Mystery – One of the many alternative names for the American Indian main resident spirit

Desta's cross-country team roster

Abrham, Desta

Callahan, Sam

Callahan, Tim

Campbell, Pete

Collins, Luke

Corrado, Ken

Hauser, Steve

Johnson, Jake

Miller, Ben

Murphy, Jack

Spencer, Dominic

Walker, Derek

Ethiopian Words

azmaris – minstrels

baredo – hail

doro wat – chicken sauce

goferay – afro

goma – antelope

injera – flat bread

ketema – pulpy, green grass

masinko – a single string instrument played with a bow

moseb – skirt-shaped colorful basket

quanta – smoked beef jerky

ten – honey wine

tibis – sauteed meats

About the Author

Getty Ambau was born and raised in an isolated countryside, in the high-lands of Gojjam in northern Ethiopia and traces his ancestry to the ancient Semitic peoples of the Middle East. He came to the United States at age nineteen for his education, studied molecular biophysics, biochemistry, and economics at Yale University, and later earned an advanced business degree. He has worked in research labs and run his own companies, but writing has always been his calling. He has authored the award-winning Desta series and several best-selling alternative health books on health and nutrition. His second Desta novel was featured in Kirkus Reviews magazine. He lives in the San Francisco Bay Area with his wife, Rosario.